AT HELL'S GATE
A Penzler Pick!

"Ethan Black's *At Hell's Gate* may be my favorite novel of the year.... [A] first-rate police novel.... Nail-bitingly exciting."

—Otto Penzler, *The New York Sun*

"A riveting read.... In a world of fictional cookie-cutter cops, Voort's a true original.... One of the genre's most interesting and exciting series."

—*Publishers Weekly*

"Fast-paced, creatively plotted.... Read this story and you'll be out looking for all the other Conrad Voort stories."

—*Rocky Mountain News* (Denver)

DEAD FOR LIFE

"Splendid.... Great writing. Great suspense. Great action. Wonderful reading."

—*Los Angeles Times*

"[A] clever plot."

—*The Washington Post*

"Exceptionally engaging . . . readers of the previous [Voort] stories won't be surprised at the quality and depth of this one."

—*Rocky Mountain News* (Denver)

"An intense, intelligent thriller, *Dead for Life* is well written, gripping. . . . And it moves. Don't pick it up if you have other things you should be doing."

—*Detroit Free Press*

"Black upends the standard conventions of good cop versus bad killer [and] paints a vivid picture of day-to-day life in New York. . . . Another strong performance."

—*Publishers Weekly*

"Voort, who relies more on wits than firepower, is a joy to hang around with, and readers of hard-edged mysteries who haven't already discovered this series should quickly add it to their must-read list."

—*Booklist*

"[The] suspense remains high."

—*Kirkus Reviews*

"Intriguing."

—*The Oklahoman*

ALL THE DEAD WERE STRANGERS
A Selection of The Literary Guild

"Dead on. . . . Black nails the cops' esprit de corps, but the baddies are even better, at once diabolic and heroic. . . . [He has a] flair for action."

—*People*

"Black writes nearly perfect thrillers."

—*Library Journal*

"Gripping . . . fast-paced . . . riveting. . . . Black's timely thriller addresses questions of terrorism and government corruption with intelligence and flair. . . . Supercharged suspense . . . a flawless, slam-bang conclusion."

—*Publishers Weekly* (starred review)

"Ethan Black's *All the Dead Were Strangers* is as good as it gets."
—*Milwaukee Journal Sentinel*

"[An] excellent series. . . . One of the best page-turners of the year."
—Amazon.com (A Penzler Pick)

"Intelligent and believable."

—*American Way*

"An exciting, carefully crafted novel."
—*Booklist* (starred review)

BOOKS BY ETHAN BLACK

At Hell's Gate
Dead for Life
All the Dead Were Strangers
The Broken Hearts Club
Irresistible

At Hell's Gate

ETHAN BLACK

POCKET STAR BOOKS

New York London Toronto Sydney

A Pocket Star Book published by
POCKET BOOKS, a division of Simon & Schuster, Inc.
1230 Avenue of the Americas, New York, NY 10020

This book is a work of fiction. Names, characters, places and inci-
dents are products of the author's imagination or are used ficti-
tiously. Any resemblance to actual events or locales or persons,
living or dead, is entirely coincidental.

Originally published in hardcover in 2004 by
Simon & Schuster, Inc.

ISBN-13: 978-0-7434-6421-5
ISBN-10:   0-7434-6421-4

This Pocket Star Books paperback edition July 2006

10 9 8 7 6 5 4 3 2 1

POCKET STAR BOOKS and colophon are registered
trademarks of Simon & Schuster, Inc.

Cover design by Patrick Kang;
Cover photograph © Paul Colangelo/Corbis

Manufactured in the United States of America

For information regarding special discounts for bulk purchases,
please contact Simon & Schuster Special Sales at 1-800-456-6798 or
business@simonandschuster.com.

ACKNOWLEDGMENTS

A very special thanks to Chuck Adams, Patricia Burke, Vince Capone, Ted Conover, Phil Gerard, Jim Grady, Clay Max Hall, Bob Leuci, Bill Massey, the McAllister family and tug company, Esther Newberg, Jon Plutzik, Steve Rabinowitz, Wendy Roth, and Kevin Smith.

At Hell's Gate

ONE

"What's the thing you must never do, but you can't resist doing?" asks the street preacher on the loading dock. "The extra step that you can't stop from taking? The excess that brings you to Hell's Gate?"

It's what I did tonight, thinks the man in the front row, sinking down, trying to hide, knowing he's chosen the wrong place.

It's too light in here. Too big and empty. The men chasing me must be right outside.

The street preacher wears coveralls. The eleven P.M. sermon takes place on a hot September night. The once-a-week "church" is an abandoned warehouse garage in the South Bronx. Bare bulbs illuminate folding chairs that hold a smattering of half-sprawled, half-asleep prostitutes, homeless men, and even one long-haul trucker who knows he shouldn't be here but couldn't resist looking for a certain redheaded hooker. She'll infect him with AIDS forty minutes from now.

I should have just gone to work tonight. I should have driven the taxi. I should never have come to Hunts Point. Save me, anyone, prays the fugitive in the front row.

"For each person the temptation is different. But the result is the same."

The man in the front row pulls down his Mets cap

and turns to squint toward the smashed-in garage door. Three silhouettes—large men, from the shapes—have just materialized in the shadows back there. Their heads move side to side as they scan the audience. Their features are invisible, but the fugitive feels as if their scrutiny carries weight, and darkness, coalesced into human form, needs a few more seconds to gather power, to attack.

"Hell's Gate," warns the bald, bearded preacher in a soft voice, "is as small as the last digit of a phone number you know you shouldn't be dialing, as delicious as one too many sips of scotch before you drive off on an icy night. It's as logical as an urge to please someone you love: a parent, a boss, a child."

The shadow men glide forward.

"You men! We have extra seats in the front if you'd care to sit."

The attention freezes them, but they resume moving when the preacher's attention shifts to the trucker and the hooker, who are whispering together in the third row.

Only a few years ago here—before fire closed the place—big eighteen-wheelers would back up to this dock in the Hunts Point warehouse district each night to unload fat prosciutto hams from Parma, sweet Vidalia onions from Georgia, bananas from Honduras, crates of baby peas, yellow squash, corn, black beans. Food biblical in its proportions, to feed New York. Bounty grown, manufactured, or genetically engineered from all corners of the earth.

"If you are here, friends, you have known temptation."

Homeless men eye folding tables laden with freebie Tropicana orange juice, freebie Dunkin' Donuts.

"You never dreamed you'd live in a wasteland like this."

The shadow men halt in the dark areas flanking the front row; two on one side, one—the biggest—on the other.

I never should have followed them into that bar, the man in the middle of the first row thinks. *Or asked them that last question.*

He looks pathetic, more boy, less man. His khaki shorts are as grimy as his black Keds high-tops. His sweat-stained T-shirt swells with a pear-shaped body that's been out of shape for years. His Mets cap is pulled low over black-framed glasses. Only his biceps show muscles, as if they're the only part of him that gets exercise.

He might win an arm wrestling contest. He'll never win a race.

I shouldn't have asked them about their job.

"Hell's Gate is the name we New Yorkers call the body of water only half a mile from here," the preacher announces to the blast of a tug horn, a requiem floating over his congregation in a low F flat. "It's a ship graveyard, right in our city. Down there lies the broken sloop *Irene* and the schooner *Diadem.* The tug *Vixen* and the brig *Guisborough.* The wrecks of the *Flagg,* the *Planter,* the fine old *Hannah Ann.*"

I'm too scared to stand.

"Imagine those struggling sailors as the water closed over them. But my friends, they'd reached Hell's Gate long before their ships."

The man in the front row bolts.

He runs up onto the loading dock, toward the startled preacher but away from the men. Charging past the preacher, he glimpses wide bottle-green eyes and white palms coming up, as if to ward off an attack.

The man plunges through a half-sealed doorway into the abandoned main warehouse. The dark assumes geometry. Blocky forms of burned-out machinery rise up in opaque light seeping through mesh windows, or flooding through holes smashed in sooty glass. The runner weaves past stripped-down conveyer belts, rusted blackened crane hoists, stilled winches, pushcarts robbed of wheels.

Dim, through the wreckage, he makes out a exit door at the far end of the big room.

He bangs his shin but keeps from crying out, more from vocal-cord paralysis than self-control.

Someone call the police. He sends his will out as a prayer.

The only answer is the sound of footsteps behind.

A flashlight beam swings in the dark.

What is about to happen will never make the newspapers. The homeless people of Hunts Point don't talk to police. The trucker's not about to admit he left a $110,000 rig parked alone. The preacher will make no inquiries because in this neighborhood that would violate an unspoken bargain.

Which is mind your own business, preacher, and pimps and pushers won't bother you.

Maybe the agreement will bring *me* to Hell's Gate one day, the preacher sometimes thinks.

"I won't tell," the man in the Mets cap yells as he batters his way through the two-by-fours half-nailed across the exit. Doubled with exertion, he pants back onto the street.

I won't tell.

Outside, Hunts Point presents itself as deserted block after block of warehouses, razor-wire fences, and bars in which the liquor served is more of a side business. The rare private home is squeezed between tire shops. Squad cars—when they come—seem more lost than appropriate in a place where most vehicles lack even parts to be stripped. Street names—like Tiffany and Casanova—suggest that geography itself would rather be somewhere else.

In the distance, through gaps between warehouses, the running man sees the lights of Manhattan, beyond the East River shoreline oil terminals.

"Get away from meeeee!"

His sneakers slap against glass and roadway. He realizes that he's run the wrong way. He crashes into a chain-link fence topped by concertina wire. Moonlight illuminates a municipal sign beside a long hole cut in the fence.

TIFFANY STREET PIER. KEEP OUT AT NIGHT.

Beyond that the dark river churns toward the roughest part of the harbor. The late summer air seems as thick as water down there.

I can't swim. The man pounds down the pier.

And of course here they come, as silent and purposeful as African wild dogs he once saw on TV in a National Geographic special. He'd *told* himself not to talk to these guys, but had been unable to resist asking one five-second question, the one that had made their eyes turn hard.

"Please don't hurt me."

Sinking down on his knees, he feels the moist scrape of wood and smells the tarry odor of resin. He's afraid to make eye contact as the men reach him. When a hand appears at face level, he sees the tiny tattoo below the knuckle of the index finger. He'd noticed it in the bar, a picture of an old-style cutlass side by side with a barracuda. At the time the image had made him think of pirates.

Henry Morgan. Blackbeard. Calico Jack. Captain Greaves.

When the finger crooks now, the barracuda's mouth seems to open.

"I don't know what you're doing. I don't care what you're doing. I'll go away and never come back," the man in the baseball cap whimpers.

The Mets cap falls into the water.

The hands, when they touch him, are gentle.

He hears a siren in the distance.

It's much too far away.

Hell's Gate again, seen this time through a telescope.

"You left him in the water," says Ted Stone coldly, eye pressed to the piece.

Leon Bok stands behind him, eyeing Ted's fine paintings. He is unintimidated by the severe tone. The room is silent and the two men so high up the only sound is the hum of central air-conditioning soothing away the mechanized fray sixty-five stories below. No sound from FDR Drive or the UN helipad or river walkway. Ted's triple-strength windows turn Manhattan into a diorama. The city is filled with moving toys down there.

"A police patrol was coming. There was nothing else to do," Leon remarks in his flat, dead voice.

"But you *did* go to his apartment," says Ted. "Right?"

"He had frozen pizzas in the refrigerator."

"I'm not asking about his diet."

"I know what you're asking. He wasn't the one."

Ted is tall and lean and at thirty-five he's reached the tail end of his competitive-squash-playing years. Tiny rectangular distance glasses give him a slight air of befuddlement when he looks down his nose through the lenses, but accentuate his intimidating aspect if he gazes over the top. It's the sort of look that gets guys punched in bars but works well against subordinates in offices. His eyes are as cold as marble. His face is long and remote. His sandcolored hair is thick and boyishly straight on top, cut close at the sides and beginning to show gray. His light wool suit is soft as cashmere. Red suspenders add a festive splash while enhancing the conservative core. His desk is filled with photos of a pretty, adolescent girl playing tennis. She's got Ted's limber build.

She seems like a happy kid.

Leon is shorter but wider, and well muscled in a rough, outdoor way, judging from the way the pinstriped fabric fits on his two-button Armani suit. He seems at ease, at peace. The silk striped tie is perfectly knotted. His skin is tanned as a sailor's and his face is smart, broad, flat. Combined with his soft vague accent, his intriguing features often lead women to speculate over his nationality. Wide-ranging guesses include Moroccan, Turkish, Argentinean, dark Russian. The women always choose someplace exotic. Something in the man suggests that no matter where he is, he arrived there from far away.

Leon unwraps a small, foil-covered piece of dark Swiss chocolate. "Anyway, we should be finished in five days, more or less."

"The police will find him before that."

Stone straightens up from the telescope. Bok shrugs.

"Police aren't even permitted to hit people in this country," says Leon. "So how can they accomplish meaningful things?"

"They get lucky once in a while."

"No one ever called finding me lucky."

Outside, Hell's Gate burns red, reflecting the chemically enhanced glow of the rising sun. Crimson light flows down the spires of Midtown. It spreads along the bridge cables and reddens fog patches spotting the river. Tugs look as industrious as army ants down there. They are a mechanized current threading Hell's Gate.

Inside, Ted's phones are ringing and the two men— equally matched—regard each other under the scrutiny of a dozen pairs of staring eyes. There's the imperious George III, depicted in the original portrait painted by Richard J. Barrington in 1779. The drooping condescension in the glance of the duke of Cornwall, as he poses with his sword in the left hand, right hand on jutting hip, 1693. The gluttonous desire in the black irises of the Spanish Infanta María Christina, betrothed to Prince William of England to bind two royal families. The marriage failed.

The chairs come from Christie's auction house. The glass case holds mahogany-handled pistols fired at Waterloo against French dragoons. The hunt tapestry once hid a water stain in a castle eight miles from Inverness. British troops looted the tapestry and carried it back to London, where it was eventually sold to, in order, a Pennsylvania coal magnate, a Chicago radio producer, a Silicon Valley software inventor, and finally British antiques enthusiast Ted Stone.

Maybe Bok is part French, Ted thinks, picking up the mockery in the way he regards the British paintings, and the snobbish reverence whenever food comes up. Like *they* never make mistakes? They groveled to Hitler. They sell nuclear parts to anybody. They lost a war to Algerians and had to be bailed out both times Germany attacked. But eat a Pop-Tart in front of a French office messenger who failed high school and he'll treat you like you're a gorilla.

"I want someone watching that apartment all the time, Leon."

"Of course."

"I want to know if police go there."

The impassiveness in Bok's face conveys about two thousand years of evolved indifference, as if any of his ancestors who couldn't knock down an oak with contempt stopped breeding around the time of Charlemagne, and now, after centuries, only the champs of ridicule remain. Bok's face muscles seem not to have moved in the slightest, and *still* the feeling coming off him is pure disdain, like, what do you think, I'm stupid? What do you think, I flew in from Santiago or Bonn or wherever the hell you ordered me in from because I *don't* know what to do?

"I'll need the name of any police who come, and the license on the car," Ted orders.

"Perhaps I can finish up in three days, before your lucky imaginary policeman can figure things out."

Ted feels the warm flow of relaxation spread over him, of wishful thinking. But then Bok shrugs.

"I cannot be rushed," Bok says. "It is not a science. Perhaps I will need ten days, not three."

Ted Stone goes back to the telescope as a form of dismissal. A half-minute later he hears the door close.

Down on the river, the sun's turned the waters of Hell's Gate gold, the color of doubloons, embossed stock certificates, and the Krugerrands Ted's been accumulating as the stock market tanks.

He's sweating through his shirt now, despite the air-conditioning.

I never should have started this. It can't possibly go longer than five more days. Please please let it stop before five more days.

Unconsciously, he's adopted the same stance as that of King George III, whose portrait, on his wall, was finished two weeks before the Americans won their Revolution. George looks pretty poised up there, even haughty, but maybe it was an act that day. Maybe he was consumed with fear too. Maybe he showed the painter one face, but inside he was screaming in terror.

If anyone can help me, it's Leon.

"So this is Hell's Gate," Camilla says.

Voort opens his eyes and shields them against noon sun that is as warm as a first rush of anesthesia. The gorgeous blonde on the beach towel to his right wears a black string bikini right out of a teenage boy's dream.

Voort loves her long hair. Her trim, tight athlete's body. Her tanned, smooth skin that highlights her fierce Irish blue eyes.

The green birches and oaks behind the strip of beach are filled with migrating tanagers. Two foldable kayaks, yellow for Voort, red for Camilla, lie pulled up where they'd left them two hours ago.

"I can't believe we're in the middle of New York," she says.

"Ready to head back through the Gate?"

"Falling asleep during an argument doesn't win it."

"I fell asleep because I was tired."

"You're *tired* because you've been carrying the load for Mickie for weeks. You're working without a functioning partner. If you get in trouble, who's going to save your nicely muscled ass, Voort?"

A good day, despite the edge to the banter. A relaxing day. His first day off in two weeks.

"Whatever's wrong, Mickie will work it out," he says, knowing that in all likelihood, he's just lied.

Brushing her hair, she leans close. Even when she's irritated her lips fascinate him. "That's interesting because you don't even know what *it* is," she says. "You say, 'Hey, Mickie.' He says, 'I know.' End of conversation. What is it with guys?"

"They give all their attention to their gorgeous fiancées," says Voort, who knows Mickie's problem well enough and has been jeopardizing his job by protecting his best friend.

"That's the most pathetic, condescending and bald-faced attempt at dropping a subject I ever heard," Camilla says, grinning.

"Yeah, but you liked it," Voort says, smiling back.

There's something about a woman when you finally decide on her, Voort thinks. It's a solid feeling that makes all the old questions disappear. You sleep more deeply. You're filled with a kind of certainty you'd never known existed before. You understand things you've been missing.

"At least talk to Mickie," she says.

"You know what they say about Irish women?" Voort stands and starts gathering up the remains of lunch. "They never die. They just get smaller and smaller from wind erosion. After a while nothing remains but a complaining voice by the fireplace."

"You know what they say about Dutch men?" she counters. "They never die because they were never alive in the first place."

"Okay, I'll really talk to him this time."

Her kiss still gives him a jolt. Any disagreements between them these days are nothing compared to the obstacles they've overcome. He flashes back to some of their history. There was the initial three-month period when the richest cop in New York had started dating the tough, beautiful TV producer. It had been the most sexually thrilling time of Voort's life, and her day-to-day temperament—the rhythms of her quiet times—had matched his own. But there had also been some extra quality that defied definition. Some primal connection that had driven him wild.

He'd been so infatuated he'd found himself praying for her in church each day, including her in the supplications he sent out for the family.

God, he'd say, help me make her as happy as she makes me.

Now as they store the remnants of lunch in the kayaks he remembers the second phase, when she'd started disappearing evenings, seeing a shrink, as he later found out. He'd learned of a betrayal so bad it seemed impossible he could ever forgive her.

She wanted to come back but I said no.

Which is why he'd been amazed to find himself ringing her bell one day after the Szeska case had concluded. They'd become friends again, and then lovers, and now—four years after they met—what exists between them lacks the spicy danger of the early days, but it's a mix of trust, respect, and chemistry, with just enough unpredictability thrown in to make him anticipate happy surprises in the upcoming years.

"Last one through the Gate has to limit the wedding list to two hundred," he says.

"Then it better be you, because that's how many Voorts we have at the house every night."

In the foldable Feathercrafts they push into the swift water toward Hell's Gate. At this hour flood tide is flowing in from Long Island Sound, heading south toward the East River, which is churning north. The collision zone is the S-shaped curve ahead.

Beyond that Voort sees the towers of Manhattan.

"Yippee!" Spray flying, Camilla drives her foldable out of a bubbling whirlpool and up a four-foot wave. She's a former college kayak champ, a TV news producer laid off by NBC. She spends hours each day at the Hudson River boathouse, building custom models for private clients, having made the transition from professional woman to unemployed athlete without a hitch.

Voort keeps pace easily, a lean man, with good shoulders, bronzed by the sun and powdered by beach salt. He's the guy women notice in offices, churches, supermarkets, jazz clubs.

Overhead is the railroad bridge linking Queens with the soccer fields of Randall's Island. At Voort's back is Brother Minor, the island where he and Camilla had eaten their picnic of warm French bread, smoked Gouda, pink strips of prosciutto, and ice-cold Evian water. No people live on Minor. Its ruins and woods are filled with migrating birds. Even farther astern, from the prison windows at Rikers, inmates jeer at anyone on the water who's having fun.

"Watch out, Camilla!"

A big square-prow tug chugs toward them, twin engines roaring, diesels set at full thrust to push through Hell's Gate. The captain blows his horn at the kayakers—to him, Voort guesses, irritating specks on the waterway. Pleasure seekers who have no place clogging up a business highway, a commercial thoroughfare for real river men, not a playground for yuppies and their two-thousand-dollar toys.

"Fuck you too," Camilla shouts, getting out of the way easily. She's dainty as a schoolgirl one moment, tough as an eighteen-wheeler driver the next.

The tug sends up a wake that hits a wave that churns into a whirlpool. Seventy feet below, from a mountain of rock, tons of water bubbles up toward the sand barge towed by the tug's thick ropes.

"He's trying to slow me down, Voort."

"That, Camilla, is impossible."

Ahead, something white and big spins in a whirlpool. *I hope that isn't what I think it is,* Voort thinks.

Is that an arm?

The day so far has been a journey—as any metropolitan trip is for Voort—through three centuries of family history. It had started at eight this morning when they'd carried the foldable Feathercrafts in their knapsacks from his house on Thirteenth Street, a property Voorts have occupied since the end of the American Revolution, when the Continental Congress gave the family the land and any structure built on it in perpetuity, tax-free.

"It was a reward for keeping the British from landing in New Jersey," he'd told Camilla on their first date.

They'd walked under the FDR Drive to the Twentieth Street "beach," a strip of sand, rock, and washed-up pilings jutting twenty feet into the East River. They'd assembled the shock-cord frames and rolled on the Duratek skins of the foldables as fascinated onlookers, chess-playing oldsters, looked on.

"The British chained American POWs together in prison ships, off this point," Voort had told her.

The ninety-minute journey upriver had taken them through a panorama reminding him of family tales. Here was Roosevelt Island, to which Voort cops had ferried the city's orphans at the turn-of-the-previous-century. Here was the UN, where Voorts had held back protesters hundreds of times since the building opened its doors. Here was North Brother Island, to which Voorts had rowed the waitress Mary Mallon—"Typhoid Mary"—to live out her days in isolation.

"She sang all the way out," Voort had told Camilla.

Fact is, Voorts have protected the city since the Dutch first settled it. They patrolled the mud streets on foot in

New Amsterdam. They drive electrically rechargeable Hondas in Central Park today.

"What's *that* in the water, Voort?" Camilla says now. "My God!"

"He moved! I think he's alive!"

Voort paddles hard to give the man something to grab, but a whirlpool sucks away the body.

I'm caught too.

It's impossible to keep the kayak stable and reach out at the same time to grab a black-Ked-clad foot. Then the foot is gone but fists are spinning above the surface, as if the man twirls underwater like a Rollerblader enthralled by music on headphones, like skaters in Central Park.

The maelstrom pushes the forehead to the surface.

I was wrong. He's been cut up by propeller, or ship. No way is that guy alive.

On land, meanwhile, in Astoria Park, people are starting to realize something dangerous is happening twenty feet from the shore rocks.

Voort tips left, rolling dangerously. He's going to get dumped. He thrusts the flat of his paddle into the current and uses its counterforce to right himself. Camilla has driven her Feathercraft into the floater to try to push the body to shore.

"Together!" she shouts. TV producers have a need to produce.

They inch the corpse toward the softball field in Astoria Park.

The game has halted. Players in red or blue uniforms line the rocks, spread out to help if the kayakers can get close enough. Men extend bats, which are much too short to reach.

"Grab it!"

Someone screams, "Watch out!" and Voort spins the kayak left to avoid a heavy timber shooting past.

Camilla hits the riptide suddenly and her kayak gets caught between currents. She spins. She flips. She's upside down. Voort's heart goes to his mouth, but in that fraction of a second she surfaces again, cursing, long hair flying, muscles straining as she drives the prow into the body with renewed force, gaining another two feet.

"Camilla, get to shore and call 911."

A fisherman has removed the hook from his line and replaced it with bobbers and weights, to cast it farther as a makeshift lifeline. Falling toward Voort, the red and white plastic bobbers resemble Christmas tree decorations dropping from the sky.

"Camilla, go ashore! I'll follow the guy!"

But the current gives them a break, spurts them toward shore so the ballplayers haul up the body and kneel and grab the kayaks. Hands reach, grip wrists, pull hard until Voort and Camilla half crawl, half scramble onto land, blowing hard, out of breath.

The last thing Voort needs is some two-hundred-pound ballplayer shouting in his face, but the guy is doing it anyway.

"I'm a cop," he yells as Voort notices the team name—Thespians—on the man's blue shirt. "Are you crazy to go out there? You goddamn people! Crazy nuts! Your buddy's dead! Are you out of your mind?"

"The current's not even a class two," retorts Camilla, puffing up to them, coming to Voort's defense. She's right, Voort knows. Without the body to handle, passage would have been simple. They plan to honeymoon on more difficult stretches of water in Andalusia four months from now.

"Camilla, you hurt?"

But she looks fine and says, "Your cell phone's in my front compartment." Meaning, to call 911.

Camilla adds, "Excuse me, honey."

She leans over and throws up.

Voort introduces himself to the cop and takes over. He orders the off-duty Blue Guy, "Keep everyone away." He adds, recognizing shock in the man, "You did a great job. Tell your pals thanks."

After calling 911 he phones his partner, Mickie, on Long Island, at his waterfront mansion.

No one answers there. Nor does he get a response on Mickie's cellular phone.

Which has been the way things have been going even when they're on duty lately. Mickie's just not there.

Hell's Gate churns behind him as Voort bends and examines the body, the gashes, feels for breaks, studies the face. It's cut up but not puffy, so the death occurred last night or today, Voort guesses, maybe as recently as the last few hours, although his experience with floaters is limited, so he could be wrong.

The arms took a beating. The right hip seems caved in. The skull has suffered one hell of an impact, probably from boat, rock, timber, whatever shredded the T-shirt down the man's back. Blunt objects in the river flow down every few moments, coming at targets in multiple choice.

"Who is he?" Camilla asks, beside Voort again, staring down in horror, and yet he hears in her voice the TV pro-

ducer's ability to dehumanize a situation, the instinct—
whether she's working or not—that never goes away.

Voort orders her away from the body.

"I *found* him, buster."

A quick look from Voort and she's backing away.

"Do you think," she asks, "he jumped or fell?"

Voort kneels again, frowning. "Look how his pockets
are all turned inside out. The current didn't do that. Peo
ple did."

TWO

Dusk now, and all over the city people indulge in risky excesses. A film agent decides to work instead of attending her sixteen-year-old son's playoff soccer game. She'll dwell on this memory when she's dying of cancer twelve years from now. A pilot waiting to take control of a 747 sips from a Jack Daniel's miniature in a locked stall in a JFK bathroom. It's just one drink, he tells himself. A secretary heading home from work, in a rush, cuts through a thickly wooded part of Central Park instead of skirting it. A high school gym teacher driving to an Atlantic City casino takes his bank card along despite his wife's entreaties. This way if I run out of cash I can get more, he excitedly thinks.

"How's the fiancée, Voort?"

"Fine, Tina."

"Here's that fax you wanted."

The office of assistant medical examiner Tina Tadesse is small but comfortable. She's one of those people adept at making the best of things. The terra-cotta walls are hung with blow-up photos of the beaches of Somalia, where she'd been born. The odor is floral thanks to the riot of potted palms, tulips, and orchids that block out worse aromas from the hallway outside. Voort gets a small thrill as their fingers touch when she hands him the fax sheets. Tina's a head turner, all right, a tall, gorgeous Yale graduate who spent her girlhood in Switzerland with diplomat parents. Her investment-banker sister is engaged to one of Voort's cousins. He's worked with Tina and likes her. He'd once considered dating her, but she'd had a boyfriend at the time.

Since breaking up with the boyfriend, she's occasionally let Voort know she's available were he to find himself single again.

"Set the wedding date, Voort?"

"December."

Her eyes are black magnets. Her skin is velvet. Her glossy hair is cut at neck length. Even though she works in the death house, she manages to smell of good perfume.

Voort took her out for coffee a month ago, told himself it was to talk about a case, realized it wasn't, and never phoned again. But late at night he sometimes finds himself thinking about her. Occasionally he envisions her naked when he makes love to Camilla. Imagining that slender body is harmless fantasy, he tells himself.

Everyone has fantasies, he thinks.

"Large wedding or small, Voort?"

"Big Dutch family. We'll put a tent on the roof for the overflow from the house."

He hates the morgue, the way that in the exam areas and halls sound echoes, the way the smell gets in clothing, the way cops and doctors bend over gurneys, the way tubes stuck into bodies carry life's fluids out but never in.

He hates the gleaming cabinets and air-conditioning set at temperatures to accommodate dead people. He hates the way, after bad fires or air crashes, pallets fill hallways and ambulances line the parking lot outside. Visiting the morgue always makes him want to go to church afterward. It makes him feel like he's walking inside a steel coffin. It makes him feel clocks ticking, time passing. It makes him want to take the day off and make love to Camilla, to feel alive.

Some cops get over it—make jokes about corpses or smoke cigars to keep the smell away. Voort thinks those cops have lost a little edge.

Brought to the old morgue by his dad when he was eight, he remembers, he'd asked, "Why does it smell like a hospital if there's no one to cure?"

"If you become a cop, you'll come here often. You'll do it to keep other people from making the trip too soon."

But afterward his dad had taken him to Lucky Tim's Pizza, ordered a double cheese with extra sausages and pepperoni, black olives, sweet green peppers, hot onions. All his favorite additions. As if to apologize for showing him something ugly and celebrate food, drink, air.

"What's the fax, Voort?" Tina asks now.

"A missing persons list."

Her slender leg swings up and down, giving him a flash of stocking through the slit of her baby-blue surgeon's gown. "I moved your floater up in line. Not that anyone in front of him complained. Want to watch?"

"No," he says, standing anyway. When she walks her body sways to some personal hormonal music. Her high heels set down directly in front of each other. A man couldn't walk that way even if he tried.

Glancing at the missing persons list as she picks out instruments in autopsy bay B, he sees the list starts out with a Beth Aarons (White) and a Harvey Clarke (White) and a Cleon Francis (Black). There's a Marcel Paul and a Clarice Sanchez, and he sees the name Erica Max and the name Peter DeGrange, age 42, nose scar as an identifying feature, home address in Katonah, New York.

The names are at the moment mere rearrangements of letters. They lack faces, passions, dislikes. But Voort knows each one represents an anguished phone call to the department. It means that some daughter, husband, lover, or friend is sitting by a telephone, or watching out the window, living in terror of a squad car pulling up to disgorge a detective sent to escort them to this horrible place.

"He drowned, probably," Tina says at length, bending over the sliced-up slab of body. "There's water in the lungs. The diatoms are from the East River. I can confirm it later. But I'd say ninety-five percent sure."

"Did the major bleeding start before or after he died?"

"After," she says, probing professionally. "And the angle on the postmortem trauma corresponds with damage caused by being struck by a ship, or ships. From the swelling I'd say he was in the water less than a day."

"What about the pockets turned inside out?"

Tina looks up intently, but there's slight amusement in her eyes, as if she is waiting for him to realize something. "I missed the class on pockets in medical school."

"But you found something extra." His pulse has quickened.

"I get pleasure from watching a smart man think."

He looks down at the slice line, the flaps, as if the corpse represents two John Does: before and after. The white, puffy skin area is spotted with curly, dark hairs.

The red, moist trench is filled with gray, orange, and blue viscera.

"These small bruises." His rubber-gloved index finger hovers above an arc of purplish dime-sized marks on the left shoulder blade.

Her head floats up and down like a model's. Her eyes are approving and the hollow in her throat pulses as she speaks. "These are not from a boat. Look at the pattern, the spacing."

"Fingers."

"That's what I think, with the larger bruises coming from palms pressing down. These are ruptured blood vessels. When you rupture an area, blood seeps into the intercellular spaces. Look at the other shoulder. And inside the left forearm and along the biceps. See? More of them."

"Like someone bent his arm back, held it against his back." Voort mimes it. "Shoving him along. These other bruises? More people restraining him."

A shrug. "Good guess."

"They drowned him? Held him down?"

"It's open to interpretation, cheri. I'll agree that several people fought with this man prior to his death. But the marks could come from being pushed up against a wall. His back is too smashed up to tell. The fight could have occurred hours before he died. For all I know, he was robbed, disoriented. He falls in, or he's pushed or jumps to get away."

"The currents are so crazy in Hell's Gate that he could have gone into the water anywhere within five miles north or south."

Tina's face seems close suddenly. "Do you ever fear

for yourself, dealing with people like ones capable of doing this to someone?"

"Mark the death open, Tina."

"He's special for you?"

Voort thinks about it. "Finding him made it special. And there was a moment when I thought I could save him. That did it, I guess."

"I'm off in twenty minutes." Meaning, do you want to go somewhere with me?

"I have guests at home." But there's no denying the tingle in his groin and the speck of disappointment he experiences at his own self-control.

Hell, I'm a dog. I can't help it. A dog in love with Camilla, but a dog all the same.

"Well then," she says, "congratulations again on your engagement, Conrad."

When they shake hands her fingers feel long and silky. Her smile tells him there's still time to change his mind.

"I lost the house. I lost the car. I'm broke."

Nine P.M. now, and Voort and Mickie sit in Voort's third-floor study in the town house that his family has occupied for two hundred years. Party noises—jazz and laughter—waft up from below. Voort hears the sounds of his nieces running in the hallway. His house has been the center of his extended family since the presidency of James Monroe. It's a haven that never closes. His ancestors stayed here when they came home from wars, or lost jobs in the Great Depression. Voort cops still bunk here if they have to be back at work in a few hours and their home in an outer borough is too far away.

"I was sure my tech stocks were going to rally, Con Man. So I borrowed and bought more."

The man in the stuffed chair across from Voort—his best friend—takes a long draught of Laphroaig and stares down at the woven colonial-era carpet. His shame is palpable. He's half-drunk, in shock, going on about a blow that had seemed only months ago inconceivable to him. From the hole he has fallen into, Mickie looks out at Voort as if a deep gap separates him from what used to be his own life.

"How much did you borrow, Mick?"

"I know I haven't been doing shit at work either. I know you've been carrying me. You're working two jobs basically, champ."

"Did you tell Syl what happened?"

"I barely admitted it to myself."

"You need money?"

"I need a genie in a bottle. I need a Frank Capra movie ending. I need a time machine to go back and buy two percent T-bills instead of thieving Tri-Star Energy stock. That's what I need."

Mickie drains his glass of single malt scotch.

"Please, Mr. Dickens, I want some more."

The crumbling economy has closed restaurants and bars and halted construction on the city's skyline. It's forced the mayor to lay off cops and firemen. It's left bridges rusting and expressways dotted with holes. Universities have stopped hiring professors. Pension-fund managers are testifying before Congress. Libraries are limiting hours of operation. Every other lamppost in residential neighborhoods has been turned off to save electricity at night.

"I heard on CNBC that the brokerage houses will be cutting bonuses on Wall Street, Con Man. Those companies pay thirty-five percent of the city's taxes. Goddamn Congress would try to privatize oxygen if they could figure out how to do it. Goddamn president would privatize breathing if he had the chance."

The phone starts ringing. Voort glances down at the Caller ID to see that Hazel, his favorite computer girl at One Police Plaza, is on the line. He'd asked her to monitor the missing persons list earlier, on top of working on half a dozen other cases he and Mickie have been assigned.

"How much did you lose, Mickie?"

"I had twelve million dollars a year ago. *Twelve million*. When I was a kid I figured only Rockefellers had that much. I couldn't even *say* a number that high. And then I actually figured out how to get it. And now . . ." He trails off.

His voice sounds like another man's, not Mickie's.

"Syl's a surgeon, Mick. She makes a good living."

"She's the woman," Mickie snaps as if Voort's comment was the dumbest in the world.

"What are you, a triceratops?" Voort says.

"Con Man, no matter what women say, they lose respect for you if they make more money. And then you lose respect for yourself. Ah, what do you know about it? You were born rich."

The phone stops ringing. Voort hopes Hazel is leaving a message on the answering machine.

Distract him. Get his mind on work.

"Mickie, when I saw that body . . ."

"All I had to do was pull out of the market. The warnings were there. But I told myself, I can make a killing. Last time I checked I *owed* over a quarter million. I took out a second mortgage. I fucked that up too."

As late as three months ago, Voort remembers, a *Daily News* article had called the partners "the richest cops in New York."

Mickie had come roaring out of the 1990s like a slum-kid genie of finance. He'd taken his salary and doubled and tripled it, and then tripled it again. Other detectives had nicknamed Voort and Mickie "Merrill and Lynch," "Paine and Webber."

Mickie had spent it as fast as he made it. "You can't enjoy it when you're dead," he'd said. His waterfront home in Roslyn sits in a gated compound including a carriage house, boathouse, private dock, two-car garage. He dresses like a *GQ* magazine model. He'd hired a private decorator to redo their office, stocked a mini-fridge in it with expensive coffees, cheeses, beers, breads.

"Just because we work in shit doesn't mean we have to live in it," he liked to say.

"Come downstairs, Mick. Eat something."

"Why? Eating makes the brain sharper," Mickie says, getting up and reaching for more Laphroaig.

The phone starts ringing again as Mickie taps his head shrewdly. "Let's go out and dull the memory, not improve it." Mickie grins. "I'll buy."

"You're going to have to tell Syl."

"Nah, I got a plan. I'll let the moving men do it. See, I found this apartment in Astoria. It's really great, Con Man. You don't have to shout over the street noise to be heard, 'cause the place is so small, and there's a washing machine in the basement. The exterminator comes once a month. It's paradise. I can't wait to show her, once she finds out what happened. She's liable too for what I lost. We fell in love the old-fashioned way. Joint accounts."

"Why don't you move in here awhile," Voort says. "You do windows, right?"

Mickie laughs, but the truth is, like the city itself, the reversal has robbed him of some essence. His bull neck has sagged. His jet-black hair is streaked with gray. A booze gut is starting to strain out over his belt buckle.

Our strengths are our weaknesses, Voort thinks. Mickie's always been an absolutist. There's no bend to him. He's as unforgiving with himself as with others. Watching him now is like watching a 747 crash.

"You know what I was thinking about today?" Voort says. "The time you showed up in the police launch after I got dumped in the river. On the Bainbridge case."

"You were wet."

"Cold."

"I saved your ass."

"Move in here until you figure out what to do," repeats Voort. "It's a big house. Camilla would love it. We'd be like one of those Idaho communes. You can milk the cow."

Mickie bursts out laughing. But when he looks up, Voort's surprised to see a glisten in his eyes. "Answer your phone, Con Man. One of us has to be responsible."

He stands unsteadily and weaves toward the bar while Voort picks up the phone.

"Voort? It's Hazel. I updated missing persons, like you wanted. A description came in that might interest you."

"You're the best girl."

"White guy. Thirty-eight years old. Hundred eighty, ninety, and out of shape, like you said. Brown eyes and hair. Maybe it's your floater. The name is Colin Means. His sister called it in."

"Any special marks?"

"A diamond-shaped birthmark inside the left thigh."

Voort feels a surge of adrenaline. "That works."

"So does the clothing. The report says he was probably wearing khaki shorts with lots of pockets. And ready for this? Black Keds."

"It's him."

"Before I give you the name, I've been suffering from Voodoo beer withdrawal. You don't happen to have any in your little fridge, do you?"

"Mickie stocked us up with Saranac. Help yourself."

"Tell that man I need stock tips. When the market goes back up, I want to ride it with you two geniuses all the way."

"I'll pass it on."

"Okay then, the sister's name is Rebecca Means. She's in Little Neck, at 21 Grady Place. If you're wondering how Colin made it onto the list so fast, Rebecca went to high school with a detective from the one-eleven. He did her a favor."

"Details, Hazel."

"Colin never reported for work yesterday. He's a cabby with Pioneer Yellow. Never misses work. Always calls home."

"The brother and sister live together?"

"They have separate apartments in the same house."

"Did the sister say where he might have gone the night he disappeared?"

"End of bulletin. But she's self-employed, so her home and office is the same."

Voort gets the name of the detective who took Rebecca's call. When he hangs up, Mickie wags a finger at him drunkenly. "My foster father used to disappear in Vegas, all the time. He didn't come back for two months once. I ever tell you that? He landed up in Gamblers Anonymous. But I don't need GA. That stupid higher power. I can stop myself."

"Did I mention Gamblers Anonymous?"

"I'll change. I'll be gangbusters, man. Plenty of people are worse off than me. I have a great wife, great friends. I have the infamous Con Man in my corner. What are we carrying now, anyway? Six, seven cases?"

"Eleven."

"When did *that* happen? Eva's really dumping on us," he says, jumping from one topic to another. "But hey! Once a Marine, always a Marine. Marines can get through anything."

"I have some papers for you to sign."

"I'm feeling good, optimistic. Maybe the market will even go up tomorrow," Mickie says, reaching for a pen. "If I can dig up some cash I can reverse the losses. Anything's possible, right?"

Voort feels like he's drowning as he opens a drawer and hands Mickie filled-in report forms, complaint forms. He's been completing them for his partner, late at night on the tie-in computer, or mornings, at home, before he goes to work.

"Sign here. And near the bottom. Date it."

"Isn't it possible the market will rebound?" Mickie sounds like an eight-year-old asking about Santa. He signs the papers that give the department proof, on paper, that he's been diligently working cases with Voort.

He saved my life. You don't abandon a friend because he hits a bad patch.

"Get a grip, Mickie. It's money. It's not like you have cancer."

"Only money? Fuck you. Better yet, give me yours."

Voort tells himself Mickie's slide is temporary. He tells himself as he goes downstairs that Mick is tough. Everyone goes through bad times.

As for Colin Means, I'll drive out to Queens early to-morrow. I'll take Mickie if he's sober, but I have a feeling he'll be sleeping off a bad night again.

The hallways are hung with portraits—a timeline of Voort cops; men with muttonchops and handlebar mustaches, men riding in motorcycle sidecars during the 1920s, when they busted up illegal distilleries and arrested whiskey smugglers from Canada.

"Just the furniture in this highly decorated detective's five-million-dollar town house is worth another three million easily," *Fine Homes* magazine had written last year when they did an article on the place. "The desks and armoires and even much of the good silverware came into the family as Revolutionary War booty, taken from Tory homes after the owners evacuated, or pillaged from British ships."

Voort grew up here. He left to live with various relatives after his parents died in a plane crash when he was nine. But he returned within two years at his own request—and the family's agreement—to live here with bachelor uncles until he reached age eighteen. No one had wanted the house empty. It meant too much to them.

On Voort's birthday that year, the last uncle to live with him—a detective lieutenant—had taken him to watch a Mets game from the family box and then he'd moved out, after which Voort had resided in the house by himself while attending NYU, then the police academy.

But he's never really been alone here. He's the head of the extended family, and this is their capitol building. Family carpenters and electricians work on the house when it needs repair. Two years ago his cousin Matt lived here while undergoing successful chemotherapy. Last year a dead cousin's widow—dispossessed by the World Trade Center disaster—moved in with her son until she found a place to live near the boy's school.

"On the morning of the arrest we walk into the hedgefund office," booms a voice from the kitchen. Voort recognizes it as belonging to Uncle Vim, a retired detective with the DA's fraud division. "Where our arrogant CEO—he's been laughing at us for months, right? He's sitting in his corner office, Bruno Maglis up on his mahogany desk. You should have seen his face when I put on the cuffs."

Voort pushes through the swinging door into the huge, warm Dutch kitchen. Half a dozen relatives sit with Camilla at the big antique table. Voort sees a bubbling stew pot, and on counters, platters of steaming corn, squash, garlic mashed potatoes, macaroni salad, wine bottles, cold cider jugs, a perking coffee machine, and a half-dozen pies, brought down by the Hudson Valley group, or in from bakeries by the Queens Voorts.

Tradition is, each visiting family brings food. People serve themselves and clean up when they leave.

Camilla's a Voort now in all ways but legal, he thinks. Head cocked sideways, she sits at the head of the table, chin in palm, listening intently. Her eyes glow with pleasure when she realizes he's come into the room. She's wearing denim overalls and a pink T-shirt. Her hair is up, so Voort can see her turquoise stud earrings. He's warmed by the light of the diamond ring on her wedding finger. It was his mother's, and before that, his grandmother's. Someday they'll pass it on to a daughter, or daughter-in-law, Voort thinks, massaging her shoulders.

Uncle Vim is saying, "You know what the guy does when we get him to the station? He takes one look at the holding cell and actually pisses on the floor. He says, 'You're not going to put me in with real felons are you?' I said, 'Real? *Those* guys burglarized a house and stole six hundred dollars. *You* ripped off the bridge painters' pension fund, the nursing home ladies. *You* defrauded enough to build a subway to JFK.'"

"I love this part," says cousin Matt, nodding to Voort.

"*He* says," Vim continues, "'I'm not going to have to go to a regular prison, am I? Can't I go to that nice prison in Pennsylvania? The one for businessmen?'"

Camilla winks at Voort. She's heard the story three times before.

Matt finishes the tale. "Vim says, 'Roger, I hope they put you in a cell with the biggest fudge packer in Sing Sing, and you're a soprano by the time your first week's through.'"

The laughter's got a rough edge. The city seems to be getting meaner, as if everyone is waiting for bad things to happen, as if everyone is looking for someone to blame.

Camilla tells Voort, "You sit. I'll serve," and heads to the industrial-sized stove to bring back a stew that makes his mouth water. Voort spoons up chunks of savory beef, yams, peas from Matt's farm, cauliflower, okra, and spicy radish bits and black pitted olives.

"You talk to Mickie?" she asks when the others go into the living room, to give the engaged couple privacy. The family has a finely tuned sense of when to leave Voort alone.

"You bet."

"Everything okay?"

"Absolutely," Voort lies.

"I have a special dessert for you," she says, leaning close. Her hand brushes his thigh. He feels a lovely tingle in his groin.

"Hmmm. Is the dessert ice cream?"

"It's warmer."

"I better leave room, then," he says as the door swings open to admit Mickie, who weaves into the kitchen, looking embarrassed and drunk.

"Hey, Con Man, I'm sorry but I spilled my drink on your reports. Then I tried to retype them but I think I did something to the computer. . . ."

"What?"

"The screen froze. I can't get it to respond to commands. Hi Camilla, did you make that stew? It smells great."

"It smells to *me* like whiskey just now."

Mickie's palms come up. "I don't blame you for being mad," he says. "Con Man's been covering for me. It takes time away from you. You have every right to be pissed."

"I'm glad I have your okay."

"Camilla," Voort says sharply.

Mickie looks dizzy for a moment. He steadies himself against the wall. He says, "I just wanted to tell you about the computer, Voort. I bet you'll fix it in two seconds. I'm a dinosaur when it comes to those things."

"I'm sure it won't be a problem. Are you hungry now?"

"There's, uh, also a little booze on the keyboard, but I wasn't sure how to clean it without hitting the wrong keys, you know, sending wrong commands. I didn't want to mess things up."

Camilla says, "How thoughtful."

"You eat. I'll check," Voort says.

"Yes, sit down, Mickie," Camilla says, getting up to fetch food. She adds, "Before you fall down."

Upstairs, Voort sees that Mickie's knocked over more than a "little" Laphroaig on the keyboard. Ice melts on the keys, with little pools of water atop letters *t* and *g*. A watery mix sloshes beneath other letters and runs in rivulets off the desk. He needs half an hour to clean it and reboot, then another thirty minutes to get the program running, reprint, and shut the thing off. He pulls the plug. He scrubs the whiskey smell off with scented soap and paper towels.

By the time he's through the music has stopped downstairs. So has the laughter. Lights are off in the hallways. Snoring comes from the extra guest room, which means

Mickie stayed over, instead of trying to drive home, which is some small relief.

But when he reaches his own bedroom Camilla's under the covers, back to his side of the bed. The small table lamp is on. Her back rises and falls erratically under her extra-large T-shirt. She's awake.

"Camilla?"

No answer.

"He saved my life, Camilla."

She rolls over. She looks hurt and confused. She says, miserably, "I know. I was in the water too. When he showed up in that boat at first I thought it was a mirage."

Voort says nothing. He just starts undressing.

"You're right," she says contritely.

"So he spilled a little whiskey."

"I guess I'm mad at myself because I'm angry at him. Mickie's not supposed to be weak. You and he are the strongest men I know. And I'm angry because he's taking up time when you could be with me. It's selfish."

She turns away again.

She's out of work. I've been ignoring her for weeks because I'm covering for Mickie. I don't even know what she does every night while I'm typing his reports. I'm too exhausted to ask. Truth is, these days she's more present at family functions than I am.

"You're not selfish," he says.

Voort kisses her on the shoulder. Naked, he slips under the covers. She smells terrific, of perfume and talcum and essence of girl. When he wraps his arms around her, he's already hard. Groin presses buttocks. Perfect fit, he thinks.

"That dessert you mentioned. Might it still be available, miss?"

She rolls toward him. She kisses his cheek. But then she turns over again.

I guess not.

Camilla lies toward the open window, preferring to face the street noises, the late-night discontent of the restless of the city.

After a while Voort falls asleep and dreams of Tina Tadesse.

Her black eyes stare up at him and her lean strong arms hold him close. In the dream he smells a warm musk odor tinged with perfume.

"Come inside me, Voort," she whispers. It's fantastically exciting.

Even in sleep, he's ending the day by going too far.

THREE

"Why do we have more money than other people?"

Eight-year-old Conrad Voort stands in his Little League uniform, on the roof of their home, looking up at big Bill manning the smoking Weber. It's a gloriously hot July night. The Panasonic is tuned to the Mets game. Half a dozen uncles sprawl nearby in Adirondack chairs, drinking Red Stripes, laughing about Stallone's bad acting in *Rocky III*, admiring the Oakland A's speed-demon base stealer, Ricky Henderson.

"Billy Martin's the greatest manager that ever lived."

A great summer so far. Ron Reagan is president, and Mayor Koch—commander in chief of the NYPD—has just returned from a goodwill visit to Cairo.

"Will the ruins of New York have the same grandeur as Egypt's a thousand years from now? I don't think so," Koch announced when he got back.

Bill Voort looks down at his son as if he has always known that the money question would come one day. "We have more because your namesake won a battle instead of losing it. Because Voorts invested wisely. You and me are lucky, big guy. You need some luck in life. Why do you ask?"

"Because the first baseman on Powell's Raiders said I was a stupid rich kid and my life is fun only because *his* is shit. He said *his* father told him that."

Uncle Bram calls over to them, "Hey Bill, the commissioner's turning into a little Commie. Send him to one of those Russian collective farms."

The uncles laugh.

But Voort feels bad thinking about the other kid, an angry eight-year-old, a beanpole filled with rage. Voort remembers the way when the game was over the boy trudged out of the park in the direction that poor kids live, toward a different part of the island. The part he hears sirens heading toward sometimes. The part mentioned in *Daily News* crime headlines. The part he sees on Channel Two when it shows fires, shootings, drug arrests, a riot.

"Want a steak, Khrushchev?" says Uncle Bram, extending a plate. "Or would you rather eat the slop Russians eat? I fought the Reds in Korea so kids like you could eat steak."

"Lay off him," says Uncle Vim, one of Voort's favorite relatives.

Next morning Voort wakes to see Dad sitting on his bed, watching him with the expression that always makes the boy feel warm, appreciated, but tested too. Bill says, "I thought we could go buy that bike you wanted today."

"Thanks!"

"We'll chow down on blueberry pancakes at Athens Diner. Then head over to Bike City for one of those models that's light as a quarter, and so fast, pal, that next time we race the loop in Central Park, I'll have a coronary trying to keep up with you."

An hour later Voort and Dad are in the big Buick heading north up Sixth Avenue toward the Triborough Bridge and, Voort assumes, fabulous Bike City, which sells about every two-wheel contraption in the civilized world. Only instead of Bike City, Dad drives into Harlem, past 125th Street, past the liquor stores and funeral parlors, until he turns onto Stowe Drive and pulls over across from a row of burned-out tenements and a rubble-strewn lot.

At ten thirty the day's already so hot that a dozen boys and girls run in and out of hydrant spray across the street. Water sparkles in the bright sun and mists down on a busted-up Mister Softee truck leaning against the curb, stripped and abandoned.

A hundred degrees out with WABC promising a day of broken temperature records. Without air-conditioning, the car fills with humid heat. Voort rolls down his windows.

"Why are we here, Dad?"

"Just sit, buddy."

"Can you turn on the air-conditioning?"

"Not right now, chief."

Voort, by now, has accompanied Dad on occasional jobs; visits to crime scenes. He spends many weekday afternoons at One Police Plaza where he's become a kind of detective mascot. He's no stranger to Harlem, but is unsure why they have come here today, as there's no crime to solve.

Then Dad starts the car and electrically rolls up the windows. The wash of cool air bathes Voort as the Buick heads away from Harlem, north, and finally sails into the massive parking lot of every kid's dream emporium, Bike City, in the Bronx. The model that Dad picks out has a super-light aluminum frame and SunTour derailleurs, a shock absorber, a cool, gleaming black paint job, and best of all, fifteen speeds.

It's better than a regular bike. It's the kind of bike that every boy dreams of. The kind, when you're riding it, that makes you imagine yourself driving the Indianapolis 500, fleeing bandits, battling alien spacecraft, driving the damn bike into the blue sky like the kid in the movie *E.T.*

"Like it, Conrad?"

"It's the *best!*"

"We can buy *this* bike, or," Dad says, rolling it disappointingly away from the cash register and up another aisle, "the Peugeot, which costs half. But that way we can buy two of them and give one to a kid at the hydrant. Or to another poor kid, like your pal in the park."

Voort frowns.

"Or," Dad says, walking toward another display, "we can buy the Raleigh, which costs a third of the first bike, and buy *two* bikes for other kids or, if you want, we'll drive over to W. S. Roth's and get ten of those discount models, and give *nine* away. Your choice. I'll spend the same amount of money today no matter what. We're on a budget."

"I don't know those kids."

"All for you, or split it up?"

Voort senses curiosity. The father wants to learn about the son.

"What should I do, Dad?"

"Make up your own mind."

"Is this about what I asked yesterday?"

"It's about figuring out who you are."

"One for me. One for another kid," Voort decides. "Is that the right answer?"

"Why ask me? How about ten bikes for the other kids and none for you? You already have a Schwinn."

"I want this one." He feels content with the decision. A weight's off his back. But he's unsure of the lesson. "What is it?" asks Voort, wanting to please Bill.

"Someday Mom and I won't be around. I hope it won't happen for years. But after that *you'll* own the house. *You'll* be the center of the family. *You'll* be the one they look to, and only *you'll* be able to figure out the balance between what others want and what *you* want. You have more than other people. Unless you screw up, you'll probably always have more, and that makes you a little different. Not better. Not special. Just different. But what you want and what *they* want won't always be the same, even when you love them, even when you want to make them happy."

Within the year, his parents are dead in a plane crash.

He's remembering the bikes as he steers his Jaguar out of the Midtown Tunnel and heads east against the flow of pre-rush hour traffic toward the outskirts of the city, where Long Island meets Queens. The buildings are shorter here. The congestion eases, but the glamour falls away. He passes a vast gray-stone cemetery, a staple factory, and a zipper factory and the railyard for the LIRR. The city is a mini-country. He's in its heartland now. Queens is the Iowa, the Wisconsin of New York.

What do I do about Mickie?

His partner's back on the second floor of the town house, probably waking from another drunk.

He misses Mickie's surly company. He misses the way Mickie never shuts up. He misses the wisecracks attacking every news bit on the radio, every politician's pronouncement, every excuse that suspects make, and half the decisions Voort makes in his personal life.

Just give him a week or two, I told Camilla.

But the truth is, Mickie's getting worse, fast.

Right about now his best friend will be unsteadily making his way down to the kitchen, where Voort's pissed-off fiancée will be packing a lunch to take to the boathouse.

I need to think about Colin Means now.

He exits the Long Island Expressway at Little Neck Parkway. Urban becomes suburban. The homes are nice, and big, with green lawns and hedgerows and oaks shading well-kept streets. Public- and private-school kids wait for their respective transports at adjacent bus stops. On all-sports radio, tennis star Amit Amos is looking forward to the US Open, about to start near Shea Stadium in Forest Hills.

Following Hazel's directions, Voort winds his way down to commercial Northern Boulevard and a block of well-kept clapboard homes behind the one-story shops lining Little Neck's main drag. These cheaper houses form a buffer zone separating the bars and groceries from the better homes that begin farther back.

Pulling up before 21 Grady Place, he checks the mailboxes to find the upstairs apartment receiving mail for COLIN MEANS. Downstairs is occupied by the sister, Hazel said. The woman who answers Voort's knock has the same pear-shaped face as the corpse's, and similar wheat-colored hair. The light-brown eyes—growing fearful at the sight of his badge—are set wide like the eyes of the floater. This woman's got the same kind of doughy body as her brother, the kind that Voort associates with bad diet and no exercise. He judges her age between thirty and forty; she's a fireplug of a woman stuffed into baggy jeans and a lemon-colored tank top that accentuates the fat arms and saggy breasts. Red plastic cat's-eye reading glasses hang from her neck on a string.

"Oh God. It's about Colin."

He'll never get used to delivering death notices, even if he stays a detective for twenty more years.

"My name is Detective Conrad Voort."

Tears spring out on her face. The woman stumbles as her knees give way. Gravity sucks her onto the hard stoop as Voort reaches to help.

"Something happened to Colin," cries Rebecca Means through the "homeless man's" earpiece, as he monitors what's going on across the street. The watcher's a large, strong man in grimy clothes, sprawled against a Dumpster in the alley behind the Shamrock Tavern. From his recessed alcove his view encompasses the Means house and corner. He puts down the Egg McMuffin he's been eating and turns the audio up so he can hear every word.

"This may not turn out to be about your brother," says the voice of the blond man who'd pulled up in a Jaguar minutes ago.

What kind of detective drives a Jag?

The watcher jots "Voort" on a pad, and the pronunciation of the name. "Sounds like fort." He's got a good view and the sun is hot, which is pleasant.

Suddenly the cop turns his way, which is not.

The cop seems to freeze and stare directly at the watcher.

But that's impossible. There's no way he could know I'm here.

The cop shields his eyes with his palm. He doesn't move for a moment. The watcher's heartbeat speeds up.

Then the cop slowly turns back around, and helps Rebecca Means stand up.

Of course the police would match the floater to the missing persons list. Leon said it'd be no big deal if a cop showed up.

Still, the homeless man writes down the Jag's license number, which will give Leon access to the Social Security number. Once you have that, you can learn more about people than their family knows, half the time.

The way he stared this way gave me the creeps.

And now over the earpiece the cop is trying to calm the woman, like he really cares? Repeating that it's possible his visit may have nothing to do with her missing brother, but he has to check out a lead. Blah blah blah. The watcher's mood swings toward amusement. The cop asks, "Would you mind looking at these photos, Rebecca?"

"It's him!"

Her cry so loud that the listener almost jerks out the damn earpiece. Her anguish blending with traffic noise on Northern Boulevard. Buses. Asphalt trucks.

Voort and fat sister disappear into the clapboard house.

Switch from the porch to the living room mike.

The watcher hears high-pitched wailing so loud that he turns the volume down. Christ, he thinks, she must be sitting a foot from the bugged phone, on the ugly green sofa. Her mouth must be six inches from the damn transmitter.

"That's okay. Lean on me," says blond cop's all-American voice.

The homeless man grins. Some guys will fuck anything, even that hundred-sixty-pound sack of lard.

The woman cries, "He *drowned*?"

The watcher picks up his McDonald's bag. Might as well eat while he listens. We don't want our Egg McMuffin to get cold, do we?

Voort saying, "Would it be all right if I asked you questions?"

More sobbing.

"How about if I make coffee, Rebecca. Is the kitchen that way? I'll be right back."

The watcher finishes the last bit of tasty McMuffin and starts on the potato. I added too much salt, he thinks. His legs are splayed and he hears a cat meowing in the Dumpster. In the thirty hours he's been on surveillance he's been impressed with the neighborhood. The cops patrol regularly, so he stays in the alley. The homes look well kept. So far he's seen only one rat.

Footsteps return to the living room now.

"Sugar?"

"Thank you."

"Milk?"

What is this, a damn cookie party? the watcher thinks.

Now comes an irritating sucking sound like old people make when they drink tea through dentures. He envisions the apartment, which took him about two seconds to break into while she was at the dentist's office a day and a half ago. It's a pigsty, with about a thousand straw hats, or pieces of them—brims, tops, sheeting—all over the place. 1890s-type hats. What kind of nut sits around all day making hats? And not even different kinds. Just the same model, over and over again, like she's a flesh-covered machine.

The cop asks, "Did Colin say where he was going?"

"No."

"Was he having problems with a neighbor, girlfriend? Maybe someone at work?"

"Even when he was a kid he ran away from fights."

He certainly tried, the listener thinks, remembering, grinning.

"Did your brother owe anyone money?"

A sniffle. "He saves everything he earns driving that taxi. But what does this have to do with him drowning? Why are you asking these questions?"

The cop going soft, oozy, touchy feely, the way they're trained to do. "I'm sorry, Rebecca, but it's possible that your brother was in a fight before he died."

"A *fight*?" She's hyperventilating.

"We don't have to talk now if you're too upset."

"I want to know!"

"Well, he was so banged up it's hard to understand exactly what happened, but it's possible that he scuffled with people before he drowned. His pockets were turned inside out. No wallet. No watch. No rings. There was no alcohol or drugs in his blood."

"You're saying he was mugged."

The homeless man envisions the cop shrugging. The cop says, "It looks like two or three people held him down."

The homeless man jerks up. *How did he know it was three?*

The sister sounds dazed, and is weeping softly now. "Where did you find him?"

"Near Astoria Park. But with the currents so strong he could have gone in anywhere within twelve miles. Forgive me for asking, but was Colin depressed about anything recently?"

"Oh God. Colin. What am I going to do?"

The homeless man coughs as a piece of potato goes down the wrong way. By the time he clears his throat the woman is saying, "No, I don't mind if you look around his apartment. I'll take you up."

Shit.

"Rebecca, are there many homeless people in this neighborhood?" the cop casually asks.

Who is this guy?

"I never see any," the woman replies.

Footsteps fade now and become louder as detective and sister come into range of the hallway bug.

The watcher envisions the scene in there from the creaky sounds. Cop and sister are walking up the stairs, over threadbare carpeting, stepping around Colin's junk on the upper landing; boots, an old umbrella, a rusted snow shovel, a rack with peaked caps on it; a Sony hat, a Red Sox hat. She's unlocking the Medeco. Crisper footfalls indicate they're in the pine-floored foyer of the cabby's stifling flat.

"I love him, but he's a slob," sister says.

The watcher envisions Colin's mismatched stuffed furniture, old black-and-white console TV, homemade cinder-block bookshelves, and lots of cheap prints of eighteenth-century wooden sailing vessels battling storms at sea.

"Colin loved ships, but the closest he ever got to being on one was the Staten Island Ferry," the woman says. The watcher imagines Voort pivoting, looking around.

"A lot of books about pirates," Voort's voice says to muffled knocking sounds.

He must be pulling out volumes. Well, there's nothing there to find, asshole.

"He loved pirates," the sister says. "Do you know Captain Kidd actually buried treasure on Long Island? Colin told me that. When we were kids he'd walk along Jones Beach and look for doubloons. What a nut. Ten thousand bathers around and Colin figured if he looked hard enough, he'd see something shiny."

Get off this subject.

The cop says, "If you don't mind me asking, if he's a slob, who cleans this apartment?"

The homeless man sits up straighter.

"Why?" the sister asks.

"Well, there's dust on the TV, shelves, floor. But see how the bookshelves are wiped clean?"

"I guess he dusted them," the sister says.

The watcher loses his appetite.

"Must be," the cop says in a way that indicates he may be entertaining another, more accurate idea.

The footsteps move off and the watcher imagines Voort in the bathroom now. He hears the squeak of a cabinet opening and the clinking of Voort moving around the dead cabby's Zovirax, fungicide cream, Barbasol, acetaminophen. Then the footsteps enter the bedroom and the volume goes haywire again. Voort sounds like a goddamn panzer division roaring around in there.

"Do you mind if I look through Colin's closet and desk, Rebecca?"

"If you want. But why?"

"Maybe I'll get an idea where he went, who he talked to. Maybe he kept a calendar or wrote himself a note."

He didn't, you piece of shit. I checked.

"Everyone liked Colin," Rebecca says.

Sounds of hangers moving in a closet.

That room has nothing for you, the watcher thinks, but he's sweating slightly now.

The woman saying, "What's special about his shoes?"

Uh-oh.

The cop asking, "Does anyone else have a key to this place?"

"Not that I know of, Detective."

"Any workmen here recently? Electrician? Plumber?"

Shitshitshitshit . . .

"The exterminator came in July."

The watcher stands in agitation as the woman says, "What *about* the bed?"

What are you doing with the fucking bed?

"Well Rebecca, see how the sheet is stuck between the mattress and box spring in the corner here?"

"Colin never made his bed."

"Right. This is probably nothing but watch what happens if I pull out the sheet. It hangs free, see? But if I lift up the mattress the corner of the sheet gets sucked underneath. If I drop the mattress the sheet stays there."

The woman says, "So what?"

This cop is too smart. And things seem to be going out of control now, because a dry-cleaning van pulls up outside the house, and a deliveryman gets out. The watcher stares in agitation at the plastic sheeting slung over the delivery man's shoulder, at the bulky shape of a man's sport jacket inside. In the earpiece, he hears the front bell ring.

What is this, Murphy's Law?

The woman takes the jacket from the delivery kid.

And of course the blond cop asks—even a moron cop would—"Is this Colin's jacket?"

And of course Miss Cooperation says, "No I don't mind if you check the pockets." Followed by, "Hey, it's a piece of paper inside! A list!"

The watcher pulls out a cell phone. His fingers are trembling.

Voort saying, "Hannah. Mary Ann. Bridge. Are these Colin's girlfriends?"

"Those aren't women. Those are ships that sank."

The watcher punches in Leon Bok's number on his cell phone.

The woman says, "Oh, Colin and his stupid treasure."

"Treasure?" says the cop.

"Bok," says the oddly accented voice of Leon Bok over the phone.

"*You* know. The *Hussar*," the sister tells the cop.

"No, I don't know," says the cop.

"I'll call you back. I have to hear this," the watcher whispers, frantic, and clicks off.

"Oh, Colin's been blathering about that ship for so long I assume everyone knows about it," says Rebecca Means' voice in the earpiece. "The *Hussar* was a British ship that sank in New York two hundred years ago. Colin said it was carrying jewels or silver. I stopped paying full attention to this stuff twenty years ago. Colin's a treasure nut. Captain Kidd. Captain Black . . . you have to understand, Detective. My brother could watch *Treasure Island* twenty times in a row and never get bored. He loved sea stories, loved reading about pirates. He was a taxi driver who lived in fantasy. I loved him, but he was a big baby."

"Tell me more about the *Hussar*," says Voort.

A long sigh in the earpiece from the sister.

"Why? This can't relate to anything you need to know," the woman says. *"Treasure in New York?* I told him, give me a break. Don't you think if there was treasure someone would have salvaged it a century ago? It's not like the *Hussar's* a secret. Colin drives into Manhattan to that special library all the time, to read about it. Or he parks on rainy nights and stares out at places where he thinks it sank. Oh God! *That's* what happened. I bet he went too close to the edge and fell in. Or that's where he got mugged. In Hunts Point or Astoria. I didn't even *think* of that."

The watcher groans.

The woman tells Voort, "A couple of times Colin even tried to raise money to find it. He wrote letters to Donald Trump, Ted Turner. They never answered, of course. He wrote to real treasure hunters, like Mel Fisher in Key West, to apply for jobs. But Colin couldn't even swim. *Real* divers work on these projects, not cabdrivers. So for Colin it came down to one last fantasy. If he didn't find *this* ship, he'd never find any. He'd have to accept that he was a fat high school dropout. I love him, but that's what he was."

"Where's the special library in Manhattan?" asks Voort.

The woman's voice speeds up, as if she is arguing with

her brother, or trying to block out the present by conjuring the past. "I used to say, Colin, the East River's *narrow*. It's not like a ship went down in the *ocean*. Boats with sonar go through Hell's Gate every day. Tugs. Yachts. The current's had centuries to wash up anything valuable. The police send divers down all the time. I told him, go to night school, law school, *any* school. But Colin would say, no, it's there. I'll raise money. I'll find it. We'll be rich. You'll see."

"He sounds dedicated," Voort says.

So do you, the watcher thinks, sweating freely now.

The woman's voice goes soft and teary. She's blubbering. The news is sinking in. As the watcher hits Bok's redial button she tells Voort, "A cabdriver and hatmaker. What a pair. My parents would have been real proud of us."

"I like your hats," the cop lies.

Bok's phone starts buzzing.

"Straw hats," the woman says with disgust. "Colin and I both stopped developing after age twelve. He saw *Treasure Island* and never got the chest of gold out of his head. And me? God knows where the idea for these hats came from. I can't stop making them. I sell them through a distributor in Chinatown."

"You again," says Bok over the phone.

"My grandfather had a hat like that," Voort says.

"He knows someone searched the place," the watcher says, more terrified of Bok than the cop.

"Mr. Voort, people buy my hats on the Fourth of July. Barbershop quartets wear them. On New Year's Eve I see people wearing my hats. Then, after midnight, I spot them in the street. People smash them after they use them. They're gags. Stupid hats."

Sound of drawers opening and closing in the earplug.

"Colin had a file here about the *Hussar*. A fat file. Where is it?" says the sister.

"I'm sorry about your brother."

"Did you leave prints?" asks Bok's emotionless voice.

"The file had drawings in it, and articles," the sister is saying. "Colin's been adding to it for years. There was a map he found at that library."

"I wore gloves," the watcher insists to Bok.

"It's not in *this* drawer either," the sister says. "I don't understand."

"Don't worry about it," the cop soothes, as if he knows the file won't be there, knows someone took it. "Rebecca, someone has to identify the body. I can drive you to Manhattan and back if you want."

"Oh God. I can't!"

"Perhaps the detective used magic," quietly suggests Bok.

"I just can't do it," the sister says. "I had to identify my parents when they died. Can I have a friend go? I couldn't stand to see Colin that way."

"Perhaps the detective spread magic dust in the apartment," says Bok.

"You *told* me to hurry. I hurried," says the watcher.

"You have a point," concedes Bok after a dangerous pause.

Voort's voice says, scratchily, "Of course a friend can go. Here's my number."

The front door has opened. Cop and sister stand on the steps. From a distance Voort could be a political canvasser, a door-to-door salesman. The day is getting hotter.

The homeless man is sweating but not from heat. The cat leaps from the Dumpster and, glancing back, sensing the watcher's violent capabilities, it flees into the Shamrock Bar through a gap in a window.

Maybe the cop forgot about the library.

But then the cop says, *"Where's* the special library your brother liked to visit?"

Bok saying, "As long as he doesn't go to the Seaport . . . and by the way, don't cops have partners?"

"Not this one," says the watcher, his words drowning out whatever the sister just said.

Voort's gone silent in the earpiece, like he's pondering something. Then he again turns toward the alley and stares in the watcher's direction. Like his eyes are binoculars or X-ray machines. Like his senses are as finely tuned as Leon Bok's.

He's going to come over here.

The watcher feels inside his army surplus trousers, touches the hard surface of his Glock. The day is totally, completely going out of control.

Voort telling the sister, "Oh, it's no problem."

Taking a step toward the alley.

Voort says, in the earpiece, "The Seaport's on my way to work."

FOUR

"Pirates?" laughs Mickie over Voort's car phone.

"I told you, they were his books, not mine."

"Treasure?" snickers Mickie with the old half-welcome sarcasm. At least he's paying attention. "Maybe Colin drowned after Bluebeard made him walk the plank."

Voort sighs. "Remember the Bettinis?"

"The cousins who wanted to rob Bank Leumi."

"Except their tunnel would have broken them into the pizza shop next door."

"They fell out before they got halfway," Mickie says. "The mechanic shot the barber. What's your point?"

"That it's not important whether *you* think treasure's under the river. It's what *they* think."

"Who? Mermaids?"

Voort hits the brakes and looks ahead, gazing over three lanes of exhaust-belching steel. He's in the biggest parking lot in the world, the Long Island Expressway. Crawlway would be a better name for it. Wastingtimeaway.

Enough cars blocking him so, if they disappeared, replacing them could jump-start the national economy.

"Shiver me timbers," Mickie guffaws.

At least he's at the office, hungover but working, Voort thinks. At least he's going through files; making notes and getting ready to go out.

"Con Man. The apartment was tossed? You're sure?"

"I think so. His file was gone. And he was a slob, Mick."

Which refers to the fact, they both know, that the hardest apartments to search discreetly are dirty ones, where dust has built up over time. In movies, the clever policeman sets traps to enable him to tell later if his premises have been entered. He sticks a hair between a door and doorjamb. He scatters powder on the floor to retain imprints of shoes.

In real life, undercover cops learn, *be a slob.*

"Leave shit everywhere, dust everywhere. What's the guy who breaks in supposed to do, bring Mr. Clean?" Uncle Vim used to say.

"Believe me, Mick. There was dust a quarter inch thick in the closet, but the shoes sparkled. No dust on drawer handles, but plenty on the drawers."

"Treasure. Give me a break."

Traffic speeds up to a breathtaking five miles an hour. Starting and stopping, Voort crawls toward the tollbooths serving the Midtown Tunnel, inches forward in the fan-shaped mass of vehicles squeezing into the tunnel's only open lane.

And that homeless man walking off bothered me. The way he looked back.

"How's your head after last night?" Voort asks.

"I'm on my third gallon of tomato juice. And Voort? You're not having sex with your fiancée enough. She was so cold this morning we didn't need air-conditioning in the house."

"Because you got her so mad last night we didn't need heat."

Voort hears papers ruffling. Then, slightly embarrassed, "By the way, Con Man, what exactly is this Ozawa case I'm supposed to be working on? Eva dropped in and asked about it."

Voort sighs. "Frank Ozawa," he says, naming a state supreme court judge, "has a nephew who was arrested for stabbing a prostitute to death in Midtown South last week. The Blue Guys found his credit cards in her purse, and his skin was under her fingernails. His neck was all scratched up. But Ozawa's fine lawyer J. L. Corrigan maintains that yeah, he screwed her but after he left she brought another john to the hotel and the other guy did it. He says she lifted the cards. She scratched him during sex."

"So we need to place the nephew at the hotel."

"Or on the block, at the right time. We need a witness," Voort says. "I've been giving out our number."

"I have some vague recollection of this. Voort, do you really think you should be taking on new cases on your own? We have a lot as it is. But in other news, the market's up one hundred fifty-five points, man. The rumor's that IBM is going to acquire Zephyr."

Mickie's breathing is quickening with Voort's disgust. "The market's bottomed. Now's the time to get back in."

Voort hangs up.

New York's South Street Seaport was, in the 1800s, one of the most thriving harbor areas of the city. The East Side of Manhattan from the Battery to Twenty-third Street was lined with a solid mass of piers and ships. Clippers laden with cargo from a hundred countries—wines, clothing, spices, caviar—ran the tides to and from the Verrazano-

Narrows. Swift Lighters—workhorse sailing craft—ferried goods to and from warehouses across the bay. Brigs and schooners waited for berths, and bars on shore did a brisk business while serving as makeshift seaman halls and prostitute watering holes.

Voort foot patrolmen assigned to the Seaport had been among the busiest in the city.

Now, getting out of the cab—having left the Jag at home—Voort finds himself standing outside one of those interchangeable glass-enclosed "waterfront restorations" that dot America's harbors. The modern Seaport could be Faneuil Hall in Boston or Baltimore's Harborplace. Instead of sailors he sees tourists—from Berlin, Tokyo, San Francisco. There's a J. Crew store, Belgian waffle stand, ice cream emporium, pizza-on-the-run.

He finally locates the library along a narrow cobblestone street running north/south directly behind a row of three-story ex-shipping company town houses comprising the west wall of the Seaport. A hand-scrawled sign on the locked outer door reads "Duke and Mr. T need a calzone fix. Back in ten. Wait here or else."

Somehow even signs imparting information come across as threats in New York.

That homeless man moved awfully fast back in Little Neck. He just disappeared.

Sitting on the stoop in the September sun, Voort tries to pinpoint what else had irked him about the vagrant. He envisions his dad dressed for undercover work, when Voort was a kid. Bill Voort smeared with more grime than a boy takes on in a football game. Smelling like a trash can in August and looking with his phony beard like a member of the Charles Manson family Voort had seen on TV.

Do I look like a bum, Conrad?

Yes and no.

What's not right, Sherlock?

You look too proud.

Dad grinning, and ruffling his hair. Dad explaining, "The average guy on the street looks into your eyes or avoids them as an equal. Homeless people are in your face, wanting something, or skittish, nervous, out-of-place."

That man was dressed right, Voort thinks now. *But the way he looked at me was wrong. Or am I imagining it?*

He spots two forms approaching, a tall, stooped, thin man, and a Chihuahua keeping even with its master without the benefit of a leash. The guy slurps a dripping calzone from a napkin. The dog growls threateningly, in a quivery Chihuahua way, when it spots Voort on the stoop, blocking its path.

"I'm Detective Conrad Voort."

The guy clutches his chest theatrically. Between the note he left and the silly grin, Voort gets the feeling everything is a joke to him.

"I didn't *see* the little girl," the man gasps. "It was *raining*."

"Can we go inside, sir?"

The man swoons on the doorstep. "Lepke . . . Lepke . . . The feds are closing in. I hid the dough in the graveyard."

"Ruff," says Duke appreciatively, or is the dog Mr. T?

"It's important," says Voort patiently as the man unlocks the library. He makes the joker as young, twenty-six, but already his black hair is receding over a high forehead. A tomato sauce stain dabs his white button-down shirt. From the pockmarked skin and bad movie lines, Voort suspects this man's life is lived between work and his DVD machine.

"My *God*," the man cries as they enter the tiny one-room library. "I left the body next to the desk, but it's not there. *Don't tell me Dr. X is still alive!*"

Voort drops the politeness. "A man drowned yesterday, sir. Not in a movie. Not by accident. Cut the crap."

"Sorry." Suddenly the librarian looks like a meek kid. He's gone beet-red. "No one ever comes here. I get carried away when they do. Who drowned?"

The dog snuggles into a pillow atop a cleared rectangle of bottom shelf. Voort takes in the library. Three aisles go back fifteen feet, lined with stuffed bookshelves. Oak-plank floors support a lone creaky reading table and a librarian's desk. The hard-back chairs look a couple of decades old. Oil paintings of tugboats line the wall above a Dewey decimal system card catalogue and below a rotating fan. There's an utter lack of electronics, and a smell of paper going brown and brittle as printing on it fades.

"Ever hear of a ship called the *Hussar*?"

"*Again?*"

From the real surprise on the face, Voort surmises that the man's not joking this time.

The guy frowns and says, "You're the fourth person asking about that old treasure this month."

The John Paul Jones Club—named for the American naval Revolutionary War hero—is a very private, exclusive new marina near the Brooklyn Bridge, along a formerly commercial strip. A small stone breakwater shields boats at anchor and the lushly furnished floating barge clubhouse, just as the harbor's most famed restaurants—Manhattan's Water Club and Brooklyn's River Cafe—is moored to land too. The club paid handsomely for a ninety-nine-year lease.

Ted Stone's a member. The marina is a short cab ride from his penthouse apartment and his office, both near the UN.

Content at the moment, he's sipping fresh, pulpy orange juice with his beautiful fourteen-year-old daughter Candace in the bar-grill area, by the picture window. He's watching the dock boys bring his Orson-57 up so he can take Candace to Queens for today's afternoon session of the US Open. Doing anything with Candace makes him happy.

Catching sight of Leon Bok entering the grill does not.

"Daddy, I can't *wait* to see the Alon-DeVille match!"

Bok halts under the *Endeavor* painting like a force of nature. He's in faded jeans and a yellow windbreaker. Bok mouths, "A word, Mr. Stone."

Outside are members' toys: a fifty-foot Kanter Atlantic and a Grand Banks 42 Classic. A very well-kept 76 Hatteras and a sleek Ferretti 53. In Ted's rare pessimistic moments he regards these crafts as lifeboats serving the island. He recalls old newsreels of Havana, on the night Castro took over, when people who owned boats like these flooded the docks with their bonds and jewelry, started up their powerful engines, and fled.

"Just a minute, honey. I have to talk to that man."

"We'll *miss* the beginning."

"Nonsense. We can do thirty knots on the *Candace*."

He kisses her smooth forehead, loving her freshness, excitement, intelligence, youth. Bok, seeing him coming, slips from the grill room, where conversation carries, into the main lounge area, which is more discreet.

Club colors are pastels. Paintings show clippers, steamships, the old, grand yachts of J. P. Morgan and Malcolm Forbes. The carpet is thick enough to sleep on comfortably. The chairs are studded leather. Potted palms quiver from the silent rush of air-conditioning, and the room is flooded with slanted natural light.

Bok big, quiet, imposing, waiting.

Explaining about the detective.

Bok adding, "I didn't want to do things without your okay."

"You did right to come. I hate phones even when they're protected. If one can block out listeners, one will eventually invent something to break through and hear."

"Detectives can have accidents like anyone else."

Stone frowns, concentrating, telling himself there are no good options here, only grades of risk. He shakes his head slowly. "If the police decide it's not an accident we'll have an army to deal with. I have to live here. You go home to wherever you're from."

"Then there are other ways."

Bok lists some as through the doorway Stone watches Candace pacing in front of the picture window. The boat's ready. She wants to go. He loves that to her a tennis match seems so important.

In low tones, Bok tells Stone how he shut down a reporter in Spain once.

"He killed himself after."

"I should think so!"

"Hey, I didn't do it personally. I paid other guys."

"But I don't want him to kill himself," Stone says stiffly. "That would have the same effect as you doing it. What if he's made notes? What if he leaves a suicide note? No, he's got friends in the department, and relatives, you said. Civil servants," he adds disparagingly, "get hot about personal things. It's in their blood. I need something to shut him down but keep him alive, at least for now. Alive outside. Dead inside."

"Mister Stone, there's no magic button here."

"I'm sure you're up to the challenge."

Bok thinks for a moment. "I could do a variation on Spain," he suggests.

"Jesus," Ted says, awed when he hears it. "But doesn't he have a partner?"

"Not yet."

Stone blows out air. "Okay then, but only if he connects Mcgreevey."

"Nothing succeeds like excess."

"Probably he'll miss Mcgreevey or use up a few days first, in which case it won't make a difference. So if six, seven days pass and he leaves Mcgreevey alone, forget about him for now."

Stone waves to Candace, who's in the doorway now, furious.

"Plenty of time, honey," he mouths to her.

Smiling his dad smile, he walks back into the grill room.

Candace tells her dad, "I can never see too much tennis."

Dad tells daughter, "Too much is seldom enough."

"Tell me about the *Hussar.*"

Alone with librarian Lyle B. Moskowitz, as the name plaque reads on the skinny man's desk, Voort bends over a table eyeing maps and articles about the old treasure ship.

Duke lies on his pillowed bookshelf, watching Voort with one bulgy eye. Tugs in paintings steam through the harbor. Lyle B. Moskowitz, calm now, is actually likable in a nerdy, lonely way.

"Do you know anything about the Revolutionary War period in New York, Detective? Most people don't," the kid brags.

"Always like to learn," says Voort, not mentioning the weekly lessons he received when he was a boy, the records in his library, the family journals, the glassed-in artifacts displayed in his house.

"Okay then," Lyle says, spreading his hands as if, in his mind, creating an imaginary scene. His eyes shine. "It's November twenty-third, 1780. New York's an occupied city. British troops are quartered in private houses. British guns fill the harbor. American POWs are locked up on ships, shackled like animals, sick, chained, dying. Healthy prisoners row the dead ashore in Wallabout Bay each morning, and bury them in shallow graves. We're talking eleven thousand prisoners dead from smallpox and yellow fever. Dysentery. Hell, only seven thousand Americans died in combat in the whole war."

"The *Hussar,*" Voort prompts.

"Meet the ship," says Lyle, stepping back, nodding out past the stacks toward the river, as if, were they to exit the building, they'd see furled sails and masts and hear the creak of wood and clank of shackles. "One hundred and fourteen feet long. Thirty-four feet wide. The HMS *Hussar* is a twenty-six-gun, three-masted frigate."

"Carrying prisoners," Voort says, remembering from the old diaries that at least half a dozen Voort soldiers disappeared during the Revolution.

"And payroll gold," whispers Lyle. "Nine hundred and sixty thousand King George the Third guineas. Bound for troops in Newport, Rhode Island. That's about six hundred million dollars' worth today."

Voort whistles, impressed.

"The day is sunny. Blue sky. Warm." Lyle's hands move left to right, signifying the ship sailing. "Hell's Gate was different then. The reefs were more dangerous. Rocks poked up top, like in this old lithograph."

He points out an article in which an old black-and-white drawing shows a wooden ship keeled over in a fierce storm. The sail is tattered. The sailors look terrified. The hull is striking a looming rock that seems to be in the middle of the sea.

Voort says, "Wait a minute. That's *inside New York*?"

"Do you have any idea how many ships went down a few miles from here?" Lyle says. "It's funny, you think of treasure, you think South Seas. Palm trees. Grottos. Who the hell thinks of the South Bronx?"

"Go on."

"Sometime around noon the current drives the *Hussar* to port. It hits Pot Rock. The hull starts to fill. The prisoners are screaming to be unshackled. But the Brits figure they can keep the *Hussar* from sinking. The Captain," Lyle says, jabbing a harbor map with his skinny index finger, "tries to gain a point off Port Morris so he can run aground."

"He fails."

"Understatement."

"They unshackle the prisoners."

"Sorry, and the water's eighty feet deep. The Brits get off but the prisoners go down, and according to the American version, so does the gold."

"What's the British version?"

"That it was taken off before the *Hussar* sailed. That it went by land to Rhode Island."

"So why are you grinning?"

"Because the British version is full of shit," says Lyle. "If they were right how come within two weeks they were frantically trying to salvage the *Hussar*? What on it was so important? The guns? Maybe, except for what happened later. The prisoners? Right."

"Salvage couldn't have been easy in those days."

"You said it," says Lyle Moskowitz, fountain of lore. "There were no oxygen tanks. No air hoses. No way to fight the bends. We're eighty feet down in diving bells. They're basically inverted bathtubs, filled with air. You send down the diver. He breathes inside the tub. He swims out to look for wreckage. He's a slave or prisoner since half the time they drown or die of nitrogen bubbles in the blood."

"So they never found gold. And that's the story of the *Hussar* search until today."

"Nope. Until Thomas Jefferson."

"President Thomas Jefferson?"

"You might ask," Lyle grins, becoming more likable in his nutty way by the minute, "how come he waited till *after* he left office to fund an expedition. How come *when* he was president he didn't do it. Hell, he used public money to send Lewis and Clark to Oregon, didn't he? But when it came to the *Hussar*, he waited."

"So he'd get any payoff himself?" finishes Voort, getting the feeling that this story is just beginning.

Lyle winks. "I am but a humble librarian. But remember, as president, Jefferson had spies and diplomats in London. He learned things average people didn't. Was the *Hussar*'s cargo one of them? Even the Shadow doesn't know."

"I take it Jefferson failed."

"And so did everyone after him. For *two hundred and forty years*, every three or four decades, someone's gone looking for the *Hussar.* In 1880 it was George Thomas and his corporation Treasure Trove. He made a deal with the U.S. Treasury Department to share what he found. In the 1930s it was Simon Lake, who'd worked on submarines. In the 1990s it was Barry Clifford, the treasure hunter who found the *Whydah*—the eighteenth-century pirate ship— off Cape Cod."

"No luck either."

"A few coins. A plate. Tchotchkes," Lyle says dismissively, using the Yiddish word for small, valueless items.

"You'd think with the river being so narrow, someone would have come up with the wreck by now."

Lyle the landlocked sailor shakes his head. The dog

makes a disgusted "rff-ing" sound, as if even a canine knows Voort's question is dumb.

"The currents," explains Lyle. "And the muck is worse than the La Brea Tar Pits. Not to mention, a hundred years ago there was major demolition in the river. Tons and tons of rock smashed up. Divers say you can't even see your hand in front of your face, and even if you *could,* there's over a dozen wrecks down there, each on top of the other. Add concrete poured, and fifty thousand tons of garbage dumped since 1780. Cars. Freight boxes. Dead mob guys, ha ha. Illegally dumped chemical canisters, probably. Fucking horseshoes."

"Some story," says Voort, remembering the tales he's heard from police divers, confirming visibility problems. "Mind if I read awhile?"

He thinks about the story while he peruses articles, which add more information, but Lyle turns out to have been accurate as well as entertaining. The dog wanders up and sniffs Voort's ankle, looks up, and seems to wink.

There are two kinds of dogs, Voort's decided. The kind that seem like animals, and the kind you'd swear understand everything humans say. Duke is the latter. The bulgy eyes never leave Voort's.

Next time he looks up, Lyle's on his cell phone, playing electronic games. Little beeping noises come from the phone. They turn out, when Voort steps closer, to represent laser blasts as Earth antiaircraft batteries on Manhattan rooftops repel UFOs attacking New York.

"Don't you need a permit from the state to look for a wreck, Lyle?"

"From the Department of Education. That's where the state archaeologist works. But they never say no."

"Who were the other people who asked you about the *Hussar*?"

Lyle turns off the intergalactic war game. At the moment, it's unclear which side, Earth or alien, is ahead.

"One was a cabdriver. Colin Means. He's been coming here for years. He's a treasure nut."

"Did he say anything special about the ship last time he was here?"

"What he always says. That someday he'll find it. That guy lives in a dreamworld," says Lyle. Then he blushes. "Like me, I guess."

The dog says, "Ruffff." Voort has a feeling the Chihuahua just told the kid not to be hard on himself.

"Who else, Lyle?"

"McMannis? McGovern? What was that second guy's name?" says Lyle. "Wait. He signed the register. Everyone has to. You too, by the way."

"Show me."

Lyle leads Voort to a small wooden lectern upon which lies a large open hardback ledger. Visitors have scrawled their names on yellowing pages stamped by date.

"Mcgreevey!" Lyle says, after flipping to a section dated two weeks ago. "He was a tugboat captain. I remember now. Nice guy. He said he and his brother own a small tug company on Staten Island."

"What did he want to know about the *Hussar*?"

"He didn't ask questions like you. He just went through the file. But he liked the tug paintings. That was what he talked about. He wanted to know who's the artist."

"And the third visitor?"

"The guy before Mcgreevey. He signed right here!"

"Marcus Sanders," reads Voort aloud, noting the double spiral on the upper loop of the *S*. "What do you remember about him?"

"Good-looking guy in a rich way, with that calm, cool attitude. White. Late thirties, maybe. Had that kind of waspy George Bush look, lean and remote. Soft-spoken. I remember some kind of fancy watch. Blue, with a silver rim. Polite guy, but not friendly. I remember he kept getting calls on his cell phone. He was the only reader here that day so I told him it was okay to talk on it. The calls were about tennis match tickets. He kept saying, 'Don't worry, honey,' 'don't fret, honey. . . .' "

Lyle the human tape recorder.

"I think he was talking to his daughter. It was the way he said 'honey.' By the way, you can use your phone too here if you want, even though it's a library."

"Rfff," says the dog, as if it's okay with him.

But considering the fact that Lyle clearly monitors every word, Voort walks outside to call Hazel in the computer section. He asks her to access any records on a Kevin Mcgreevey, of 902 Mason Terrace, Staten Island, and on a Marcus Sanders, who lives at 1289 Broadway, the ledger says.

"Marcus with a *c* or *k*?"

"*C*."

"I'll need a few hours. I'm busy right now. You're not the only detective I work for, you know. Just my favorite."

Then from his PDA Voort punches in the cellular number of his cousin Captain Greg of the tugboat Voorts, whose homes and three-boat business are located across the harbor in Staten Island.

"Greg here!"

"It's the commissioner calling."

"Heyyyyyy! We're coming over tonight. I caught a big mako off the point this morning and he's on ice. Little white wine, chopped garlic. Little thyme and saffron. I figure we'll have shark steaks on the smorgasbord table, eh?"

"You working now?"

"We just docked a Volvo carrier in Port Elizabeth. I'm heading home. Why?"

"You ever meet a couple of tug owners named Mcgreevey?"

Silence. Voort thinks the connection's broken.

Then, in a soft voice, Greg says, "You're on *that* case?"

Voort feels the low, steady pulse of suspicion burst into something stronger. The dryness in his mouth signifies he's just graduated from poking around the periphery of an investigation to throwing himself in.

"What case?"

"They died," Greg says. "The brothers. The mate. If you don't know about this, why'd you call? Ah, goddamn Manhattan never pays any attention to Staten Island. To you we're like Indiana. It happened a week ago." Greg sounds angry about it. "Where are you?"

"The South Street Seaport."

"I *knew* that inspector didn't know what he was talking about." Greg mutters something else that sounds like, "a stick up his ass."

"Tell me about Mcgreevey."

"Walk down to the dock on the south side of the Seaport, Conrad. Wait at the end, by the tall ship. I'm coming over. I'll pick you up. I'm taking you to meet someone who'll give you the story. Son of a bitch, Conrad."

"They were friends of yours?"

"Someone will bring you back to Manhattan when we're through. Those poor guys."

FIVE

Even dangers facing policemen seem to have changed since Voort became a detective. Threats preoccupying the city have become more insidious, harder to spot.

At Shea Stadium a Blue Guy stares into a knapsack at a mayonnaise jar filled with amber liquid. He would have assumed it was scotch, not explosives, five years ago. A woman trying to rent a Piper Cub near Long Island finds her driver's record and employment references being cross-referenced by the FBI. A customs agent phones the Anthrax hotline instead of Drug Enforcement when he spots a bag of white powder in a suitcase. A Brooklyn mail carrier eyes the contents of his bag nervously.

He used to fear dogs along his route, not the actual mail.

In a way Voort feels his jurisdiction has become the whole planet. But his beat remains limited to one small block.

"A problem came up," Greg says.

Paranoia or wisdom? Monsters or ghosts? Voort stands beside Greg in the pilothouse of the *Anna*. As the tug pulls from the Seaport, he's struck by changes in the harbor nearby. To the north, like steel dragonflies, military helicopters sweep over vessels approaching the United Nations building. Gunboats escort even familiar tugs past.

"I may not be able to take you to Mcgreevey," Greg says.

From where will the next blow come? Voort wonders. The sky again? The sea? From the pleasure boat being boarded a quarter mile south, by the Coast Guard? From the cruise ship piers where he's participated in anti-terrorism exercises, and where trained dogs now sniff trunks of cars entering the passenger drop-off zone?

"I take it you called the Mcgreevey family," Voort says. "And got chewed out for telling me things."

"House rules?"

Which means, will our conversation stay as private as talk does on Thirteenth Street? Can I invoke the family code as powerful as the oath you took when you joined the NYPD?

"I don't know enough yet to say."

Normally Greg is bullish and direct, so now his hesitation is disconcerting. Voort tells him, "I'll do my best but it's up to you. Turn around if that's not good enough."

"Hypothetical, then," Greg offers as the tug passes within view of the Statue of Liberty. He's gambling that in the end Voort will help the Mcgreeveys.

"Hypothetical."

Voort eyes Lady Liberty, gazes at the armed Coast Guard patrol boat bobbing off her left foot. Time was he could paddle his kayak almost up to the hem of her green tresses. Last time he tried, sailors with machine guns shooed him away.

"What if," Greg begins, "there was an old man. A good guy. He lost his two sons. It just about killed him."

"Lost them how?"

"In a fire on their tug."

Voort closes his eyes.

"His wife's still alive," Greg goes on. "But neither of them can eat, or sleep."

"Parents outliving children. There's nothing worse."

"What if our seventy-six-year-old guy is also sick. And in financial trouble. The insurance company denied payment. He's desperate. He's cleaning out his son's house one day, which is hard enough, and in a closet he finds money. Cash, Conrad. In a shoebox. He has no idea where it came from, but basically it's all the money he has. His tug business is finished. He has mortgage payments to make. Hypothetically, if you found out," Greg asks uncomfortably, "would you feel compelled to report it if you were investigating something unrelated?"

Voort blows out air. "Let's also add that the guy is a friend of my beloved cousins. He wants to find out what happened to his sons, but he needs the cash. Why did the insurance company deny payment, hypothetically?"

"House rules?"

"I don't *know* yet if it's unrelated."

"Hardass." Greg frowns, weighing bad choices. "Do you mind if I ask what *you're* working on that led you to ask me about Mcgreevey?"

But Voort's not about to mention the nutty notion of sunken treasure in the harbor.

"I appreciate your problem, Greg. I'll do my best. I promise. Meantime, tell your hypothetical friend that if he pays his bills with the money now, it'll be harder for the city to go after it later. They'd be more likely to make a deal with an old man. After all, he just found the cash, right?" Voort winks. "He assumed it was legitimate."

A beat. Voort's cell phone starts ringing. Not recognizing the number, he doesn't answer. If he breaks off the conversation just now he feels Greg may turn the boat around.

Greg sighs. "Cap'n Mcgreevey said it was my decision whether to bring you or not."

He steers with his elbow outside the sliding glass window. Marlboro smoke swirls in the pilothouse behind. He's Voort's age, early thirties, with curly black hair and eyes like blue icebergs. He has the biceps of a weight lifter, the belly of a beer drinker, the permanent facial stubble of a Yassir Arafat, and a steel-trap mind that made him runner-up for valedictorian at NYU.

"How much was in the shoebox, Greg?"

Pride of the Voort fleet, the *Anna* was built in 1977 at the Iron Works in Houma, Louisiana, and named for Voort's great-grandmother. The tug's 123 feet long and driven by 114-inch propellers. Net weight, 118 tons. Radar by Sperry. Steering by Vickers. Double-drum towing machines by HBL wrap two-inch-thick steel cables that have helped dock some of the biggest ships in the world.

"Twenty-two thousand, four hundred and sixty-seven dollars," says Greg.

"So someone's been adding to a stash little by little. Or taking away from what started out."

"Knowing the brothers I'd say taking. They're not the regular-payoff type. One time, maybe. Once."

"You probably wouldn't have guessed before this that they'd take a one-shot either."

Greg snaps, "That family lives hand to mouth."

"When did the fire happen?"

"Ten days ago on their main boat, the *Linda*."

Two of the four men who signed the ledger in the library—who looked up the Hussar—*have died.*

It also occurs to Voort, *My name is one of the two left.*

But all he says to Greg is, "If the insurance company denied payment they must have thought the fire was arson."

"Oh, even Cap'n Mcgreevey thinks that."

"Then what does he want from me?" But then Voort sees it. "It's who did it."

"Yeah, if the sons *didn't*, who did?"

Ahead, coming up, he sees the familiar rust-ridden shore of Staten Island, a patchwork of ferry terminals, tug yards, and abandoned lots.

"Give me some background on the family." Voort's thinking, *For all I know the sons are guilty.*

The *Anna* chugs down the narrow Kill Van Kull Channel separating Staten Island from New Jersey. The smell is a mix of vaporous chemicals. Squat, round oil terminals look as if they've been screwed into the ground on the Jersey side.

"They're little guys, Conrad. One of the last family tug businesses. Used to be hundreds. Now there's just us, the Browns. McAllister . . ."

"McAllister's big."

Greg nods. "Megacompanies and little companies. Moran and McAllister get ninety percent of the business. Small guys get leftovers or assists. At the bottom is Mcgreevey's barge jobs. And not even *all* barges because their tugs are old single-screw models and the law says you gotta have two propellers or you can't move oil. Mcgreevey tugs were powerful enough to help tow ships thirty years ago. But ships have gotten too big now."

"They're discount guys, then," Voort says.

"Right. You need a sand scow moved, a crane, get a price break from Mcgreevey. But money's drying up. Couple more years, half the family operations will be gone."

Voort weighs his obligations to strangers. To a taxi driver found floating in the water, and a grief-stricken old man who's a friend of Cousin Greg. He asks, "Could someone who works for the Mcgreeveys have started the fire? Mcgreevey could collect the insurance money if a family member's not responsible—if it was some kind of grudge."

"They only had one mate. He died too. It's a mom-and-pop company, Cousin. Cap'n Jack can't work tugs anymore. His right leg is useless. He stays home as dispatcher while his wife, Alice, does the books. The sons man the tugs. They all scrounge for work. Every once in a while they luck out and get a TV job, y'know, a camera crew rents the boat for a day. But mostly it's scows, day after day."

Voort's cell phone buzzes. This time Mickie's calling.

Walking out onto deck he sees the Voort tug yard coming up as the *Anna* closes on a patched-up pier where men in welding masks work on the docked *Marie*. If Greg's not turned the boat around by now, Voort knows, they're going to Mcgreevey.

"Hey Con Man!" Mickie says. "Your new girlfriend sounded sexy on the phone."

Voort gets an image of Tina Tadesse, followed by a surge of guilt.

"First name Lucy," Mickie says. "Last name never

mind. She wanted to talk to the 'cute cop' who handed out his business cards along Thirty-first Street, looking for information on Ozawa."

"She can place him?"

"Well, our sex-bomb caller wouldn't tell me shit when she learned I wasn't the *cute* cop. I gave her your cell phone number ten minutes ago. It's tough being cute."

"I'll check my messages." Voort's hope rises at the possible break. He's been canvassing prostitutes on the West Side to see if any of them remembered seeing the suspect in that case.

Now he hears "Lucy's" message. "(Giggle) If this is the detective who was asking about the attack on Thirty-first Street, I'm not sure if I saw the man but I *did* talk to a guy that night on Twenty-eighth . . ."

Another spot for cruisers.

". . . who was stooped over like you said, and he had something wrong with his mouth. He talked sideways."

Voort's excitement soars. The killing had occurred a day after Judge Ozawa's nephew had undergone a messy tooth extraction. On the night of the killing the surgery could easily have affected how he talked.

Lucy says, "Do you still have that girlfriend who was in the Internet article on you? Are you really rich?"

Voort curses inwardly. Memory ID tells him the caller used a public phone. There's no way to call her back.

"Meet me tonight, at ten, in front of 692 West Twenty-seventh. I'm small with long black hair. I know what *you* look like. Come alone or I won't talk to you. I can only get away for ten minutes. My boyfriend doesn't like when I disappear."

You mean your pimp.

Calling Mickie back, he says, "I didn't mention the dental surgery to the girls. I only found out about it afterwards. So this could be real."

Mickie laughs about the Internet crack. "Know what Marilyn Monroe would say if she was alive today, Voort? The Internet's a girl's best friend. Let's hook up at nine-fifty, at the Churrascaria next to Jimmy's Burritos."

Meaning, I'll go with you as backup. No way are you meeting an anonymous caller alone.

"Jealous, Mick?"

"I'm a happily married man. Well, at least married. Well, a man whose wife'll leave him as soon as she sees our next PaineWebber statement."

Voort figures he should head home for dinner before the meet, see Camilla, smooth away the rough edges. But he doesn't want Mickie to be alone later. These days, Mickie alone equals Mickie walking into a bar.

"Let's hook up earlier and chow down. My treat," Voort says. He'll tell Camilla he's working late again, which is true, sort of. He can make up with her after Mickie heads back to Long Island. Voort figures he'll be home by eleven, tops.

I knew Mick would get back to normal.

The tug eases in beside the dock. Greg steps from the pilothouse. "I should tell Cap'n Mcgreevey to spend the money, huh? Good idea."

"What money?" says Voort.

The Mcgreevey house is small and boxy with a turquoise paint job that contrasts with the brown lawn, in need of watering. Homes on the narrow, hilly street were built identically, just after World War II, for soldiers coming home from overseas and planning new families. The lawn ornament, an orange tug, tilts half keeled over, as if starting to sink.

Although the funeral was two weeks ago, it feels as if it just happened when Voort gets inside. It will probably feel that way in here as long as Jack and Alice Mcgreevey live.

"Greg said I can trust you," Cap'n Jack Mcgreevey says, glancing from Voort to Greg.

Through the bay window, Voort notices a white plumbing van going up the street for the second time in as many minutes. His attention returns to Cap'n Jack, whose straight-backed form juts up in an old leather sitting chair strategically situated by the window in a shaft of late-afternoon sunlight. Like a reptile, the white-haired man spends his days trying to keep warm.

"I'm sorry about your sons, sir."

Old men, Voort's noticed, decline into the detritus of their professions. Time after time he's walked into the homes of the elderly to see the results of decades of commitment to one particular job. Plumbers get knee problems. Typists rub swollen knuckles. Corporate types chug ulcer medicines. Ex-lawyers sink into senility needing to fight somebody, anybody. Waitresses. Toll takers. Dog walkers.

The need to do battle is ingrained.

Captain Mcgreevey's leathery skin is dotted with scars from skin-cancer lesions. His pale eyes are magnified by thick lenses as if his vision was burned off by too many watches in the sun. His withered thigh, Voort learned, is the result of a cable snapping back fifteen years ago.

Mcgreevey's forearms show gouges inflicted by razor-sharp railings on scows.

"Greg promised you'd help."

Voort kneels down so he's lower than the old sailor, so he's looking up at the face, not down. "Tell it any way you want, sir."

There's always one part of a man that never ages. Hair. Lungs. Eyesight. Sense of humor. In Mcgreevey's case the vocal cords still seem as strong as a radio announcer's. He speaks with the kind of deep tones that strangers obey in emergencies, that can calm a crowd into evacuating a smoke-filled theater in single file.

"Four A.M.," he intones, as if starting a film clip that he will spend the rest of his life reviewing. "They're always at the dock by then. Bud first. Kevin sleeps late. The mate was Byrd Martie. We've used him for years."

Mcgreevey's liver-spotted hand trembles. The insurance form he clutches, stamped DENIED, rustles a bit.

"They were supposed to tow a crane to Brooklyn at five, for pier repair work."

He suddenly can't talk.

Voort gives him a moment and then prompts, "They were getting the boat ready to go."

"That's not the way Mr. Clark Weill of Reliably Best Insurance sees it. *He* says my boys had no intention of working. *He* says they were there to burn down the ship. We owe money, Mr. Voort, to just about everyone. *He* says Bud and Kevin spread accelerant around the galley they'd grown up in. Into the pilothouse that they used to play in.

Down toward the bunks that they *sleep* in. They had a homemade, time-delayed ignition device, Weill said. No one denies that *someone* used accelerant. From the burn pattern, down into the deck as well as up, it was arson for sure."

"What else do you know about the device?"

Mcgreevey's voice gets stronger as he grows angrier. "Household items, Mister Voort. Everyday, innocent stuff. Weill taped together two gelatin capsules and said my boys had filled one with plain old glycerin, the other with crystals used by doctors as a mild astringent. Headache pills and antiseptic. Weill found both in Bud's medicine cabinet."

"Innocently inside their bottles? Or inside capsules?"

"Some damn evidence," Greg scoffs. "Headache pills."

"The chemicals are harmless unless you mix them together," Mcgreevey says. "Do that, and sixty seconds later they go white hot."

"Hell, I have headache pills in *my* medicine cabinet," says Greg. "Maybe I'll burn down *my* boat too."

"Shut up," says Voort, glancing out the window at another army helicopter in the distance sweeping over the waterfront. "Cap'n Mcgreevey, what happened next?"

"Well, see-all-know-all Weill gets foggy on that. He *says* my sons accidentally loosened a valve too early on the propane line into the galley from the tank outside, although I'd like to know how you can accidentally open a valve that needs a wrench to move. He said the stove pilot light set the explosion off. That's just one of the problems with his version."

Voort says gently, "The explosion killed your sons?"

Mcgreevey blinks a few times. For an instant Voort thinks he's going to start crying. Then he says, "They died from smoke. Weill figures Kevin collapsed first and the other two tried to drag him out. Kevin was on the bottom."

"Forgive me for asking, sir, but what else is wrong with the story? You said there were other problems."

"Well, why burn down your own boat at four A.M., when everyone in the goddamn world knows you're *on* it. Four is when tug men get to work."

Voort nods as if it's a good point, but he's thinking, if stupidity was a reason to eliminate suspects, half the convicts in Sing Sing wouldn't be there.

The sons could have planned to start the fire and claim it was an accident, and it backfired. It's happened before.

"Also," Mcgreevey says, "they always stop at Fred's Eat-In before going to work. They have coffee there, not on the boat. They don't make coffee until later."

Voort thinks, *So what? They can't make more coffee?*

Greg tells Mcgreevey, "The money, Jack."

Mcgreevey stares into Voort's face a moment, then reaches down and brings a shoebox out from under the chair, where it had been hidden behind fabric.

"You tell me, Detective. Why burn down a boat you love, that you stayed up nights trying to figure out how to *keep?* Why do *that* for money if you already have *this?*"

Which of course is the interesting point, especially combined with the death of Colin Means.

Mcgreevey's eyes blink, bright, wide, wet.

Voort doesn't touch the money. He won't want his fingerprints on it if he has to take it in. "Did anyone see other people near your tug before the fire started?"

"Other crews along the channel were getting their own boats ready at that hour. No."

"Did the nearby crews notice other boats in the channel?"

"No."

"Was there any indication that anyone besides your sons and the mate was on your tug?"

"If there was, it burned up," says Mcgreevey. "Like they wanted."

"By 'they' you mean whom?"

For the first time the old man looks irritated at Voort. "It doesn't take a genius to connect it to the shoebox."

"Any idea how Kevin got it?"

Mcgreevey shakes his head at Greg disgustedly. Voort figures he'll check the fire and police department reports on the fire after he leaves the house. He'll drop in on other boat crews. He'll check Coast Guard records to see if any crews might have reported in from the Kill Van Kull Channel around the time that the fire began.

Mcgreevey says, "They got paid off for something. What do you think?"

Drugs?

At eight forty-five Voort's sitting at a small, round table at the Churrascaria, the Brazilian grilled-meat palace west of Broadway. A candle casts a romantic ambiance on the empty plate across from Voort. He's jotting notes as he waits for Mickie, but he's filled with a sinking feeling. Mickie answered his cell phone fifty minutes ago and said he'd be here shortly. "Shortly" has come and gone.

"Try some Cachaca rum, Voort, on the house."

"Thanks but I'm working, Fabio."

"Where's your stock genius partner, who steered me wrong on TeleMax South?"

"If you find out, let me know."

"Smuggled cigarettes?" Voort writes.

He stares down at the names and diagrams in his notebook. "Colin Means" has a circle around it. "Mc-greevey" and "mate" are circled too. A line links the circles as if in real life they were connected. But Voort's also added a question mark over the line.

"Treasure?"

It feels stupid even to write it.

"Everyone sees tugs in the harbor, but they also *don't* see them. Know what I mean?" says old Captain Mc-greevey in Voort's mind.

Voort remembering back to the little house, hearing Greg join in the explanation. "You get inquiries, Cousin. All the time."

The Churrascaria is filled with boisterous eaters at large round tables. A world-record-sized salad buffet runs the length of the theater-sized room. The restaurant's specialty is meat, enormous quantities of it, grilled and offered as long as customers can keep eating. Voort eyes hunks of steaks floating by, chunks of veal, and skewered sausages. Meat clings to bones. Meat drips with fat. Knives flash as waiters expertly slice succulent slabs of hot meat onto plates.

"Would you like some ribs, sir?"

"I'm waiting for a friend."

Eight fifty-five.

"Women are always late," the helpful waiter advises, emanating an innocent befuddlement that implies that the man will always interpret life wrong.

Voort's phone buzzes and he pulls it out, checks the number, but it's not Mickie. Hazel is calling, working late in the computer section.

"There's no Marcus Sanders or any Sanders at all at the address you gave."

"Big surprise."

"I also checked for any references to the *Hussar*. You were right, Voort. The state issued a search permit for it three weeks ago. Salvage Experts International. That's the name of the outfit. The permit gives them permission to look up and down the East River."

"Home address for the company?"

"In the Caymans, like every other corporation that keeps its finances and officers secret."

Voort sighs. "Someone had to sign the application though. Who?"

"Just their lawyer. Let me find the name. I'm scrolling. Here it is! Theodore Stone! He's in New York."

She passes along an office address which Voort writes down.

Voort remembers being on the river yesterday. "Do you know if they've started the search already? I was kayaking near Hell's Gate and I didn't see a thing."

Then again, what do treasure hunters look like? Do they use divers? Sonar? I could have passed right by and had no idea.

He realizes he's getting angry looks from a couple at the next table as Hazel sighs, "I hate you, Voort. I'm stuck in the office without even a window and you're out kayaking?"

The man at the next table hisses, "Talking in restaurants on cell phones is rude, mister."

"So is talking with your mouth full," Voort replies as he clicks off the phone. He beckons a waiter. To hell with Mickie. He might as well eat. In his mind, he goes back to Mcgreevey's living room and the lesson on harbor graft that had gone on for a half-hour.

Mcgreevey: Guys want to move heroin. Or cigarettes without tax stickers. Half the time scows are empty. The Coast Guard never checks inside. But my sons wouldn't move drugs.

Greg: We get offers, believe me.

Mcgreevey: A man named Lu wanted to move *people*.

Greg: It's like, hey man! Can I just hand you this package before reaching the docks? Give it to me later, in a bar, after I'm through customs.

Mcgreevey: A guy wanted to be ferried *out* three miles to meet a ship one time.

Some of these scams are familiar to Voort. But some are new.

Greg: How about this one? Turn on your lights at night, head out off Jersey and come back past the reefs. Another boat was going to follow.

Greg and Mcgreevey playing "top this."

Mcgreevey: There's always something new. You're taking a ship in and they want to give you presents. They're not asking for anything, just offering a TV or crate of whiskey. One time a car. *They* would have wanted something major. But until now we always said no.

Greg to Mcgreevey: *We* were offered five thousand dollars from an Interpol agent. Well, he *said* he was an Interpol agent. He wanted to pretend to be a mate. He said he was investigating a shipping company but he wasn't supposed to be working in the U.S.

Voort: How come I never heard about this?

Greg: Uh, house rules?

Mcgreevey: The Coast Guard are clowns. They rotate personnel every year. Those guys don't know shit about the harbor and by the time they learn their stint is up.

Voort had said, "You're certainly narrowing down the possibilities."

"Senhor, some chorizo sausage?" a smiling waiter asks him now.

He eats fast. Waiters carve portions of rump steak, flank steak, sirloin. He stays away from liquor. He tries to call Mickie again but gets the automatic message. Hell, maybe Mickie's right outside, at this moment, climbing out of a cab.

Sure he is.

"If you get this message meet me at Twenty-sixth and Eleventh at five to ten. I'm heading out now."

Declining dessert, he pays the bill, his excitement growing because it would be great if "Lucy's" tip turns out to be meaningful, if the girl really got a good look at Ozawa that night.

The weather has gotten colder, wetter. A pre-autumn wind whips in from the Hudson. The chill has people scurrying for taxis, into restaurants, into subways as they head for home. Voort hears thunder. He turns up the collar of his sport jacket. He buys a two-foot-wide umbrella from one of the Nigerian street hawkers. It's unclear which will prove to be stronger, the umbrella or the wind.

I could have eaten dinner with Camilla, he tells himself, punching in her number as it starts to rain.

"Sorry about last night," she says.

"I've been working too hard," he says.

"Everyone in the city is on edge."

"How about some jazz later? Ginny's Blue House? I'll pick you up. I'll be the one with the roses."

Mickie is not waiting at Twenty-sixth and Eleventh. No cab pulls up carrying Voort's partner. No voice calls out to him from a doorway, which Mickie's ducked into, out of the rain.

I've had it with him. And to Mickie, *You're not screwing up another night for me. And you're not screwing up this meeting.*

Prostitutes, of course, are notoriously unreliable. Their behavior follows a self-destructive inconsistency the exact nature of which only they and their pimps comprehend. He turns the corner of Twenty-seventh and Eleventh knowing that "Lucy" might not be here. She might be in a hotel with a customer. She might be nodding off in the crack house. She might have forgotten she ever phoned at all.

If the city has changed, its need for prostitutes hasn't. Twenty-eighth, one street over, he knows, provides a dark background for the nightly circus. The auto-repair shops are shuttered there. The warehouses are closed. Cold rain drums down on sporadic circling cars, their lone male occupants eyeing the young women who stand like apparitions between parked vehicles. Everyone is fearful, the men of disease and robbery, the women of police, pimps, and psychos.

But Twenty-seventh, Voort's rendezvous point, is silent. The buildings are gutted. A Con Ed repair job has the street blocked off, but the workers are gone. Traffic glides by fifty feet away, beyond the corner along Eleventh Avenue. Voort sees a Mobil station, closed, and a ratty-looking diner, closed, and a narrow alley at his back, between a half-burned boarded-up tenement and a closed auto-parts shop.

"Ooh, you're cuter than your picture."

He turns toward the voice. It must be "Lucy," on a work break. She's still too far away on the other side of the street, for him to make out her features in the rain. As he starts to move toward her, he feels a sharp, hot sting in the back of his leg.

"Ouch!"

What the hell?

He looks down in pain and astonishment.

Something's sticking out of his pants back there.

Voort hears running footsteps now behind him.

Oh shit, he's thinking.

The thing in his leg is a dart.

SIX

The drug starts working almost immediately. He can't move, can't scream, can't even blink. Yet Voort remains completely aware of what the three attackers are doing.

They're carrying me toward the closed Mobil station.

He sees with exquisite accuracy the brick walls along the alley going by, and the eye slits of the mens' balaclava masks. He feels hands gripping his ankles, wrists, shoulders. Rain pours in torrents from the black slat of sky between rooftops. The grease and trash smells seem overwhelming. A harsh taste like iodine—from the drug probably—fills the back of his throat.

His gun is gone. His voice is gone. He wills his legs to move but nothing happens.

Voort's had versions of this nightmare his whole life. It's the one where you can't move while danger—a bus, a monster—rushes near.

Like the bear, he thinks more as a flash of memory than a complete idea; a split second of images that ratchets up his terror by providing context for what is going on.

Voort seeing himself in western Massachusetts, in the woods, on a July Friday. Voort hiking with Camilla and Matt and a ranger friend of his cousin's. The ranger raises a scoped rifle at a bear looking down from thirty feet up in a pine.

They darted me like an animal.

Quick cut of the bear swaying and swatting weakly at the dart in its haunch. It topples into a mesh net, and Voort, standing close, stares into the frozen yellow eye looking back.

"Is he afraid?" Camilla says.

"Terrified," the ranger says. "That's why we use a drug mix, an immobilizer and tranquilizer. Otherwise he could have a heart attack just from fear."

"He's fully aware?" Voort says.

"Super-alert. But he can come out of it fast so stand back while I tag him for the study."

God let me come out of this fast, Voort prays now, trying to stay calm.

They'd hit him silently. They'd come at him like pros. They'd known the pressure points and cop holds. They'd reduced him in seconds to a five-year-old trying to punch adults.

This isn't the way things are supposed to be.

Meaning, of all the threats he and Mickie have visualized over the years, trained for, talked about, dreamed of, planned for, being drugged by a dart had not been in the mix.

This can't be happening.

He's heard the same words countless times from stunned victims at shootings, fires, assaults, wrecks.

It's not the mob. They don't use darts.

He tries to fight off panic by thinking logically.

Control your mind. Figure out who these guys are.

The top half of a steel door swings open. White light floods his pupils and he wills his eyes shut but can't even close the lids. He never knew light could hurt so much. It's like electricity spiking through his eyeballs, burning through synapses, lashing into his brain. All sensation seems magnified, as if it is compensating for his inability to move.

There's a plastic tarp on the floor, so these guys were here earlier. I'm in the bathroom of the station. But why the tarp?

To catch blood?

Don't think about that. Watch for eye color behind the balaclavas. These men have to speak sooner or later. If they were going to kill me they would have done it right away. Remember voices. Remember smells.

The tarp crackles when they lay him down. He hears the door swish shut and the lock click. The room comes to him as if through a long tube blocking peripheral vision. He sees a bit of enamel toilet and swath of white tile. An S-shaped pipe on the underside of the sink drips with condensation.

The burglary alarm's not hooked to the restroom. They must have scouted the location before the girl made the call.

From behind, a man's voice says, quietly, calmly, "He looks fine."

The ranger said those exact words about the bear.

"Breathe in, Detective. Breathe out."

Voort notes the unusual inflection in the accent. The way the speaker slightly elongates the vowels *e* and *i*.

He smells ammonia, tobacco, the raw odor of testosterone. Two sets of Reebok running shoes—both large—stand in front of his face. He notes the colors—white and green—the ribbed socks and straight-legged frayed jeans stained with grease and white paint, as if owned by workmen. Perhaps the third man stayed outside as lookout.

If it's not the mob, who sent these guys? Ozawa? That's the logical first choice. Why the masks? To keep me from seeing faces? Or to shield their faces from witnesses?

His heart sounds louder than the city. His eardrums fill with the crashing of his own rushing blood. He's managing to keep panic at bay, but it's palpable, hovering a foot from his face.

"Cover his eyes."

This is like a military or SWAT team assault.

A hand appears and lifts his head. A cloth blocks out the light and plunges Voort into dark.

I saw a tattoo on the knuckle of an index finger, but it moved too fast for me to get a good look. Are these guys here because of a different case? Mickie and I have a dozen cases.

Shit. Mickie was late.

He feels the tarp against his cheek.

Find clues. If you can find clues you have a little control.

Something touches the upper part of his face.

In Voort's mind he jerks away from the object. In reality he's as frozen as the bear.

"Voort?"

Whatever the thing gliding on his cheek is, it's smooth and sharp but blunter than a knife. He feels warm skin. He envisions a sliding fingernail on his face. He envisions the tip of the finger lingering.

"You'll be able to make sounds in a few moments. Little sounds. Like a small animal. A mouse," the voice says, dead and flat with an unidentifiable accent.

Hands loosen his belt now.

"Nice leather," the voice says. Voort can't believe it. The guy's admiring his shoes.

They're sliding off my pants.

Oh no.

The men above rotate him over onto his belly, taking care that his head doesn't hit the floor. Sneakers crackle on tarp. Water bubbles in a pipe. Voort smells urine and Lysol. Warm air drifts against the lower part of his face, probably coming from the crack under the door.

The finger is on my ass.

He can't help himself. *Nonononono.*

He tries to kick out, push the men away.

I have no control.

In cop-training movies, and hostage and assault exercises, there's always a strategy to enable you to exercise at least a modicum of control. You talk to attackers. You reason with them. You look for weapons in the environment: vases, rolled magazines, pencils, candlesticks. You try to make friends with people you'd rather shoot.

"Ever wonder what happens to men you send to prison, Conrad?"

Are these guys people I arrested?

"Cruel and unusual punishment," the voice says, chipping away at will, resistance. "The Constitution prohibits cruel punishment. But getting fucked by a con with AIDS is cruel even if it's not unusual. It makes a man angry, makes him want to do the same to someone else. Mild men become wild men. Following my drift?"

Voort's perspiring like crazy. He feels the sheen of sweat like a film of oil on his skin.

You're not going to get to me.

But they've rendered him less functional than a quadriplegic. At least quadriplegics talk.

"I bet," the voice says, slowing down, weeding into the part of his brain controlling even the speed of Voort's thought, "that you sit around with those uncles of yours every night in the kitchen on Thirteenth Street, hmmm? Stuffing your faces. Laughing at guys you sent up."

Voort feels the men spread-eagling his wrists and ankles. He hears a vague muffled protest—just a long note—start up in the room and realizes it came from his own throat.

They're tying me to pipes.

The voice says, "Or maybe you and Camilla joke about it in the third-floor bedroom? You get in that special shower, the one with the four nozzles . . ."

How do you know about that?

"Camilla says, Conrad, soap my belly . . ."

The finger brushes along his spine.

"Conrad, I love when you do that."

Voort feels like throwing up.

But he makes himself think, *It's not a New York accent.*

Which narrows the speaker down to about three million residents and visitors in the metropolitan area just now.

"Still trying to distract yourself? I'm impressed."

Eastern Europe? Did I send anyone up who had eastern European accents?

Sure he has. He envisions them to keep control. A parade of faces. Russians from Brighton Beach. A couple of Polish painters/house burglars. Big blond guys. The Romanian car-accident insurance bunch. A whole ring of con artists.

"A guy gets rammed in prison, Voort," the voice says as he feels oily liquid dripped on his back, running in the crevices, "and he's never the same afterwards. He looks normal from the outside but he found out he *liked* it, or he's all ripped up inside."

Voort can't help it. He remembers the AIDS guys in prison hospitals. Thin and ill, hacking up phlegm. Riddled with dime-sized lesions.

Get away from me.

"Or would you rather we gave AIDS to someone else in that big family of yours? We could tell them we did it because of something you did."

He tries to kick out. The smallest, almost inaudible squeak slips out.

The voice remains unemotional. Letting the demons come.

"Cousin Matt? He's easy. Head north on the Taconic. Right on Route Twenty-three. Left on Tallyrand. Pass the barn with the quarter horses."

How do you know about that?

"Camilla," the voice says, "has a great ass. Uncle Bram? He's off to Bermuda in two weeks. Uncle Vim? The more you think, the more frightened you get."

The finger runs down his back with the kind of gentle glide that Camilla wakes him with when she's feeling randy. Then there's a grunting sound and he feels the hard points of knees, pressure, on the inside of his thighs. He smells onions, tobacco. Something warm and fleshy slides along the back of his thighs.

"You're helpless. And cute, my pals here think."

Voort's blood pounds crazily as if his arteries are swelling like balloons.

The hand tussles his hair.

"Make one of those pathetic little noises for yes. Two for no. Should we do one of them? Or you? You might as well get *some* sort of choice."

Voort feels sweat pop and clog his nostrils and drip into his mouth through the drenched gag. The tip of what he knows must be a penis has stopped on his ass.

"You then, bitch. We're going to ride you."

Hands pry his buttocks apart. Voort hears himself trying to beg them to leave him alone. But he can't even talk.

The hands lift away from his ass.

Please don't do this.

He hears the drip of water in the sink.

Voort loses control of his sphincter. Urine trickles down warmly between Voort's groin and the floor. The bear had also pissed himself in fear.

"You can't protect yourself. You can't protect your family," the voice says in disgust. "You can't protect anyone." Voort squeezes his eyes shut beneath the gag. *I won't feel it*, he makes himself think.

"Tell you what, though. Maybe we *won't* do it. Maybe you'll do *us* a small favor too. It's a question of will, not ability. Easier than you think. Little favor on your end. Shall we keep the great detective's cherry intact? Spare the folks at home?"

Does he mean it?

I'll trade. The thought comes unbidden.

The man on top lies full length over Voort now.

"Do you have the will, Conrad?"

Yes, he tells them in his mind, lying, meaning it, trying to talk, not knowing what he means, blindly wanting them to stop.

"Are you trying to say you'll do the favor?"

I'll do it.

"See, we're big and you're small. We're in the department. We're in the computer. We know things about your family. We always know where you are."

He hears the drone of a jet overhead. It seems a thousand safe miles away. True humiliation, Voort sees, means stripping away even a man's ability to get angry. It means making him admit he needs you. It blunts hate into shame, and subdues rage into permanent fear.

The worst things happen, an old cop used to say, between hell and breakfast.

"Next time there won't be warning. You'll walk into a restroom. You'll step out of a kayak. You'll leave a bar. Or someone else in the family will. But the good news is, all we want is for you to *take a vacation.*" The hand moves away. The man on top of him is gone. "That's right. All this fuss for a vacation! It's amazing how a small bit of co-operation keeps so many promising lives on track."

Voort gasps, trying to breathe, trying to fathom what he is hearing.

"Tell your lieutenant you want time off. Say you're sick. Leave the city and wait two weeks. Hell, have a good time. Then return and go back to normal. Pick up where you left off. No one will know what happened except us. And Voort? We'll know where you are the whole time."

From outside, muffled by distance, he hears a voice shouting. "Con Man!"

Mickie.

Voort envisions the man above him pausing, frowning, head cocked.

"Con Man! Are you here?"

Mickie's call is fading. Mickie must be walking off. The stranger's voice gets close again. Voort feels the tickle of breath on his ear.

"Elope with the fiancée."

Voort feels something break inside.

"Women love romantic whims."

Voort feels the man's eyes on him as if they are hands.

"Make one of those pathetic little squeaks if you'll take a vacation."

Yes.

"Or are you just saying it. You'd say anything to get out of here. I think you *won't* take a vacation."

Voort grunts and moans. He'll take a vacation. He means it. He realizes he can now move his head a bit, an inch either way. In the bear's case that had meant a twenty-minute lapse until the animal could rise again, tagged, recorded, normal from the outside, permanently damaged, Voort now sees.

The man kisses him on the mouth.

Then suddenly they're uncuffing him, pulling the tarp out from under him. He hears a high-pitched electrical grinding, the kind that handheld vacuums make. He feels the men roll him onto his back. Instead of tarp he now feels cool tile beneath him. He hears plastic crumpling.

They're rolling up the tarp.

He can still taste the kiss.

Tingling begins in the tips of his fingers. It feels like blood flow increasing when you come in out of the cold. A low buzz hisses in his ears. His elbows grow warm. The warmth spreads down his forearms and up into his biceps. His throat is dry. His eyelids itch. His body goes light, as if his hemoglobin has been replaced with some new chemical and a life force of a different nature runs through his veins.

In the Massachusetts woods, Voort recalls the ranger saying, "The bear'll be wary of people now. That will be better for him. The two don't mix."

Something soft as a mosquito brushes his face. He tries to lift a hand to push it away. It's still too great an effort.

The odors change suddenly. He smells vinegar, tuna fish, and a sweet, thick blood smell he associates with old Tampax in a toilet or can of bathroom trash.

Then the door creaks and warm air wafts across his face but the flow stops when he hears the door shut.

The sound of rain comes back to him. He hears distant traffic and the squeak of brakes. He hears scurrying rodents inside the walls.

The sense of other people being in the room is gone.

At length Voort gropes and lifts his arms. Sluggishly he pulls off the blindfold. His head throbs. He's thirsty as hell.

Around him on the floor are items that had not been there before: a Snickers wrapper, busted crack vials, grime, crumpled toilet paper. The bathroom looks as if a homeless addict broke in.

They cleaned this place beforehand and dumped false evidence after. The wrong fingerprints and DNA are here now.

A bare bulb shines down on Voort crawling to his knees, heaving up his dinner. He sees his shadow throwing up, on the wall. But he can't dislodge the taste of the kiss.

I couldn't protect the family. I couldn't protect me.

He's too dizzy to stand. He lies back in a corner, shivering like a withdrawing addict. He's cold, but whether from fear, release, or drugs he does not know.

I remember Cousin Alf, the prison guard at Sing Sing, who was taken hostage. I remember he was never the same afterwards. I remember him quitting and moving away, being drunk all the time. Talking about having no control, and being dependent on the cons.

A few small marks on his wrists seem the only evidence of what just happened.

The "prostitute" who phoned me is gone, if she was ever a prostitute to begin with. I never saw her face or profile. I doubt Lucy was even her name.

When he pulls his pants up, his trembling legs look thin and yellowish.

The ranger had said, "Now that we've tagged our bear we'll know everything about him. Where he sleeps. What he eats. From now on, his secrets are ours."

Voort stumbles into the night, and a city unchanged in its indifference. The rain seems colder. Traffic is bright and loud. Rounding the corner onto Eleventh Avenue he is merely one more pedestrian looking down as he walks.

He still feels the kiss, hands, pressure of flesh on his ass as if they've been tattooed on his nerve endings. The rain doesn't make him cleaner. The powerlessness is so overwhelming he is surprised he can move. He finds himself staring up at a billboard above a light on Eighteenth and Eleventh, and the grinning NBC news team, a quartet of splendidly dressed, coifed men and women who probably never deviate from a familiar comfortable lifestyle moving them between the studio, five-star restaurants, and luxury apartments high above the streets.

WE KNOW EVERYTHING THAT HAPPENS WHILE YOU SLEEP, the caption says.

I don't even know which case those men want me to stop looking at. Or if they're planning something in the future or covering up something in the past. I feel dirty.

A horn blasts and he realizes he's standing in the middle of the street, looking up at a clock tower. It seems inconceivable how little time has passed.

I won't tell anyone what happened.

The rain gets colder. He stumbles along the river promenade. No one else is out, even dog walkers. At Chelsea Piers, the high-end amusement area abutting the Hudson, he passes the glassed-in gymnastics area where little girls inside seem to be balancing too precariously on their wooden beams; the glassed-in basketball courts where little boys in jerseys seem to be hitting each other too hard under the basket, trying to inflict pain, not just to win. He passes the boathouse where he and Camilla store their kayaks, and later the old site of the World Trade Center, where three of his cousins lost their lives trying to save others.

I would have agreed to anything.

His worst nightmares had anticipated pain but not debasement. Threat, but not surprise. What police officer *hadn't* imagined how he might handle a gun pressed to his forehead. Or a phone threat. And what cop hadn't buttressed those visions with knowledge gained from confessions, tips, testimony. We chopped him up, perps admit. We buried him in Connecticut. We kept hitting him with shovels. We made sure his belly was open so he wouldn't float back up after he sank.

Late at night, after a few drinks in taverns, he and Mickie had told each other, "If someone threatened me, I'd keep going. But if they threatened my family, I'd stop."

Bar talk.

At length he finds himself in Greenwich Village, his neighborhood, although he's unsure how he got there. The clock over the Jefferson Library says two thirty. The rain has stopped. The streets glisten. Sixth Avenue is spotted with people even in the wee hours. A few bars are open. At a French bistro, waiters serve omelets under an awning. The Greek diner actually has a small line outside. He hears the tinkle of piano-bar music— something by Barry Manilow—wafting into the again-warming night.

"Is that Conrad Voort?"

He peers at a woman in front of him and her leashed flat-coated retriever, wagging its tail. He vaguely recognizes a neighbor who lives two town houses away.

"What happened to *you*?" she says.

"I got caught in the storm."

Talk seems painful. He regards the woman—a soap opera actress—from across an immense divide.

She walks off and Voort lurches along Thirteenth Street, toward his house.

And here it sits, warm and lit as a refuge. Golden light blazes from the downstairs sitting room and kitchen windows. He recognizes cars parked outside, beneath the maple trees. Here's Cousin Matt's Prius. Here's Cousin Marla's 4Runner. Here's Mickie's BMW.

I don't want to go in.

He starts to turn away but voices call his name. The door is open. The light blazing out seems to reignite the pain in his skull, or is the drug kicking in again? The worried family has been waiting for him. They've been calling his cellular phone. Why hasn't he answered? Mickie showed up hours ago looking for him, saying that Voort had disappeared after a meet.

"I was working. It's no big deal," he says.

"You're drenched." Their faces seem enormous and elongated. Their concern fills him with shame, as if somehow he's failed them as well as himself.

"A little water never hurt anybody," he says.

"Sorry I was late, Con Man." Mickie looks mortified, his face pale, drained, lined. His eyes are black raisins and his mouth a useless hole, like that of the man screaming in the Edvard Munch painting.

Mickie says, "I was late. Five minutes late. I can't believe it. I cannot believe I showed up late."

"Don't worry about it."

"Money? Fuck money. I can't believe I was upset about money. Family and friends are the important thing. I don't know what happened to me but I'm back, Con Man. I'm behind you. I'm in front of you. I'll never be late again."

"There are worse things."

What's the old song line? You wanna get better but you'll never get well?

Voort hears himself talk as if his voice reverberates out through an empty chamber, or floats from a hole in the ground.

Cousin Marla kisses Voort on the cheek, as she leaves. He restrains himself from recoiling. *I don't deserve affection.*

"Gotta open the main store early," Marla says. Greg saved a prime cut of shark steak for Voort. "Thanks for helping out with Captain you-know-who. You're a pal." Vim starts telling a story about when *he* got caught in a storm once on a stakeout, but Aunt Maeve shoos him out, onto the sidewalk.

"Vim, do everybody a favor for once and shut up," she says.

Camilla wraps her arms around Voort when they're alone, finally, in the foyer.

"I was scared," she says.

"Why? I've worked late before."

"It was the way Mickie was talking. I've never seen him like that." She's talking too fast, which happens when she's nervous, a rare occurrence. "I think this woke him up. He was terrified that something happened to you."

"I'm tired," Voort says, turning to walk upstairs.

I'll go to sleep. I'll sleep it off. I'll wake tomorrow and figure out a way to handle this. They only threatened things. Nothing really happened.

He still feels the man on his back.

She's coming up the stairs behind him. She's following him for Christ's sake.

He wishes she would go away. He needs to be alone. He doesn't want her in the bedroom as he strips off his sopping shirt and trousers. He wants to burn them, but she picks them up helpfully and takes them down to the washing machine. Voort slips into the bathroom and runs the shower hot.

He starts soaping himself, rubbing. He rubs very hard.

God, he thinks, *help me out here.*

"Is this cell block B?"

Grinning flirtatiously, Camilla is getting into the shower.

"We have to stop meeting this way," she jokes. "The other cons are starting to suspect. Hey big boy." She takes the soap from his hands, slathering up lather. "Turn around. I'll do you."

"Do you" are the words the man in the bathroom had used.

He can't stand her touch. He hates the way her hands feel on his skin. She reaches down to soap him but he jerks away when her hands touch his ass.

"What's wrong with you?" she says, looking hurt. Water runs down her breasts and tummy. It drips off her nipples and thatched V of hair. It pools at their feet.

"Ticklish," Voort lies.

"Since when?"

"I'll finish up myself," he says, taking the soap.

It was a mistake to come home, at least tonight, he sees. He should have rented a room. He should have phoned and said he was working. He should have given himself time to sleep, think, pray, whatever.

"I'm sorry about last night again," she says when he comes out. She's sitting on the bed, legs crossed, naked. It's a pose he always found beautiful before. Is she actually blaming herself for his bad mood?

"I can't even remember last night," he says. "It seems like a long time ago."

"You're wearing pajamas? You never wear pajamas."

"I got cold in the rain."

She grins. She pats the quilt. Her body looks strange to him, soft and lumpy and pink.

"I'll warm you."

He doesn't move. Then he says, "Let's go to Spain."

"What?"

"Let's just go. Why wait months? You might get a job again by the time we get married and you know how TV work is. You can never get away. Hell, if Mickie's feeling better, let *him* pick up the slack for a change."

"Well, sure, I'd love to go but—"

"Good! I'll change the reservations," he says, hoping his smile looks normal. He pulls a chair out by the Dutch writing table. He sits instead of getting into bed. "I have vacation time coming. I've been putting it off. I was thinking about what you said yesterday and you're right. We could both use a trip."

I'm overexplaining.

"Great idea, but this is sudden," she says, as if something about the notion bothers her but she is unclear why.

"So what? We'll plan it over the next couple days."

His smile feels stretched, rubbery, lopsided. "I'll call Lieutenant Santini in the morning. Hell, he's been asking me to take time off. We can go anywhere. It doesn't have to be Spain. We'll save Spain for the honeymoon. Get an atlas. It'll be great. We'll take the Feathercrafts."

"Sweetie," she says. "Come to bed."

Lights off, he lies beside her. He can't stand it when she snuggles up. He hates the moist heat coming off her, and her breathing against his chest. He hates her legs pressing against his, parting his legs, slipping between.

Her foot glides up his calf.

"I'm really tired, Camilla."

The foot pulls away.

"Being in the rain knocked me out."

He stares up at the ceiling. He hears rain drumming outside again.

I never knew that kind of fear and helplessness was possible.

Voort tells himself his mood is temporary. He's sat with plenty of sexual assault victims, interviewed them, comforted them, soothed members of their families.

That's different.

Why?

They're women.

He tells himself that most women get over it for the most part, and function normally.

Do they? How the hell would I know?

Are they watching the house now?

He doesn't fall asleep until dawn.

SEVEN

Voort notices the Ford Explorer behind them on the way
to Kennedy Airport. It follows his car-service Lincoln onto
FDR Drive, north past Hell's Gate and into the E-ZPass
lane for the Triborough Bridge.

Sometimes it falls back. Sometimes it switches lanes.
Voort always finds it when he looks. There's mud on the license plate.

"Argentina," says Camilla excitedly, "sounds so romantic."

Each mile takes him farther away from the family he
has been brought up to protect; people who have no idea
they've even been threatened. Voort asks himself who he
is trying to protect by leaving. Them? Or himself?

*Watch the other cars too. The Explorer could be there
by coincidence. Red's a bad color for surveillance. Or do
they want me to know they're behind?*

Gazing out at the city, Camilla's dressed for travel in a
loose-fitting, cream-colored pants-jacket combo. Silver
hoop earrings glisten between strands of her straight
blonde hair. Wraparound Armanis reflect back dusk sun
drenching light traffic on the Grand Central Parkway,
moving fast for a change.

Voort thinks miserably, *I've been looking over my
shoulder for three days now.*

Camilla flips pages in a book entitled *Go Argentina!* "They recommend two places for kayaking, Voort."

His eyes flicker to the rearview mirror. Through the Explorer's tinted windshield he makes out two figures. Both look like adults.

Camilla reads, "The Paraná River Delta, near Buenos Aires, is filled with beautiful islands and channels. Patagonia is mountainous with spectacular rapids and lakes."

"We'll do both," he says, "with the foldables."

"I never knew you were this impulsive," she says.

"I'm full of surprises."

When she kisses him he manages not to pull away. Her tongue feels hot and sticky in his mouth. The car swings left to pass a Honda Odyssey. The Explorer matches lanes, five cars back.

I couldn't just leave her here. It's bad enough I left the others.

But he relaxes a bit when his Town Car takes the exit for Kennedy Airport, and the Ford keeps going straight, toward Long Island. Then he thinks, *That blue Chevy was behind us on the ramp too.*

The truth is, a five-star-quality watcher can be anyone. The Chevy veers off toward the Delta Airlines terminal, but ten minutes later Voort notices a young, dark-haired woman in the Aerolíneas line at Terminal Eight, eyeing him.

She's looking at everyone. Not just me.

A businessman type in a gray suit, also on line, seems to be concentrating hard on his *International Herald Tribune,* but he never turns pages.

Just how badly do they need me out of the country?

Voort wonders. Just how rich or important is the prize?

Just before he reaches the ticket agent an older man ahead in line turns and asks Voort something in Spanish.

"I'm sorry, sir. I don't speak the language."

Voort looks into the handsome face of a professorial type, a white-haired man in a green cashmere sweater. Pleated wool trousers brush the tassels of polished loafers. The posture is excellent. The smile is white. The effect is of superb self-preservation during a gracious slide into old age.

"Forgive me," the man replies in accented English, but not the accent Voort had heard in the Mobil station. "I thought I recognized you from the flight up last week."

"We've never been in Argentina," Camilla volunteers, friendlier on vacation, already shedding her Manhattan veneer for something more trusting of strangers. Voort wishes she would shut up.

"Where will you be visiting in my lovely country?" the man inquires.

"We haven't decided," Voort says.

"May I suggest particularly excellent destinations?"

"That's so nice," Camilla says, getting out her ever-ready PalmPilot to jot down tips.

The man takes her wrist with three fingers. An elderly man can touch another man's fiancée in ways a young man could not. "Perhaps I can take a few hours and show you Buenos Aires. The city can be confusing."

The business card he gives Voort identifies him as Dr. Emmanuel Farkas, gastroenterologist, retired.

"We have plans," Voort says.

"Telephone if you change your mind." Dr. Farkas

bows slightly in a way that reminds Voort of German diplomats in 1930s movies.

"Why did you say no?" Camilla asks as they enter the plane's business-class section. "We have no idea what we're doing tomorrow. He seemed like a very nice man."

How do I know when I get back that they'll leave me alone?

"I thought we'd keep things more private. More romantic," he says.

Hurtling down the runway, he feels a momentary lift of cares, a sense of shedding problems that he knows is illusory. But he lets himself experience it. Manhattan falls away. The spire of the Empire State Building is lit green and red, the colors of casinos or Christmas trees, of wishful thinking.

Ship-running lights dot the harbor. He gets a pang when he sees the space in the sky where the World Trade Center used to be. He avoids looking at the neighborhood around Twenty-eighth Street, where he'd been attacked.

Camilla giggles lasciviously.

"Did you hear what I said? My friend Debbie Atlas joined the mile-high club last week."

Those men wouldn't harm anyone in the family while I'm gone. If they did, I'd tell what happened. It's like we've made a deal.

Voort says, "Who wants to make love in a bathroom anyway. It's cramped."

"We could be inventive."

He experiences a wave of revulsion so powerful that he unclasps her hand. For an instant the jet seems filled with the odors of Lysol and urine. A hard ticking starts up in his head.

Camilla's fingers run down his forearm. "Debbie and her boyfriend also did it under a blanket on the flight."

"Do you tell your friends everything *we* do too?"

"That would make them unhappy with *their* sex lives."

"If only I didn't have this damn infection. Doctor Strahan said another week of medication and I'll be fine," lies Voort.

Shoes off, she's curled up on her inclined seat, sipping from a glass of champagne. A whiff of her new perfume, Deceit, comes to him. Its commercials show a man and woman undressing in a hotel suite, while a chorus of voices whisper, "De-ceit!"

At ten P.M. the jet heads south over the eastern seaboard. The cabin is warm. On Voort's tray are the remains of a meal of Argentinean beef and green salad. There's a crystal glass of Mendoza Red. A cheese selection on a china plate. A stewardess rolls a cart past, offering hot fudge sundaes.

"The movie's coming on," he says. "I've wanted to see *The Green Mile* again."

His dick feels like a rag, a traitor. It hasn't hardened in days, even when he wakes from his nightly bad dreams. It doesn't deserve satisfaction.

Camilla sighs and picks up *Go Argentina!*

"If you love polo, you'll love Buenos Aires," she says, reading. "Can we see a match?"

A prison movie is the last thing Voort needs. He pulls on the flight mask and tries to sleep. Dozing, he finds himself back in the Mobil station. He smells tobacco and sweat. The pipe beneath the sink is writhing, trying to detach itself. He's desperate to get out. He looks up to see that the attackers have taken off their masks. He's horrified to realize that it's his family up there. Vim and Matt regard him the way cops eye suspects in interrogation rooms.

"Don't rape me," he begs.

"Wake up!"

A stewardess looks down at him sympathetically. Camilla's shaking his shoulder.

"You talked in your sleep, honey."

Sweating, Voort says, "What did I say?"

"I couldn't make out the words."

Thank you, God, for small things.

Behind the stewardess, a woman he had not paid attention to earlier watches from three rows back, over the top of a *TIME* magazine. Trying to remember all these faces is exhausting. Voort figures her to be in her early twenties; a petite, sour-faced passenger with her stockinged legs crossed.

"Voort, you look so tired," Camilla says.

She rests her head on his chest, like a kitten snuggling against an agitated human heart. Her breathing sounds like purring. Moments later she gently falls asleep.

But Voort doesn't want to sleep. He stares out the window at blackness and feels the throbbing engines and waits for morning. The woman in 8B is now snoring lightly.

It's not like I could leave the plane, Voort thinks. *It's not like she'd have to keep watching all the time.*

Buenos Aires appears out of the clouds at nine, immense and spreading along the west side of the rust-colored estuary of the Río de la Plata. He sees a mix of modern buildings and tile-roofed, white-walled houses, wide European-style boulevards and tin-roofed shanty slums. He feels, watching the earth get closer, the demons of last night evaporate. Nobody followed them onto the plane. No one is waiting here. The resources required to keep track of Voort are too costly. Whoever threatened him will do exactly what they said they'd do, nothing, if he stays away.

Reading from her travel guide, Camilla says, "Avenida nine de Julio is the widest boulevard in the world."

Dr. Farkas reappears abruptly out of the crowd at the luggage carousel, to ask if they would care to dine with him tonight or be his guest at a performance of tango?

"I confess that a handsome woman like yourself reminds me of my deceased wife, Emilia. We celebrated our thirtieth anniversary in New York, ten years ago. People were kind to us there. We saw a great show."

"What hotel did you stay at?" Voort asks, checking the story, nodding at the reply.

"Ah, the tango. We cannot manage government in this country but we dance quite well," Dr. Farkas says.

Voort asks Dr. Farkas *which* Broadway show he saw ten years ago. Farkas's references to old restaurants seem accurate. The story about hearing jazz at the now-closed Hawk's Nest rings true too.

But Voort declines the invitation again. "We'd planned a few days alone."

The doctor's smile conveys a masculine appreciation of romantic privacy. He bows and walks off, looking frailer from behind, limping slightly, rolling his little travel bag.

"You sounded like you were interrogating him," says Camilla, in the taxi. "I feel bad for him. He looked lonely. Let's call him."

"I lost his card."

"They have telephone books here, you know."

Voort gives up. "What do you know, his card was in my pocket," he says, pulling it out, acting surprised.

They spend the morning walking the old city, buying antiques—a silver snuff box, a silver-plated gourd for a popular drink named maté—on Florida Street. He feels dead. They sip coffee in an outdoor café by the Plaza de Colón, and stroll the gorgeous botanical gardens. She admires the way that, in the subways, real paintings hang on platforms, and there are glass cases filled with historical artifacts— old swords and uniforms—which nobody steals.

"The city feels safe," Camilla says. "I love it."

They order a rental car for tomorrow's drive to the Delta. They dine at ten with Dr. Farkas, who picks them up in his antique Mercedes, and drives them to a ballroom-sized restaurant where a whole cow rotates on a spit in the window, and diners sit elbow to elbow along rough, long tables. Waiters in starched white aprons serve succulent grass-fed steaks, french fried potatoes, thick cuts of sweet onion and red tomatoes, and a bold Argentinean cabernet that both Voort and Camilla liberally drink.

If Farkas is the one, I can't do anything about it. I might as well go with him tonight. We'll lose him tomorrow.

"Was that so bad?" she asks after Dr. Farkas drops them near their hotel at midnight, at the Plaza San Martín.

"You acted at the airport like you thought he was going to mug us."

"When you're right, you're right," Voort says.

"Abstinence makes the heart grow fonder," she says, taking his arm as they stroll toward their hotel across the plaza. Here we go again, he thinks in disgust. Oaks ring walkways. Couples kiss on benches. Regal-looking General José de San Martín—hero of the Argentinean revolution against Spain—looks down from horseback with a stern expression that makes Voort flash back to his own ancestors and flush with shame. The sky is starry, but the stars look so different in the Southern Hemisphere that even Voort, not a skygazer usually, notices alien patterns that confirm that he's in transit, not at home.

Why did I bring her? he asks himself. But the answer is, *How could I have left her home?*

In the distant past—five days ago—they'd been unable to keep their hands off each other. He knows that if he acknowledges the reference to sex it will invite inventive escalation—considering their repertoire—despite his lie about passing along a urinary tract infection. But not to play along would be out of character too.

"A few more days, we reinvent the *Kama Sutra*," he promises, noting as they reach their room that the hair wedged in the hall door is undisturbed. So are the ones inside the closet.

"I love you," says Camilla.

"I love *you*."

"I'm so hot, Voort. Let's masturbate each other," she says when she comes out of the bathroom, in a white lace teddy that shrivels him up like a dead worm.

There's no way out of this.

"Get over here," he says.

He can't even masturbate. He feels used up, old. She reaches to arouse him but the instant she touches him the Mobil station floods into his mind.

At four A.M. he's up again, gasping, sweating, sitting up in bed with the smell of Lysol in his nostrils. The repulsive feel of hands on his ass will never go away.

Distract yourself with work.

What was I close to discovering back home?

What comes to him instead is a different thought. Break up with her. You're no good as a man anymore.

Quit the police.

A new, modern eight-lane highway carries them north through industrial zones and farm zones and into the Pampas and a strip of semitropical forest. Following maps they find a parking spot overlooking the main channel of the Paraná River, a wide, clay-colored flow coming from the Amazon, hundreds of miles away. The roads here are red dirt. Thick, gnarled trees are covered with vines. Garbage litters the roadside. Barefoot boys on one-speed bicycles pedal past.

"Do you think there are alligators here, sweetie?"

"I don't think the guidebook would have recommended kayaking if there were."

They heft the knapsacks containing the foldables out of the trunk, assemble the crafts on a grassy bank, and slip into the water.

"Look, Voort! Parrots!"

He's starting to think that no one is behind them. No

cars followed them off the highway, and as they have no itinerary, no one can be waiting at whatever destination they choose to stop tonight.

I don't think the attack was payback. If it was, why would they care if I left New York or not? Why wouldn't they have just carried out the threat right away?

Who are they? he screams inside.

Camilla reads, "The many channels of the Delta region are beautiful but deceiving. It is easy to lose yourself in the maze of islands. Beware!"

The day is hot and the sky blue and neither Voort nor Camilla has mentioned his physical failure of the previous night. Within minutes civilization seems gone. There's no visibility beneath the dark, swirling river. They cut through the oily wake sent up by a passing rust-bucket freighter that looks too dilapidated to pass inspection in New York.

They turn into one of the narrow channels. Stilt homes lean sideways in forest clearings. A gray, bloated dead tapir drifts past. Pairs of brightly colored parrots squawk in the treetops. Occasionally a modern powerboat roars past.

"New York feels a trillion miles away," Camilla says.

She's wearing a *Target* T-shirt—after her old show—over her bikini. Voort's in an NYPD softball team shirt and baggy Lands' End trunks and they both have on ankle-high neoprene boots in case they have to walk in the muck.

At noon they pull onto a mud bank and picnic on fresh bread, cheese, salami, bananas, and cold bottles of mineral water. "Just out of curiosity, why are you paying cash for everything instead of using your credit card?" Camilla asks.

"They charge extra here if you do, the guidebook says."

But she's a news producer. She doesn't drop subjects that seem odd to her. She brings the issue up again that night as they dress for dinner in their small Delta hotel—where the clerk had accepted cash.

"Remember that show *Target* did on the FBI's Most Wanted list, a couple years ago? How the FBI tracked them down through credit card expenses?"

"You figured me out. The FBI is after me."

"We did another one on a truck driver transporting illegally cut trees from national forests. He hated doing it, but he couldn't bring himself to turn in his boss. I waited him out. Finally, when he was comfortable, he told."

"Any particular reason you're bringing this up now?"

Their third-floor balcony overlooks a plaza. Voort puts on chinos and a dark blue sport jacket and a button-up white shirt. Camilla zips up a calf-length floral-print skirt over her strappy sandals. Her pale green sleeveless top matches her button-up light-wool sweater. Delta evenings can take on a chill, the book said.

"If you don't want to tell me what's going on, fine," Camilla says mildly. "But don't lie to me."

The breeze smells of vegetation, diesel fuel, a whiff of barbecue, and something that reminds Voort of apple butter, but it's more foreign than that.

"I thought it might be a woman at first, in New York. But this has nothing to do with a woman," she says.

"No."

"Before I got married last time, my husband, my ex, courted me like crazy. Then the morning after the ceremony I remember I scrambled eggs for him. While he was still asleep. He came downstairs. He looked at the eggs. Something in his eyes changed. *He* changed, but I pretended for months afterwards that I hadn't seen it, or I'd misinterpreted. All he said was, 'I hate scrambled eggs.' But it wasn't what he meant. I promised myself I'd never fool myself like that again."

"I love scrambled eggs."

"Why are you afraid? You're making me afraid. This isn't like you. You're a strong man. You're the strongest man I know. You're better than any problem."

"I'm starving," Voort says lamely. "Let's eat."

They take the north/south highway out of the Delta and into the wide, flat pampas. He drives for miles, hours, a day in a direction that takes him in farther away from New York. He drives into a vacuum. They barely speak. He drives off the edge of the world. Cities fall away and so do towns, and they are in a desert, still heading south.

It grows cooler. They are driving toward Antarctica. The landscape reminds Voort a little of New Mexico. It is dry and filled with sagebrush. But he also sees volcanic snowcapped peaks to the west, and a stiff wind blows always, and there are no animals, only a long two-lane road filled with potholes. The trees are small and scraggly and seem to tip south, as if vegetation itself is trying to rip its roots out and fly off. Indians in thick sweaters sell them Cokes and ham-and-cheese burritos at tin-roofed rest stops.

"Now I know why travel agents call vacations 'escapes,'" Camilla says, sitting as far away from him as possible in the front seat of their rented Peugeot.

The land goes greener. The road starts to rise. Ahead in the distance is a solid line of vast, dark, cloud-capped mountains. Sagebrush becomes brown grass and brown grass becomes pine forest. Clouds hover like sentries in the distance. Huge bolts of blue-green lightning chase each other across the vast sky.

"Patagonia is one of the world's most beautiful wild places," she reads aloud from her book.

Bariloche, when the road climbs to it, resembles an alpine tourist town in its collection of gingerbread-trimmed hotels and narrow streets, and in the number of ski shops, souvenir shops, restaurants. Many cars are twenty-year-old American models, gleaming and well kept, as if their owners know there are no second chances here for vehicles that fall even mildly into disrepair. Voort sees the ribbony lengths of ski slopes in the mountainous distance, although in September, Argentinean spring, they are closed.

"Do you accept cash?" Voort asks a smiling clerk in the first four-star hotel they visit.

"Yes, but I need to take a credit card imprint in case you run up extra charges."

Voort thanks the clerk and they try the next hotel, where the policy is the same.

Four blocks later Voort finds a lovely guesthouse surrounded by blooming alpine flowers, behind a white picket fence. The owner records the names of his guests in a ledger, by hand, and also accepts traveler's checks.

"I'm taking a bath," Camilla says in a tone of voice that tells him she wants to be alone.

"I'm taking a walk."

He's furious at her even though she hasn't done anything, angry at her for existing. His growing rage is a bubbling chemical.

"Is this what marriage will be like?" he says.

She turns away.

"You're from New York, aren't you?"

Voort turns around slowly. He's on line at a bookstore. Horrified, he sees the girl from the airplane who'd been sitting three rows back. She's with a guy now, both of them in down vests and boots and baggy corduroy hiking pants. She's apparently going to buy the trail map in her hand.

"I'm Rachel. I live on Seventy-third and Amsterdam. I remember you from TV last year. Hey Chuck," she tells the guy, "he was on my plane. He was on TV. He's a cop."

"What a coincidence," the guy says, eyeing Voort as if Voort just made a move on his girlfriend, a rude but natural reaction. Or is their whole appearance an act?

How could she have known Camilla and I were coming here? Wait a minute. Camilla told Dr. Farkas.

"Your name is Voort," she says. "Right?"

"What a good memory."

"You're the detective who tracked down that serial killer last year. Sempa or Stampras? The name started with an *S*."

"Szeska."

"A real hero," Rachel tells the guy. And to Voort, "Are you staying in Bariloche? I heard Ted Turner bought a house near here, and Sylvester Stallone. It's like a hot new destination."

"What brought *you* to Argentina?" Voort asks, heart pounding.

"Chuck lives here. He's a ski and kayak bum. Do you ski or kayak, Voort?"

Voort says, "Excuse me. I have to meet someone."

Could that nice old man on the plane, Dr. Farkas, have been working for the men in New York? And if he had, how could *two* people on the plane have been working for them?

I'm acting paranoid. Lots of tourists visit the same towns.

"You're checking out? You just checked in," the confused clerk says when Voort gets back to the hotel.

Is this how life will be from now on?

Camilla says, as he pulls down the suitcase from the closet, "What the hell happened that night in the rain?"

The car takes them south, past cliffside hotels overlooking glacial lakes. It's spring, but they're close to Antarctica, and wind from Antarctica is supposed to be an engine for the world's weather. The car rattles from gusts sweeping through the pines. A branch falls on the side of the road.

"Stop, Voort."

He pulls over by a steep overlook.

"I hate this," she says. "If we're not going to talk, let's at least paddle."

Below the overlook is a zigzag path through forest, leading, a sign indicates, to a pebble beach. Voort looks down at a blue, oval lake. The surface is broken by whitecaps.

"I'm going down," she says. "Do whatever you want."

He has not escaped anything, he sees, not even distraction. In the Peugeot they change into cold-weather gear; Kokatat drysuit shells with latex seals at the neck, wrists, and ankles. Neoprene zipper boots for wading, and Seattle sombreros against the sun and wind, and rubberized gripper gloves.

They've dreamed of taking this kind of trip since they met, and now they're here and as happy as a couple in divorce court. He leads the way down. The path is narrow, and rocky, and when he asks if her pack is too heavy she snaps, "Keep going." It takes twenty minutes to reach the beach where he sees that the waves are more violent than they'd seemed from up top. The troughs churn. Foaming whitecaps crest at over four feet. Other than this volcanic strip beach, the lake is ringed by granite walls and boulders. There's no other place to get out of the water, once they're in.

Get dumped here and it'll be so cold you can function for a few minutes at most, even in a wet suit.

She says, "Why did you ask me to come anyway?"

Waves crash into each other from different directions, seemingly in defiance of natural law.

"Look at the bright side," she says. "You won't have to check the rearview mirror out there."

The foldables creak when they launch into the water. Voort drives forward, hunched over, spray drenching his shell, gloves, and face. He likes the challenge, distraction, punishment. He likes the way all his attention is required to keep from capsizing here. The way he's overcoming obstacles by exerting control. At least he and Camilla are moving through water together, in separate crafts, but sharing something that isn't a fight.

"Beats Hell's Gate," he says.

"You're driving me crazy," she says.

The waves get larger and the wind drives cold into his teeth, where it seems to harden. Camilla paddles with great, muscled strokes. He hears her grunting with exertion.

"This is better than sex," she says. "At least the sex we've been having lately."

"I told you. The medicine," he calls over the wind.

"The medicine? If you're going to make up a story about medicine, Voort, put pills in your kit, or pick someone else besides a journalist to fall in love with."

Ninety minutes later on the beach, they're exhausted. His shoulders are on fire. His fingers cramp when they disassemble the kayaks. His thighs hurt when they carry the forty-pound knapsacks back up the cliff. The sky has gone a dull, winter gray and the late afternoon wind heralds the oncoming gloom of Patagonian night.

But all his anger is gone for the moment.

God, help me out, he prays, driving again, warm again, as she dozes beside him in the car. *Help me make myself normal, and treat her right. That shouldn't be so hard.*

No answer.

Dad? Are you there?

Dad doesn't come. It's the first time in twenty-four years.

Things seem to be building toward culmination.

He finds a small hotel overlooking a rushing river. Rapids churn below and disappear into a cave. The clerk takes cash. The room has a fireplace and huge oak bed with a thick handmade quilt, and there's a fruit bowl, and a bottle of Argentinean white. Downstairs there's a comfortable-looking restaurant that has candles on the tables. The restaurant smells of fresh-burning pine.

"I dreamed of a place like this, Voort."

"Me too."

"Should we order steak? Steak? Or steak?"

Voort laughs. They try lake trout and fresh vegetables. A temporary truce has been called for the evening. All the hostility has been lanced back at the lake. But he understands that for both of them this meal is a hiatus in battle, precious because it is temporary.

She looks so beautiful that he feels the great beat of love start in his heart and spread until his chest is throbbing. He feels as if his guts have been hollowed out and his muscles have been removed. He feels as if his blood has thinned into uselessness and he is as old as Dr. Farkas.

They did this to me. They laid me on that floor and took off my clothes as easily as if I'd been an infant. They touched me in private places. They threatened my loved ones and I was helpless to aid anyone, not even myself.

The trout has no taste. The candle seems like flickering ice.

It won't be any better in New York, he sees, holding her hand across the table. Voort floats above the hemisphere. Distance overcomes illusion. From now on, wherever he is, life will be just as dead. Reflected in his wineglass, he looks the same as a week ago. But he's not. Everything is different.

Later she sleeps and there's a toasty fire in the room. He dresses warmly. He walks out of the hotel and into the forest. The full moon gleams coldly on the A-shaped pines.

It whitens the froth far below the cliff from where he stares down at the hissing river.

The image comes by itself, with the natural force of gravity. Voort imagines a tiny figure cartwheeling in the moonlight, spinning like a helicopter rotor as it plunges into the humpbacked boulders below.

I can't believe I even thought that.

Never in his life has he thought that.

He kneels and picks up a pebble. He extends his hand over the side of the cliff and opens his fingers. Accelerating, the rock disappears into the darkness. The water drowns out the ping of its landing below.

Then he has the idea.

Voort trudges back through the forest, brushing branches from his face, lost in thought. His fingers are numb when he lets himself back into the room.

He's thinking, *It's not the best idea, but it's best under the circumstances. It's that or give up.*

Voort's rage is a range finder, zeroing in on the right target.

The woman sleeping ten feet away has loved him and waited for him. She's overcome her own fears of betrayal to become a unit with him. She's family. She's kept her core intact while meshing with him into a third personality, their couple personality. Him and her.

I'm sorry for what I'm about to do to you.

He pulls a chair to the bed. He sits looking at the contours of her face. The flames sculpt her cheekbones. Her hands move beneath the sheets, as if paddling, as if in a dream she is trying to reach some important goal.

Then her eyes open sleepily as if some sixth sense has told her he is watching.

Her hand moves under the covers.

It extends out and takes his.

"You're cold," Camilla says.

Her skin feels warm, and he can smell her unique mix of bodily musks, not just her perfume. It's a smell he misses already, even though it is present. Her fingers rub his knuckles. It is as if she is trying by friction to reignite a spark, laboring to coax heat from charred, damaged wood.

He will need all his energy and talent, he sees, all his ability to think and pressure and convince, all his luck, contacts, and wealth to accomplish what he needs to do, and survive.

Voort moves closer to Camilla.

Am I going too far? Am I doing this for the family, or me?

It's crucial that she trust him.

Voort feels the full flood of anger now, finally. A transfusion.

He begins by telling a lie.

EIGHT

War criminals need vacations like everybody else. They get tired at their jobs, and yearn to relax at a Broadway musical, buy a Game Boy for their eleven-year-old son, sip a margarita without having to worry that the hotel lounge will be blown up by rebels, check out the *Jewelry of the Steppes* exhibit at the Met.

"You throw a great party, Ted," says Tolo Sundra, gazing over the stern of the cabin cruiser *Candace* on this warm, starry night. "My cousin was right."

Major Sundra, or "the Butcher of Kinabalu," or "Sword of the Devil," as he is known in remote areas of Indonesia, sips his Bombay Sapphire over crushed ice, savors the juniper-berry nuances in the gin, and turns appreciatively to regard the other two guests on tonight's cruise along the West Side of Manhattan. He's a powerful man with thick, close-cut, shiny black hair and a soft melodic voice, and he's dressed in a crisp-looking, cream-colored suit, his button-up silk shirt the blue of the Sargasso Sea, his tie sporting a festive crimson stripe pattern. The *Candace* is passing Harlem on its loop around the island. Offices and apartment buildings are all lit up.

Neither Ted nor Sundra invited their wives.

"Someday my people will enjoy the advantages of

electric power as extensively as you do here. They will enjoy better health care, diet, lives," Major Sundra remarks.

"You care much about your people," Ted Stone says, thinking, *Puh-lease!*

Major Sundra, Ted knows from his extensive sources, is not the *top* target currently under investigation by a Brussels commission. He's second-tier, not a headline-grabber. He's better known locally, but that hasn't prevented him over the last ten years from grabbing—investigators say—a chunk of UN highway contract money for Borneo, a percentage of AIDS pharmaceuticals—U.S. aid—for resale in Europe, a small but lucrative cut on illegal cigarettes, and there are rumors of a prostitution ring sending adolescent boys to Taiwan.

"I am a people person," Major Sundra humbly says.

If the accusations are right, which they probably are if Sundra is in New York, the man's very special problem must be solved legally, on U.S. soil.

"Specialize when you grow up," Ted's dad always said.

But tonight's goal is to attract a friend and explain convolutions, and so, getting down to *exactly* what parts of people Major Sundra loves, Ted looks back at the slim blonde leaning over a teak table inside the cabin. Her creamy cleavage is visible above the low line of her black velvet evening gown as she bends to sniff up another line of powder. Her services cost one thousand dollars a night.

The fourth passenger, the thin, sexy redhead, told Ted she never uses drugs. She's downing her fourth lemon Stoli and Ocean Spray on ice instead. She's not a hooker.

Ted thinks lasciviously, I'm a people person too.

Ted doesn't like to pay for sex. He prefers to impress less intelligent women for it. Hookers go home when the clock runs down. Women you've impressed pleasure you at your convenience. *You* determine when they do things. Not money. And not them.

"Anyway, as I was saying," Ted remarks as his secure cell phone starts chirping, "Austria is where . . ."

"No business tonight," interrupts Sundra pleasantly. "Tonight is for pleasure." He waves his drink at the blonde. "Tomorrow I may visit your office perhaps?"

"At your convenience."

"Is nine thirty too early, sir?"

"Nine thirty is perfect, sir."

His eyes lock on the blonde's. She smiles and stands with a slight wobble implying tipsiness, eagerness, and a rampant self-destructiveness that appeals to a certain kind of man. She turns and walks down the carpeted stairs toward one of the well-appointed cabins. Johnny Hartman music pumps softly over hidden speakers. Fresh tulips stand in cut-glass vases. The bar is stocked with Stoli, Bombay, Maker's Mark. Ted steers the *Candace* and enjoys the way the swells lift and bob it and imply that he's partnered up with a great power. He maneuvers through the harbor as an equal of gravity's vast natural force.

I feel so much safer with that cop gone.

"Would you excuse me?" he asks, reaching for his phone. Sundra's broad, straight back recedes down the narrow passage leading to the cabins and the blonde.

"Ted Stone here."

"I have good news, and good news," jokes the dead voice of Leon Bok, which sounds the same whether he's announcing a lottery win or plague outbreak. The only things he seems to get animated over are stylish shoes or cuisine.

"You're about to be happy, Mister Stone."

Ted's heartbeat soars.

"I'll know for sure in an hour."

"And the other part? Is it the cop? I can't go through all that stuff again."

"He's still booked to return a week from now. We're into the airline's reservation system, so if he changes plans, we'll know. If he walks through customs, we'll know. When he uses his credit cards, we know, and anyway, the second he tried to pick up where he left off . . ."

"So if he comes home early, I'm fine."

"Believe me, he was broken. If he could have talked he would have begged."

Feeling good, lucky, prosperous, Ted turns philosophic. "Blood greases history."

"You're safe."

But then an hour later, Bok calls back.

"I need more time," says the voice, so filled with impassive malevolence that it might be coming through earth, wood, fate itself . . . so soft that the telephone electrical system—accustomed to reassembling the voice molecules of normal humans—has to strain to broadcast Bok's words.

"How *much* time?" Ted asks unhappily.

"Patience, the beggar's virtue," Bok says with a sigh.

"Can you keep a secret?" Dad asks.

Voort looks up excitedly from his third-grade homework assignment. He's at One Police Plaza on a cold November afternoon, visiting Cousin Mark of the IAD, Internal Affairs Division. He's spent the last two hours alternately writing a report on Aldous Voort, the night watchman who caught New Amsterdam's first serial murderer, and learning from Mark that even police officers steal money sometimes, work for mobsters, beat suspects, use heroin.

A bittersweet day for the IAD, when Mark had explained that they've made a case against an undercover cop in Inwood.

"The Sparrow'll skip, Conrad. He'll be fired, but he won't go to court."

"Why not?" the offended boy had asked.

"Departmental interest, whatever that means."

"Why do you call him 'the Sparrow'?"

"The mobster we taped named him, called him a small bird with a big appetite."

Voort asks Dad now, as he grabs his coat, "Are we going to a crime scene?"

"No."

"To court to hear a Voort testify?"

"Not at night," Big Bill replies with the mix of gravity, affection, and curiosity that mark police lessons, Voort has learned.

"Give me a hint."

Instead the LeSabre takes them to Harlem and over the George Washington Bridge, which Voort Blue Guys guarded against Nazi saboteurs in the 1940s, after the troopship Normandie burned down at its berth in the harbor.

"Everyone thought the Germans sank it," Dad says.

They turn north onto the Palisades Parkway at Fort Lee, where Voort detectives—part of a tri-state task force—spent weeks in a hotel room in 1952, babysitting Albert Siciliano of the Bambara crime family. They played checkers with him and screen-tasted the baked ziti brought in for him. They shielded him with their bodies while transporting him along different routes to federal court each day.

"Conrad, how did you feel when you heard about the Sparrow?"

The boy repeats Cousin Mark's assessment. "He reflects badly on all police."

"Uncle Vim thought you're too young to come tonight, but I told him," Dad winks, "that the commissioner knows how to keep a secret. I'm training him *and* you. So house rules. No blabbing to your friends, teachers, even your pals at headquarters about what happens."

They pull into a small parking lot fronting a gray-stone church by the Palisades, south of West Point. Below Voort sees the wide, calm Hudson River. The rising moon is bright on the fall foliage. He recognizes cars in the lot. Uncle Vim is here, and so is Bram. Sergeant Mark from IAD came, and so did Inspector Willis Voort, and Cousin Dieter, just out of the police academy, and the boy sees the Ford belonging to Lt. Jayne Voort of Bay Ridge.

He knows the church. He visited it on one of the regular family outings. It was once a way station for smuggled silver that Voorts transported during the American Revolution—bound for France to pay for arms.

"We have a special relationship with this church," Dad

says. "We donate money. They let us hold special meetings here."

"What kind of special meetings?"

"Patience, pal."

Inside, everyone looks serious, talks in low voices, and wears civilian clothes. It's unusual for so many Voorts to gather without at least one in uniform, the slightly intimidated boy thinks.

The tension rises. It's chilly in the church. Wind blows down a chimney to scatter ash in a meeting-room fireplace. Dad sits him on a carved chair out in the hallway, looking up at a stern-looking portrait of a long-dead clergyman wearing a high, lace collar. A bloodied Jesus is tied to a cross behind the man, floating in the night sky.

"For Pete's sake, Bill," Vim says. "He's only eight."

"Finish your homework. Wait for us to come out."

The door reverberates against stone when it shuts.

Over the next forty minutes he hears muffled speech punctured by raised voices of argument, but the walls mute sound, so he only makes out a few words. He hears "punishment" and "Sparrow." He hears "disgrace" and "traitor." Vim says clearly, "That fucking scum."

It's late when they emerge. They don't look any happier. Vim tells the boy, "Someday you'll be in there too." Then Dad takes him to a diner and over cheeseburgers says, "I'm endlessly fascinated by things you notice. Figure anything out?"

Voort pours on ketchup, takes a bite, frowns. "One person came from each part of the family. One from the Bronx. One from Queens. It's like what I learned about Congress."

"Sometimes you scare me," Bill says in a way that tells the boy he's just been given a compliment. "But we don't make rules. We just hack out problems."

"Rank didn't make a difference. Queens sent a sergeant but a captain came from the Bronx."

"That's like Congress too. But think of it more like an Indian tribal council, which is where your ancestors got the idea. No one *has* to do what we say. We spread news."

Voort knows that Dad is waiting for more but he hates making mistakes.

Bill prompts him with a smile. "Guess."

"I think Mark told you all about that crooked cop, the Sparrow. I think you talked about doing something to him."

"Why would we care, big guy?"

"Because he's a bad policeman?"

Bill shrugs. "There are thousands of cops. We don't call a meeting every time one does something wrong."

Voort chews a french fry. "The Sparrow hurt a Voort?"

"You're getting warmer."

And suddenly the boy sees it. Awed, upset, understanding the entire thrust of this educational day, he gasps. "The Sparrow *is* a Voort."

"He's your cousin Al. The department can sweep this away, but not us," says Dad. "Remember how Mark said everything IAD does is secret? He jeopardized his career by telling us about Al. But now *we* know what the DA knows, what the commissioner knows, what the newspapers will never find out, at least not from us."

"What did Al do?"

"That's not your lesson."

"Will you hurt him?"

"Not the way you think. He's exiled. No invitations. No aid, jobs, help. Meetings take care of family, Conrad. Cousin Mark had a responsibility to tell us *and* the department what happened. We have a responsibility to treat Al fairly in case the department screwed up."

"What if somebody in the family *likes* Al and helps him anyway?"

"That's their business. It usually doesn't happen."

"Is that what you meant when you said, there's department policy and family policy?"

"The old saying is, 'In a time of test, family is best.' "

The customs agent at Mexico City frowns while looking between Voort's face and passport. The airline steward makes a cell call immediately after directing Voort to his seat.

"Flight time to New York will be approximately seven hours. We expect a relaxing trip."

I paid cash for the AeroMéxico tickets. I'm still in the American Airlines reservation system to fly from Buenos Aires to New York next week. If anyone's checking me out on the computer they'll think I'm still in Argentina.

The plane pitches as the stewardesses begin serving breakfast. The woman beside Voort grabs his hand like a nervous flier. The attractive brunette—not Camilla—has been concentrating until now on her *New York Times*.

His heart is pounding as if he's already landed, as if the half-truths he told Camilla have already transported him home.

They held a gun to my head. They knew the family habits. They said they're in the police computer.

The jet shakes and claws for height and the sun hangs in haze like an eye peering through the Plexiglas window. In his mind—back in the hotel—a log snaps in a fireplace. Sparks fly up in release and glow and drift to die like fireflies against the steel-mesh curtain.

I have no way of knowing if they paid somebody in the department or hacked into the computer, Camilla. Or even if they told the truth. But they're going to do something bad in the next few days, I think.

She'd been almost paralyzed with fear for him, which had made him feel worse. But he'd been unable to tell her about the man on his back, the sour-sweat feel that lives inside him, the kiss, the utter debasement. The rage starting up inside.

I have to find them.

"Are you crazy?" she'd gasped when he'd reached the part he'd figured out on the cliff. "You want me to stay *here?*"

"Only for a few days. I'll make calls. I'll use connections. I'll hire private security to protect you."

"Protect *me?* I can call my pals at NBC and find their fixer here and get my own security. This isn't about security, lover. It's about you playing John Wayne."

"You're an investigator," he'd said flatly, implying a whole range of argument. "And you chose a cop to marry, I told you. If we go back together it's easier for them to know I'm home."

"And what about the rest of the family? You going to fly two hundred Voorts out of the country too?"

"I *told* you what I want to do about that."

He'd tried to calm her. He'd explained his plan again, as

if it could really work. He'd said, not meaning it, "I understand if you won't do it and I won't go back if that's the case. We'll just continue along here."

"Just finish our laugh-a-minute vacation, huh? That's not fair and you know it." She'd practically been crying from anger. "You haven't slept. You haven't touched me. You're in another world. If you don't do something about it you'll burn yourself up, and blame me. I hate every man. I'm going to become a nun."

Now the turbulence gets worse and Voort recalls the deal he'd urged on her, asking for trust, saying trust me, please trust me.

"Don't you trust me?" he'd said.

"Voort," she'd said, "if you lied, if you don't check in every few hours, if you don't use me as your computer link I'll be on the next plane home."

"Fair enough. Hazel works wonders without leaving her office. Do your magic here. You did great on the Nye case."

Which is when she'd slumped in temporary surrender, and even tried a sour joke. "Remember those old grade-school essays? What I did on my vacation? Man, if Mrs. O'Toole could see me today."

"Planning a party?" the woman beside Voort asks now.

He turns to see wide blue eyes and thin, dark brows dipped prettily. The lips are full and glossy. Voort smells Chanel.

"I hate flying," she says. "Talking calms me. You're listing names, I see. When I do that it's a festive time."

His hand-scrawled list starts with "Ozawa" and ends with "Ted Stone."

"Birthday party," he says. But the names represent

people he'd never want in the same building, let alone the same room. Lyndon Child is a blackmailer who'd sent Voort a letter that said, "You kept me from getting parole." Julie Twain had fed her husband poison. "You think you're safe because you're a detective?" she'd hissed as she was led from court. Ted Stone's the lawyer representing the treasure-hunting consortium that Voort speculates may have something to do with the floater and dead Mcgreevey brothers. Baldwin Brennan was an ad salesman who'd wept when Voort and Mickie arrested him for sexually assaulting a fifteen year old girl.

"I'm afraid of being raped in prison," he'd moaned.

"You'll get used to it," Mickie had said.

The list will keep Camilla busy for days. And research on these people will really help me out.

The plane is over Pennsylvania now. The woman beside him goes back to reading. Voort's list gets longer. He stares at names of suspects, sources. Men and women he's arrested. Guys who got off but hold grudges anyway.

I don't think the attack was about a grudge. Why would a grudge have anything to do with me staying away for two weeks?

"How do you protect yourself?" the woman says.

He whirls. She's holding up the *Times*, with its headline of the latest Mideast atrocity.

"Terrorists," she says. "We can't seem to stop them. You can't protect everyone. How do you even start?"

"By figuring out who they are."

They didn't identify which case they want me to lay off, so they must not care if I go back to it. Why?

The woman says, "I'm scaring you too, I bet. Whenever I fly, my husband tells me, 'Take a Valium, Yasmine. Shut up and sleep.'"

In the lavatory mirror the stranger who stares back at him has dark curly hair and a neat mustache below round wire-rimmed glasses. Heel wedges add to his height. Cheek wedges make his face rounder.

The suspect is supposed to be the one resorting to disguises. Not me.

"We'll be landing in forty minutes," the captain announces, pleased with their progress. "We'll be at the gate early. A nice surprise for anyone waiting for you."

The plane breaks from low clouds and below, seething in a dirty chemical soup, the megalopolis sparks like a prehistoric ocean filled with mindless, groping life. Bits of glowing plankton.

The Airbus's wheels touch the runway. Voort hears the screech of brakes trying to stop the barreling craft.

I'm going to lie to the family, unless of course I don't even make it out of the airport.

Have I lied to myself too?

AeroMéxico flight 347 parks at gate 4A at Newark Airport, not JFK, Voort's original departure point. He waits until the plane empties before walking out into the arrivals area. A silver-haired Port Authority police captain is leaning against a wall out there.

"Is that *you*?" says Cousin Ellis Voort. "Say something so I know it's really you."

"Steal any Snickers lately?"

"Want to tell me, James Bond, what the hell is going on? Where's Camilla?"

"Am I okay with customs?"

"They'll stamp you on the tarmac. I told them you're undercover. I swore you're not carrying drugs."

"Does aspirin count?"

"Why isn't Mickie here? Why'd you call me?"

"Ellis, even when you were a kid you knew how to keep secrets. Your father almost killed you over those stolen Snickers, but you never gave me up. Let's go."

The New Jersey Turnpike takes them to the Palisades Parkway and after that it's the same route Voort drove with his dad twenty-five years ago. When they pull up to the gray-stone church the modern cars are smaller. He re-members how the carved chairs used to be so high that when he sat on one his feet didn't touch the floor. The claw-footed conference table had stood at eye level. Now it comes up to his thighs.

Only the stern-looking clergyman in the painting looks exactly the same.

Dad, I'll tell them what they need to know. They don't need to know everything.

The faintest voice in his head answers, "Anger can make you sharp, pal. Or anger can make you go too far."

Voort feels the breath seeping out of him. He pushes his father away. He tells himself it wasn't really his father talking. It was just guilt.

From the head of the table he looks over the current council. *His* council. Vim's still there but now Cousin Matt is too, from the civilian side of the family. Shapely Spruce Voort is here from Flushing Meadows, beside Uncle Vim and Lieutenant Margaret Voort of the 68th Precinct in Bay Ridge. That Conrad is back early from

Argentina underlines the importance of this meeting to them.

He starts out by saying, "The family's been threatened. You. Your kids. Your wives or husbands. Everyone."

Family rules are, don't interrupt. Let each person finish. Ask questions or argue when a speaker is through.

He gives the version he told Camilla, that he was threatened with a gun. He sees outrage on their faces but he's unsure how they'll react in the end.

Vim, the biggest of them, a white-haired bear, starts off gruffly when Voort's through. Usually he's a big supporter.

"You should have told us right away."

"There was no threat if I left, Uncle. Only if I stayed."

"Or came back too soon," says Spruce.

"Conrad, it wasn't for you to decide," says Ellis.

"A dart? Who uses a goddamn dart?" Uncle Vim snaps. "They treated you like an animal. You dart a dog."

Matt looks ashen. "They knew Rachel leaves her window open? Excuse me."

Matt walks out, gripping his cellular phone. Voort outlines a broad sketch of what he wants to do, without giving traceable specifics.

"You'll make yourself bait," Vim says thoughtfully.

"Bait gets eaten. I prefer lures."

"But you'll drop the whole thing if we ask you to, right?" asks Spruce, staring into his eyes. For Voort the temperature seems to rise in the room.

"I'm not sure that's a good idea," he says.

"*Promise* you'll drop it if we say."

The argument's in full swing as Matt comes back.

"Give them what they want. It's just for a week."

"If they get away with this once it'll happen again!"

"You don't have children, Bram!"

"We'll get everyone protection," says Vim. "We'll work out schedules. Pull together. We'll figure out who they are before they know we're even *there*. We'll back Conrad up."

"I don't care what you vote. I want a goddamn car outside my house twenty-four hours a day," says Matt.

"Hold on, hold *on*. This is complicated."

"Everything important is complicated. *Let's vote.*"

The recommendation is, stop now. Get back on a plane. Finish your trip overseas. Keep us safe. Sorry.

Six to five, but it might as well be eleven to zero.

Voort feels dizzy. He feels sick. This isn't the way things are supposed to be. The relatives are growing smaller by the second. They can't control what he does, but he wants their approval. He's never gone against a decision. He needs to try again.

"I was afraid in that gas station," Voort hears himself say, "in a way I didn't know possible."

His throat hurts and his spine hurts and the back of his head is throbbing. His voice sounds strained and disembodied to him, as if coming directly out of his brain without passing through his mouth.

"There was a moment when I would have agreed to anything. Do you understand what I'm saying? They reduced me that much."

Silence.

"Jesus," says Ellis.

"What happened was terrible, but don't compound

it," Spruce says, shaking her head. "You're mixing up your personal problems with the family's. You can't put us all at risk because you were humiliated. It's not our problem."

Vim says gently, "Anyone would have been afraid in that room. It has no bearing on you as a man, or a cop."

"Try therapy," Spruce says.

"Maybe it was a bluff," Ellis says.

"Maybe they're crazy fucks and they'll do what they say."

They vote again. Six to five, against.

"I'm sorry," says Matt afterward. "Drop it. Come back after. Investigate anything you want *then.*"

"After," Voort tells him, "may be too late."

"For duty? Or too late for revenge?" says Spruce.

Matt looks stricken. Until now he and Voort have been practically best friends. "Look, if one of the kids gets hurt how will you handle it? The brave thing is to drop it. Those guys have us by the balls."

"Appropriate expression," Voort says.

"I'd back you on anything else."

"I'd teach *my* kids to fight, Matt."

"No, you'd let yourself be shot to protect them."

Voort tells Ellis, in despair, "Let's find the nearest bar."

Spruce saying, "Go against a vote and you're dead, Cousin. Pull it off and maybe we'll forget we opposed you, if you're lucky. Fuck up and at best you'll end up like Cousin Al, without a family. An old fuck who none of us even knew anymore when he died."

Walking out he recalls one of Dad's old expressions. *A family divided perishes together,* Bill used to say.

*   *   *

"Did they go along?" Camilla asks over his cell phone, thirty minutes later. She's calling on a powerful model he'd bought in Buenos Aires.

"Of course."

"Even Matt?"

"Especially him," Voort says, lifting his second Laphroaig, watching Ellis head off to the bathroom, probably to call the others and report if Voort's going along with the vote or not. Tonight's Mets–Dodgers game plays over the hum of conversation. "Tell me what you found, Camilla."

"I got lucky. My old staff is helping. I told them this might turn into a story I'd pass along, so they're hot for it. None of the people on your list got out of prison lately. No one's up for parole. No trials scheduled. Nothing in the news about developments on any of your cases. Nothing special on Colin Means."

"Then with only a few days to play with we pick one direction and concentrate and hope we're right."

"Well, whoever worked you over has recourses and none of your official cases are high-level. Ozawa maybe, if you stretch it. And those men did get to you by mentioning that case."

"They could have learned I was working on Ozawa from the newspapers, or in the department. Hmmm. A treasure-hunting consortium would have money."

"I thought of that too. I e-mailed Mickie like you asked and he's been working your *regular* cases—*not* the treasure, and everything seems fine, he said. And by the way, he's kept up on Ozawa and no one's threatened *him*. I didn't tell him what was going on, like you wanted."

Voort thinks a moment. "Ask your pals at NBC about that lawyer, Ted Stone. Cases. Clients. Credit. News. He's the only connection with the consortium."

"Be careful." They break the connection.

There's a sudden warm breeze in the room and when he looks up he has the oddest, most powerful sensation that Dad is here. He even smells a whiff of Old Spice aftershave.

He's never doubted the truth of visitations. He hopes this is a real one now. The voice in his head seems clear.

"I'm proud of you, son. You told the family what they needed to know to protect themselves. But when are you going to tell that fiancée of yours the real truth?"

"I might drop the whole thing, Dad."

"You knew you'd never get a unanimous vote, so six–five or ten–one, what's the difference? Also, you missed a clue, pal."

"What is it?"

"It's been staring you in the face for days."

Voort feels his heart ticking faster. "Does that mean you'd go ahead with this even after the vote?"

"Only once or twice in a guy's life," the voice seems to say, "does something really big happen. How you handle it determines who you are for the duration."

"They're planning something . . ."

"I wish we knew if it involved lives or only money."

"If they harm one of the kids . . ."

The presence seems to get closer, and for a fraction of a second he feels pressure on his right shoulder, where Dad used to guide him along while they hiked. He wants to cry.

The voice seems to say, "I don't envy you. Consequences seem bigger these days. But all the lessons, Conrad, were to teach you that good against good is never easy. You told the other Voorts. They'll take precautions."

"Did you ever decide beforehand not to bring someone in, Dad?"

"You were a kid. That's not the sort of conversation you have with a child, even a gifted one."

"I want to hurt them."

"Revenge never goes unrevenged."

The presence is gone. The music grows louder and a gust blows through the bar from the open front door, as if Dad took the human way out, exhausted from the effort of communicating. Voort supposes even ninety-year-olds miss their dads.

He picks up the phone. He punches a number in from memory. He's made the decision.

"Con Man!" Mickie says, astounded. "Hey, I'm dry, guy. Not a goddamn drop since you left. You're *back*? What's wrong? Tell me what you need."

NINE

"Waking the generalissimo at midnight will boost our careers, big time," Mickie says an hour and a half later.

"She'll need to okay what I want in the end so we might as well start here."

Getting out of Mickie's BMW—which is for sale—they walk up a narrow flagstone walk toward a small Cape Cod home in Forest Hills, Queens. With its neat lawn and picket fence, it looks like a thousand other cop homes Voort has visited. The night is warm. The porch light comes on three minutes after Voort rings the bell.

"This better be extra good," says Eva Ramirez, New York's first female chief of detectives, answering the door herself.

As one of the department's five top "super-chiefs," Eva's a contender for the commissioner's job should Warren Aziz leave. Petite, attractive, and tough, she rose through the ranks by compiling an award-winning record stretching back eighteen years. At work she favors dark-colored, well-cut skirt-and-jacket business suits, not the pink terry-cloth robe showing a fringe of nightgown at the hem, which she's wearing at the moment. Her copper-colored hair, worn up at the office, falls even with her olive-colored jaw. Her green eyes, which cops see through contact lenses, scowl out through rose-rimmed glasses. Divorced, she lives alone.

The rabbit-head slippers don't exactly scream police.

Even Mickie, who generally distrusts brass, has a high opinion of Eva. She has a reputation for fiercely backing subordinates caught in a jam.

Voort says, "A six-hundred-million-dollar scam. Three murders. Threats to a dozen officers. Is that worth waking you up?"

"If it turns out that's really what it is."

It's a cop's house, Voort thinks, following her into the eat-in kitchen. Basic wood paneling. Lots of ceramic knickknacks—little goats and sheep and kids in lederhosen playing flutes. Lots of framed photos of Eva's rise from cadet to undercover ace to detective lieutenant. Her ex-husband's in a couple of shots. Rumor is he's still a Blue Guy, and a drunk.

"I'm waiting," she says, putting a kettle on the gas stove, and then three china mugs on the Formica counter.

Voort gives her the gun-threat version, not the near-rape version. As he speaks her face goes hard, angry, thoughtful, suspicious.

"You were threatened and you just left," she says when he's done.

"I felt it safer for my family to look like I was cooperating at first."

"You didn't even tell Santini?" Meaning, Voort's new lieutenant.

"They said they had a source inside, Chief."

"Any evidence of that?"

"I didn't want to test it."

Eva puts Twinings bags in the mugs. "You think it's Santini?" she asks with disbelief.

"I needed to tell my family before I took another step."

"And they want you to proceed." Eva's brows rise in admiration. She's worked closely with Voort before, and likes him.

"Actually, they'd prefer I drop it."

Eva upends the hissing kettle and blows out air herself. "That's tough, with *your* family. What do you want from me?"

"A P&P." Voort pushes away the family part as if that will make it disappear.

She looks surprised, but then nods thoughtfully. "P&P" means "pad and package," a 1960s term for providing temporary residences and IDs to witnesses, key sources, and undercover cops. "Package" means a ready-to-use passport, driver's license, Social Security number, credit cards.

Just add photos.

"Pad" means an apartment seized or borrowed under court settlements for NYPD use, in the same way the FBI confiscates drug dealer cars. Pads often come equipped with hidden video cameras, microphones, and motion detectors. After being used once, they're sold or given back.

In an hour, Voort knows, if Eva gives authorization, arrangements will be set in motion with the phone and electric companies, voter registration office, motor vehicle bureau, post office, to give Internet life to a false identity. But no one except Voort, Eva, and Mickie will know who the new identity is for. At any given time two or three P&P jobs are under way.

IDs run the gamut. Undercover cops have walked

streets as members of the gravediggers union, disbarred anesthesiologists, offtrack-betting parlor clerks, playboy millionaire heirs.

"You want to be a different *detective*?" Eva says.

"I need authority to investigate. I figure we only have a few days to figure things out."

Eva nods. "So we put your new ID into our system in case your friends have access."

"We *monitor* access," Mickie says.

"If we miss it? Or they come after you anyway?"

"At least my family's safe," Voort says. "They go after the phony guy. Unless the whole thing was a bluff. And if that's the case, the family's okay anyway."

When Eva stops pacing, the rabbit-head slippers seem to nibble at the shag carpet. The smell of chamomile tea fills the kitchen, but steam's stopped rising from Voort's mug.

"I wish I could arrange protection for your family," Eva says, and Voort knows she's hamstrung by the budget crunch and work slowdowns, and the fact that extra detectives will be needed this week at the UN, the National League playoffs, the US Open. A permanent contingent siphoned off for anti-terrorism duty has cut Eva's options even more.

"I appreciate it, Chief."

"I'll see what I can do about increasing patrols in their areas, discreetly. Give me a list of who they are."

"I already wrote it up."

"Make sure they call their precincts if they even think something screwy is happening. Voort, you'll be alone."

"What am I, invisible?" Mickie protests.

"You," says Eva, "were two minutes away from suspension. You think those phony reports fooled anyone?"

Mickie the ex-Marine turns crimson. "I cut that out, Chief."

"Report to me directly, Voort. If you find these guys, restrain yourself."

"It's my best quality."

"Why do you think they didn't just kill you in that bathroom?"

"They didn't want to trigger a larger investigation. They believed they could scare me away."

Which they did.

Mickie says, "They were confident that by the time Con Man came back they'd be finished. There wouldn't be evidence or they wouldn't care. They'd be gone."

"Do you really think it's possible a six-hundred-million-dollar treasure's under the East River?" Eva asks, with real curiosity, and Voort can see she's envisioning piles of ducats, jewels, padlocked chests coming out of the water.

Voort speaks slowly, as if testing the validity of his thinking. "My dad used to say that complicated problems have simple solutions. All I know is, the biggest thing on my plate before the attack related to the *Hussar*. A six-hundred-million-dollar find. A dead man in Queens who was fascinated by the ship, and *two* dead tug operators who took a payoff and worked near Hell's Gate. The attack happened the day I found out."

"Get on the river," says Eva. "Check out that operation, if they're still there."

Voort says, "I keep thinking about my cases. This

seems like the best bet. Nobody from the state supervises divers, Chief, so if they're recovering treasure secretly, they don't have to pay off investors. They don't have to share it with the state. They don't care if I come back later because they'll have walked off with a fortune nobody will ever miss."

"Six hundred million," Mickie sighs. "Tax free."

"Don't start," says Voort.

Thirty minutes later Voort and Mickie are on the Long Island Expressway, heading to Mickie's waterfront home in Roslyn. No way is Voort going home to Thirteenth Street. The new IDs won't be ready until tomorrow, Eva said.

"My house is on the market," Mickie says without a trace of moroseness. "Every penny to go to Citibank. MasterCard. Uncle Sam."

"You told Syl what happened then. Good."

"You were right. I'm an asshole and she was furious, but you get things off your chest and feel better."

I can't tell Camilla. Not yet. Maybe not ever.

Voort just looks in the rearview mirror, frowning.

Mickie sighs. "About me being late that night . . ."

"Forget it."

"Nothing would have happened if I'd been there."

"They would have darted you too," says Voort, not meaning it, leaning closer to the mirror, pulling back the collar of his shirt to get a better look.

"What are you doing?"

"Dad *said* it was staring me in the face. One more piece and I didn't want to see it."

"Dad? You mean like your *dead* dad? Take my advice.

Sleep," says Mickie. They've reached the Roslyn exit. "You've been up for what, twenty hours?"

"I need to use the car. Let's drop you a couple blocks from your home."

"Eva said to stick with you."

Voort raises his eyebrows.

"Since when do you listen to Eva," says Voort. "And it's better if I don't stay out here anyway. What if they're watching? Think about Syl."

He remembers the block—in upscale Brooklyn Heights, overlooking the Promenade and East River. He'd dropped Tina off here last time they'd seen each other, but had declined her invitation to come up. The apartment houses are well kept. The block is lined with trees. The parked cars seem newer and shinier than autos on most city streets.

The lobby guard hands him the house phone after Voort shows his badge. Tina answers sleepily on the fifth ring.

"When I said come back any time I meant before two A.M. But this must be important. Give me five minutes. I'll unlock the elevator. It opens right into my loft."

She breaks out laughing when the door slides open, and she sees the wig. "I like you blond better."

"It itches," Voort says, pulling it off.

Barefoot, she's in a powder blue Juicy Couture velour pants and hooded sweatshirt suit that clings fetchingly to her tall, lean body, and is unzipped to the edge of small cleavage, a faint swell. The loft smells of incense, wood soap, baby powder. The potted-palm fronds almost touch the high ceiling, and Voort sees lots of blow-up shots of East Africa—Peter Beard originals—on the clay-colored walls. Masai women with neck-rings. Lions at dawn.

"You look taller, Voort. Wedges in your shoes? I thought you more secure than that."

Over her shoulder he glimpses a fabulous view of the lit-up Brooklyn Bridge and Manhattan's East Side. Floor-to-ceiling windows frame the South Street Seaport and night traffic on the river. One Police Plaza is lit up as if generating its own electricity through industriousness.

Brooklyn offers the best view in New York, he's always thought.

"I don't mean to make fun," she says.

Barefoot, Tina leads him over the polished plank floor toward a living room area—a square formed by couches facing each other over a coffee table—with a tiptoe progress implying that she's in high heels even when she's not. The butcher-block kitchen is adjacent to a glassed-in bedroom. He sees a tousled double bed in there, dimly lit, covers rumpled, purple satin pillows piled on the side where she'd slept.

Voort can't believe his physical reaction.

For the first time since the attack, he feels himself getting hard.

"Tina, remember the finger marks on the floater?"

"I have photos at the office."

"I was attacked too, the next day."

She stops smiling.

"The guys who did it were professionals. I think the pattern of my bruises match his, but I'm not sure."

"Take off your shirt," she says.

The couches are dark leather. The carpets, orientals, are patterned in vegetable dye colors—blues, greens, orangy reds. Voort sees his reflection in the window superimposed over the lights on the bridge. His shirt comes off. The air seems more fragrant. Her long fingers come closer and touch him. He can't help his physical reaction as she traces the marks on his neck and chest.

"Turn around," she says.

Smooth hands warm dormant nerve endings. His mouth is dry. His head is throbbing, but not from pain. He is excruciatingly aware of her slender body behind him. Two elements burn toward combustion.

I didn't know if I'd be able to get hard again, or at least not for a long time.

"They used the same holds on you," she says. "That's fairly evident."

"Professional ones."

"I can measure the gap between bruises," she says. They've faded from their original blue to a faint strawberry color. "I have a caliper here somewhere. I could get a rough idea of finger-spread, hand size. Did they hurt you badly?"

"No." The breath catches in his throat.

"Anywhere else?"

The other marks are on his thighs and ankles but Voort says, "You can get an idea from what you see."

"It's up to you but these bruises are evidence. I have a Polaroid. I have the caliper. If I can match up both victims it might help you in court."

He takes off his pants.

Her face is close, her black eyes close. Her lips move toward him as she bends to measure with the caliper. "These must have been pretty painful."

"You should have seen the other guys."

"I hope I do. On the front page, when you bring them in."

His pent-up desire is exploding. He can't understand why he's had no reaction to Camilla but now the blood pounds so powerfully in his ears that it is hard to think.

Or is this what I wanted to know?

"You can cover up those cute legs again," she says, stepping back from him without seeming to move away. "Where's the fiancée?"

"Argentina."

Her brows rise. "You look tired."

"I flew up today."

"The couch folds out. I'll get a blanket."

He knows he should leave, but he sits instead.

"I don't have pajamas for you, sorry."

Something about the apartment makes him feel safe, and with that comes exhaustion. "Thanks, Tina."

She kisses him on the cheek. Her lips are warm, and they linger. The apartment smells of spices he had not detected before. Smells beneath smells in here.

"Good night, Voort," she says, turning the light off, allowing the urban glow in. Outside, cars glide along the bridge and a jet blinks across the sky. He senses her in the bedroom thirty feet away. A beautiful woman can work magic. She can make danger disappear. She can erase problems. She can obliterate history temporarily and obscure everything on Earth except desire.

"Need anything else, Voort?"

What she's really saying is, *You have to start this. All you have to do is walk into the bedroom.*

He wonders if watchers can see into the apartment from the bridge. He wishes he'd spot them. He sees himself heading over there, with his Sig Sauer.

In the dream he's back in the AeroMéxico jet, except this time Camilla sits beside him, not a stranger. Vim sits behind him, he realizes. Spruce sits across the aisle. Looking back as the plane starts shaking, Voort sees with horror that the whole cabin is filled with family. Dad's here, beside Mom. Greg is reading a magazine. Tanya, Camilla's Russian ward in the "little sister" program, is watching a video with her headphones on.

"Meet me at ten," says the captain's voice over the intercom as the Airbus starts to buck.

Voort gets up instead of fastening his seat belt. He needs to tell the pilot to change direction. He fights his way down the pitching aisle. The cockpit door is locked.

Suddenly the plane goes into a dive as Voort bangs on the door of the cockpit. Only instead of the cockpit, when the door opens, he sees the Mobil station bathroom inside.

Instead of a pilot, Voort sees himself tied and naked on the floor.

Three men wearing balaclavas look up.

The one with the strange accent says, "You haven't the slightest idea of what's really going on."

When he wakes he's sweating and sunlight is seeping through the picture window and glowing on the spires across the river. He hears the sound of a child running in the apartment upstairs, playing happily. New York residences seem filled with other lives.

"Bad dream?" Tina's voice says.

She's in the kitchen area behind the butcher-block counter. He smells coffee brewing. Her high heels click and snap like music. Her calm seems a fixture. Dressed for work, she's in an open-necked blouse-and-skirt combo. Hoop earrings dangle and toy with the light.

New beginnings always seem to wipe troubles away for a while.

"You're in some difficulty, I think, Voort."

The room reeks of incompletion, desire, regret.

"I'd appreciate it if you don't tell anyone I'm in New York," he says.

"Coming back tonight?"

Quite softly, he says, "No."

She busies herself in one of the wooden cabinets. "You don't have to decide now. I'm leaving the key on the counter, and my card with my cell number. I liked having you here. I think it felt nice to you too."

"It did," he says.

"I'm a veggie. You'll find Kashi and granola and dried fruits in the fridge. Help yourself to anything here." She smiles. "I always go to the gym before work. Got to keep the muscles fit. All I do is look at dead ones all day."

"Thanks for everything, Tina."

"Oh, I'm selfish," she says, letting her amused eyes rove down the smooth fabric of his blanket. "But then, everyone is, I imagine. And those things are like dogs' tails, aren't they? Fido gets excited and perks right up."

*   *   *

"Where were you?" asks Camilla over the phone. "I got worried. You said you were going to check in."

"I slept for ten hours straight," Voort says. He's called her from the police impound lot on the West Side of Manhattan, where he's to meet Mickie, and pick up unmarked cars.

"Good. You needed rest. But meanwhile I haven't been able to get much on Ted Stone. It's funny how hard it is to learn things about the guy. Lawyers are usually all over the place. *Who's Who*. Alumni organizations. But one of my old interns said she thinks *That's the Story!* tried to investigate him a couple years ago. She's making calls to see, but even the network people don't want to talk. It's weird."

"Eva ran Stone through the criminal databases last night and nothing came up either," Voort tells her. "What about the company he represents? Treasure, Ltd.?"

"It's registered in the Caymans. The officers are secret. There's no mention of it anywhere in the LexisNexis database, which is also a little odd because treasure hunters *like* publicity. It helps them raise capital. Anyway, the treasure-hunting community is small. I called a few places, said I was with the network. No one I contacted heard of these guys. But they *did* know about the *Hussar*. They seem divided on whether the treasure's really down there or not, but with treasure that's always the case."

Voort sighs. "Even if the company's crooked, the lawyer might not know it. He might just be signing papers."

"You going top or bottom, Voort?" Meaning, does he intend to start his investigation by questioning people on the search boat, if it's still there, or the lawyer?

"Both. By the way, how's your own security?"

"Very handsome. Captain Martinez is in the next room."

"I'm jealous."

"Finish up fast and I'll come home."

As they click off, Voort spots Mickie getting out of a cab outside the seizure lot, off the West Side Highway. He's already handed over Eva's authorization "for the bearer of this note" to use any two cars here for business. The midnight-blue Volvo he selected for himself comes with leather seats. Quadrasonic sound system. Tinted windows.

"If they ram you, it has side airbags too," Mickie says, handing over a brown-wrapped package. "Here's your P&P. I'll use that piece-of-shit-looking Chevy. It goes with my new status in life."

As Mickie screws new plates on the Volvo and Chevy, Voort checks out the package. Eva took digital photos before they left last night, so they are already laminated into his new ID for "Detective Frank Heffner," and his new driver's license, passport, DBA card, NYPD card, Social Security card, HMO card, MasterCard, and two sets of keys for an apartment in Whitestone, near the Throgs Neck Bridge.

"Eight years on the force, huh, Frank? You don't *look* familiar." Mickie grins.

Voort walks off and punches in a number on his cell phone. After a moment, a voice says, "Harbor Police. Sergeant Rabb."

Voort gives Frank Heffner's badge number and gets connected to the Coast Guard liaison post. He requests an immediate inquiry as to the name of any boat on the river today searching for the *Hussar*. Since 9/11 any time the UN General Assembly is in session, boats working near the building have to register with the authorities. Otherwise, they're blocked or boarded.

"If you hold on, Detective, I think I can call Captain Jax, over there," the liaison says, and four minutes later is back on the line. "The *Wanderer*'s the name of the boat. Someone's still looking for that old wreck, huh?"

"Thanks."

Next call goes to cousin Greg on his tugboat. Voort's unsure what type of welcome he'll receive after the arguments in the church last night.

"Man, I heard what happened," Greg says. "You split the family wide open. Half the Voorts want to back you, half to kill you. We'll be taking turns watching the kids and houses. Vim called an hour ago. He'll be sitting in my tug yard with Bram and a couple of shotguns tonight."

"I need help, but I'll understand if you say no."

"That's what I've been trying to *tell* you. There are plenty of us with you. Hell, I'm the one who *told* you about Mcgreevey. I'm not going to turn my back on you now."

Voort fights off a wave of emotion. "You have to do exactly what I say, Greg. No going off by yourself."

"Not like you, huh? Only you can do that."

"Do you know any good salvage experts?"

"Chip Levant's the best. He's a friend of mine and he worked with the Mcgreeveys too. He's out of Greenwich."

"I'll double his rate."

"I doubt he'll accept pay for this."

"I need to go out with him—or whoever you get—today. *It's got to be today.* I want to know if somebody is diving near Hell's Gate, searching for a wreck. He'll know what to look for, right? Sonar? Radar? Whatever divers use when they hunt for an old ship. 1780."

"What the . . . tell me later. He da man."

"Don't go yourself. Stay away from there. Call me as soon as you get somebody and I'll be down right away. I don't want these guys knowing someone's interested in them."

"Actually, we have a job through the Gate today. We're taking a junked freighter to the Merchant Marine Academy near the Throgs Neck. The cadets will use it as a classroom. You and Chip can come if you want. No one will notice a tug going past."

Clicking off, Voort tells Mickie, "Remember, we only talk by cell phone from now on." Both their models have scramble chips. "I tell you where I'm going and you get there first, see if someone's waiting. You watch my back when I leave."

Mickie breaks into song. He's a terrible singer.

"I'll be there," he bellows.

"You better be. And find out the status of the Mc-greevey case, but don't give your name. Now let's go visit that lawyer, Ted Stone."

U Thant Plaza, named after the former Secretary General of the UN, is a sixty-five-story copper-colored steel-and-glass tower in Turtle Bay, near the UN. The building is occupied by international aid agency offices, lobbyists' offices, NGO offices, and several foreign news services.

Ted Stone's office is on the top floor, Camilla said.

Voort leaves the Volvo double-parked with its police visor out, in a row of double-parked cars with diplomatic plates. He feels sorry for the traffic cops on this beat. Foreign diplomats don't have to pay tickets, and can't even be held for trial for crimes in the U.S. without permission from their countries. But the countries always request that big offenders be flown home, and the department ignores small ones. Turtle Bay precincts provide One Police Plaza with a steady mass of unenforceable violations and petty crime.

Voort shows his new ID to the security guards in the lobby.

Inside the packed elevator, he hears a hodgepodge of English, French, and Asian languages. He gathers from the babble that a special UN meeting's in progress on maritime issues. Dumping. Mining. Offshore boundaries.

"Not to mention smuggling," says a man with an Indian accent to a woman who looks Japanese. "Of drugs. People. Arms."

Suite 6541, belonging to THEODORE STONE, ESQ., as the gold plaque reads, turns out to be a modest-sized, well-appointed office with a five-star view of the East River. Voort instantly takes in the British paintings and antiques.

This man would be interested in the Hussar, *all right.*

The receptionist passes him on to Stone's secretary, a slim, dark Italian-looking woman wearing too much lipstick and a conservative, repressed look. Voort's badge doesn't impress her. She sizes him up instantly along lines that he suspects have to do with perceived wealth. Ted's out at the moment, she says, gazing up from her *Commentary* magazine. Clearly Voort's not here for business, so he's apparently not worth a second look.

"He's with Candace on the *Candace*," she adds, looking down at the headline, EUROPE'S BORDERS! GOING, GONE!

"Excuse me, Lizzie, but who or what is the *Candace*?" he asks, trying for a personal note by using the name on her desk plaque.

"I'm not Lizzie," she says as if he's the dense one. "Ms. Aarons is out sick. I'm Mr. Lewis's secretary, on double duty this week. Candace is Mr. Stone's daughter *and* the name of his boat."

Following her glance, he sees a framed photo of a white cabin cruiser over the couch in his office.

"He has a box at the US Open," she says in a tone implying that Voort's abilities as a detective should include mind reading, or that anyone who doesn't have a box at the Open is a loser.

Usual procedure is, if you're trying to break open a company, you go after the top *and* bottom. You squeeze. You look for the chatty secretary, ignored intern from the Xerox room, pissed-off rival by the watercooler, man or woman who got passed up for promotion, humiliated at a sales meeting, turned down for a date, downsized and let go.

But Voort doesn't have the time, doesn't even know if he's looking in the right direction.

He tells her there have been thefts in the building. "I'm checking to see if you lost anything too."

"We didn't."

"No need to bother Mr. Stone then. Thanks."

Camilla calls sixteen minutes later, while Voort and Mickie are on FDR Drive, headed for the US Open.

"Ted Stone's apparently quite the monster," she says. "Watch out for yourself, Voort."

TEN

Theodore S. Stone, future "monster," future murderer, rising bureaucrat and petty marital cheat, trots across the tarmac of Nairobi, Kenya's Wilson Airport toward a mammoth ex–Soviet-bloc transport and paratroop plane—a twenty-year-old Antonov—filling with other nervous-looking civilians. It's 1993.

"I'm sending you to investigate a war criminal," his boss, Mr. Yoruba, had told him in New York.

The apprehensive accountant, and law student at night, is dressed for his first trip outside the U.S. in pleated khakis, white Van Heusen button-up shirt, and brown-striped tie from the outlet mall in Secaucus. His faded tweed jacket is slung over a forearm. Inside the plane he squeezes a snap-up leather briefcase between his knees as he straps himself onto the gray steel bench running the length of the fuselage, beneath red jump-lights. Passengers face one another across the aisle, as on the 7 train that Ted normally rides to Manhattan each day, from Queens.

"Mohammed Aiwad has been responsible for the deaths of thousands," Mr. Yoruba had said. "But he'll be nice to you, I think."

The massive motors start up and the Antonov—with its blue UN markings—lumbers slowly into the sky. Small clouds hang like ack-ack bursts in the distance. The other passengers are probably relief workers from Doctors Without Borders, CARE, Christian Vision. After all, no commercial flights land in Somalia anymore. The government has collapsed. The country is divided by warring clans. There is no effective capital, money economy, functioning school system, electricity grid, or even safe roads.

"Why would Mohammed Aiwad let me check his books?" Ted had asked his boss.

"The *rules* say," Mr. Yoruba had answered sternly, "he must allow UNOB monitors in or lose his aid."

UNOB is the United Nations Oversight Bureau, where Ted has gotten his first post-undergrad job.

"Rules are," strict Mr. Yoruba had continued, "even though he's probably running guns, that's not your problem. *Your* problem is to make sure food aid gets where it's supposed to go—that he's not stealing it."

"I'll check manifests against contracts," twenty-eight-year-old Ted had said. He was a graduate of Pace College, a young dad, and the first Stone to go to law school and work for the prestigious UN.

"Eyeball the operation. Follow up any references to European bank accounts. You're working in tandem with staffers in Europe. We're sure he's laundering money, but is it ours? Ah, Ted. The world is so compartmentalized now."

Mr. Yoruba had been munching on an avocado-and-cheddar burrito from Benny's. He was a small, neat Nigerian, always in a black suit and bright bow tie, a sour, proper man who'd been running UNOB's Africa desk for thirty-one years.

"Don't tell anyone what you're up to. Don't go anywhere in Mogadishu without Aiwad's guards. International aid rules are, he has to protect you."

Below, East Africa flows by through portholes, as stripped forest, small maize farms, private game preserves where the last wild animals on Earth eat one another as paying tourists look on. Dots down there—worms snaking along red dirt roads—represent UN convoys, a cornucopia of goodwill or pity funneling out of Washington, Berlin, Paris, unloaded from ships in Mombasa, or from planes out of Melbourne, London, Madrid.

Ted finds it all sort of . . . well . . . exciting.

"We are crossing into Somali airspace," says the dark, pudgy man on Ted's left, an Indian or Pakistani.

Ted is the newest man in Mr. Yoruba's underfunded office, a warren of partitioned cubbyholes on the eighteenth floor of the UN. Back there on Ted's corkboard, beside the photo of Candace, are flow charts monitoring contracts for grain, tetracycline, energy-efficient woodstoves, battery-powered radios, jerricans, bicycles, water-purifying tablets, textbooks, string beans in vacuum cans.

"Are you the accountant?" the Indian shouts over the roaring engines as the Antonov hits an air pocket and drops five hundred feet.

"How did you know?"

"I manufacture windows. I am a friend of General Aiwad, which is how I got a ride. I am hoping that when the fighting stops I will get the glass contracts in his area. Many windows will need to be replaced."

Ted also meets the smiling man on his left, a surprisingly elderly but stylish-looking Parisian in a dapper blue jacket and open-necked shirt. The silver-haired, tanned Remy Truelle introduces himself as "a friend of Mohammed Aiwad. I advise him on investments in Europe."

"Investments in what?" Ted says, heart beating fast.

"Stocks. Bonds. The general has banana plantations. This legitimate income is going north. If the peace accord is signed he may move to Paris." Truelle winks. Ted takes it to mean that if the peace accord is signed, Aiwad will flee.

Are these guys double-teaming me? Ted suddenly thinks.

The plane gets lower. It is impossible to land in Mogadishu's main airport, says the Indian, because it's bombed out. But Aiwad controls a private airstrip, normally used for the transport of kat, a mild narcotic leaf that, when chewed, provides daily relaxation for the warweary population of Mogadishu, and more "legitimate" income for Truelle to invest.

"There are so many new ways to hide cash," Mr. Yoruba had sighed back in New York.

Turn right on a street corner and life goes on unremarkably. Step left and you're in *People* magazine.

"I see you are interested in treasure hunting," remarks the Indian, reading Ted's book over his shoulder.

"Yes. This ship, the *Hussar*, sank in New York with millions in gold and art in it, in 1780."

"Art is expensive," the Indian says.

"I just read about it."

"It is sad to be unable to afford things you love."

The plane begins landing. Below, the yellow-dirt runway is lined by truncated palms and Toyota trucks manned by ragged-looking men shooting guns into the air, but not at the plane. When the hatch opens Ted ducks out into the bright light, to more gunfire and the cries of black-clad ululating women, all wearing veils.

Had he actually been riding the 7 train only forty-eight hours ago?

He's never imagined moments like this existed.

He experiences a surge of unexpected joy.

Young Ted thinks, *Hey, this is fun.*

And eleven years later—in Flushing Conrad Voort shows his new ID at the US Open Tennis Center and a security guard waves him through a turnstile onto the packed, busy grounds. The rage inside him is a living presence. It seems to feed on the crowd's demonic energy, to absorb it.

"You know the difference between cop records and reporter records?" Camilla brags over the phone as he walks. Blue Guys monitor crowds flowing in from parking lots, the IRT subway, the Long Island Railroad. Guards peer into purses, knapsacks, fanny packs, binocular containers. They confiscate water bottles. Cops don't assume that clear liquid is water anymore.

I don't see Mickie. He's supposed to be watching me.

"*Your* records say who got arrested. *Ours* say who got accused," she brags.

Camilla's voice is so clear she might be calling from inside the grounds, from one of the two stadiums, row of restaurants, or amusement tents. Voort asks a guard for directions to the administrative offices. He's directed to the mezzanine level in the main arena.

"Master of innuendo. That's you," Voort says.

"*That's the Story!* looked at Stone five years ago but dropped it. The producer quit TV. He runs a bike shop now in Massachusetts. My friend Melanie—she was the AP—says he never talked about what happened. He just left."

"Why was NBC looking at Stone in the first place?"

Static.

"Camilla?"

"I'm back. I heard you. His name came up on a fishing expedition. The story started out as a look at UN aid. Think about it," she says, excited, like a producer covering a big story. "In sixty years there's never been a major scandal out of the UN. *Billions* allocated. A *hundred* governments involved. Dictators, warlords, thieving administrations in a dozen countries. *Never one big public fraud?* Give me a break."

Voort pushes his way up the ramps into the main stadium. The crowd seems more orderly here than at Shea Stadium, where the Voorts have a box. A sign directs him toward the US Open offices. Hopefully someone there will give him the number of Ted Stone's seats.

He says, "Get to Stone."

"The main *theory* was, no one screams about UN graft. Donor countries don't want to make enemies. Poor ones are afraid to scare donors off. UN aid is feel-good money. It's not *supposed* to be efficient. Nobody rocks the boat. Stone's name came up in relation to food aid that might have been sold for profit overseas."

Voort feels a pulse start up in his throat, usually a signal that an investigation has become fruitful. He's unsure how Camilla's story could relate to treasure in the harbor, but "Once guys start breaking laws," Dad used to say, "they get greedy. They go too far. Always remember, Al Capone got caught for tax evasion, not murder."

"How was Ted Stone supposedly involved, Camilla?"

"That's the part where there's not exactly proof."

"This is like pulling teeth. Are you going to make me ask everything?"

"Hey, I'm stuck here. I'm lonely. My only fun is to torture you. We're talking rumors, remember, not charges." She pauses dramatically. Even the natural rhythms of her conversation reflect television presentation.

"When the investigation reached Stone, the source and her two kids got wiped out."

Ted's convoy stays beside the two-lane coast road as it heads toward the embattled capital. The road, lined by date palms, is bombed and cratered, and the danger from mines is so great that drivers never venture onto the asphalt itself, but keep parallel to it, to be safe. Nomads watch from camels. The convoy halts for prayers. Fighters spread straw mats on the ground and bow east to the call of a muezzin. Toyota Technicals—trucks modified to carry antiaircraft guns as artillery—surround Ted's vehicle.

"Against ambush," the Indian explains.

"Scared?" the Frenchman asks.

"Are you kidding? This is *great*."

The Frenchman looks surprised.

It's true, though. It's like being in some fascinating movie. Stone feels a swell of unanticipated excitement. Long-dormant nerves respond to the rampant anarchy apparent even in the landscape. Men can live their whole lives in an orderly universe and never even imagine the things that would truly excite them. Now the civil servant has the oddest sense of coming home. He suspects almost instantly—not as a concrete thought, but an instinctive recognition—that there is no check on raw power in this place.

He senses from the awe on the faces of passersby—farmers or nomads—that he has crossed onto the preferred side of a once unimagined boundary. Even colors seem brighter on this side.

"This is so different from Queens," says Ted. The air smells of frangipani and lemons, and a breeze off the Indian Ocean brings a whiff of natural corruption. In the blue water swim hammerhead sharks, the Indian has said.

The feeling swells his heartbeat, constricts his throat . . . it's all so unlike his orderly home and commuter's schedule and sense in New York that there should be more to life than neighborhood-watch meetings and antique magazines.

"All guys feel antsy," say his old college buddies, who are making better money at big accounting firms now, and whom he is starting to envy. "Get laid. It goes away."

And getting laid helps, sure, in some momentary way that lets him feel power and control, but it doesn't solve the fundamentals. Back in New York he's taken to picking up the occasional secretary, restaurant hostess, shopgirl, stewardess. Uncomplicated liaisons dull the restlessness, but within a few weeks it's always back.

"What a coincidence," the Parisian tells Ted now, drawing his attention back to the present. "You're staying at the Deep Sea Hotel? Me too."

The Indian grins. "We can all have dinner together!"

The convoy starts up again. The moon and sun—dark

and light—hang in balance over banana fields and clay farmhouses with flat sunbaked roofs. The indolence accelerates Ted's blood flow.

"There are opportunities here," the Indian man says.

The outskirts of Mogadishu strike Ted as a combination of sleepy seaport and ravaged ruin. Cut telephone wires hang from broken poles. Lavender and turquoise buildings are spotted with rusty bulletholes, blood streaks, graffiti. The convoy twists through narrow streets half buried with sand and dotted with burned-out Technicals. Dogs' eyes glitter in headlights. Residents crouch in doorways before wood fires, chewing kat leaves. There's no sound except for the engines of the Technicals.

Ted's not a violent man, but he's thrilled by the proximity to raw danger.

"Do good in life," his dad had always told him, back in Bayside. He was a bus driver, proud that his son had a job at the UN.

"Your life is so glamorous," his mom had said. She was a crossing guard at Carr Junior High.

The hotel turns out to be a two-story Italian villa with a private generator for electricity, a glass-topped protective wall around it, and guards wielding AK-47s on the roof. Ceiling fans whirl. Potted ferns vibrate from unnatural airflow. The fawning owner refuses Ted's payment, insisting Ted is General Aiwad's "friend," and the only other guests seem to be a trio of blonde women he glimpses through an arched doorway, playing billiards beside the small but well-stocked bar.

"Three of them. Three of us. A coincidence," says the Indian. The heat exaggerates strong temptations.

"Perhaps we'll have a little party," suggests the Frenchman. "I have a delightful Beaujolais."

Hell, getting laid has nothing to do with doing the job right.

Big things have small beginnings.

"Only a little party?" Ted says.

"Tell me what happened to the source and her family," Voort asks Camilla over the phone eleven years later, pushing his way through the crowd on the stadium ramps, heading for the US Open office.

"She was a pissed-off divorcée, her husband a UN functionary. He'd left her and gone back to Europe. She was out of her mind with rage. She comes into NBC after hearing we're looking at the UN, and she tells a great story. She says there's looting going on. A New York lawyer is involved, and what *really* pissed the woman off was, her ex used to party with the lawyer—Ted Stone—on his boat after they did deals. You know: Do coke. Get laid."

"Why didn't she go to the police?"

"She wanted a job in TV. She wanted to be an assistant producer if we did the story."

"And?"

"Testy, aren't you? Our producer visits Stone and thirty-six hours later the woman and her kids die in an accident."

"Let me guess. A fire."

"Then the ex-husband is killed in a car accident in Switzerland."

"Keep going."

"Melanie said that Stone was ex-UN by then. He'd

become some kind of financial adviser, taken speech lessons, tennis lessons. He'd started out as a bean counter. He landed up, as of five years ago, with a Mercedes, cabin cruiser, a two-million-dollar apartment, and more colonial-era British art than even you."

"We stole ours the old-fashioned way. In war. Camilla, was it possible the fire *was* an accident?"

"The cops were all over Stone at one point. They came up with nothing. But Voort? Normally if you're on an investigation and a source gets killed, you get *more* interested. In this case the producer quits NBC that week. He leaves TV. The VP at network orders the whole thing dropped. Weeks of work go into the trash."

"You think someone threatened them?"

"The VP's at ABC now. Arnie 'the Asshole' Haft. He's not a news guy. He's one of those MBAs who ruin everything they touch. An ass-coverer. He's on Sixty-sixth Street. Talk to him."

Voort finds the administrative office and fights his way into a carpeted suite besieged by journalists, camera crews, irate ticket holders, and one tennis star's mother—whom Voort recognizes from TV—shouting that the air-conditioned locker room is giving her daughter a sinus headache, damaging her serve.

Staffers shout into phones. Flat-screened TVs broadcast the match of the moment. Showing his badge, "Detective Frank Heffner" learns from an attractive Asian woman that Theodore Stone owns field-level box 39JZ, ten rows up from the court.

Once I talk to Stone, if he's the one, I'll set everything in motion. He'll send his people after Frank Heffner.

The corridors are almost empty while a match is in progress. Voort hurries past bored vendors manning empty refreshment stands. He's struck by differences between the Open and Shea Stadium, only fifteen minutes away by foot. At Shea the stream of fans never stops moving. At the Open ushers block entry during play. At Shea fans never stop shouting. At the Open, he sees from behind a cordon, waiting to be allowed in, fans sit raptly, heads moving right-left-right, quiet as congregants in church as the ball bounces. No beer hawkers. No dancing mascot. No air bazookas firing balled-up souvenir T-shirts into the stands. During a match it seems impolite even to chew food.

If I'm going to quit, the time to do it is now, before I meet Stone.

At Shea the advertisements are for sports radio and electronics. At the Open they're for JPMorgan. Paine-Webber.

God, help me do the right thing here. Protect my family. Mickie, you better be watching my back this time.

Eyes moving between the seating chart in his hand and the boxes visible through the open doorway, he finds the right aisle, box, and makes out the long blonde hair of a teenage girl, and then the father, if the secretary at Ted's office was right.

Is that the man who ordered me attacked?

Voort's rage blooms suddenly but he knows he must contain it. He can't jump to conclusions. He has to locate the right person.

The stadium smells of Lysol suddenly. Voort's stomach clenches. His cell phone is buzzing. Cousin Greg's name swims up on the Caller ID. Has he found the salvage expert to take Voort to Hell's Gate?

But as Voort reaches to answer, the attendant lifts the cordon, waving the crowd in before the next set begins. Voort is drawn toward the box thirty feet ahead, close to courtside.

I want Stone to be the one. I want anyone to be the one. I need to know who attacked me.

Voort enters the stadium to the boom of applause. But his heart sounds louder.

In his head, Camilla says, "That poor woman. Her kids . . . obliterated."

As if sensing Voort approaching, Ted Stone turns around.

And eleven years ago Ted steps briskly into a snowstorm at Kennedy Airport—back from Africa—to see Annie waving from beside their battered green Plymouth. Little Candace is in the backseat, dozing. He takes the ignition key from Annie and jerks as a car backfires in the unloading area behind.

The airport smells like wood smoke suddenly, and camel's milk—a sour-sweet, dunglike, pungent aroma.

"Have a good time?" Annie asks. Ted's still amazed at how easy it had been to walk back through customs, once he flashed his UN ID. No one had even checked his luggage. There'd been no need to hide General Aiwad's special present.

"I *said*, a new Rite Aid drugstore is going up at the mall," Annie says. "Isn't that great?"

Ted—trying to hold on to memories—sees the three

blondes from the hotel in bed with him. The Swedish girl is going down on him. The German is on her knees, butt up, high heels on, wiggling her luscious rump. The brunette from Iowa is chewing kat leaves and washing them down with Jack Daniel's. She leans forward to kiss him. She passes more J.D. into his mouth.

Annie says, "I made pot roast for dinner. Your fave."

He leans forward and turns the key. As usual, the damn car won't start right away. The smell of mildew comes from the carpeting. The front window won't even roll down. The snow outside is dirtied the instant it hits the ground.

"I understand you like antiques?" says Mohammed Aiwad's voice in Ted's memory. It's midnight. Ted's finally doing the books in the warlord's villa, after a glorious two weeks in Somalia. The actual job is a crescendo to the trip. There have been a dozen orchestrated "delays" at getting to see the books, while the warlord was "away" or "giving a speech" or "fighting the Aidid clan"—days when Ted got to enjoy the blondes, chew kat, drink with Remy, go shark fishing, eat wonderful meals . . . and also, once or twice, eyeball actual food-aid distribution.

Ted standing on those days in a shattered courtyard piled with sacks of Kansas-grown grain. Ted—fingering his new watch, a gift from Remy—watching skinny guys in rags heft the sacks over their shoulders and disappear into the maze of Mogadishu's sand-covered streets. Were they really civilians? Or were they Aiwad's soldiers? Who could tell?

And now it's the last night in the big old villa, which sounds more impressive than it is, as the doors are blown off, the toilet must be flushed with a bucket, the refrigerator is only half-working, and the books in the downstairs study seem decomposed from heat. The walled grounds are packed with soldiers sleeping on the ground. The sickle moon and North Star hanging outside balcony windows look like a Moslem crescent on a foreign flag.

Ted looks up at the clan leader, digging in the pockets of the combat fatigues that seem to be his only clothes. He never seems to stop unwrapping or sucking on peppermint hard candies.

Ted looking down at Aiwad's big, old green-leather ledgers as the clan accountant, a scowling octogenarian in a woven white skullcap, fingers his AK-47 and slurps thick tea with leaf bits floating on the surface of his tin field-cup.

"See? Everything in order," Aiwad says, and walks out.

Ted eyes rows of numbers. Some have been crossed out. Some have been erased. Some have little strips of paper taped over them. Some have Arabic notations on the side.

The whole goddamn thing is a big joke.

"It is customary when a friend departs for home to give him a gift," the accountant says, holding out an envelope, surprising Ted with his New England accent, not the gift.

"You speak English?"

"I attended the University of Vermont."

Eleven thousand, nine hundred dollars, the exact amount that can be given tax-free in the U.S., thinks Ted, with a tug of disappointment. Couldn't it have been a little more?

Now Annie pulls his attention back to the airport. "There are some thrilling new movies at the mall."

"All I've been doing is working, honey."

"I have exciting news," says Mr. Yoruba the next day at

work. "You will attend a seminar next week, about new techniques for tracking money."

Whoop-de-fucking-do.

Ted remembering how, at work each day, chewing kat had produced the loveliest lethargy through his whole body. And made sex better.

Torture. That's being home. The 7 train seems suffocating on the way to work each day. The heating system on the Plymouth breaks during a snowstorm. Candace needs foot braces—not covered by insurance—to correct a pigeon-toed condition.

"You seem distracted," Annie says after they watch the new Bond movie at the Clearview Cinema that week.

He goes out. He picks up a shopgirl. He gets laid. It doesn't help.

He takes Aiwad's cash to a Christie's auction of British furniture that weekend, but it's not even enough to top bids on one damn chair. He settles for a small painting, an Alfred Massey original, of a sloop on the Thames River. Buckingham Palace is in the background.

Ah, Christie's! It's like a museum where you can buy the art. He's never dreamed that so many beautiful pieces are actually purchasable, so you can keep them in your own home, and see or touch them any time you want.

"You spent nine thousand dollars for a *painting?*" Annie cries at home that night. "We can't even pay the plumber!"

Ted buries his head in *Fine Art* magazine. He hates marital confrontations.

"Did you hear me? You sell that painting. If you want art, buy a poster. Where did you get that money?"

"I won a trifecta at offtrack betting. Yoruba took me. Whoever would have thought that old stick-in-the-mud likes to gamble, huh?"

The restlessness worse than ever now. The unhappiness and yearning keeping him awake in his little Queens bedroom at night.

Ted sitting in the "Follow the Money" seminar at UN Plaza, being trained on new ways illegal money gets shifted around the planet. Each year, it moves faster.

"Over *four billion dollars* disappears annually from the world's books," says the Treasury Department speaker at the podium, reading from notes.

I really liked that chair. It isn't fair that other people can buy things and I can't.

The speaker drones on. "There are four major stages of money laundering. The aim is to reach a stage of virtually unrestricted use of stolen funds."

I am so bored.

"As our first chart shows, phase one assets can still be traced by owner, or location of funds. Which is why señor cheating presidente doesn't want too much of what he's stolen kept in his own country. If he's overthrown, he needs assets overseas."

I am so horny. That German woman was fantastic.

"In phase two, the money has been moved overseas but authorities can still apply political pressure to locals. Swiss banks take anyone's money, no questions asked, but demand a thirty-five percent fee, and the Swiss are susceptible to pressure. How do you think those old Nazi accounts were discovered?"

Ted gets up to leave. He'll head over to the Roma

Hotel bar. Stewardesses and grade-A prostitutes hang out there. He must get laid right now. His groin is on fire.

"By stage three, assets are hidden through European corporate ownership. Luxembourg. Liechtenstein. The Channel Islands. The Grand Caymans. Although secrecy laws are breaking down and many safe havens are evaporating, although banks are obligated more to give up names, you can still open accounts in, say, Austria, with no identification, by mail. Coded, pseudonymous accounts. Austrian banks are geared specifically toward the need of foreign investors. Even in the U.S., legal loopholes protect launderers. For instance, if you don't *know* you're laundering money, it is perfectly legal to do it. If Treasury can't prove you *knew* money was laundered, you go free."

The speaker looks surprised and shrugs theatrically, acting like an accused launderer.

"Hey, I didn't *know* it was drug money," he says.

Ted picks up *two* stewardesses at the Roma that night. But the cash from Aiwad is gone, and when his American Express bill comes, he starts to sweat. He can't even pay off the plumber. Annie was right.

Later that night, Ted has the big idea.

Ted sits in Shun Lee Palace, one of New York's five-star Chinese restaurants, with Mr. Yoruba, who is sucking down his second mai tai through a straw. For the first time since Ted met him, Yoruba is relaxed. He loved the crispy Peking duck.

"It is kind of you to take me out for my birthday," Mr. Yoruba says. "I have no family."

"I've learned so much from you."

"I'm grateful to have such an eager student."

"I'm only a reflection of my teacher," Ted says. "I feel like I have only barely started to learn. I must admit, though, I used to have a more benevolent view of the UN."

Yoruba's in his signature black suit and bright bow tie, this one splashy yellow, and the rum makes him talk more than usual. "The UN is a *wonderful* organization," he says. "A few bad apples. That's who I hate. They steal at home. They spend it here. A president's nephew, brother, uncle. That is who comes to New York. People with connections. They're here for ten years. Then a new crop comes in when the president is overthrown. Walk around the building," he says, shaking his head. "These ambassadors who were *clerks*. These generals who were *privates*."

Ted nods sadly. "Few rise through merit, like you."

Mr. Yoruba has tears in his eyes. Everyone likes to be appreciated, and Yoruba—a gadfly—is generally not.

Ted leans forward. The hour is late. He signals the waiter, pointing to Yoruba's empty glass so his friend will be served a third mai tai. Yoruba loves the fruit.

Ted's heart is booming. He wonders if he's capable of doing what he has planned, if he'll actually try it—even if Yoruba has the information.

Yoruba saying, "You are a good man and I am going to promote you."

Ted saying, "In your opinion, sir, which delegation at the UN is the worst?"

"Excuse me? Are you Ted Stone?"

And eleven years later, in Flushing, a stranger bends toward him in the aisle of the US Open, holding out a wallet. Ted's heart leaps into his throat. He's looking at a detective's shield, and then up into hard green eyes that seem to drill into him, hate him. Everything about the man, his gaze, posture, the quiet in the voice, speaks of suppressed fury.

They found out. Oh God. It's over.

"I'm Frank Heffner," the detective says flatly. "Did you think you'd get away with it, Mr. Stone?"

ELEVEN

"See that nice-looking young man sitting by my desk? Do you think he paid someone to murder his grandmother?"

Eight-year-old Conrad Voort stands in the entrance of Dad's squad room on a Saturday afternoon, a wedge of hot pizza in one hand, a Styrofoam cup filled with Coke in the other. The boy's horrified that a person might actually hurt his own grandmother, but is thrilled, as always, when Dad gives him a test.

Big Bill balances his tuna hero, chips, and steaming large coffee on a tray.

Countdown: five minutes to the boy's first real cop job.

"You knew he'd be here when we got back from the cafeteria, right, Dad?"

"I might have wanted him to stew a bit. You get an A, pal."

You *never* know when a test is coming, Voort thinks. Dad surprises him when he watches detective TV shows sometimes. *"What mistake did the cop make?"* he'll say. Or at the bank: *"Notice the bulge under that man's jacket? Is he a guard or a robber?"* Or even while strolling in Washington Square: *"See the tall man on this side of Fourth Street and the short guy on the other? How come they eye each other each time a woman with a purse comes up the block?"*

Dad says now, "He phoned me. He offered to come in and talk. But was that to help me, Sherlock? Or trick me?"

Voort guesses the maybe-murderer is in his early twenties, same age as Cousin Gus, with a brushed, sand-colored cowlick, turtleneck sweater, and jeans. The guy looks around as if enjoying the ambiance. His crossed leg swings casually. He nods to officers going by.

"Dad, you said to collect facts first."

Bill nods, sitting down at a nearby desk so the guy doesn't realize they're watching. "He owns a brownstone on Seventy-first Street. He inherited it. He wants to sell it, and he even had a great offer, but the last resident—his grandmother—refused to move. On Tuesday she went shopping and was knifed in the street."

Voort gasps, picturing an old lady rolling a shopping cart down a busy block. A man comes up to her swiftly, then runs away into a crowd. Voort doesn't put a face on the man yet.

"Where was *he* when it happened?"

"At his office."

Frown lines wiggle on the little boy's head. He takes Dad's tests seriously. "Do you think he paid someone to do it, like that other man you told me about in Battery Park?"

"A friend of the grandmother's said he threatened her. She was afraid of him. Eat your pizza while it's hot."

Voort chews while the guy across the room gets fidgety, like he's getting angry waiting. Voort says, "But you said never to believe things people say without proof."

"I'm proud of you."

"That means *you* have no proof."

Dad takes a bite of pickle and waits for more questions. Life as an immersion into professional suspicion. The boy feels the taxing and pleasant weight of future responsibilities, and a covert thrill from studying the guy.

"Watch a suspect if you can, before talking to him. You need every edge," Uncle Vim likes to say.

The man just looks irritated. The worst people can look normal. It's not like there's a sign on the man screaming "murderer." Sure, *after* someone is arrested, it seems obvious that they did it, but beforehand, Dad says, lots of times, even the killer's family doesn't know.

"You said you only have a few days to figure things out. Then other cases get important, Dad."

"So we have to make up our minds fast."

"Is it time for the old eye-detector test?"

Dad laughs at the familiar joke. *Watch the eyes,* he always tells the kid. And, *How you approach someone can make all the difference.*

"Can I help?" Conrad asks suddenly with a boy's surging yearning to be part of things, wanting something more than a test. He's thinking, *The killer should be arrested.* He's in the grip of the frustration of guesswork that will mark the rest of police life.

Dad shakes with silent mirth and wipes tears from his eyes. "That's terrific. Wait till Vim hears this. *You* want to ask the questions. Oh, Conrad. What a guy."

But then Dad pauses, looks thoughtful, eyes his son appraisingly. And minutes later Voort finds himself shaking hands with an actual maybe-murderer, feeling the warm skin of the man's smooth hand. He's never met a maybe-murderer. His heart pounds in his little chest. The guy smiles down at him like any adult, but it's amazing how once you *think* someone might be a criminal, everything about him seems suddenly tricky.

Do it right, Voort thinks, feeling a chill.

"Thanks for coming," Dad tells the man, acting tired, disinterested, even yawning. "Meet my son, Conrad. He's eight. He wanted to come in and see what it's like to be a cop. I told him, two guys in the same family shouldn't make the same mistake."

Both adults laugh. *"Do* you want to be a policeman?" the maybe-murderer asks, looking down with baby-blue eyes.

"Or an astronaut."

"Good-looking kid," the man tells Dad. "But if you don't mind, I have a meeting uptown at four."

"Sure. Sorry for the wait, uh, I appreciate you coming in. Saves me a trip. Let me find something to write on. There was a pen here a minute ago. Damn. I lost it."

The guy watches Dad fumbling around, pretending to be a klutz. "I want you to find the scumbag who killed Oma," he growls. "I'm posting a reward. Poor Oma. She had a tough life. Nobody's safe."

Dad says, "I'm really sorry. I'm always losing pens. My questions will just take a few minutes."

Voort breaks in at the signal sentence. "But Dad, *you* said you *found* evidence and—"

"Conrad!" Dad cuts the boy off, glaring, furious-looking, utterly transformed and astounding Conrad with rage even though he knows it's an act.

"Go play in the hallway," Dad snaps.

And looking up, the boy sees, gaping, that the maybe-murderer's facial muscles have rearranged themselves.

The cords are bunched at the jawline. The lips have thinned and gone white. The eyes seem wider, the nostrils big, like a horse's at Matt's farm.

The change lasts only an instant. Then the nice face is back.

Dad orders Voort. "Now."

And takes him out for a congratulatory hot fudge sundae that evening. A double.

And two weeks later, the landlord is locked up.

"Did you think you'd get away with it?" Voort asks Ted Stone, twenty-five years later.

He's vaguely aware, concentrating on the face, of tennis fans moving around him to get through the aisle. The stadium is smaller than Shea but the energy is high, just quieter. The crowd is orderly, less pushy than at Shea. Twenty feet away, at courtside, the pros sit and fan themselves or drink water. Everyone looks calmer than they feel. The power here lies in containment.

Stone's not nervous on the outside, just curious, Voort thinks, judging the face before him as late thirties, white, long, oval, remote. Beneath the high forehead, pale-blue eyes regard him. Stone has an excellent tan. Voort spots a silver-edged, blue-faced watch, and his excitement ratchets up.

Like the third man who visited the Seaport museum.

The teenage girl beside Stone says, "Is something wrong, Daddy?" *She* looks scared, all right.

"Only with the way Amit Amos blew the last match, oney," Stone says, squeezing her arm. And to Voort, "May see your ID again?" He's crisp and unintimidated, irritated that Voort's scared his kid, which is totally normal under the circumstances.

"Detective Heffner," Stone says, dragging it out just a bit, or trying it out.

"As in Hugh."

"Did I think I'd get away with what?"

"Taking a day off from work," Voort grins like a bad joker, an obnoxious loudmouth, wanting to push and piss the man off fast.

If you're the one, send someone after me. You already did once.

"There are perks in being a boss," Stone replies smoothly. "Taking a day off is one."

This is no boy landlord, and he's been grilled by police before, Camilla said.

Stone asks, "Do you mind telling me why you're here?"

"To talk to you about one of your clients."

Now the look turns apprehensive, but again in a normal way. "Did something happen to someone?" Stone asks, radiating concern for the health or safety of an associate, or a loss of business, which for some guys is worse.

"It's better if we talk in the hall," Voort says, turning toward the exit without checking to see if the lawyer is following, which, of course, he is. Reel him in.

Get the guy outside his turf, Dad used to say.

The corridors are busy. Refreshment stands sprout lines. Using the phony ID, Voort gets an attendant to unlock a small VIP lounge. It's empty of people inside.

Keep Stone off balance.

He shuts the door and the room grows quiet. *This dis-*

guise better have worked. There's a couch, and a table displaying platters of fruit wedges and four kinds of bagels. Coke and Sprite cans sweat in a plastic bucket, and Voort sees a cookie tray near the TV. Refreshments for VIPs are free.

"You frightened my daughter," Stone says.

Good. You don't know what to expect. You're not used to being dicked around with, not this way. I frightened your daughter? Or do you mean I frightened you?

From the officiousness in Stone's manner Voort pegs him as used to giving orders, not taking them. He decides to play the petty tyrant with Stone.

"Mcgreevey Tugboats," he says accusingly.

"What?" With a blank look that reveals nothing, not even attitude, Stone waits for more. Either he's hiding zippo or he rolls with bad news.

"Kevin Mcgreevey. Bud Mcgreevey."

Stone steps closer. He pulls himself up. He's equal height with Voort, healthy and prosperous-looking, and he radiates authority even in casual clothes: a lightweight Lacoste shirt over twill khakis, shiny loafers, no socks. His hair is tousled as if he's been boating.

"What are you talking about?"

"Three A.M. September second. Mcgreevey."

"Look, Detective. You clearly have something on your mind, so why not share it so we can have a productive conversation? Or would you rather throw strangers' names at me and waste both our times while I miss the match?"

Voort crosses his arms as if in weary amusement. "Are you telling me—"

"And do it politely." Stone cuts him off, equally poised

here and by the court. "I'm more than willing to talk to you. You can ask the same questions courteously or obnoxiously. I always cooperate with police. I don't appreciate your attitude. Try again."

But Voort is pitching his approach to the scared Stone, who he hopes is inside the confident shell. He wants his whole attitude, posture, and tone to be insulting. He's committed to the attack. There's no time to fear offending an innocent. Let the guy complain if Voort comes on too strong. Add Camilla's warning about Stone to the assault at the Mobil station, and Voort knows if Stone's his quarry, *I want him flushed as fast as I can.*

"I'm investigating several murders on the East River," Voort says, and watches the blue eyes turn surprised, and then register again appropriate wariness and fear. But is it fear for *himself* or someone else? Stone the innocent suspect. Stone the unaware dupe.

"Murders?" Stone asks, softer.

"Attacks against people who have an interest in the treasure ship *Hussar,* which *your* client is hunting for Treasure, Ltd.? Your name's on the permit application. We need to look at that company. Someone there may be involved."

Ted looks as if he's having trouble absorbing the possibility that a client could actually be involved in anything so heinous as murder.

"Those names you mentioned," he says. "Are they the victims?"

Instead of answering, Voort pushes. "How's the search going, Mr. Stone?"

"That's not something I deal with."

"I'd like a list of personnel on the project."

"You've come to the wrong person, then. I just sign contracts. I'm not familiar with the operation outside of paperwork," Ted says, but the vaguest hint of some new note—defensiveness—has finally seeped into his voice.

"Then I want to talk to your clients. I'm not asking what they tell you, so there's no problem with attorney-client privilege. I want to know who they are."

Voort pulls out a little pad and waits. Major eye contact now.

Ted Stone blinks for a moment, thinking. Then he wilts a bit.

"I don't actually know that."

Voort gives him the cop look. The one he used to practice in the mirror when he was twelve, and that he's perfected over years of real police work.

He repeats, amused, "You don't know your client."

The tone perks Stone up again. "I'm contacted by a law firm in Vienna. They ask me to sign contracts. They need a New York rep, okay? That's how these things are done."

"What's the firm's name? Write it down for me. Foreign names. I always get 'em wrong. Then I have to come back to check. I just keep coming back and back."

Stone understands the threat and consulting his PalmPilot, scribbles "Mueller & Rosenberg" on the back of his business card. He adds a phone number, including the international access code. He seems rattled by the accusation against his clients, but that would be normal for an innocent man too.

Voort hands Stone Frank Heffner's business card.

"This is my home address and phone number. I live alone. All I do is work. Don't hesitate to call if you decide you want to tell me . . . more." Voort smiles.

"What's that supposed to mean, 'more'?" Ted taking umbrage at the insinuation. On TV, near the platter of ladyfingers, the crowd claps as two players in white walk onto the tennis court.

Voort repeats, "You don't know your own clients."

"You're a diligent man," Stone says. But the look on his face is flat and white now. It's rage.

"Yeah, well, I'm type double-A, my ex-wife used to say. I don't have a life. I spend all my time catching guys. That's why I'm on the cold case squad. That's why even a triple-murder from five years ago—a mom and two kids—still interests me."

"Sounds like a fulfilling life, all that work," Ted says.

"Not *ful*-filling. Just filling, as in, filling up Sing Sing. Or Danbury, for white-collar guys. Prisoners who spend the days counting lines on the tennis courts. That sort of thing."

Stone is red now, but who wouldn't be at this point? Nothing in his attitude says guilty so far. "I haven't read about these murders in the papers, Detective Heffner."

"Maybe that's because the victims don't live on the East Side."

"That remark was uncalled for. I don't appreciate that steel chip on your shoulder. I was persecuted five years ago and I won't put up with it again. You hear me? I want a phone number. Who's your superior?"

"At work? Or on the social scale?"

"I want your badge number."

"Maybe I'm like you. I don't know who I work with. Anyway, what would *you* do with a badge? Felons can't work for the department, even as guys who sweep up."

After Voort walks out, and the door clicks shut, Stone reaches for his secure portable.

His hands shake as he punches in Leon's number. It seems like the temperature's risen to about ninety degrees in here. He can't breathe. His stomach is burning.

"Another detective showed up. I have his home address and phone. He . . . he's coming after me."

"Describe him."

Stone does and Leon says thoughtfully, "That doesn't sound like Voort."

"I told you. It's not Voort. His name is Frank Heffner."

"That's not the name of Voort's partner. Who's *this guy then*?" frowns Leon Bok.

ABC Network headquarters occupies a high-rise on Sixty-sixth Street near Broadway, a block from Central Park. The lobby is filled with blow-up photos of the smiling hosts of news and national talk shows. The elevators are packed with staffers whose conversations cast more accurate light on the personalities whose famous faces greet visitors downstairs.

"That bitch told me I'm the best producer she ever had. Then she tried to get me fired."

"Is this what I went to Stanford for? To guess the anchorman's mood based on whether he's wearing blue or black?"

Everyone seems harried. On the sixth floor—the new power floor—Voort follows hurried directions and threads a warren of cubicles to find VP of news programming Arnie the "Asshole" Haft occupying a prestigious, sunny corner office overlooking Columbus, and Lincoln Center two blocks away. Emmys fill shelves. Voort sees the usual honcho shots implying friendship with or at least access to well-known people: Haft with Julia Roberts; Haft with Senator Kyle Landon the John Bircher, Ralph Nader the anarchist election-wrecker, Freddy Foxx the Yanks' third baseman, Oswald Stark the famous swindler.

Closeness to fame is the important thing.

"I have a meeting in ten," Haft says self-importantly, without standing up. He'd been working the phones when Voort entered. Several buzzers and beeps are sounding at the same time. Haft waves vaguely at a chair in front of his oversized desk, but doesn't seem to care if Voort sits or stands up.

"What can I do for you? I'm in a rush."

The VP is young, dressed in a three-button suit, crisp white shirt, and red suspenders, Wall Street style. He's prematurely bald on top with a fringe of brown curls ringing his skull like a monk's tonsure. He seems on the pudgy side, despite the expensive clothing, so he's probably in awful shape with the suit off. He's got the wan color of a man who lives in a cave, casino, or bomb shelter, and thrives in a world of unnatural light.

"I want to ask about an investigation that you shut down at NBC five years ago," Voort says.

"Who remembers ones you shut down?" Haft says, reaching for a can of Mountain Dew. "If I shut it down, it was shit."

"Ted Stone," Voort says.

The transformation is instant. The manic movements stop. The Adam's apple bobs. The body goes still. The man has just completely focused. The gray eyes slip sideways a millisecond before the man starts talking, so Voort suspects whatever's coming now will be a lie.

"Who?" Arnie says.

He's an ass-kisser, Camilla had said.

Voort recounts her story, but implies it came from "several sources" at NBC. Frankly, he says, he has no interest in what happened half a decade ago inside the network. Meaning, man to man, he won't tell anyone if Arnie really chickened out when threatened. Voort says that details might help solve a murder now, though.

"I don't know who told you this shit," Arnie says angrily. "It's a complete fabrication. No one threatened me. I barely remember what you're talking about. That UN investigation was going nowhere. That's why I shut it down."

"No phone threats in the middle of the night? No one saying they'd hurt your family."

"Hey, I'm a *news* exec. I don't scare," Arnie says. "You wouldn't believe the backbiting crap that goes on in TV. People'll spread any rumor to fuck over your career."

"Why did the producer move away?"

"How do I know? People burn out."

Voort sighs. "Then you have nothing to worry about when I talk to Leona," he says, not needing to mention the last name of the new president of the news division, whose ferocity against slackers is legendary among the city's upper echelon TV people, whom Voort and Camilla regularly run into at cocktail parties. Leona's firings of execs regularly make the gossip columns, and her purge of the sixth floor made the evening news last year, when Arnie got his job—probably from her.

Arnie says quietly, "You know Leona?"

"I'd rather keep this between you and me. I only want to know what happened five years ago. Lives are at stake, Mr. Haft."

As the VP starts drumming his fingers on the desk, a woman sticks her head in the door and complains, "Diane's making up stupid questions again. She wants to ask the fucking secretary of state what's the most important thing he's learned about love? Can you believe it?"

Arnie snaps, "Deal with her."

Voort waits while the woman withdraws.

Arnie wipes his shiny forehead.

In a lower voice he says, "You promise? Just you and me?"

He closes the door. The force goes out of his face, and Voort gets a glimpse of the fat kid Arnie had probably been in the school yard. Mr. Brash looks suddenly terrified.

"I never heard a voice like that before," he whispers. "The guy called at four A.M. The voice . . . it was dead. It was talking and dead at the same time."

That's the same man who was in the bathroom with me, Voort thinks, experiencing a thrill of fear.

"He knew where my wife worked. He said he had someone at the network. I never found out if that was true. He said he'd know whatever I did."

"So you stopped looking into food aid being stolen?"

Haft looks ashamed and humiliated, a phony caught playing big news exec.

"It only started with food aid. You have to understand who Stone is. He's the legal designee for over half a dozen dictators or their pals in New York. He has power of attorney on contracts; signatory power on offshore accounts. Over the years he's worked for people in Angola, Serbia, Zimbabwe, Pakistan."

"Revolving door. Government to private."

"By the time I shut the story down, we'd heard rumors of stolen AIDS drugs too. Shipments diverted for sale. Tens of millions a year. Payoffs to UN peacekeeping officers who actually ran the stuff. But it was just rumors. There was absolutely no proof. After I got the phone call," Haft says in a humiliated voice, "I deleted all our files and tapes."

"I'll ask you again. Why'd the producer move away?"

"I assume they scared him also."

"Where'd he go?"

"Cal Quinones and his wife opened a bike shop up in Otis, Massachusetts. I heard he died of cancer last year."

"That helps."

What could any of this have to do with treasure?

Voort takes the 9 train from the Upper West Side to the Fulton Street stop near the South Street Seaport. Walking east, he keeps looking around for Mickie, but his partner seems to have disappeared again. Voort notices a black kid from the train staying behind him.

Food theft. Drug theft. What's the treasure link?

When the black kid walks into a computer store, nobody else on the street seems to pick up the tail.

No Mickie in sight either, though.

As Voort reaches the nautical museum, his cell phone rings.

"I've got your salvage expert," Greg says. "When he heard you're after the guy who killed the Mcgreevey brothers, he said forget money. He's on his way over. He'll stay with you as long as you want, and there are a hundred other river guys willing to help. When do you want to go out?"

"Give me an hour."

Voort phones Mickie. "Where are you, at your broker's? I don't see you anywhere."

"Go to hell, Con Man. But before you do, look left, down the row of stores. Souvenir shop. Ice cream shop. Keep going. Clothing store. In the window. Hel-lo!"

"I'm impressed."

"I'm the invisible guy. No one followed you from the stadium and no one showed up here before my best buddy, Frank Heffner, did. You look like a Frank, y'know? You have that ducky kinda Frank walk. Maybe you should change your name."

"What did you learn about Mcgreevey?"

"Investigation closed. Final determination arson."

Voort finds the librarian at his desk, playing electronic games again as the Chihuahua looks on from its pillow on the lowest shelf. The man doesn't recognize Voort in disguise, but the dog's ears perk up. The librarian asks, "Can I help you?" and Voort—going hoarse to disguise his voice—asks for a book on tugs.

"Please sign the ledger," the librarian says.

The electronic game issues laser-blaster noises and tinny carnival-type music.

Voort doesn't care about tugs. It's the ledger he wants to see. He flips pages until he finds the phony "Marcus Sanders" signature and then compares the writing to Stone's jotted-down name of the law firm in Vienna. Voort's spirits lift. He'll need professional confirmation, but the double loop atop each *S* looks the same. So does the *e*.

The rage in his head is a steady, mounting beat.

You sent those men.

"Do you have a Xerox machine?" he asks. The kid barely looks up as he waves Voort toward a supply room in back. The dog wags his stumpy tail. Thank God dogs can't talk, Voort thinks. They seem to have a wire into our brains.

Afterward, outside, he calls Mickie, who picks up on the first beep, complaining.

"I can't even buy a shirt anymore without worrying about the price. No more surveillance in stores. This sucks."

Voort asks Mickie to get hold of Stone's driver's license photo so they can show it to the librarian. Then he explains what he wants Mickie to do while he's out with the salvage expert. Mickie balks.

"I'm not comfortable leaving you alone," says Mickie.

"Neither am I."

"I've never seen you this angry."

"Do it," says Voort.

Voort stands on the bridge of the SS *Kukulka*, a junked freighter being towed by the *Mary Ann Voort* and *Alice Voort* up the East River, toward the Merchant Marine

Academy. Lacking power, the ship is basically like some immense barge, moving in silence as migrating butterflies—thousands of small turquoise ones—line the railing, making it seem to undulate. The river unwinds like a dark ribbon flecked with gold. Voort feels as if he's floating in a balloon, looking down on ferries, sailboats, the occasional motorized pleasure craft.

"I once looked for the *Hussar* myself," salvage expert Chip Levant says, beside him. "Ten years back."

Like the skeleton crew, both men wear white coveralls that read "USMMA" on back. To anyone gazing at the ship they look like any one of a dozen academy students and staff helping baby their new floating classroom home.

Greg's down on the *Mary Ann*, receiving instructions from the third man on the bridge, the river pilot. Putting Voort on the freighter had been his idea. "You're *supposed* to be watching the river from up here," he'd said. Now he issues periodic instructions by radio to the tugs—which stay close like pilot fish. Push the bow. Push the stern. Untie a line. Hell's Gate coming up.

"We didn't find the *Hussar*, but I always thought it's there," the salvage expert says.

Chip Levant is youthful gray, with thick brushed-to-the-side hair matching his mustache. In his sunglasses, tight jeans, plaid shirt, and Sauconys, he's handsome as a Gap model. He shields his brow with a tanned hand and occasionally lifts a field radio to his mouth—but doesn't speak into it. From a distance he'll look as if he's working. Voort does the mouth-to-radio act too every few minutes, to be safe.

"Thar she blows," Chip says, gazing northeast toward

a fiberglass boat in a narrow loop of channel several hundred yards south of Hell's Gate. It's not far from Astoria Park, where Voort had found the floater only a week ago.

Throat dry, Voort reads the name off the stern. The *Wanderer*, a twenty-five-footer, cruises parallel to shore and against the current, much slower than other motorized traffic. Two figures occupy the stern, one crouched over a roll of cable, tending machinery, one standing to monitor a computer screen. A third man drives the boat, beneath an awning.

Three men attacked me. Three men on that boat.

"They haven't found the *Hussar* if they're pulling a fish," Chip remarks, his gaze moving aft. Voort spots something silvery on the surface, thirty feet behind the *Wanderer*, skimming the water like a hungry barracuda.

"You're sure?"

He experiences a wave of disappointment. The theory that he'd proposed to Eva—that the treasure has been secretly found—had made sense last night.

What am I missing?

"Maybe they're only pretending to look," he says. "Maybe they found it. They marked it. They go through the act to fool investors. At night they bring the treasure up."

"That happened in Florida," says Chip Levant.

Voort's spirits lift.

"But forget it here."

Voort sighs. If Greg swears by the salvage man, he's the best. Chip's worked up and down the East Coast, on reef wrecks, river wrecks, harbor wrecks, in deep water. "He dived for the navy in the Persian Gulf," Greg had said. "I think he still does, but he's not allowed to admit it."

The movie-star face scowls. "In this current," Chip explains, "if you find something, you bring it up before it gets away. You mark it with a buoy, or lay down a grapple hook and go down hand over hand. There's eight inches visibility down there, maximum, and the current can move a buoyant find four miles either way in a single tide. You don't screw around if you find something lost for two hundred years. Pretend it isn't there and thirty minutes later it may not be. And you don't leave a marker either, where three thousand people will spot it while you're gone and go down."

"They're really looking," Voort says. Part of him had doubted all along that treasure could really be there.

Chip doesn't answer. He leans forward, peering with renewed interest into his binoculars.

"On the other hand," he says, and trails off.

"What?"

"Hmmmmmm."

The sun is bright on the dark, roiling water. The day is hot and the sky blue. Their Coast Guard escort, a gunboat, had dropped away half a mile north of the UN, to pick up an oncoming sailboat.

"What are you looking at?" Voort says, impatient with the man's silence.

"See the cable attached to the fish?"

"They're pulling it up."

"That's a Klein 3000 side-scan towfish. Definitely not Geometrics. Yep! Cable's attached at center top. Silvery black tailfins in V-shape. Yep! A Klein."

"Do you mind speaking English?"

The northern tip of Manhattan goes by, and a dark channel flows out of the Harlem River. The air smells of salt, diesel fumes, acrid cleaning compounds. The cadets have been scouring the ship for days with industrial-strength compounds that could wipe out a plague.

"Sorry," Chip says thoughtfully. "It's just . . ."

"Just *what*?"

"Well, if I'm using side-scan to find something buried in muck, I'm looking for *clues*, see? More than the actual thing. See the guy at the monitor? As the fish passes over the bottom he gets a rolling picture, like aerial photography. But a treasure ship will be buried so he's looking for an outline on sediment, or maybe a piece of wreckage sticking out."

"Which means what?" Voort says, trying to curb his impatience, knowing only that something has struck the expert as odd.

"Everybody works differently." Chip's backpedaling.

"Just tell me what you were going to say."

Nope. Chip's a techie and talks like one. He starts with little things. He takes you step by step through the process. He drives you crazy waiting for conclusions. He's unshakable in his commitment to piece-by-piece logic as he examines his own thought process for flaws.

"Well, you could use ground-penetrating radar too, but I wouldn't in an estuarine environment. In freshwater, sure, but in New York the salinity takes up radar energy, dissipates the pulse. Like watching a fuzzy TV. Who can see the football? Side-scan's better."

"The football?" says Voort.

Slowly, the merchant ship pulls abreast of the salvage

boat. From his perch, Voort can see more of the stern and, on it, diving tanks, secured, and little piled swatches of rusty machinery, or small pieces of boating equipment. He suspects it's debris the divers brought up.

The *Wanderer* crewmen, tending equipment, don't look up.

Even if they did I couldn't recognize a face.

Chip says, "Which brings us to magnetometers."

Voort gives up. There's no way to rush this guy.

"Magnetometers look like a different type of torpedo and they help you search for buried metal."

Voort gets it suddenly, or thinks he does.

Pulse hammering, he says, "Are you saying they're using the wrong type of equipment?"

"Well, it's all personal preference, but if I were looking for the *Hussar,* I'd use something else."

Voort eyes the small pile of debris brought up from the bottom. He picks up his binoculars. Suddenly the items jump out at him, extra clear.

Everything they've brought up looks electronic. Or it's fiberglass. Plastic. Modern, not old.

The soaring certainty inside is a boom of rushing blood in his chest. "They're not looking for the *Hussar,*" he says. "They're looking for something else."

Chip stares at him. "I don't get it. Why even apply for the permit? Why go to the trouble?"

But of course it makes sense, perfect sense. Voort feels a big piece coming, feels now that he is right.

"Because with security so tight," he says, starting out slowly, "you can keep diving. The Coast Guard checks you out the first day. You show the permit. After that they know your boat. You stay away from the UN. You become part of the scenery. Since you're looking for something illegal, you need a legitimate reason for being there."

"Then what *are* they searching for?" Chip asks.

"Treasure," Voort answers. "A more modern kind. But what?"

TWELVE

Leon Bok smells bananas. A bad sign.

Am I being watched?

He waits until the tugs pass before allowing himself to glance away from the side-scan monitor and follow their progress. The boats—Voort tugs from the tri-colors—recede north into the churning waters of Hell's Gate.

The smell grows stronger but there's no fruit on the *Wanderer,* just Bok's mercenary crew, cable roll, dripped oily river water, and strapped-down diving tanks.

Bananas take him back. He's twelve, run away again from his foster home, hungry and angry and he's broken into a Paris grocery where he gorges himself on foods he'd never otherwise eat. Mr. and Mrs. DeLavery would rather lock him in a fucking broom closet than feed him anything more than scraps. They're chefs, for Christ's sake, and spend their lives oohing and aahing over food like kids opening Christmas presents. But they'd never share with *him* the delicious treats on which he gorges himself now.

As the gendarme appears out of the back room, where he's been watching, Bok's finishing a plump banana and ignoring the sense he's had for the last few minutes— the vaguest interruption in culinary happiness, the softest infringement in consciousness and itch at his flight mechanism—that suggests another human has focused attention on him from somewhere nearby.

It's Leon's first big lesson in law-breaking. The problem with instinct is that people ignore it. But he tells himself that he'll never ignore the twinges again, and later he learns during the truant days and military days that the smell of bananas means he feels watched.

Now he resists the urge to pick up binoculars. If a pro were looking back he or she would just turn away. So what's the point of revealing suspicions?

If the police could prove anything, they'd be here, Bok reasons, *so who is watching?*

Which leads to the next question.

Who is Frank Heffner?

The problem had come with Stone's frantic call two hours ago, and Bok's been unable to reach his police source to do a check.

Stone's description of the man didn't match Voort. But I don't like coincidences. I don't like that two separate investigations zeroed in on Stone in two weeks.

He remembers Voort on the floor of the Mobil station, tied down and pathetic. There had been no mistaking the terror and sense of debasement in the man. But Bok knows that every once in a while a victim—the rare dangerous one—will snap back and come raging out against you. He's seen it on a battlefield. A cowed soldier charges the other line. The only way to stop him is to put him down.

Which boils to, *Is Voort really away?*

Bok doesn't feel fear as other men do, as a ratcheting up of heartbeat, a dry mouth. For him it's a mounting of logistical questions, a sense that he must push himself harder, be more careful.

He rarely gets angry either. Emotion causes excess.

And the truth is, he admits now, on the river someone is *always* watching. That's a fact of working in a public place. The narrow channels make his boat more noticeable. The volume of traffic doesn't help. The Coast Guard is a constant danger, whether he has a diving permit or not. Police launches pass every day.

If they knew what was on the bottom I'd be surrounded.

But hell, challenges make life fun.

"I fixed the fish, Leon," says his screen man, an ex–French Navy sonar expert, ex–UN peacekeeper, smuggler, wanted-for-murder merc named Andre.

Bok sighs as the cable unrolls. He foresaw the obstacles when he accepted the job. It's why he demanded triple pay and why Stone agreed without protest, knowing he'd purchased the services of some of the top help in the world. Knowing Bok's perfect record, his point of pride.

To the south now, a U.S. Army helicopter swoops over the harbor, making one of its periodic anti-terrorism sweeps to assure citizens that their government is protecting them. Bok smiles. They're useless to spot anything except the most overt threats, worthless until terrorists are getting away. The tugs are gone. The city looks back through a hundred thousand windows. At any moment he's in view of over a million people, but they lack the knowledge to understand what they're seeing in front of their eyes.

"Leon, I don't understand why I can't find it," growls Andre, looking over the side. "How can it just disappear?"

"Perhaps the current swept it beneath something else."

Time is running out. Studying the monitor as the boat proceeds along today's grid, Bok gets a bird's-eye electronic view of three centuries of urban effluence. A Studebaker lies sideways on the bottom. So does a cannon muzzle. A sunken sloop, iceboxes, wagon wheels, horse skeletons, a sand barge, a big aluminum container filled with Chinese illegals, a box of Civil War uniforms, a crate of Depression-era Canadian whiskey. It's a museum of deterioration down there.

Bok sails over a junkyard of history, an unrolling education in rejection, uselessness, outdatedness, decay.

"Take me to the dock," he orders, still pondering the detective problem.

"But it's still daylight."

"Stay out here. Call if something comes up."

"That a pun?"

During the sixteen minutes it takes the *Wanderer* to reach landfall near Long Island City, at a new marina, Bok punches in a call—an international access code and a number in Delhi, India, best place in the world to contract out low-cost, top-quality computer experts, as any multinational exec knows. India's security agencies are not tied into Interpol or U.S. enforcement. The line offers Bok superb voice quality. From the tone he could be conversing with someone eight feet away, not eight thousand miles.

"Singh here!" Bok hears Indian music, a sitar and cymbals, and an irritatingly high-pitched woman's voice singing in the background.

He gives his account number. No client names used on this line. He's never met Singh. In the global age, decentralization is the key to so many successful businesses. Why not crime too?

"Good to hear your voice, sir," Singh says.

"I need you to piggyback into the NYPD system," Bok says. His source inside the department has not called back yet.

"It is not a piggyback, sir. It's simple access. I can use one of the passwords I've been provided with by you."

"I want to know everything about a detective Frank Heffner in the cold-case squad. Social Security number. Work records. Family info. Decorations."

"I'll hop exchange through Finland. Even if someone is watching, they won't be able to trace."

"Whatever. Write down his name, address, and phone number. Hit all your databases. Cross-reference this man. U.S. ID number. Driver's license. Credit history. The usual U.S. search. Tell me if anything looks wrong."

"I will not go home until you are pleased, sir. And on the other matter, Conrad Voort used his MasterCard twice yesterday in Argentina. He bought an antique chest, and fish dinner for two in a restaurant in La Plata. He is still reserved to return to New York next Saturday. He confirmed the flight from BA today, our airline liaison says."

"Check Camilla Ryan's reservations too."

Bok hangs up. Something still seems wrong.

He recalls Stone saying, *Heffner said he lives alone. He has no social life. All he does is work.*

Was that a threat? Or an invitation?

The *Wanderer* leaves Bok at the small marina, and he

locates his ten-year-old Accord—bought, not rented—in a dirt parking lot. Choosing one of two pre-packed plastic bags in the trunk, he fixes on a dark wig, Phillies cap over his cutoff Hofstra sweatshirt, and Ray-Bans. A Band-Aid covers the knuckle tattoo. Stick-on pads thicken his shoulders and give his washboard belly a gut.

Use a disguise once, then get rid of it. That way if someone's snapping photos, the clothes will be gone.

He consults a detailed street map then heads into Queens, listening to all-news radio's rundown of the day's excesses. The dollar is dropping. War looms again in the Mideast.

Twenty-two minutes later Bok drives up Frank Heffner's block as if looking for a parking spot, which he is not. He could have sent someone else here, but his sixth sense tells him the job calls for heightened awareness. The street rolls by as a series of props for potential ambush, an urban diorama into which enemies can insert themselves.

He eyes small box houses and neat green lawns. The Norway maples are still blooming in late summer. He rolls past a redbrick apartment building, built in blocky post–World War II style. Heffner lives here, according to the business card he gave Stone.

I see two kids on bikes. No delivery trucks. No utility trucks. No moms pushing strollers. If somebody's watching they're on a roof or in a window.

The second time he cruises by—New York drivers circle looking for spaces—he spots the white guy in a parked Camaro, and calls in the license to Singh. Motor-vehicle records are as easy to access from Delhi as from Queens.

"Borders," Stone had told him once, condescending

when secure, stating the obvious, "make the best protection."

He parks two blocks away and strolls back. The Camaro is gone. It's quiet in the neighborhood, even with school out. A kid in shorts and T-shirt walks a beagle. An old lady pushes a shopping cart, stopping every few feet to catch her breath. Two teenage girls giggle and pretend to ignore a boy mowing a lawn, who watches them as if disappointed, feeling unnoticed by people he wants to impress.

Bok walks into a small park diagonally across from Heffner's building, and opens a *Daily News*. There's no alternative to ratcheting up this risk. He feels the hard surface of the H&K nine-millimeter at his hip, beneath his cutoff sweatshirt, and an S&W .360 PD on his ankle, beneath the jeans. The knife sheathed to the right side of his torso is Swiss.

Okay, Frank, let's get a look at you.

No doorman in the building. The front buzzer works, he sees, because visitors have to wait to get in. Heffner's business card puts him in 4B.

Bok discreetly scans rooftops, hedgerows, cars. He looks for a swish of curtain, the glint of sun on binoculars or a camera lens, a head poking over a dashboard as a watcher who's fallen asleep wakes and peers out.

Nothing. But don't stay on a bench too long.

Bok walks two blocks to a commercial zone and an Associated market, where he buys enough groceries to fill one large bag. Packaged Folgers coffee. Ramen noodles. Polish dills. Little Debbie sweetcakes. And most important, three thick bunches of red-leaf lettuce. I hate these big supermarkets, he thinks. The food is never really fresh.

"You from around here?" the checkout lady says, giving him the sexy eye.

"I'd like a paper bag please, not plastic."

Plastic bags you carry at your side. Paper you carry in front, which is the point.

On the way back he pauses, bends, slips the S&W into the shopping bag. The safety is off. The gun, cushioned by lettuce, makes no noise clinking against the bottle and can.

Singh phones back as Bok reaches Heffner's block, timing his approach to catch the opening outer door of the building when a resident goes out.

"Frank Heffner has lived at that address for five years, according to phone and tax records. He owns one credit card but he's bought nothing with it. That is the part that strikes me as odd, sir."

"Double bonus, Singh."

"Also, Camilla Ryan just changed her airline reservations. She'll be returning home tomorrow morning on American Airlines flight 23, due in at Kennedy Airport at nine thirty A.M., sixteen hours from now."

"But Voort is still scheduled to fly out Saturday?"

"Perhaps they had a fight and the woman is returning home early."

Dryly, Bok says, "Nine thirty A.M., eh? Nothing like a good homecoming."

Bok gets into the building easily and takes the elevator to the fourth floor. Elevator empty. Hallway empty. Bok treads softly, smells frying fish, considers which apartment—based on sounds coming from behind closed doors: a news show, an argument, classical piano—suggests an occupant who would best react to a "Doesn't Lenny Schuster live in 4B anymore?"

Knocking, he remembers how once, in Africa, he saw villagers lure a leopard into a trap by tying a lamb to a stake, and hiding.

Bok doesn't get angry about it. After all, he chose his life of violent logic.

Bok thinking, *Plenty of time to meet her flight.*

Voort gets the all-clear from Mickie and pulls into Captain Mcgreevey's front driveway in Staten Island. The grass has been mowed, the house painted. He sees other cars at the curbside. Tug families are pitching in, Greg had said, to help the old couple out.

I was attacked after visiting Mcgreevey last time.

Waiting for the captain to answer the door, Voort keeps going over his conversation with Chip Levant the salvage expert. Voort seeing them on the bridge of the *Mary Ann.* Voort asking, "If those guys *weren't* looking for the *Hussar* but something smaller, a different boat or piece of cargo, how small a thing *can* you find with side-scan sonar?"

"Hmmmmmm, good question." Levant taking his time.

Voort rolling his eyes in memory. Here we go again.

"One time I found a rifle off Miami, for ATF."

"That small?"

"But that was in the ocean, on clean sand. You mean in the East River, right?"

"Right."

"The river's pretty crowded so a rifle would be hard to find. Nope. Sorry. No rifle without lots of luck."

"I didn't say it was a rifle. I asked what you *could* find, not what you couldn't," Voort recalls having said.

"Welllll, you'd have to set the sonar differently for something small, use a shorter range. It would depend on the depth too, of course."

"Of course."

"Welllll, in Holland, police actually experimented with bodies. Side-scan worked well finding bodies in the ocean, but not in cluttered canals. For centuries the Dutch have been dumping shit in those canals."

Voort sighs. "So a body is out too."

"Probably. But not conclusively. A shopping cart's possible. A chain and anchor . . . especially if the chain is long. A wooden chest. In Long Island Sound you could find a lobster trap. So many things fall off boats I don't know where to start."

"What things?"

"Anything you can load, you can lose. Containers. Hell, even missiles."

"Missiles?" Voort's heartbeat picks up.

"Once I found an air-to-air missile for the navy. They're about two meters long, eight to ten inches in diameter. I can't tell you where. I'm not allowed. Of course a bigger missile would be easier to find. But missiles don't go through Hell's Gate. At least I don't think they do. They're certainly not *supposed* to."

Voort sweating as he remembers it. Voort's head hurting as Captain Mcgreevey opens the door, looking older, whiter, thinner, stooped, as if he's aged years in days.

When he sees "Frank Heffner's" badge he shakes his head wearily. "Go away," he says. "I already talked to police." The door starts to close.

"Sir, it's me, Greg's cousin. Conrad Voort."

The door stops closing and magnified, watery-blue eyes squint out in puzzlement through thick lenses. Mcgreevey says, "Why are you dressed up like that?"

"Whoever killed your sons attacked me too."

Mcgreevey freezes. Rage gives him color and focuses his eyes. For a moment he looks younger.

"You're hiding from them?" he asks.

"I'm working. Can I come in?"

Inside, the house smells wonderful; of tomato sauces and garlic, onions, spicy fried chicken. Of life. Of temptation.

"Someone's always here from the tug families," says Mcgreevey. "They say they're just dropping in but they come and go in shifts. God bless 'em. You Voorts are the best."

"I need to talk to you in private, sir."

Mcgreevey leads him past the kitchen, where two women wipe dishes, and the living room, where Mrs. Mcgreevey sits with more women, drinking coffee, playing cards. The back-room office is furnished with steel desks and file cabinets, a fax machine, several phones, and piles of papers and cardboard boxes. On the wall are cheap paintings of tugboats. The room smells mildewy after only three weeks of disuse. A film of dust coats the desks.

"That's the first boat my family owned," Mcgreevey says, pointing to an oil of an old twin-stacked, coal-driven model. "Built in 1909. My great-grandfather helped bring in the battleship *Hood* once on that tug, before the *Bismarck* sank it."

"I hate to have to ask more questions."

"Catch the people who killed my sons."

"I'd like to check your financial records, and your sons' too. Bills. Bank accounts. Purchases. Warranties."

Mcgreevey glances at a pile of taped-up cardboard boxes in one corner.

"Kevin's are at his house. But Bud was a bachelor. We cleaned out his place. That's his stuff. Can I help?"

He looks like he needs the job, so Voort says, "Sure, let's sort out the financial papers."

Together, they go through boxes. Voort sifts through a CD collection, signed baseball collection, a box marked "Salvation Army" filled with sweaters.

Mcgreevey says, over the top of a different box, "Here's his bills."

Voort eyes the dead man's last paid electric, gas, and AT&T bills. Nothing interesting leaps out. He'll have Mickie check out phone numbers called. Voort finds a warranty for a Sony big-screen TV.

"Bought on August twenty-seventh."

He feels a slight ticking start up in his head when he finds another warranty, for a microwave, purchase date also August twenty-seventh, and the kicker, the waving red flag.

"Paid for with cash," he says.

"Here's a receipt from Filene's," Mcgreevey says. "New suit. Shirts. Ties. Son of a bitch. Cash. Same day."

"What's the time of the purchase?"

"Eleven A.M. If he was shopping we had no jobs.

You're thinking they got paid off that morning or the day before?"

"I don't know. Let's keep looking."

At Voort's suggestion Mcgreevey phones his daughter-in-law the widow to ask if Kevin had also made any big purchases in late August. No, he tells her in response to a question, nothing's the matter but would she mind checking the drawer in the kitchen where she keeps warranties?

He pauses, listens, interrupts her and says, "Just tell me." When he hangs up, he's blinking away tears. "Cruise tickets for me and Edna. She always wanted to see Alaska. They were going to give them to us on our anniversary next week."

"I'm sorry, sir," says Voort.

Then Mcgreevey thinks of something else and starts rifling the top drawer of the file cabinet. His bent neck looks frail and skinny, and Voort sees the bone structure at the skull base, the skin papery and peppered with liver spots. Age always looks worse from behind.

"Upkeep file," Cap'n Mcgreevey mutters, pulling it out.

Voort steps closer, looks over the cardiganed shoulder at a stack of invoices, bills, canceled checks.

"They ordered a whole series of jobs. Paint. New stove. New nav equipment. On August twenty-eighth. New bumpers, the fancy kind, not the old tires. Now *that's* useless. That's two thousand dollars! They hired a diver to check the rudder too."

"They hit something," Voort muses.

"It's possible. New paint. New bumpers. The diver. It's *possible*, but upkeep happens regularly."

"If they hit something, they didn't report it," Voort says. "Nothing came up on the computer."

Mcgreevey shrugs. "I could see that happening. Yes, I could see them taking money for not reporting an accident. You work it out between yourselves, especially if damage was minor. Why call the Coast Guard? Why risk a bad report and have your insurance costs go up? Maybe it was foggy. There was a collision or maybe just a near miss. Maybe something fell into the water."

"Where are the logs from the twenty-seventh and twenty-eighth?"

"Burned up."

"Great."

"But I have a list of jobs we did those days. Remember, I make the deals. They do the jobs."

Voort notes that Mcgreevey has just slipped into the present tense, as if his boys are still alive, and are out on the boat, working. The instant the tense shifted, his posture straightened.

Mcgreevey clears a pile of *Ship 'N' Harbor* magazines off a swivel chair and turns on a computer. His fingers punch keys with surprising dexterity. A list of jobs swims up.

"August twenty-eighth. Nothing," Mcgreevey confirms. "That was spend-the-money day, I guess. Twenty seventh? We took a garbage scow to Jersey in the morning, had a crane job to the old navy yard at twelve thirty. Last one was at night. They towed a barge up the East River to Queens."

Voort watches the cursor pulsate. Each beat conveys a jolt of fresh energy to him. Like a finger tapping against his brain.

"Did they go through Hell's Gate?"

"Right past LaGuardia."

"What was on the barge?"

"Just sand going from a dredge site to a landfill."

Voort envisions the barge. It's night. He sees the mound of sand and the roiling water. He adds stars. He sees a Coast Guard launch falling in as the tug passes the UN.

"Would the Coast Guard ever check under the sand?"

"If they board you they check the tug, not the barge. And even then it happens only once or twice a year, usually for drug tests."

Voort's thinking, maybe Mcgreevey's sons were paid to transport something and it fell into the water. Maybe the Coast Guard was coming and the sons freaked out and threw the cargo overboard, off the tug or barge.

Mcgreevey is shaking his head in agitation, as if guessing Voort's thoughts. "My sons wouldn't *do* that. No drugs. No illegals. Maybe they weren't carrying *anything*. Maybe they just *saw* something or had the accident and got paid off."

"Don't tell anyone I was here, Captain Mcgreevey."

Mcgreevey grips Voort's sleeve as he is leaving.

"Fathers should never outlive sons," he says.

Dusk is falling. The investigation seems to be opening up, not narrowing, Voort thinks, frustrated, remembering what Chip Levant had said about missiles.

The possibilities are getting worse.

He heads north to the Whitestone Bridge, then up the Hutchinson River Parkway into Connecticut. He takes Route 8 from Bridgeport to the Massachusetts border.

The road narrows to two lanes. The air becomes chilly. Fall has arrived early in New England. Roadside fruit stands are selling apples, signs say. Maple leaves in the headlights show red fringes. He smells chimney smoke. He turns on the heat in the car.

Cal Quinones, the producer who quit NBC, moved to Massachusetts, Haft said. *He died of cancer. He left a wife.*

Voort tries to reach Camilla and gets no answer. He feels a stab of guilt. He's been working so hard he hasn't checked in with her since this morning. It's nine thirty now, *thirteen hours since we talked.*

He's about to try again when his phone buzzes with Mickie calling.

"Good news and bad, Con Man."

"It's important to live a balanced life."

"Someone's accessed Frank Heffner's employment records. The entry came from outside the building, but the password belongs to a Lieutenant Tom Boynton, of the Two-Nine. He wasn't at work when it happened. Ever hear of him?"

"What's the bad news?"

"You gotta even ask? They're after you. And Boynton was one of the investigators on the arson deaths five years ago. He interviewed Stone."

Voort whistles softly.

"Yeah, incoming," says Mickie. "Eva says to play it your way. You want we sweat him or watch him?"

"Sweat him for *what*?" Voort says. "All we can prove is his password accessed a file."

"Push here, there."

"No," Voort says. He's on a country road, passing pastures, a chicken farm, an occasional house. In the dark he goes slowly so he can read names on mailboxes. They're the kind of mailboxes that have little metal flags on them. He says, squinting, "The second we come down on Boynton, Stone'll know we're figuring things out. The idea's to lure him in, not scare him off. Get him to make a move."

"What's wrong with you? You sound like you *want* the guy to take a pop. Why *not* scare them off? You think they're going to come after a cop's family with the department watching?"

"What about when they come back a year from now," Voort says. "You giving guarantees then too?"

"Con Man, is this really about protecting family, or is it payback for what they did to you in the Mobil station? I've known cops who were never the same after being threatened. Me, I believe in payback. But it's new for you."

Voort feels his pulse throbbing in his forehead. He doesn't want to think about the question. He says, "They killed at least six people and we can't prove it. They shut down a TV network investigation. They bought at least one cop. They shot me with a goddamn dart, and if I heard right, stole enough money to pay off the national debt."

Voort goes on about what he's learned today. He fills Mickie in on the Haft visit, Mcgreevey visit, tug ride. Hitting the brake to avoid running over a waddling porcupine, he concludes, "It's not treasure down there. But what the hell is it?"

"Why not send down police divers and blanket the river?" Mickie says. "Find it first?"

Voort's headlights pick out a steel mailbox with white lettering on it that says QUINONES. There's a long dirt driveway climbing up a hill, through trees. He can't see the house. Looks like the wife still lives here.

"Find *what* first? There's six inches of visibility down there and whatever they're after could be the size of a TV. *They* know what it is and they *still* can't find it. Better to watch. Get them when they bring it up. Or make them come after us first."

"*You* first, Con Man."

Voort bumps up the dirt driveway as Mickie snorts derisively and adds, "Yeah, all we need is people to watch 'em twenty-four hours a day—divers, helicopters, night scopes. Call out the army. Eva will go for this big time, considering manpower cuts. What jobs do you see her pulling guys off? The National League playoffs? And what'll *really* clinch it is that you don't have one clue what Stone's looking for, one piece of proof that it's against the law, or even that he's behind it. Everything you said is speculation."

"At least I'm consistent."

"All right, goddamnit, I'll watch Boynton. We'll check his calls. Maybe we'll get lucky and he'll phone Larry King and confess everything on national TV."

"Good-bye." Voort shuts off the headlights as he pulls up before a sturdy-looking white Victorian house. Lights blaze from downstairs and upstairs windows. There's a picket fence on a widow's walk and a swing on the front porch. He sees a couple of mountain bikes leaning on railings, and a hammock. Getting out of the car, mounting the wooden steps, he hears the sound of PBS nightly news coming from inside.

When he rings the bell, the TV shuts off, and then he

hears the thud of heels on a wooden floor. The main door opens. The screen door opens. The woman who looks out didn't even ask, "Who's there?" first. Voort's outside of New York, all right. He's looking into a pretty face, maybe forty years old, with cropped dark hair and soft lines at the almond eyes suggesting kindness and likability. He smells cinnamon and chocolate. He hears footsteps running upstairs. Cal Quinones left kids, Voort recalls, showing his badge.

"This is a New York City detective shield," the woman says. She's wearing a denim jumper. "Are you lost, Detective Heffner?"

Actually I am.

Some wives know their husbands' secrets. Others never find out. It's probable that whoever attacked Voort two weeks ago threatened and maybe killed Cal Quinones. It makes Voort feel close to this woman instantly and he wants to reveal his real name, but he doesn't. He dislikes lying to her but he does it to be safe.

He's come on a long shot, he says. She doesn't have to talk to him, not legally, but lives may hang in the balance. He believes that her husband left NBC five years ago because he was threatened. He believes the same people who threatened him may have murdered four people over the last two weeks.

She nods. Her lips look pretty when pursed. She does not look surprised. "You're here for the tape, aren't you? You found out Cal made a copy."

"Yes," Voort says, stunned.

She sighs and seems to withdraw into herself, goes back to some private, painful memory. The door opens wider. She steps back to allow him inside. The hallway is filled with teenage items, innocent things—baseball mitts, a skateboard, dirty sneakers, schoolbooks.

"I don't know why I kept it," she says. "Cal used to watch it and watch it. Whatever they did to him tortured him every single day."

Voort feels that he's about to get some answers.

Mrs. Quinones asks, "Want a slice of chocolate cake?"

THIRTEEN

"I married into a family of thieves and liars," Antonia Nidal says on the tape.

The basement is warm, the lights low. Dorothea Quinones sits curled in a club chair, feet tucked beneath her in a posture Voort associates with TV watching, magazine reading. He hears kids running upstairs. He smells chocolate cake from the plate on the end table. A TV room is supposed to be a sanctuary, but in this house it's a torture chamber to which Mrs. Quinones consigns herself, as her husband had regularly, with the copy of the NBC tape.

"I had no idea what Jaffa was really like when I married him," Brooklyn-born Antonia—the ex-diplomat's wife—says on the tape.

Voort strains to hear every word. The tape is excellent quality, and the woman in her late twenties, Voort judges, with golden skin and rich blonde hair, but her lips are thin, drawn tight with permanent dissatisfaction. Whatever sweetness or sexiness she might once have conveyed is vanishing, it seems, word by word.

"I thought he was elegant and cultured. He turned out to be a drug and sex addict."

An interior decorator, she'd met her husband when she'd been hired to redo his East Side luxury apartment. "I became one more decoration," she snaps. Voort guesses the apartment has the same overstated look that she does. Antonia's black Armani pantsuit is sleek and expensive, but the emerald broach and ring are oversized, the mascara too thick, the lipstick too red. She's nightclub, not museum. Britney, not Bach.

"Jaffa's family runs half the construction businesses in Palestine. I'd fly over at Christmas and see beggars in the streets. After the UN sent aid, the cripples would still be there, but the family would have new cars."

She points at photos on a table.

"A private detective took these shots of him on Ted Stone's yacht."

In the blow-up photos Voort sees a handsome, dark-haired man wearing black bikini underwear and sunglasses, down on all fours, as a large-breasted naked woman straddles his back. The woman drinks from a bottle of beer. The man's face is shiny from drugs and sexual excitement. He's howling and laughing, playing the dog.

"That was taken from shore. Stone the lawyer sends his crew home during special parties. He makes his deals on the boat, Jaffa said."

How many of her accusations are true? Voort wonders. And how many are a reflection of hurt and anger?

Either way, chalk up one more person who'd died when his life intersected Stone's. Making this tape, this woman had no idea that within days she, her children, and her husband would be dead.

"I don't even know where Jaffa lives now. He's off in Europe, living it up."

The woman glares into the camera, expecting her audience to share her rage. But there's something disingenuous in the indignation. It's too strident and righteous, Voort thinks.

"I should have known something was wrong."

Dorothea Quinones sighs, "She had no idea. Right."

"Life was fun," Voort says.

"Jaffa started getting drunk at home. He did drugs in the apartment. He bragged about things and wouldn't remember. He was drunk when he told me about Ted Stone."

For Voort, just hearing the name seems to heat up air in the room.

" 'Mister five percent,' Jaffa called him. He said Stone worked the UN, knew who was tied into corruption overseas. Not necessarily high-level people. Connected people. Stone would show them a good time, explain that sure, everything was great for them back home now, but what if it went sour? Look at what happened in the Philippines, Iran, Panama? Stone became a funnel for illegal funds. He set up his own private security system to monitor journalists and police in countries where they work—you know, to make sure the news never gets back here. They do horrible things to people."

Mrs. Quinones whispers, "Like burning genitals."

Voort stops the tape and Antonia Nidal's face freezes, huge, distorted, enraged. He turns his attention to the living woman on his right, who is looking away.

"I saw the scars," Dorothea says, staring into a corner. "They never heal all the way. Cal stopped having sex with me. He wouldn't go to a counselor. Whoever hurt him told him I'd be next, apparently. Want to know something crazy? I blame myself for Cal's collapse. He was trying to protect me."

Her words fill Voort with shame, and he flashes to Camilla. Is she far away, alone also, blaming herself for the terrors in Voort's head? The face on the screen remains frozen. Mrs. Quinones won't meet Voort's eyes. She's locked into a private memory that runs like a tape loop in her head.

Voort says, "This may not mean much to you right now, but I talk to a lot of people who blame themselves for things they never could have prevented. You'd think the screwups would do it, but it's the good ones who suffer every time."

Dorothea turns back and wipes her eyes. Her round face is soft with vulnerability and gratefulness. Voort feels as if he's involved in a four-way talk between Stone's victims: Mrs. Quinones, Cal, a dead woman, and a damaged cop.

"Dorothea, the worst part of being a caring person is that you can't do the impossible, but you keep wondering if you could."

"Whoever tortured Cal *wanted* to debase him," she says. "To them he was no more important than an insect. There wasn't even anger in it, just calculation. The lack of importance hit him the worst."

And Voort can't breathe suddenly, remembering the hiss of a man's breath in his ear, the hard press of flesh on his rump.

"The tape reminded Cal of what had happened every day. He'd never imagined he could be diminished so much."

Voort remembers the hands parting the cheeks of his ass. He restarts the tape. Offscreen, a confident-sounding

Cal Quinones asks Antonia Nidal, "How did Stone set up his money-laundering system?"

"When he worked at the UN, he spent years getting assigned to places where aid was disappearing. He made friends with people doing it. Later, money was routed to Stone through legitimate law firms or banks overseas."

"But there's nothing new about money laundering," Cal says. "What was different about Stone's way?"

Mrs. Quinones hits the pause button.

"The scale was *huge*," she says. "Cal told me his theory. I'm better than Antonia at explaining it. But there was no proof. Just allegations. And people living very, very well."

"I'd appreciate hearing it anyway," says Voort.

"Stone works loopholes in laws. By the time investments reach him, they've been washed through so many transfers no one can prove a thing. His clients are war criminals. He buys up water rights in Arizona for them. Real estate on Long Island. Stores. Condos. Cal said the government screams bloody murder when Americans shift money *out* of the country, but makes it easy for funds to come *in*. Cal was collecting lists of war criminals or crooked businessmen overseas who had vanished when their governments went down. He thought they're living here now. That Stone brought them in, set them up."

Dorothea hits the pause button again and the tape resumes. On screen, Antonia Nidal's bitterness pinches her skin and makes her look older. It's like watching a speeded-up tape of life passing. Her future becomes her present.

Cal Quinones asks, "Tell me about the other part. Stone's security system."

"Leon Bok? My husband calls him 'Dead Man Talking.' He says whenever he shows up, someone dies."

Voort freezes at the description. His breath catches in his throat.

Antonia pouts suddenly. "Look, you said if the story pans out you'd help me get a job."

"I will. But tell me more about Bok," soothes the producer, thinking he is in control of his story, that he is clever and protected. Asking one too many questions as he dreams of outwitting opponents who are already two steps ahead.

"Nobody knows where Bok lives or where he comes from, or even if Bok is his real name. My husband said in the old days you would have called him a mercenary. A man hired to overthrow some African dictator, or by the dictator to train his troops. My husband said if you want Bok you contact him through the Internet, wait for him to show up, and pay what he wants. His reputation is, he never stops, fails, or calls off a job. My husband said Bok's a killer, but an honorable one, with a private code, whatever that means. My husband talked a lot about Leon Bok and honor when he was drinking." She shakes her head disgustedly. "Honor. I should have known."

"And what is Bok's private code?"

"Jaffa was babbling. Once you take Bok on, he'll never screw you, never double-cross or disappoint you. That kind of thing. My husband used a Japanese word for Bok."

Every time she says "husband," her voice tightens.

"What was the word your husband used?"

" 'Ronin.' Jaffa said Bok was like one of those old Japanese warriors after they'd lost their master. They still value personal honor. But they work for anyone who pays."

"So Bok was in the military once?"

"Ask *him* if you get him on your show."

"Wasn't Jaffa afraid that he might be hurt if he told you about Stone or Bok?"

For the first time the woman's voice smooths out with satisfaction. She's achieving some revenge here, she thinks.

"Oh, he was terrified. When he sobered up he insisted he'd never mentioned Bok. But how could I have *known* about Bok if Jaffa hadn't told me? So Jaffa said, no matter what happens, never talk about Bok. He was so scared it was funny. Well, I want to see them all in jail."

"Detective Heffner?" Dorothea says, stopping the tape again. "Do you think Leon Bok hurt my husband?"

"I do."

"Can you find him?"

"I hope so."

"There's something in your eyes that I used to see in Cal's. An intensity. It was there when you came to the door. If you don't mind my asking, is this inquiry personal for you?"

Voort whispers, after a pause, "Yes."

"They did something to you too, or someone close to you?"

Voort's head hurts. He's exhausted. He says, "The tape's been helpful. Can I take it?"

Dorothea shuts off the VCR and retrieves the tape. With the set silent Voort hears canned laughter from a sit-com upstairs.

"My husband thought he could forget what they did

to him, and that's what destroyed him, not the attack. It was living with it that ate him away."

Their hands touch as she gives him the tape.

"Do you understand what I'm saying? I trust you. I sense good in you. You said things to me that only a good person would say. Whatever you're planning, do it for the people they'll hurt if you don't."

The tape feels warm to Voort, from the VCR machine. It contains damaging accusations but not proof. Just words.

"An eye for an eye," Dorothea Quinones says savagely, standing there in her denim jumper. "If you spare the guilty you'll injure the rest."

Fog is rolling in when Voort gets outside, two hours later, after a nap on Dorothea's couch. He's still exhausted. The moon disappears. Stars blink out. The air turns clammy and a roiling blanket of mist beads the windshield as if it is drizzling. But it is not.

Wipers slashing, Voort heads south, the tape beside him on the front seat. He has to squint to see the road. The farms are gone. Towns come up as a blur of clapboard homes or blinking lights at rural intersections. The fog lifts momentarily to show a hillside cemetery, and tilting headstones. It closes in again. The headstones disappear.

He tries to reach Camilla, but it is after midnight and he gets no answer. Perhaps she is asleep, her phone turned off. Perhaps she dreams of a life of normalcy.

But as he clicks off the phone buzzes. His hope rises.

"Camilla?"

"It's your favorite tug captain," says Cousin Greg with a mean edge. "They're diving. Now."

Voort feels a surge of protective panic for his loyal cousin. "I told you to keep away from them. Where are you?"

"Where do you think? On the tug. Did you hear what I said? They found what they're looking for. They've got the diving light on. Do something!"

"Are you deaf?"

"They didn't see me."

"Dillinger said that before the shooting started."

Greg sounds confident. To him, civilians on the water never notice things. They drive their little boats obliviously past bends, snags, sandbars, wrecks. To Greg it is impossible that a newcomer on the river could outsmart a veteran or even notice an observer.

Voort curses himself for ever asking Greg to help.

Greg huffs, "I thought you'd want to know. They've been in the same spot for hours. I checked with one of the McAllister tugs. And don't worry. I didn't tell them anything. Zip-mouth. That's me."

"How about hiring a blimp to fly over. They won't notice that either," Voort snaps.

"They murdered my friends."

"They're suspects. That's all."

"Don't give me that shit. When you want help, they're guilty. When you decide I should stop, they're not."

Voort has to brake to maneuver around a series of sharp curves. His headlights come back at him. Fog blinds him as he drives.

"Let Mickie and me handle it. Okay?"

"Conrad, I know what divers look like when they're just looking, versus recovering. These guys are excited."

The mist hems in Voort and squeezes together time and necessity. He needs more sleep. Exhaustion bunches the muscles in his shoulders and wrists. The headlights drift toward a wall of trees and Voort jerks the wheel left. Greg promises to go home, "if you promise to call a patrol."

"Hello? Mickie?" Voort is on the next call.

"You still in Massachusetts? The fog here is unbelievable. Accidents all over the place. Drive slow, bro."

"Greg says they're diving out there."

"Well, if they found something, that makes sense. No one can see what they come up with in the fog."

"Try to get a patrol to check them out, maybe ask if they're in trouble. Make up a story but don't spook them in case Greg's wrong."

"I'll call Mike Egee in harbor patrol."

In Winsted, Connecticut—still two hours from New York—Voort pulls into a BP station and buys gas, a ham hero, and two coffees. The road widens to four lanes and the speed limit hits sixty-five, but drivers seem too wary of the fog to move even as fast as legally allowed. The caffeine buzz is a vibration in Voort's throat and behind his eyes.

"At the US Open today, a small misstep ended a promising bid for championship," a radio announcer says.

In his mind, Voort replays the tape, tug ride, talk with Dorothea Quinones. He sends his thoughts to the McGreevey house, slows them down and sees Captain McGreevey going through his files.

"Damn! The files!"

He takes the next exit—for downtown Waterbury—and pulls over beneath an overpass. Through gaps in mist the deserted neighborhood looks New England–industrial; seedy and spotted with clapboard homes and a small Shell station. Even streetlights are off. Within seconds, without the wipers moving, the windshield mists over. Voort clicks on the interior light and searches his Palm for a phone number.

Everything that's happened involves the river, which is where Stone entertains his clients on that boat.

"Is he dead?" asks the smoker-hoarse middle-aged man who answers on the first ring, and doesn't seem embarrassed when Voort identifies himself. Voort imagines the judge on the other end, in pajamas and bathrobe, at home in Riverdale. It pays to be a multimillionaire detective when calling a judge with political ambitions after midnight to ask for a search warrant. It helps that the judge will need campaign funding for a Senate run next spring.

"Sorry to bother you, sir."

"I thought you were my wife. Her father's dying of cancer. I'm expecting her call any minute now."

"Then I'll be quick."

"Ah, I can't sleep anyway, and we have call waiting. My father-in-law's a great guy, Conrad. He used to be a weight lifter. Now he's as thin as a stickball bat. Don't put life off. You never know when you'll lose the opportunities. I'm getting maudlin. Tell me what you need."

Voort explains his rationale for requesting a search warrant for Stone's boat, office, and apartment. The killings on the river. The tape. The interviews with Haft and Mrs. Quinones. The treasure search. The files.

"That's interesting, but I'm not sure it constitutes probable cause," says the judge after some thought. "Also, Stone's a lawyer so you'll risk violating attorney-client privilege if you go through his files. Ever think of that? You could screw up your own case."

The judge is a good judge, Voort thinks, and might make a good senator. But they both know the only reason he's staying on the line is that Voort contributes money to candidates. His $100,000 helped defeat a mayor who tried to remove the tax abatement on his home a few years back.

Voort presses. "Sir, please reconsider. I have a reliable informant on a tape made by professionals. It's no amateur home movie, Judge. A VP at NBC admitted the tape was suppressed after threats were made. The producer was tortured. I believe a look for records relating to money laundering is justified under the circumstances. And if I tumble on something incidental while I'm at it, that's admissible too, I bet."

"Which law school did you graduate from?" But the judge sounds amused.

"I should tell you the sonar expert considered it possible that there's a stolen missile down there."

The word "missile" does it. All an aspiring senator needs is to fail to issue a warrant in a case where a stolen missile later gets fired.

"Want me to fax you the warrant?"

"Actually, you live in Riverdale, right? I'm driving down from Connecticut. Could you leave it in your mailbox? I

won't even knock. And sir? I'm undercover. I'm not supposed to be in New York."

"I'm on Lafayette Place, 8674. Take the exit for 246th
Street off the Henry Hudson. I'll write up the warrant
now."

The caffeine buzz is still intense as Voort heads back
onto the highway. He takes the Merritt Parkway to the
Cross County and Sawmill Parkways, south past Yonkers
and into the pricey North Bronx.

If they're diving, time is running out.

The judge's three-story Tudor lies on a narrow street
that looks more like a country lane. The warrant is in the
mailbox. The fog is so thick that Voort can barely make out
the light in the upstairs window, and the judge's silhouette
looking out.

Four-fifty A.M.

By the time Mickie reports back, Voort has been de-
layed by an accident and is on Harlem's 125th Street, heading crosstown toward FDR Drive and Ted Stone's marina.
Even cabbies seem fearful of driving too fast in the cloying
fog.

"No luck, Con Man. I went out with the boat. Those
divers weren't bringing up anything. Greg was wrong.
They were cooperative. They even invited us to come on
board."

Voort bats off disappointment. "You checked IDs?"

"Yeah, but you said don't spook 'em. It was casual."

"Find anyone named Leon Bok?"

"No. I'm running the names. An Aussie and a Frog."

"But why dive in the middle of the night?"

"They said they thought they'd found the *Hussar*. Th

sonar had picked up a ship. They need flashlights down there anyway so it didn't make a difference whether they went down during day or night. They were afraid the wreck might move."

"What about their accents? The man I remember had a dead voice. Weird accent."

"Nope. I gotta tell you, in this fog they could raise the *Titanic* and you wouldn't see it unless you were five feet away."

"Ask the patrol to keep swinging back and to search them again when they move off."

"I'll try. But Egee has to move around."

"And head for the marina. Once I show up there, Stone will know where I am."

A beep on the sat phone tells him another call's coming in, so he clicks off with Mickie.

"Frank Heffner."

"When I'm finished with you you'll *wish* you were Frank Heffner," Camilla says.

"Where are you?" Despite her anger, a wave of relief washes over him. "I've been calling for hours!"

She rages, "I'm in the air, that's where. In a plane."

His relief turns to panic. For Voort, oxygen seems to drain from the car.

"I'm over the Gulf of Mexico. I can't believe you lied to me. *You lied, Voort!*"

Voort calculates distance quickly. Gulf of Mexico means she's at least two and a half hours out of New York.

"Where are you exactly, Camilla?"

"Don't use that tone with me, and don't say another word until I'm through. I e-mailed Spruce. I was worried about *you* when you didn't check in, you shit. Did you really think I wouldn't find out what happened?"

Voort's jaw starts to throb.

"Spruce told me the family voted 'no.' They told you to stop. Well, I warned you I'd come back if you lied. What else did you lie about? Huh?"

"Calm down."

Two words guaranteed to inflame any enraged, out-of-work type-A TV producer.

"If you can't trust a person, what's the point of being with them?" she says.

"We have to talk."

"Oh, now you *want* to talk? I wasn't even going to call until I landed, but I've been *sitting* here getting *angrier* and *angrier.* I warned you. My husband lied to me."

Voort's tone reflects a calm he does not feel. "Please tell me your flight number."

In the silence he imagines her plane touching down. He imagines Leon Bok at the airport. He remembers Antonia Nidal saying, 'When Bok shows up, someone dies.' It will take him thirty minutes to get to Kennedy Airport from Manhattan, or is Camilla coming into a different airport?

Is she still even on the line?

"What time are you landing, Camilla?"

He hears her breathing. So she's there. Thank God.

"Nine thirty," she snaps. Which is three and a half hours away.

"What airport?"

"Kennedy."

"American Airlines, still?"

She hangs up. It's her way of saying, Fuck you. Find something out for yourself, jerk.

A sign ahead reads EAST SIDE MARINA.

I still have time to search Stone's boat.

Concentrate, Voort thinks. In the fog the Volvo floats into the parking lot. He experiences the sense of things ticking toward culmination. Time fractures into delays and questions. It speeds up and slows down at the same time.

Will there even be anything incriminating on the boat?

It is six A.M. along Manhattan's Gold Coast, where, if her denizens are to be believed, money can buy anything. The rent-a-cop at the gate grows nervous when she sees Frank Heffner's warrant, but it's less from fear of police than from being caught between her employer's anger and the municipality's demands. She's young, blonde, petite, in her twenties. Her uniform's too big. Voort notices a statistics textbook in her free hand. The night job helps put her through college, he supposes.

"All boat owners have to leave keys at the office, but I don't know what to do," she says. "If there's a break-in I'm supposed to call the police, but you *are* the police. Nobody told me what to do if you just show up."

"Let me in," Voort orders, sidestepping the question. If she chooses to call Stone first Voort may have to wait.

The harbor smells of diesel oil, salt, and there's a fishy flavor wafting up from the old Fulton Fish Market. The fog is alive with bells and horns, as if ships out there are scattered beasts, a mechanized herd talking in a language Voort does not understand.

As Voort follows the guard down a floating dock, she

says over her shoulder, "Mr. Stone will have me fired."

"I'll say you tried to stop me. You put up a fight. I'll complain about *you*. But get me on that boat."

Hulls creak against rubber. Bumpers rub docks. Voort hears the low, muffled tones of Coleman Hawkins playing "Sancticity" on his tenor sax. Somewhere in the marina a jazz fan passes time as dawn nears.

The *Candace* is berthed at the end of the dock, her gleaming-white fiberglass hull beaded with moisture, her name in gold. He recognizes the deep V shape and forward-set main-deck superstructure from the Quinones video and photo in Stone's office.

Be damaged, he hopes as the guard steps up on the stern with a ring of keys. The first one doesn't work. The yacht's an Orsid-57 with an extended flybridge and fishing chairs in back. The sliding glass cabin door is misted. From Voort's angle the boat does not seem to have suffered a collision, so maybe the repair work listed in Mcgreevey's tug files was a false clue. But Voort cannot yet see the bow.

"How long have you worked here?" he asks.

"Six months. I'll try another key."

"Has the boat been here every night the whole time?"

"Except for when it was refitted."

Voort hides his excitement. "When was that?"

She opens the aft cabin and stands aside. "Let me think. My boss said it was okay for visitors to use Mr. Stone's berth for a couple weeks, because the *Candace* wasn't going to be here, and *he* was going on vacation the next day, so it was late August, the twenty-ninth or thirtieth."

The day after the Mcgreeveys started spending money.

"Was the boat in an accident?" Voort asks casually.

"Boats get refitted all the time," she replies as Voort walks past her along the deck. He starts checking over the side. It's smooth and undisturbed but it could have been repaired.

"Do you know where the boat was refitted?"

"No."

"Does the marina keep records of when boats leave or arrive?"

"No."

Does a possession have personality? Does it absorb the passions of people it serves? Voort has spent hours in suspects' cars, homes, planes. He's gone through bills and e-mails, peered into boilers and under sinks and into dark, clammy crawl spaces. As far back as when he was five, his dad had played "find the clue" with him. They'd visit an uncle's house and Dad would say, "There's a spot of ketchup in this room. Find it." Or, "There's something out of place in the kitchen." Or, when he was older, "Is *anything* wrong? Answer right and get a pizza. Answer wrong and buy me a Coke."

"I've never seen police do a search," the guard says with real curiosity.

"And you won't now."

Stepping down into the salon he feels the deck slide as if gravity has shifted. The porthole dips. Somewhere on the river, something heavy and dangerous has passed.

Voort's first pass takes him through the master stateroom, VIP forward cabin, cockpit, lower helm.

Nothing in plain view. What did he expect?

The decks are teak, the furnishings cherry. The flybridge features a wet bar, lounge seating, and dinette. Teak stairs take him from the upper salon to the cabins. A cherrywood table shines.

Nothing. Voort wants to scream with frustration.

Camilla will be over the U.S. by now, the East Coast. *Why was this boat refitted?*

In his mind it is night, foggy, like tonight, and Stone is on the boat doing things that depend on secrecy. A tug looms. There's the crunch of fiberglass. The Mcgreevey brothers rush out on deck, horrified, to spot someone or something they were never supposed to see.

Antonia Nidal had said, "Stone sends his crew home during special parties."

But if this is about something the Mcgreeveys saw on Stone's boat, why would Stone need divers?

He starts phase two of the search, the drawer-opening part. It's night in his imagination. The tug brushes the *Candace* and something falls overboard. It's small but large enough to find with side-scan sonar. But it's *so* small that it takes two weeks in the East River for professional experts to locate it. But why would something that size *be* balanced in the first place so that it would fall overboard?

Maybe someone was holding it, showing it off.

Aiming it?

I'm tired, Voort thinks. *Stone doesn't deal in missiles. He deals in money, every source says.*

He finds nothing interesting in drawers. No warranties for new equipment. No bills of repair. No diary confessing to ordering six murders, ha ha.

The guard is probably phoning Stone out there.

Voort goes back out on the stern and gazes at the river, as if staring into fog might help imagination. He changes the scene in his mind so it unwinds a different way.

It's foggy. There's the crunch of hulls and the obvious argument. A fight starts. Men yell at each other. Someone pulls out a gun. Stone pays the Mcgreeveys to keep quiet.

Then what fell into the water? Crog's friend said bodies would be nearly impossible to find with sonar.

Try again. Again. Again. Again. Maybe the Mcgreeveys were working with Stone. Maybe something fell off the tug, not the yacht. Maybe the Mcgreeveys *towed* the *Candace* somewhere to be repaired.

He starts to laugh. Maybe, he thinks, there wasn't *any* collision. Maybe what happened is just what the marina guard said. The boat got refitted, period.

Call boat yards today. Find where the work was done.

He snaps out of the trance. The mist has coated him. His hands are wet on the railing. His scalp is slick and his clothes send up the sour-sweet odor of wet fabric. It's seven, he's been here almost an hour.

The guard is still fretting on the dock when he climbs down. She's likable but seems as if she'd be useless in an emergency. "I reached Stone. He's angry at me for letting you in without calling first. He wants me fired."

Voort takes pity on her. "Look, my friends run a law firm that hires night clerks. I can try to help you get a job if you want, or do you like security work?"

"Are you kidding? It's lonely here and I'm scared all the time. I just need a night job. I go to NYU during the day."

At least I can help one of Stone's victims, Voort thinks.

Together they trudge toward the office. Lights are on in a couple of boats. Voort hears morning radio. From the river comes the rumble of heavy engines, maybe even from a Voort tug, pulling a barge like the Mcgreeveys did on the night they did or saw something that cost them their lives.

Back in the parking lot, outside the main gate he turns one more time, peers riverward, into fog, time, and possibility, lost in the twisted realm of cop speculation. Man, he thinks, in this soup if a tug rammed a boat it would *really* smash . . .

He freezes.

Is it *possible*?

Rushing back, he presses the buzzer, holds it, hope building, as the frazzled guard hurries to let him in again.

"I need to get back on Stone's boat."

She doesn't protest this time, and onboard, Voort starts scribbling down numbers. Registration sticker number. Manufacturer's hull number. Engine ID number, and parts for pipes, navigation system, oven.

Writing, he imagines a different scene now. The tug looming, the gigantic barge behind it. The ropes straining and the yacht skimming sideways. People shouting, "Look out!"

The fog hiding the collision. The *Candace* keeling over, water pouring in. The barge shattering fiberglass, splitting the balsa core, breaking the boat into pieces, leaving a trail of debris sinking into the oozy wreckage down there.

Cousin Greg had said, "I know how divers act when they've found something, and when they're just looking."

Consulting his PDA, Voort next wakes up a lieutenant he knows who works out of the City Island Harbor Unit, whom he and Mickie helped solve a case two years ago. The loot doesn't even complain about the hour. Voort figures cops who work with boats—stolen ones, abandoned ones, drug runners—may have access to databases matching boat registration, parts, and manufacturer's numbers.

"Sure we do," the lieutenant says. "The Coast Guard came up with it to uncover pirated boats. The druggies would kill the owner. Paint on a new name. Or crash a boat and replace it with the same model, to fool us. Now we can match craft and parts. Give me your number. I'll call West Virginia. Believe it or not, that's where the Coast Guard keeps this shit."

Car owners work out private deals at accidents all the time, to avoid dealing with insurance companies or police.

"Mickie? Time to change tactics. Where are you?"

"Parked across FDR Drive, watching you. No one showed up in the last half-hour at the marina. The Shadow knows you're safe."

"Call your pal Egee. Ask him to pick us up on his boat. And to call in divers. Greg may be right. I think they found what they're looking for. They may never have intended to bring anything up. They're clearing off a wreck down there. And oh yeah, we have to be at Kennedy Airport by nine thirty."

"My creditors haven't gotten that bad yet, Con Man. It's still safe to stay in the country."

"Camilla found out I lied. She's coming home early."

Mickie whistles. "You think *Stone's* dangerous? You're *really* dead now."

Ten minutes later Voort's friend at City Island calls back to say the numbers Voort gave him do not belong to parts on the *Candace*.

"They belong to a different Orsid-57, built the same year as the *Candace,* and sold out of North Carolina last month. So where's the real *Candace,* huh?"

FOURTEEN

Seven thirty-five A.M., and all over the city, the metropolis begins squeezing. A minor slipup yesterday explodes into something worse today. New York has had three hundred years to evolve its forms of unforgiveness. Screw up for a second and pay the price for years.

An out-of-work executive finds himself trapped in a stalled F train, having failed to give himself an extra fifteen minutes to reach a crucial job interview, because he'd stayed in bed making love to his wife. Now he will lose the chance at the job, lose his apartment, and six months from now his wife will take the bed with her when she leaves.

A Little Neck author drives toward Manhattan for breakfast with her editor at Rockefeller Center, having put off a six-month check on her Honda yesterday. Seeing taillights ahead, she slams on the brakes. The pedal drops to the floor. Her scream is drowned out by the crash.

Above Central Park West, EMS attendants carry a body under a tarp from a three-thousand-square-foot penthouse. At midnight last night, the teenage boy who'd lived here had reached for a hypodermic, thinking, one last shot, then I'll quit.

And on the East Side of Manhattan, retribution takes the form of Leon Bok, standing in the parking lot of Ted Stone's marina, watching as a hundred yards ahead, on the river, fog lifts momentarily and cooperatively to reveal a police launch chugging away from the docks. On board is the detective Leon's been following, Mickie Connor, and also the one whom Stone called to rant about again a half-hour ago.

Bok's lips twitch.

Frank Heffner my ass. Connor is Voort's partner.

Bok pulls out his STU-11 encrypted cell phone and punches in the *Wanderer*. Local cops are amazing, he thinks. They switch cars and think that they've turned into Houdinis, that they're brilliant tricksters instead of Keystone clowns.

"We found the bow," says the man who answers. "It's the *Candace*, all right."

"The police are coming back."

"With divers or not?"

"Assume yes," Leon says, his words routed into the encryption chip to be scrambled and garbled. Phones are weapons, and the modern warrior must master electronics. Bok's words are protected by the finest U.S. military technology, provided by a friendly Afghan warlord using it to protect investments in the U.S.

Bok's man says, "Do we keep diving?"

"Why not?"

"We'll need a few hours to finish the perimeter."

"They'll never go down."

Bok remembering the ease with which he'd found Mickie Connor. Seeing himself back at "Frank Heffner's" apartment, learning from neighbors that Heffner the "longtime resident" had actually just moved in. Waiting for Heffner's backup. Taking down the license of Mickie's battered Chevy. Learning from Singh that the car had been seized by police in a drug bust last month.

Then I followed you home to Long Island, Mick.

Hanging up, Bok uses a disposable cell phone to punch in another local phone number, which he'd memorized even before starting the search for the *Candace*.

"Chance favors the prepared mind," an old UN peacekeeper instructor had used to say.

"U.S. Coast Guard. Seaman Kirby."

Going mideastern, Bok starts out softly. "America will pay for what you did to my family."

A pause. "Who is this?"

"You think you are rich and protected. The blessed mullah said, the punishment must fit the offense. Well, the punishment will happen today."

"May I have your name, sir?" Seaman Kirby asks, as if politeness will stop terror. Bok envisions tracking equipment—computers, satellites, frequency finders—showing the call coming from the East Side. Big deal.

"The bridge of the infidel will crumble into the Narrows," he says.

"The Bridge? The Verrazano *Bridge*?"

"The howl of explosion is the rage of God. Your spans will be destroyed like the walls of Jerusalem. Your mothers will weep at the Verrazano, as mine cried at home."

Click.

Bok hums Bach, walking toward his car, imagining the warnings exploding out across the metropolis. Not even a .22 bullet is strapped to that bridge. But it will take authorities half a day to confirm it, and every police diver in the city will be called to help.

Bok uses STU-11 number two to call Ted Stone's protected "partner-up" set. The phones talk only to each other, so no one can listen in. Stone picks up midway through the second ring.

"Talk to me," he barks in that hard way he has of giving orders. Bok forgives him. Stone's just scared.

Stone sputters, "Divers?" after Bok is done.

"You're the one who told me, no fishing," says Bok, using code words as a precaution because someday even wizardlike STU-11 encryption will become obsolete. His point is, if Voort had died earlier, there would be no problem now. But words like "kill" you avoid on phones.

Stone quiets down.

Bok goes on to suggest that although things seem under control, it might be wise for Stone to consider "visiting the museum," which produces a gasp of horror on the other end. Bok's just urged a cleaning out of Stone's U.S. accounts and the leasing of a private jet, at least until Bok is sure things are safe in New York.

"But if the boat's clean," Stone says, silence conveying the rest of his thought: There's no proof.

Bok sighs. All the technology in the world can't overcome destructive decisions. The more intelligent people are, he thinks, the more easily they fool themselves. He says, "France is beautiful. Costa Rica is terrific, and the dollar still goes far there. No extradition."

"But I don't want to go to the museum." Stone's like a stubborn kid.

Bok stays patient. You babysit the rich and powerful in special ways. He says, "I don't know what Voort's learned. I don't know who he's *told*. It's not just a question of him finding proof now, but later. He won't stop coming. His kind doesn't stop."

"What is he, some kind of nut?"

Stone sounds hurt and surprised, and the voice takes Bok back to his UN days in Africa, to evacuating men and women who had run countries, controlled armies. Powerful people stripped of influence, stunned and huddled in trucks. They'd never really believed the good times could end.

Did Stone really think that his system would last forever? Presidents hole up in palaces while crowds surge toward the gates. CEOs sink putts while investigators with warrants drive onto the country-club grounds.

"My job is to keep you safe," says Bok.

"I appreciate that." A pause. Stone's collecting himself. Thinking. "You're saying, I see, that the detective outsmarted you."

Which pisses Bok off. "Look, if you want to stay, we have to know *exactly* what he knows, who *else* knows, and what leads they have. Otherwise you're at risk."

"I shouldn't have stopped you earlier," Stone says. "It's just that I had faith in you."

Twisting the knife. Like it's Bok's fault that Voort came back.

"I have a responsibility to you," Bok says.

"Leon, you're not a father. A child adores a father. I look at Candace and know I'd never be able to explain it to her. I'll *make* arrangements. I'll be ready to go. But if there's no proof, nothing conclusive, I can weather it. Just take care of proof."

Bok sighs, realizing that Stone must have some new

connection even *he* doesn't know about, something Stone's reluctant to use except as a last resort. Something truly influential that can shut down the police.

"All right, but this time, I'll do whatever it takes," Bok says. "And you have to be ready to leave quickly."

"Whatever it takes," Stone agrees.

Bok makes one last call, to his two-man backup team in a motel near the airport. Fate smiles on preparation, which means always bring reinforcements. By happy coincidence, they're close to where he needs them. He explains where to take up position, what to do.

Alone in his car, driving toward the airport, it occurs to Bok—as he allows himself a rare excursion into philosophy—that Voort and Stone have the same problem.

They created their own difficulties.

Bok turns thought to *his* difficulties, at the airport.

Before combat, always scout terrain.

The air is the same gray color as the water. The police launch bobs, guided by instrument, not sight. Voort watches the wipers slashing. He hears the chatter of harbor radio traffic. He has lost sight of Manhattan. He might as well be moving with his eyes closed.

"I've never seen fog this bad," says Sergeant Egee, Mickie's buddy and captain of the three-man patrol boat. He's got a thick waist and a narrow chest and he wears round, wire-rimmed glasses which he keeps wiping.

Voort's palms are wet. A police tug will rendezvous with the patrol at the *Wanderer*, carrying divers.

"There's the boat, Sarge," a crew guy says.

Voort sees the smallest orange dot on the radar screen. Then comes the glow of the diver's marker light, which the launch makes a long, slow arc to avoid. He feels the engines slacken. The fog is white smoke, as if the water is burning. The bow of the *Wanderer* nods like the head of an overly cooperative suspect as the launch pulls abreast. Only a single man is on deck. So the divers are down.

They're stuck here. Chip Lovant said if they find something and leave it, it might move before they come back.

The man on deck wears a fog-wet yellow slicker, hood up. Voort wishes he could see the face better, especially the eyes. Would they match the eyes he saw peering from a balaclava? Would he even know if they did? He has an urge to yank off his wig, be Voort, see if the guy frightens. He'd like to check out the knuckles. Voort never saw details on the tattoo he'd spotted, but the placement should be enough.

"Forget something, mate?" comes over the slap of water. It's a cheery voice, Aussie, as cooperative as any pimp, drug dealer, or murderer in the first moments of contact, when they think they have a chance of fooling police. Voort doesn't recognize the voice. The launch rides slightly higher than the *Wanderer*, so he sees that for all the time these divers have spent here, they've brought up nothing of size.

Mickie said cops had searched the *Wanderer* earlier. So odds are there's nothing hidden on the boat.

Voort murmurs to himself, "What if they're not recovering anything, just destroying it down there."

"I'm glad you're here, mate," the man says. "Two boats, two pairs of lights. Less chance of getting rammed."

If you're scared of an accident, why stay out?

The guy says, "You wouldn't have coffee, would you?"

Voort's anger is a living thing, sharpening his perception, making every bead of moisture stand out. He starts to step off the launch onto the *Wanderer*, but he feels a hand on his shoulder pulling him back.

"Gotta go," Egee says, looking excited, revving the engines hard.

"But we just got here."

"Move it! Move it! Come on!"

The Aussie watching, hands in his slicker, head cocked like a dog trying to figure out some nutty human act. First the cops are boarding him. Suddenly they're leaving.

Egee ordering, "Cast off!" Pushing the throttle up so they surge forward. Everything happening very fast.

"What are you *doing?*" Voort cries as the launch swings south toward lower Manhattan, and fog swallows the *Wanderer*.

"Bomb alert. Help me watch out," Egee snaps, meaning, *for boats.* "It's at the Verrazano Bridge."

Mickie clasps Egee's shoulder sympathetically. Voort remembers him saying once that Egee lost a sister in the World Trade Center attack.

"Drop us off first, Egee."

Egee shakes his head, peering ahead like an airplane pilot flying through fog before radar was invented.

"Afterwards," he says, jaw out. "No time now."

He's going too fast, speeding to put the launch in a prearranged position. Since the terrorism started every cop in the city has participated in one form or another in training. Voort and Mickie have practiced evacuating schools, rushing into smoke-filled subway tunnels, assaulting City Hall, Cornell Hospital, George Washington Bridge, or any of dozens of other ultimately unprotectable public targets—barring the creation of a police state—that the authorities have designated as deserving special defensive attention.

Voort has to raise his voice over the engine. Even the machines on the boat seem heated up.

"It'll just take a minute to drop us on shore, Egee."

"Can't."

"It's an emergency," Voort says, each moment taking him farther from Kennedy Airport, lengthening whatever trip will be required to reach the terminal before Camilla lands.

Sixty-four minutes from now.

"It's life-and-death," Voort says.

"Whose life?" Egee says.

"My fiancée," Voort begins, but it's the worst possible way to start the explanation. Egee snaps, "Forget it," clearly thinking *domestic problems,* as he swings starboard to avoid an oncoming tug. Over the radio Voort hears snatches of lockdown preparations. The bridge is being sealed. Anchored ships are being ordered to move, and inbound ocean traffic is being halted.

"Maybe they'll reroute planes too," Mickie says.

Voort locks eyes with his partner. *You're* his friend, Voort's look says. Get us ashore.

Mickie tries, "Egee . . ."

"No."

"Egee, it's not personal like you think."

"I can't see anything in this fog," Egee says, peering ahead. "This is worse than London."

"She was threatened," Mickie says. "Whoever did it will be at the airport. It's just as bad if you get killed at the airport as with a bomb. It's not personal. Okay?"

Voort stares down at the turgid waves. He has no idea in which direction lies land. He imagines himself jumping in. He imagines the tide sweeping him in bad directions. He imagines the boat circling, cutting short its mission but not letting him swim away. He wants to scream.

The waves get larger and the boat lurches sideways. Egee cuts the wheel, bulls through crests. From the way sound has opened up, and echoes have changed pitch, Voort imagines they've reached the end of Manhattan and chugged into more open water. They're near the big-ship channels, coming up on the Verrazano Bridge.

Ships shouldn't be moving here, not during an alert.

The radio instructs Egee to take up position off the bridge on the Brooklyn side.

"Forty-eight minutes," Voort says.

Egee snaps, "Why'd you come with us in the first place if you had so little time?"

Voort calls American Airlines. "Is flight twenty-three still due in at nine thirty?"

"It's just a little late. Nine forty-five now," the voice replies, probably expecting Voort to complain. But he's been given the smallest bit of breathing space.

He calculates quickly. If the agent is right, Camilla won't walk out of the protected customs area into the main terminal until ten or ten fifteen, which gives Voort just over an hour to get ashore, find a road, *and* a vehicle, and reach the customs area exit—provided the highway's not clogged.

Or is Bok inside the protected area?

He tries to phone Eva to get another detective assigned to the airport, but the chief is not reachable during the alert.

He tries Lieutenant Santini, who is unreachable too. Extra personnel are all headed to Brooklyn, apparently.

"One fucking phone call shuts down the biggest city in the world," Mickie says. "You don't have to *do* anything to screw us up, just make calls."

"Look," Egee relents, slightly more sympathetic as they close on the Narrows. "I'll put you ashore by the bridge, on the Brooklyn side. There'll be cops all over. Get a ride."

Fifty-one minutes.

Forty-six . . .

Stone wins. Whatever was on the wreck will be gone. Even if we find the boat later, what's the charge? Not reporting a sinking? I don't know if that's even a crime.

The fog thins for a moment, and Voort finds himself gazing at the mammoth span of a ghost bridge, emptied of traffic. He hears the growl of other launches nearby. He catches a glimpse of the police tug ferrying divers, who line the railing. Every cop diver in the city will be checking buttresses, groping in darkness, shining flashlights underwater, praying the alert is phony and that unlike their predecessors, who died on 9/11, they will reach home today.

He knows Egee is right. You don't waste time in an alert dropping off a cop.

Please God, protect Camilla, the divers, the city. Get me off this boat. If something happens to her I'll never forgive myself.

The boat bumps land suddenly, against rocks.

"Good luck," Egee calls.

Voort and Mickie jump onto solid ground, scramble onto wet grass. The earth seems to be moving. All around are sirens and engines, and Voort sees red and blue pulsating lights through fog. The air is alive with men and women issuing directions. Equipment flaps as cops run. Radios squawk. Hurrying, Voort imagines the park sloping up from the river. He passes the immense base of a Brooklyn-side buttress, rising up like the leg of a dinosaur.

He has no idea as to the size of this park, or how far away the road is, but badges out, he and Mickie stumble past dozens of helmeted police and vested bomb-squad people, all heading in the opposite direction.

By Voort's estimation, it should normally take a speeding police car only fifteen to twenty minutes to reach Kennedy Airport from this part of Brooklyn, but poor driving conditions could double that, even if roads are clear.

Recriminations close in on him. If he hadn't lied, she wouldn't be coming. If he'd listened to the family, no one else would be in danger. The men who had attacked him are probably at the airport already.

The words of Dorothea Quinones are no comfort under the circumstances: *Whatever you're planning, do it for the people they'll hurt if you don't.*

"Yo! Cars!" Mickie says, pointing straight ahead like Columbus's lookout spotting land.

They stumble over a curb and into a parking area assembly/staging spot, filled with department buses, squad cars, chief cars, TV vans, mayor's office cars.

I only need one.

Squads of Blue Guys stand around doing nothing, with tense expressions on their faces. That's how you tell the difference between a drill and an alert. Everyone's posted in the same places but nobody looks relaxed.

Searching for a familiar face, Voort removes all vestiges of "Frank Heffner." There has to be someone here who he knows, and no cop will simply hand over car keys to a stranger. There will be roadblocks at the park entrance, so simply driving off with someone's car—if they were dumb enough to leave a key in it—will get him stopped before he even gets out of the parking lot.

"Lieutenant! Lieutenant Pegorari!"

Ahead, Voort's old lieutenant is issuing instructions to a knot of scared-looking Blue Guys wearing riot gear. Pegorari's a squat, bulky, monosyllabic weight lifter whose body swells against his raincoat. His thighs are so muscular that his trouser legs rub each other when he walks. Blue Guys call Pegorari "Steroids." But Voort's always found him approachable and smart.

"What?" Pegorari says flatly as Voort comes up. Not "hi." Not "What are you doing here?" Just, "What?"

Voort tells Pegorari that his car's broken down. He and Mickie need to get to the airport, quickly.

"Why?"

Remembering Egee's reaction to the word "fiancée," Voort says there are "more problems" at the airport. Let the lieutenant assume they relate to the alert.

Without hesitation, Pegorari orders a Blue Guy, "Drive him." He asks Voort, "You need to keep him?"

"Maybe."

"Let me know where you are," "Steroids" tells the Blue Guy, who seems pissed off he's being sent away.

Twenty minutes, Voort thinks, until Camilla lands. At least we have a ride.

The driver knows the streets, flicks the dome light on, and the siren, but in the fog they can't build up speed on the Belt Parkway, Brooklyn's southernmost highway looping along Jamaica Bay, and a potholed car-killer even when the sun is out. From snatches of radio traffic, Voort gathers that the alert is spreading. A panel truck has been stopped at the Whitestone Bridge's tollbooth area in the Bronx. Two Arabic-looking men are being questioned, the truck searched.

"Can't you go faster?" Voort says.

"I wouldn't advise it," Mickie says.

The Blue Guy seems the least impressed of the three of them over their mission, or the alert. "I hear they're going to lay cops off to pay for these alerts," he says. "If I was a terrorist, I'd stay home and make phone calls. What's supposed to be happening at the airport, anyway?"

"Threats," says Voort.

"Shit. An accident," says Mickie.

Ahead, brake lights glow across all lanes. Traffic has stopped. Voort can't see how far the jam extends because half a dozen cars ahead, everything disappears.

The driver swings right, into the breakdown lane, passing cars slowly, edging along Jamaica Bay swamp. But within a quarter-mile the breakdown lane clogs with civilian cars and halts.

There's nowhere for them to get out of the way. If they move any more to the right, they'll sink into the swamp.

Siren wailing, they inch forward two feet. Five feet. Voort prays, *Let this clear up fast.*

They jerk ahead twenty whole feet. It's not exactly the speed Henry Ford had in mind when he dreamed of cars.

"This is slower than chasing O.J.," Mickie says.

Voort tries to call Cousin Ellis of the Port Authority police, at Newark Airport. Maybe Ellis can phone Kennedy and have someone meet Camilla's plane. But Ellis hasn't arrived for work, it turns out. Ellis is stuck in traffic, slowed by rerouting due to the alert at the Verrazano Bridge.

"How come there's nothing about any emergency at Kennedy Airport on the radio?" the driver asks.

"It's a secret," Mickie says. "Go around that Jeep."

With six minutes to go until she lands, the swamp ends and the blue-and-white—siren screaming—bullies cars out of the breakdown lane. A quarter-mile later they break free of the accident—which turns out to be on the other side of the road.

"Gapers," Mickie says. "Shoot 'em all."

Voort calls American Airlines again. The agent tells him, "The flight is landing just about now. I recognize your voice. Didn't you call a few minutes ago?"

"I bet Camilla gets held up at luggage," Mickie says. "Last year when I got back from Chicago it took fifty minutes before my suitcase came out."

"Wait a minute," the driver says as if he's suspected for a while that something is odd about this trip. "You're *meeting* somebody?"

"Government official," says Mickie.

"What official?" says the Blue Guy.

"Are you a reporter or a cop?" says Voort.

"A chauffeur, I think."

"Then act like one. Drive," Mickie snaps.

Voort tries to call Camilla's phone. No answer.

The Van Wyck Expressway takes them past a maze of perpetual construction for the airport's alleged improvements. The monorail that falls off its track on curves. The billion-dollar rapid-rail system that dumps passengers in the middle of Queens, bypassing the heart of New York. Jockeying for position, cabs fall in behind the squad car, their drivers making better time by closely following police.

Voort watches signs pass on the airport access road. Terminal Two for Delta Airlines. Terminal Eight for Finnair.

How much damage can Bok do in an airport, a public place?

Still no answer on Camilla's phone.

Overhead, a plane thunders toward a runway.

Camilla's been down for eight minutes. But she has that gigantic suitcase. Mickie's right. All her luggage can't come out right away.

The Blue Guy sneers, "We picking up your kids too? Or just the girlfriend or wife?"

As the car pulls up Voort yanks the door open and plunges into the mass of people crowding temporary walkways outside the International Arrivals terminal.

Mickie the backup gives it another half-second. He tells the driver, "You think he'd take you off a bomb alert to pick up his girlfriend? What does that say about you, you piece of shit."

He follows Voort into the crowd, trying to keep his eye on his best friend. Voort slips out of sight, then reappears. Mickie hurries faster, watching the bobbing head.

Voort, terrified, is thinking, *No place is as solitary as a public place.*

The very layout pushes strangers together. Between construction and security barriers the area outside the terminal is packed. A temporary pedestrian walk is squeezed between the short-term parking pavilion and incoming lanes filled with honking cars, rental-agency vans, and long-term-parking-lot buses. Thousands of travelers concentrate on nothing more than getting to a gate. A million walking cocoons out here, aware of each other as obstacles, nothing more.

Pushing, Voort spots a flash of blonde hair *and Camilla is coming out of the terminal, rolling her suitcase and arguing with a tall man in a jeans jacket.*

It's not Camilla.

He follows a dozen giggling teenage girls—high school athletes carrying large gym bags—into the terminal, which is as crowded as Grand Central Station at rush hour. Camilla is coming out of the women's bathroom. No, she's hugging a little girl by a stroller. No, she's talking with a stewardess by the Avis counter.

Announcements echo. A woman is crying, "Don't leave me." Scanning the big board, Voort sees that flight 23 from Buenos Aires arrived at gate 9, ten minutes ago. Camilla could still be on the plane, or at the baggage area, or anywhere in between.

What if Bok was at the gate? What if he and his men have airport ID?

Panic is the mind-killer, Dad used to say.

Pushing, badge out, Voort says loudly, "Police. Police. Get out of the way." Loudspeakers boom. Two soldiers on anti-terrorism duty stand ahead, holding M-1s, turning toward Voort, the disturbance. They're nervous, untested, eyeing the agitated stranger coming toward them. They'll be keyed up because of the Verrazano alert.

Use them.

Flashing ID, he explains there's been a threat against an incoming passenger, and one of the soldiers gets on a radio and passes along Camilla's description: blonde, tall, pulling a black roll-a-bag and carrying a fifty-pound knapsack. Or probably a porter has the knapsack. Voort asks the soldiers to have the security office page Camilla.

"Terrorists?" the specialist says.

"Death threat," Voort says.

"Go with him, Joe," Specialist One tells Specialist Two.

Then Voort's running, knowing that he went too far with Stone and Bok. He should have listened to the family, should have left those two alone. He shouldn't have dragged others into this mess with him.

Should have means too late, Dad used to say.

Push the fat guy out of the way. Ignore the angry cry behind. Run as the curious stare and the timid just get out of the way.

Paging Camilla Ryan, paging Buenos Aires incoming passenger Camilla Ryan. Please go to the security office on the main floor.

A white arrow points toward the customs area. The hall widens into a concourse packed with travelers' relatives and friends waiting for passengers to emerge from behind sliding doors. Voort pushes to the front. The security guys won't let him into customs, even with the soldier along. Anyone could flash a badge, they say. If she's inside, she's safe. Try to push in and we'll take you away.

He cranes to see into the customs area each time the doors slide open. There seems to be a million arriving passengers on lines in there.

Camilla Ryan, identify yourself to a security officer.

If they're still paging her, she hasn't responded. Or can't.

Voort thinking in despair, *I don't even know what Bok looks like. I wouldn't know if he was standing next to me. I have no idea what his men look like. I wouldn't even hear his damn voice if he was three feet away.*

God, do whatever you want to me, but keep her safe.

A flash of recognizable color-combo—blonde hair over pale-white travel coat—draws his eyes to a figure coming through the sliding doors amid a group of men in colorful dashikis. Voort's heart starts to pound. It's her, he thinks with joy. Camilla stomps into the concourse with that clip-clip, New York–babe, pissed-off, I'm-going-to-kill-you stride.

Voort waving his arms, not caring that he's a target. She doesn't see him. Voort and the soldier shoving toward her.

Now starts the most vulnerable time.

Someone rams Voort from behind.

"Sorry," says a heavy, Mideastern-looking guy in a leather jacket.

Voort turns back toward Camilla and *she's gone*, but then he sees her again. There are too many faces here to watch them all for intent. Other people push in the same direction. They're meeting arriving passengers too.

Camilla spots him but doesn't smile. Despite his fear, she looks terrific.

Soldier protector or not, Voort thinks, I need to get her out of here fast.

Something smashes into the back of his legs. A luggage cart.

"Watch where you're going," barks a model he recognizes from Camilla's Victoria's Secret catalogue.

He's got her. He takes Camilla's arm, which is stiff, resistant. The Sig's in his waist holster and she's looking at him like *aren't you going to help me with my baggage?* He wants to laugh. But he needs both hands free.

"You," she says, ignoring the soldier, "lied."

The soldier looks confused.

"We'll talk in the cab," says Voort.

"No. *You'll* talk." She pulls her arm away. Women.

"They're calling me back," the soldier says. And leaves.

When you're protecting the mayor, or president, trained professionals help you. Blue Guys hold crowds back. Secret Service guys line the route with receivers in their ears. Police snipers lie on balconies. Helicopters fly overhead. Every foot of your path has been inspected for ambush areas, and even apartments you pass have been cleared of residents.

Now just the fifty feet between Voort and the door contains a moving mass of strangers who have not been frisked for weapons, since they never intended to travel. The newspaper kiosk shields shadows behind it. A figure stands smoking beside a Coke machine. A woman reads an open newspaper. A man who seems to be a limo driver holds a sign reading ERIC HOFFER, but he's staring at Camilla. Lots of men stare at Camilla. And then there's the guy reaching into a ski bag. Ski bag? In September?

Voort sees ski tips poking out.

When they get outside, the fog is worse. The service road between the terminal and short-term-parking pavilion echoes with horns, brakes, traffic-brownie walkie-talkies. The badge is magic. It clears the way as he breaks into the front of the cab line.

Standard security wisdom: Don't put a target on a line in plain sight.

"Hey, that's my taxi!"

Someone grabs Voort and he spins as the guy backs up, staring in fear at his face. It's a businessman type holding an attaché case out like a shield. "I didn't realize you were a policeman," he says.

Camilla hisses, "You're acting crazy."

"Manhattan," Voort tells the driver when they get inside the cab. "Move."

Bok couldn't have known I'd take this taxi.

He turns in his seat, eyes the couple getting into the next cab in line. Only then does his breathing slow, but the question is, where to take her?

He tells her as his cell phone starts chirping, "I can explain things." But he won't really. He'll figure out another lie. He simply could not stand for anyone to find out what he'd learned of himself in the Mobil station.

"Mickie? Meet us at the marina. We'll get the cars," he says, clicking on.

Bok's voice answers over Mickie's line.

"No, not the marina. And Mickie doesn't need a car."

FIFTEEN

"No one ever watches the backup man," Bok says sympa
thetically. "Don't feel badly. It's not just you."

The mere sound of the voice transports Voort, brings
back the terrible sense of helplessness. It seems for a moment that he even feels the warm brush of breath in his
ear. Bok might as well have planted a hypnotic suggestion
back at the Mobil station: When I show up, when you hear
me, you will cease to think, analyze, function.

Bok, master of domination, of control.

"Leon," whispers Voort, struggling for any advantage.
The knowledge of the name is his only edge.

"Oh, that's not my real name. People just call me that.
But use it if you want."

"What is your name?"

"How about . . . Frank Heffner?"

Voort's airport victory has turned to ashes. The taste
of failure is like dirty copper in his mouth. The consequences of poor assumptions stretch before him, a long
and private penitentiary sentence.

"A trade, that's what I want," Bok is saying.

"For?"

"Files. Information. Silence. In exchange, your best
friend's health, and safety for your loved ones, who you've
chosen to jeopardize up until now."

Voort's throat muscles work the wrong way, blocking off his breathing instead of letting in air. He flashes in a millisecond of déjà vu—more impression than concrete memory—to last summer's Colorado kayaking trip with Camilla. Dumped in a whirlpool, he'd been so awed by its power that he'd surrendered to it at first, simply watched himself swept in circles. But then he'd kicked out, broken surface, gasping.

"I want to talk to Mickie," he gets out.

"A sensible decision for a change."

"You better not hurt him." Even to Voort, his words sound pathetic.

"Who knows better than *you* what we can do," says Bok.

"Put him on."

Horrified, Camilla mouths, "Who *is* it?"

On the cabby's Urdu radio talk show, Voort hears the English phrase "nine-eleven." The ancient language has no term for the kind of modern vulnerability these words imply.

"Some backup man," Mickie's voice says over the staticky line, trying for lightness and failing. "I never saw them coming."

It's a hurt Mickie, breathing jaggedly and emitting rattling noises. Voort feels as if a piece of glass has been inserted into his belly. He imagines broken cartilage. Then more images flood in. Bok burned Cal Quinones's genitals. He killed the Mcgreevey brothers.

"Mick, nobody would have spotted them in that crowd," Voort says.

"This just isn't my month, Conrad. United Tech went down. United Assholes showed up."

Then Mickie is gone and Voort's helplessness hardens into hatred. *If Bok is calling he must need something. Find it*, Voort tells himself. Figure it out and use it if you can. That is Mickie's chance.

"Coupla weeks, he'll be all right," Bok says. "He's tough."

"I'll kill you," Voort says. Actually, he's starting to think.

Bok seems amused. "Well, that's what you want, isn't it? I love that New York expression, 'Want a piece of me?' Or would you rather hang up, Voort? Nobody's forcing you to talk."

He doesn't hang up. Bok speaks into his soul so directly that Voort wonders, did he read my detective psych evaluation? My fitness reports? Did he see any of the dozen articles on New York's richest cops, best buddies and how Mickie saved my life? Or does he just sense the bond?

Bok says, "You had a chance for safety and didn't take it. So safety's not the point with you, my friend."

"Find the *Candace* yet?" Voort asks.

"Tell your driver his left brake light just went out. He doesn't want a ticket. He wouldn't want to tangle with the NYPD."

Voort squints back into the fog but all he sees are sloshing wipers, misty windshields.

"Oh, it's not me behind you," Bok remarks. "Just a friend."

Voort tries to make out cars with only one occupant.

"Did I say one friend? Maybe it's two."

Each word calculated to drive home the feeling of

helplessness. But Voort's not tied down this time, and he senses through his fear that something is off. *Bok is pushing too hard. There's no need.* And with that comes the realization that there's something wrong with Bok's whole attack.

Why didn't he snatch me at the airport, along with Mickie? He'd have both of us then.

Voort sees it now. Bok must have tried!

He missed me. He's human. Something went wrong.

"You've decided to trade, I take it," remarks Bok.

"I'm listening."

Voort going back, trying to reconstruct the scene at the airport. A slight twinge of hope has started up inside. He sees himself rushing from the squad car into the terminal. He adds Bok's men—faceless figures—converging on Mickie the backup man first.

"This is what you will do," Bok is saying.

Voort adds a gun or hypo pressed into Mick's side. The whispered threat. Safety is an illusion in a crowd. How many times has Voort worked professional hits carried out in restaurants, on streets, once even in Yankee Stadium? Witnesses disagreed about descriptions. Anonymous hit men flew home. Crowds obliterated footprints, evidence.

"Tell your driver to pull off at the next turnoff," says Bok.

Voort imagines Bok's men steering Mickie toward a car or parking area. Killing him in the crowd would have caused screaming, and alerted Voort.

"It's not an exit, just a small breakdown area, two miles ahead," Bok says.

Voort presses into the past, sees Bok's team number two closing in on him, the perfect unprotected target as he runs to find Camilla.

The soldiers! I got help from soldiers.

Bok saying, "Camilla will continue on. You'll get into our car."

"You missed me at the airport," Voort interrupts.

A pause. "The only sure thing about luck," Bok says smoothly, "is that it changes."

He's angry, not as confident as he sounds.

"Let's concentrate on the present," says Bok.

Outside the cab the world is white and indistinct, making home, love, family, far away. Ghost cars float alongside Voort, their headlights shining vacantly, illuminating less on this foggy day than on a normal night.

Camilla presses against him, mouthing, "What's wrong?" But she's heard enough to know that something awful has happened to Mickie. She is white with fear.

Voort says, "I just get in? You call that a trade?"

"Camilla goes free. *That's* the trade. You'll talk to Mickie by phone every few minutes, check on the poor man's condition. You'll run some errands with a friend of mine along to observe. He'll tell you where to go after you're in the car."

So I can't call ahead for help.

Bok coming on smooth, fast, trying to correct his error before Voort can use it. Voort sweating, needing to keep the conversation going, anticipating what Bok wants him to do. "So I take him to One Police Plaza and he makes sure I don't talk to anyone. I take him home and gather up what you need and then go to meet you too."

"Tell your fellow officers he's a friend."

"That's my big chance?"

"That's *Mickie's* chance. Camilla's chance."

"I'm not getting in any car without guarantees," Voort snaps. His back is soaked. He prays that whatever happens to Mickie next won't be as bad as he fears. The turnoff will be coming up in less than a minute.

"I'm sorry you feel that way," Bok says.

Mickie's scream erupts from the cell phone, tinny and laced with static. Voort squeezes his eyes shut. He can't stand it. He can't not listen. The cry seems to go on, to fill the car. It's incredible that the cabby is sitting calmly up front, humming along with a commercial jingle.

The scream subsides into gagging.

Bok repeats, "Tell your driver to turn off."

Shaking, Voort fights off the urge to agree, knowing once he steps into Bok's car, it's over for all three of them. Bok will never let Camilla leave. *Even murderers try to bargain. Bok will expect it and I need time to think.*

Mickie, forgive me for what I'm about to do.

Make your voice hard. Push back.

"I'm selfish, you said. I want a shot, a real shot. So offer one."

Voort hears the sort of buzzing over the line that an electric shaver makes, or small drill. He must not imagine more. He must concentrate on Bok. He gets a flash memory of Mickie at the academy, baby-faced, in that gray plebe uniform. Mickie grinning. Then the pain sounds start again. This time the muffled cry rises and undulates and trails into, "Gaaaa. . . ."

Voort's shirt is drenched.

Demand something meaningless, something small. If you get it, you're negotiating.

"I want guarantees for my family, Mickie, Camilla. For later," Voort says as if he believes Bok will honor them. Bok won't, of course.

Bok sighs. He'll be giving away nothing if he agrees. He says solemnly, "All right. You have my guarantee."

Camilla mouthing, "What's he saying?"

Bok starts in again about the switch, except now that they've passed the turnoff, it will occur at the exit ramp before the Triborough Bridge, a few miles ahead. Voort thinking, *Everyone has a weakness. How can I figure out Bok's? What do I know about him? He knows he's smarter than me. He knows I could never beat him.*

Vanity.

"If you hurt them . . ." he says, trailing off, to make Bok think he's more pliant now that the guarantee softened him up.

"You're responsible for that. Not me," says Bok.

Great, Voort thinks. It's guns, a professional hit team, and Mickie against vanity. That and Bok's need for something from me. Otherwise Mick would be dead now.

He says, slowly, "Why don't we meet at a different place, somewhere more public. *You* bring Mickie and I . . ."

The terrible gagging sounds cut him off. Afterward Bok says wearily, "You're not listening."

I can't take any more of this.

It's obvious that a cooperative Voort makes Bok feel stronger, so Voort goes back to acting hard, fed up.

"*You* listen. If you're going to kill him do it now. I'm not getting into any goddamn car."

On the radio, an ad for Alka-Seltzer has come on.

Bok says, when Voort's done ranting, "You and me?" He sounds amused. "What is this? *High Noon?*"

"I want a real chance for Mickie and me."

Voort drives at the vanity, tries to sound obsessed, pushes unusable fear into some faraway box. "I heard about your reputation, Leon. Never misses. Never disappoints. Never screws up in airports. You're not invincible, just a guy with a scary voice. You need help even when you hit from behind."

"You're hurting my feelings." Bok still sounds amused.

"I think about you all the time. Three of you, and you *still* needed a dart. You needed to drug me."

Camilla staring.

Bok sighing patiently. Like, let the cop rant and let off steam. Then we'll get back to business.

"What's the matter?" Voort says. "Afraid if you don't have your friends along I'll take you?"

"Oh my, you've figured me out. Or maybe you want us to finish what we started in the bathroom, Conrad."

Voort prays Bok is thinking, is the cop this crazy? Could I stand to fail if we just hang up?

"You've got Mickie, which means I *have* to show up. We both do. Give me back what you took. Otherwise, the bottom line is, I'm not doing what you want. Tell Stone you fucked up. Hey, everybody does," Voort says softly, sympathetically, in a flash of vituperative inspiration, throwing Bok's opener back in his face. "Don't feel badly, Leon. It's not just you."

"How do I know you won't bring the rest?" Bok says. Meaning, police, FBI.

"Because so far you knew everything I did. You knew what happens in the department. You knew I'm back. You'd work it so your crew would spot anyone I brought."

I can't arrest Stone, or hold him for questioning. I can't even talk to him alone if he doesn't want it. There's no evidence linking Stone or Bok with any crime at all.

Voort says, "Mainly, I don't want someone else getting you. I want it to be me."

Make him think I'm damaged enough, wild enough with rage to try.

"Uncle Vim," says Bok softly. "Cousin Matt. Blonde Camilla." The cab starts up the long, buckled ramp of the Triborough Bridge. "All those relatives."

He's not agreeing. But he's weakening. Voort has maneuvered Bok's men into Manhattan now.

"You pick the place," Voort says. "Tell me what you want. Better, *I'll* tell you so you'll know I have it. You want my notes on the *Candace*. You want my leads on Stone and the UN. You want the whole case. You need to talk to me in person or you'll never be sure you got the whole thing."

Saying "talk to" instead of "torture" or "beat" or "burn."

A pause. "Go on."

"I want your word that you won't hurt Mickie more. I want your word that if I take you, your crew lets us both go. Everyone goes home except you."

"You'd believe me?"

Convince him you'll come.

"This part's about honor," Voort says, hoping the video was right and he's addressing some idiotic personal code in Bok, some self-deceptive image this man has of himself. If so, the appeal might protect Mickie a while longer, especially if nothing is at stake for Bok. Voort has seen it work with gang members, hit men, child molesters. Most people, even psychopaths, have a code under which they operate. A need to fool themselves when they do certain things.

"All right," says Bok. Even if he doesn't mean it, he'll more readily accept that Voort is on the level now.

God forgive me for what I'm about to do.

"I need two hours to get the material," says Voort.

"Ninety minutes."

"Where do you want to meet?"

Bok emits a low chuckle. "I'll call you and tell you where to go. And Voort? If we see people coming with you, or hear inside the department . . ."

"We've been through this part."

"Even a *traffic* copter, a tourist bus, a milk truck, a woman wheeling a stroller. We're gone."

"I said, this is about honor."

The cab leaves the Triborough Bridge to wind onto FDR Drive southbound, the direction of Stone's marina, the offices of the FBI, and thousands in the police department whom Voort knows he cannot call.

Bok says, "My guys will stay behind you."

"If they can keep up, sure," says Voort. "Why not tell me which car they're in, so I can slow down if they fall behind."

He's shaking with rage when he hangs up. As things

stand now, he's agreed to a double death sentence—his and Mickie's.

"You're actually going to meet that man?" Camilla says.

She grasps his arm, draws his attention back into the cab. She looks small and frightened and her eyes have taken on a lighter blue color, as if her elemental force has been sucked away from her by Voort, Bok, consequence, disillusion.

"Those were the people who attacked you, Voort?"

"Yes."

"It's my fault they have Mickie. I get angry and I don't think. You told me to stay away."

He massages her neck with one hand. It's cold in the car. Outside, across three foggy lanes of traffic, he sees the Harlem River. They've almost reached the spot where they found the floater. Could that have occurred less than two weeks ago?

He says, "It's not your fault. I lied to you. You warned me what would happen, what you'd do."

"What did Mickie say?"

Voort still hears the terrible screaming in his mind. He will always hear it. He says, "Ah, you know Mickie. He made a joke. He said buy Texaco. He never stops thinking about the market. That clown."

He reaches in his pocket, pulls out his shield. It looks like a toy now. It's lost its magic. He can't believe he'd ever believed the badge opened locked doors, altered the wills of powerful people. All his life a badge has seemed invested with power. Now it is merely metal, a decoration.

Dad, I hope I'm doing right.

The voice in his head seems to say, *I hope so too*.

Voort gives the cabby his home address. It's where Bok's men will want to see him go first. The second hand on his watch seems, through the metal and bearings, to scrape the skin of his wrist as it rotates, to peel away flesh and dig toward bone.

"What are you going to tell Syl?" Camilla asks, naming Mickie's wife, a surgeon who at this hour will probably be at Mount Sinai Hospital.

"Camilla, the men who have Mickie have killed at least half a dozen people. They have sources inside the department. They'll know if there's any mobilization. Even any *discussion* of Mickie among the wrong people and they'll kill him, and leave. With these guys, mobilization won't work."

"You mean you're not going to tell Syl anything?" She looks aghast. She's putting herself in Syl's place.

"I can't stop you from telling her. But if she turns around and makes the wrong phone call, no one will even find Mickie. He'll disappear."

And so will Stone, I bet.

"Isn't that Syl's choice to make? Not yours?"

"No, it's Mickie's, and I think he'd trust me. I have a better shot."

"You *think*."

"That's the best you get sometimes."

"You want *me* not to tell her too."

"I wanted," Voort says, "you to stay away."

"You seem not to be telling a lot of people a lot of things lately. Who *are* you?" she says. Her eyes are wide and she's staring intently at him like he's a stranger.

Eighty minutes left until Bok calls.

"Look, Camilla. In hostage situations, Aziz," he says, naming the commissioner, "rushes in. If we tell him, it's out of our hands, but still our responsibility."

"Who is Tina Tadesse?"

The cab has pulled off FDR Drive now and is moving crosstown on Fourteenth Street. It has almost reached Voort's house.

"Tina," she repeats, "Tadesse."

Shocked, he doesn't know how Camilla found out, or exactly what she knows, but he sees it's a relevant question. It's not about jealousy yet. That will come later, if he survives. But his answer will determine whether Camilla backs him. It's about trust and loyalty and how Camilla will feel if she goes along and things blow up. He goes hot inside.

"She's an assistant medical examiner on the case."

Voort's eyes holding hers. They both know that detailed explanations will take time away from Mickie. Right now his face must convey his absolute faith in Camilla, and his energy, false certainty, and resolve. That will determine her choice.

"What do you want me to do?" she asks as the cab pulls up to his house.

"Go to Greg's," he says, getting out, leaning in, noticing from the corner of his eye the way a blur of red—a four-wheel-drive—pulls up diagonally across from the house.

"Stay away from your apartment. Sleep at Greg's tonight."

"Check in with me," Camilla says.

"I'll try, but if I can't, don't go anywhere."

"Can I help?" She seems desperate to do something. Tina Tadesse is on the back burner with her too.

"Get back on the Internet. Stay on Stone. Try to find anything on a Leon Bok." Voort spells it. "I think he was a UN peacekeeper. They must keep rosters. I don't know his nationality. He's a mercenary now. Check criminal databases. U.S. military too, in case he's from here."

Something is cracking inside. Or is *he* cracking and a different Voort emerging from the bits? Even Camilla seems part of a different life.

"What happened with the boat?" asks Cousin Greg when Voort calls him.

"I'll fill you in later. Just make sure Camilla stays there with you. Okay?"

As the cab drives off with her, he rushes into the town house. It's empty of relatives for a change, and probably has been that way since the family voted for him to drop the case. The eyes in the portraits lining the stairway, of old cops, seem to follow him up the stairs in mute accusation. In the study he loads empty folders into an attaché case. He affixes a voice-activated tape recorder to his chest. He can also shut the recorder off—to save power—with a remote control he puts in his pocket.

Voort exits the house and opens the garage from the outside, so Bok's men can see the attaché case. Driving downtown in his Jaguar, he goes slow enough so the 4Runner can keep him in sight.

Fifty-six minutes until Bok calls.

Next stop, One Police Plaza, where Voort leaves the Jag parked with its cop-business visor down. He passes through the lobby turnstile and rides the elevator with Blue Guys and detectives, wondering, *Is one of you working for Stone?* The level of tension is palpable in the building. It always is during terrorist alerts.

Moving fast, in his office, Voort locks his police-issue Sig in his desk, stuffs a spare "Official Business" visor into the attaché case, and then finds Lt. Santini in his office down the hall, sticking pins into a map of Manhattan, marking spots where a serial rapist has been at work. If Santini's back on normal duties, the chiefs must suspect the alert is false.

Son of a bitch. Did Bok cause this alert?

Santini's a smart, shrewd ex–college wrestling champ who dresses in stylish Hugo Boss suits.

"I thought you were on vacation," he says, smiling.

"I came back."

"Good. I'm shorthanded."

"Lieutenant, I've been thinking. I've come in to quit."

Santini looks stunned. He respects Voort, and knows Voort's family history and powerful attachment to the blue life. In fact, they'd met last year during the Nye case, when Santini was not yet a lieutenant and Voort was desperately trying to hold on to his job—not leave it.

"What happened?" Santini sits and waves Voort toward the free chairs, but Voort chooses to stand. "Talk to me," says Santini quietly. "Guys like you don't just quit."

"I appreciate you asking, but it's personal."

"You're giving notice?" says Santini, as if not believing what he's hearing.

"Not notice," says Voort. "I'm gone. Now."

Voort reaches down and scribbles a note. He dates it. It's a resignation, effective immediately.

"Cut off my pay and benefits," he says. "I won't put in a claim. I want nothing more from the department. Once I walk out of here, I'm Joe C."

But Santini's not going for it, not this fast. He gets up and comes around the desk. He leans his butt against the desk. He cocks his head and folds his arms and his flat, intent eyes bore into Voort's.

"I got the impression from the chief that you're in some difficulty. She wouldn't go into it. It was an offhand comment she made."

Voort needs to get out of here before Bok's men get suspicious. "Don't make it harder than it is," he snaps. "You're just like my family, Lieutenant. They don't believe I'd ever go either. Well, I'm sick of the shit around here. You're not the one who should have been promoted. It should have been me."

A pause. "All right," Santini says without anger. "I accept your resignation, effective immediately."

"Do I have to sign something? Something official?"

"What you gave me will do," Santini says dryly. "But if you want me to hold on to this while you rethink . . ."

"No."

"You have some other job lined up?"

Voort opens Santini's door. Outside, the bull pen is filled with detectives.

"I quit!" he says loudly, before witnesses.

Lots of faces look up.

Voort starts to stomp out.

"Leave your ID and gun," orders Santini.

"They're in my desk." Voort's still carrying his private Sig in his back holster, and he's kept the ID. He tells Santini, "Get something yourself for a change."

He reaches the lobby, but takes the rear exit, leaving the Jag out front, within view of Bok's crew. Stepping around the concrete bomb barriers and ever-present squad/guard car, he hails a cab. He gives the hippie-looking driver an East Village address and says, "Hurry and I'll tip you twenty."

"In this fog, sports fans, if I hurry you won't arrive."

Voort, on the cellular now, calls his Jag garage on Thirteenth near First, reaches the owner, and tells him what he needs. Then he calls Stone's office and asks Ms. Snob Secretary if he can speak to Stone. He's a neighbor from Stone's condo, he says.

"Ted doesn't actually know me, but I'm soliciting votes over an important issue in the building. Whether to paint the lobby olive or fawn."

"He's in a meeting," Ms. Snob Secretary says.

"I'll call back."

So you're there.

The cab leaves him half a block from Kazoff's Foreign Car Fixit, where Voort offers Kazoff the Ukrainian two crisp hundreds for one of the loaner cars. The Jag is up-state, broken down, Voort says. As for the police Volvo, he knows, Santini will be hunting for it soon.

"Bring Jaguar for check when you get it back," Kazoff says, waving the cash away. "Take Subaru."

Ten minutes later Voort's in the elevator at U Thant Towers, Stone's office building. His heart is thundering.

Voort the ex-cop strides into Stone's reception room,

past the gatekeeper, past a surprised-looking man in a gray pinstriped suit and tortoiseshell glasses, down a hall toward the corner office, beneath the British paintings and into Stone's sanctum as Ms. Snob's protest echoes uselessly behind. Ahead, the lawyer spins away from the window out of which he's been staring, into fog, toward Hell's Gate.

"You're under arrest," Voort says, moving toward Stone, cuffs out. Moving fast to keep Stone off balance. "For the murder of Kevin Mcgreevey, the murder of Bud Mcgreevey," Voort barking.

"I want to see the warrant."

"Blow it out your ass." Voort lets the lawyer see his bald rage, his real feelings, but it's calculated.

And there it is, in the eyes, for just a fraction of a second, not just fear but deep knowledge. Stone knows exactly what this is about.

Voort spins him roughly, bends him over his desk, hears Ms. Snob's clucked outrage as he clicks on the cuffs.

You can't call Bok now.

Spun back, Stone peers into Voort's face with recognition and horror. Frank Heffner's voice is coming from a different man.

"That's right," Voort says. "I'm back."

Voort's phone starts buzzing. It's Bok, probably. Phoning on time.

"I want to call my lawyer," says Stone.

"Ah, it's better when guys defend themselves," says Voort. "Who needs lawyers?"

"I demand . . ." But Stone's recovering too late.

Voort pushing Stone on purpose. Enjoying the helplessness but also waiting for Stone to decide the cop is bungling the arrest, violating his civil rights, which means that any charges will be dropped later by a judge. Once Stone sees it, he'll come along more easily. He'll be distracted.

"This is not Nazi Germany," Stone protests.

"Sieg heil," Voort says.

"I heard that. I'm writing all this down," Ms. Snob says. And to Stone, "Don't worry, Mr. Stone."

Voort propelling Stone toward the door. Into the jamb, in front of witnesses.

"Pigs like you don't need Miranda," Voort says.

As Voort moves Stone down the hall, toward the elevator, a cleaning crew gets out of the way.

"You'll lose your job," Stone gets out, trying for dignity, but it's hard when you're being shoved into a wall.

How far is too far? Voort wonders. Or is excess itself some great circle that returns you to normalcy, if you just have the courage or stupidity to keep walking in the direction in which you started out? Maybe there's no such thing as a step too far, only one that falls short.

Voort understands that what happened in the Mobil station changed him in ways that he only now appreciates. Voort shoves the lawyer through the marble lobby of the U Thant building, the great expanse of economy and political legitimacy. In an odd way, Voort feels free.

In fact, now that he's achieved some small measure of control he sees that it's almost funny. He lives in a culture where the sexual humiliation of women is regarded as legitimate entertainment. In films and books women are regularly stripped, raped, flayed, decapitated. Voort thinks, *Bok didn't even go all the way with me. Look what happened as a result.*

Stone frowns when he sees that Voort intends for him to get into an old Subaru, not a police car. It seems off to him.

"I demand to make a phone call," he says as Voort shoves him in back, past the flipped-down front seat.

Voort takes out a second pair of handcuffs. He yanks Stone's manacled wrists around so that Stone is forced to face the side-rear window. With the second pair of cuffs he affixes the first pair to the door handle. The windows are up, and there is no back door, no way for Stone to get out except through the front.

"What kind of police car is this?" Stone says. "It doesn't even have an antenna, or police radio. Where's the dome light?"

Voort waits until any attention from pedestrians has subsided. He's leaning quite close to Stone, enough to smell the odor of cleaning chemicals on the man's suit, over sweat.

"Where's my partner?" demands Voort.

Stone's facial muscles seem to be rearranging themselves, as if he's altering his expectations. A moment ago they had included a ride to a cell. A call to a lawyer. Some manageable sum paid for bail to the municipality.

Perhaps a quick furtive ride to an airport too.

Something seems to snap inside Voort. His hands move without any conscious decision. The punch slams into Stone just below the rib cage. Voort puts his shoulder into it, his body into it, and his rage. Stone cries out once, briefly. He tilts toward Voort, groaning. There are tears in his eyes. Phlegm dribbles from his mouth.

"You'll be all right if you go along," Voort says.

"Oh God," wheezes Stone. "What is this?"

Voort has never hit a suspect, not without physical provocation, and the flood of adrenaline sickens and excites him and he feels a roaring all around him, as if the cacophony of the city—the sum total of its rampant energy—has found a new source of fury and sustenance, and as if it has tempted another soul over a line and down below its deepest tunnels and into the black, patient earth.

Voort tells Stone, pressing the Sig into the man's side, and causing him to jerk away, to grit his teeth, to breathe heavier, "Any excuse. Any one at all. Just be happy I still need one."

Outside a real squad car is passing, its occupants gazing out, taking in the street and building, and slipping idly over two men in a Subaru at the curb, who seem to be chatting. When Stone moves his eyes away from them, the car glides off, around a corner, and its exhaust gasses disappear into the gray mist.

"Leon Bok," says Voort.

"What? What did you say? What's that name?"

Voort smells ammonia, and sweat. The thick, heavy kind, worsened by a layer of sour cologne.

The phone's buzzing again. Like a hornet. But its sting is worse.

Voort gets in the front and starts the engine. Voort starts to drive. He heads west, away from One Police Plaza.

"For your sake, let's hope that Bok's as loyal to you as I've heard," he says.

Stone says nothing. He seems to need all his conscious energy and attention to maintain breathing.

But then he sees that denial is not only pointless, it's not even vaguely in his interest just now. Stone whispers in pain, "He is that loyal, but it will cost me more."

And Voort takes a breath and picks up the buzzing phone.

"Where are you?" Bok demands angrily.

"Changing the trade."

SIXTEEN

The boy learns of the sniper as he sits in a barber's chair, but the din in Supercuts is loud enough to drown out the sound of shooting even three blocks away. It's a May Saturday, and eight year old Conrad has taken the subway to Prospect Heights with Dad, and stopped for a quick trim before heading to Uncle Vim's for pot roast dinner.

Voort looking forward to throwing a baseball around with some favorite cousins. Greg. Spruce. Mark.

He squirms as a nice-smelling Latin lady oohs and ahhs over his thick hair and runs electric clippers up the back of his neck. "My sister's a casting director at ABC," the lady says. "Ask your dad to bring you in, try you out. Handsome boy!"

Michael Jackson music blasts from ceiling speakers as other boys await cuts, poring over copies of *Sports Illustrated* magazine. Voort's oddly excited at the soft touch of breasts against his shoulder, and slightly distracted by Dad—a mirrored reflection outside on the street, talking urgently to a man in jogging shorts.

There's something wrong out there, Voort sees. The jogger looks upset, talking fast, jabbing his finger west, toward Vim's block. Dad's relaxed Saturday look has been replaced by his "cop attitude": squared shoulders, head thrust forward, body lifted on the balls of the feet. He leans toward the civilian.

"Turn your head," the haircutter says.

But the boy recognizes the rhythms of interruption. They're a standard part of detective life. He's as familiar with sudden emergencies as with school fire drills, and his hand is already moving to pull the barber sheet off as Dad pushes into Supercuts, calling for him to hurry up.

"I'm not finished," the lady says.

"Keep the change," Bill says.

"We're cops," the boy says proudly as he's pulled out the door. His last glimpse of Supercuts is of other parents looking alarmed, other boys looking jealous. In his chest Voort feels a surge of protectiveness for these people.

"A man with a rifle is on a roof, two blocks away," Dad tells him as they run.

Voort thinking that someday, like Dad, he will rush toward danger when civilians flee. He will learn crucial information—lifesaving news—before other people do.

"The Two-One is on it but they need help," Dad says.

Moving fast, hand clasped in Bill's, Voort pictures a brownstone, a lean glint of rifle-barrel poking over the roof, just like when Channel Five showed a sniper on the news last week. He remembers the squad cars on TV blocking off the street, and Lt. Bozniak—Dad's poker buddy—on a bullhorn.

"Is Uncle Vim all right, Dad?"

"Stay behind me. If I leave you somewhere, don't move."

Voort's little legs taking him past slower-moving, oblivious civilians. Moms wheeling strollers. Couples walking hand in hand. His own excitement rises in direct disproportion to their calm. He has learned even by age eight that the city has two rhythms—cop speed and civilian speed. Cops jump from place to place like troopers on the starship *Enterprise*. The rest of the universe rotates normally but like Captain Picard, cops slide through hyperspace to protect civilians from harm. Sometimes, when the boy rides in squad cars, he even pretends he's on the *Enterprise*.

Now Voort and Dad hit warp speed, running down Gil Hodges Place, toward Nineteenth, Vim's block, except just before they turn the corner Dad halts and presses Voort up against a brick apartment building.

Dad kneels, grasps Voort's shoulders and says, "Calm down, son."

Which is when the thrill dies and Voort realizes he's heard no shots, sirens, or even bullhorns. A dog walker ambles around the corner. A Jack Russell wags its tail happily, its nose poking into Voort's sock.

"Well?" says Dad.

Voort feeling silly, as a warm rush of logic pushes aside pounding adrenaline. Voort's cheeks coloring as he says, "There's no man with a rifle. It's a lesson, Dad."

He hates failing tests.

Also, it occurs to him that since they left Supercuts, he's been scared. He had not realized it.

"Before running around that corner, what should you have asked?" Dad says to the disappointed boy.

"Where the sniper was?" Voort understands that the shooter could have been anywhere, even aiming down at the corner around which they had been about to run.

"What else, pal?"

"What kind of rifle he had?"

"Why is that important?"

"But you're my *father*," Voort bursts out, meaning that he'd not thought to ask because he trusted Bill. Bill would never hurt him. Fathers, the boy assumed, have intrinsic power to protect sons from harm.

A loving answer, Bill's look says, and appreciated, but wrong. Bill rubs the top of Voort's half-completed bristly haircut.

"Someday, if you become a policeman, your boss will send you into danger. Don't disobey, don't delay, but get as much information as possible first. Knowledge is worth ten cops with guns."

"I'm sorry."

"You're smart," Dad says. "The smartest boy I know and I'm not saying that because I'm your father. It's no big deal to fail a lesson. You fail lessons so you don't fail in life. Don't be mad at me, okay?"

Now, over two decades later, Voort often recalls the scene during emergencies, even after receiving the same lessons at the academy. But boys remember lessons taught by fathers best.

He asks Ted Stone, "How many guys will come with Bok?"

"Where are we going?" says Stone from the backseat instead of answering. He's still cuffed back there. Voort's driving across the lower roadway of the George Washington Bridge.

"How will they be armed?" asks Voort.

"Better than you."

A sign affixed to a passing girder reads "Leaving New York. Entering New Jersey."

The fog still seems to be thickening, giving Voort a false sense of being hidden. Traffic glides past an army Humvee—a security post—wedged into a new official-vehicles–U-turn area on the bridge.

In the rearview mirror, Stone's gaze remains calm, steady. He presumes correctly, for the moment at least, that with Voort driving, he won't be hurt.

"Let me go," the lawyer says "Do you realize that if we get stopped, you'll be the one arrested, not me? You just drove across a state line."

"You're not answering, Ted." Voort feels the warmth of the tape recorder under his shirt.

Stone's breathing is slightly labored as he's still in discomfort from Voort's earlier blow. "You seem under tremendous pressure," he says. "Even if whatever you're imagining is true, anything I told you now wouldn't be admissible. A judge would throw it out."

"Because I bungled the arrest, you mean."

"This isn't an arrest. It's kidnapping, plain and simple."

"Then it should be easy to tell me things since I can't use them," Voort replies.

Stone gazes out the window as if he's lost interest.

He's like a parent waiting for a petulant child to change his mind to go along.

"You know, an old Sing Sing guard once told me," Voort says as they turn onto the northbound Palisades Parkway, "don't make threats unless you carry them out. Otherwise prisoners lose respect for you."

Stone winces as they hit a bump.

Voort says, "So while it's true I'm not going to pull over now, when we stop I'll beat the shit out of you if you don't answer. And if you wait until later to answer, I'll *still* do it because that was the threat. My hands are tied."

"I don't know how many people he has," says Stone.

"You're not letting me finish. If you lie and I find out, it will be worse. But I can see you've made up your mind not to answer. I'll just turn on the radio. Do you like jazz? I'm bored talking to myself."

Stone tries to shake off a single dot of sweat on his scalp. He lacks a free hand to remove it.

"He has two men on the boat," he mutters.

"I didn't ask just about the boat."

"And a couple more backup people somewhere else. At least I paid for them."

"Five in all, then."

"I don't know for sure it's five. It's at least five. One against five," Stone says, the odds perking him up.

"*At least* five," nods Voort.

"So let me go."

"But then what happens to Mickie?"

"I'm not talking about Mickie," Stone says, gathering strength by increments, becoming, even with his hands cuffed, the negotiating lawyer the instant he thinks he has an edge. "I'm talking about you. You'll have no backup. You can't even call for help. You're the fugitive. I haven't broken any law."

"Then I better not call for help," agrees Voort.

"They're trained," warns Stone.

"Ah! Trained how?"

Stone presses his lips together, annoyed at himself for volunteering information. But he's made a mistake and he'll have to reveal more.

"They're specialists," he says gruffly.

"Specialists."

"Military. Special ops. I don't know where Leon gets them. But you don't want to go up against those people. Stop the car. Let me out. I'll find my way back. I promise there will be no retaliation."

"Well, if you promise," says Voort. "You look like a guy I can trust."

"What do you want? Money?"

"Tell me what was on the *Candace* when it went down."

Stone looks out the window, west, as if offering up the vast expanse of continent as Voort's safe haven. Go off to Illinois, Montana, Arkansas, Nevada, he seems to say. Pick a new village, a new state; of life, being, safety.

"You're crazy," Stone mutters under his breath.

"I bet this is Leon calling, on time," Voort says, lifting the buzzing cell phone. "Ted? Talking on these things is illegal while driving. Don't tell on me, please. Hi, Leon."

Although Voort has heard the voice only twice before, and it lacks normal emotional nuances, Bok sounds even flatter, angrier, or is that Voort's imagination? He envisions a faceless man in a car, at the ocean at the far end of the city, where Voort has sent him. Voort adds four more men squeezed into Bok's car.

But the voice does not frighten Voort anymore.

Bok says, "I'm at Coney Island. Where the hell are you?"

"I changed my mind. Drive back into Manhattan. Take the West Side Highway to the G.W. Bridge. Call when you're close."

"I'm starting to lose my patience," says Bok.

"Mohammed went to the hill," says Voort, "when the hill wouldn't go to Mohammed."

He takes an exit to loop off the parkway into the suburban hamlet of Wayne Hills—"The Town That Fooled the British"—according to a sign. Colonists misdirected the British army here two centuries ago, Voort knows, when the redcoats were chasing Washington.

Washington went that way. That kind of thing.

"Give me a break, Leon. I'm just a lowly cop. I bet you're driving around with backup, right? I have to get ready for you or I won't have a chance. Mickie and I would never get away if we met you on a beach."

Bok says nothing, but Voort guesses he's reluctantly acknowledging the point.

Voort turns right at a four-way traffic light and left by a Shell station. He enters a residential area.

He says, "No more switches. I just needed time to figure out a safe place to give your client back. I'm not in your league, Leon. I can't pull ideas out of a hat."

He drives onto a leafy street where small ranch-style homes are vaguely visible through mist.

"I warned you, Voort . . . if we see police . . ."

"Police?" repeats Voort, as if astounded. "I don't think you're familiar with the law in this country. Believe me, neither of us wants the police."

He slows, passing a black Odyssey parked on the grassy roadside in front of a small ranch house set back from the street. As he turns into the driveway, the Odyssey's driver looks out with surprise, recognizing Voort.

"Call me when you're near the bridge," Voort says and

clicks off. He pulls into the open garage and shuts the engine. It ticks, cooling.

Cousins Bert and Nils Voort, both off-duty Blue Guys in Vim's old precinct, are already out of the Odyssey, walking quickly toward the Subaru, sidearms out. It's their job to protect Voort's uncle. Although they've recognized Voort, they've also spotted the figure in his backseat.

Voort gets out of the car and jerks his finger toward Stone. "He's a friend." The cousins halt, and Nils says something to Bert, but Voort can't hear them. Neither man addresses Voort, or looks happy he's here. Last time he'd seen both had been a month and a half ago, at Bram's birthday party.

The cousins walk back to their van.

So this is how it will be from now on, if there is a from now on, Voort thinks.

"I need to use the bathroom," says Stone from the car, probably assuming this house is where Voort plans to keep him.

"This is my uncle's home. Those men are my cousins."

Stone's eyes grow huge.

"Bok threatened to have someone rape their kids . . ."

Stone can't help it. A moan slips out. He does not know the family has cut off Voort, and he's clearly suffering from fears of loyalty.

"Still want to come in?" Voort asks. "We'll be out of here in five."

I'm not even sure I'll be allowed in.

Stone turns and stares out at the shelves of paint and garden equipment, all too far away to reach.

"By the way, I haven't forgotten that you didn't answer before," says Voort. "You know. About the *Candace*?"

He heads up the short walk. *Ah, Vim,* he thinks. Just about every other retired cop has limped off to Florida or Arizona. Only Vim would move to Jersey. But Voort's uncle loves the city's museums and concerts. His kids still live in Brooklyn. Vim would stay here if New York went radioactive. He certainly would never leave as long as he's part of the family council, keeper of the church key.

Vim, you backed me at the meeting. Back me now.

"Good to see you, Nephew," says his uncle gruffly, opening the door before Voort knocks. Like other Voorts, he's probably been eyeing his front walk for days.

He's dressed in slippers and a light-gray wool cardigan that matches his thick hair and warms him against the roaring air-conditioning. At seventy-four, he's still big and vibrant, although in the last few years he's needed glasses. Other uncles call Vim "the Human Furnace." His body temperature is like his temper. It can get hot too fast.

Voort's surprised at his powerful reaction to Vim's simple greeting. He bats down welling emotion.

"Who was that in the car?" asks Vim, peering over Voort's shoulder suspiciously, even though he can't see the car. "It's not your car."

"A friend."

"Why was he in the backseat? Why wasn't he in front?"

"He has a bad leg and needs to stretch out."

"Don't listen to him," warns a sharp, recognizable voice—a woman's—from the living room behind Vim. *"He wants something or he wouldn't be here."* Shit, Voort thinks. It's Spruce. Of all the people to be visiting. Voort's odds of getting help just went down.

But Vim turns to her swiftly. He seems irritated at Spruce.

"You want to tell me who to talk to now?"

Voort's hope rises a little as he understands that these two have been arguing, probably about him.

Vim opens the door wider, steps aside for Voort. The house is modest, paneled, wall-to-wall carpeted, and filled with comfortable looking cushioned furniture. As he enters Spruce comes across the small living room at him like an incoming missile—a visceral mass of opposition. Her Gap jeans and fitted jacket show off her fine figure and slim legs. Her white T-shirt is tucked in at the waist, so her S&W is probably tucked in back. Either Vim's got three guards today or Spruce has an escort.

Voort adults travel in pairs these days, if they're smart. Is it any wonder she's mad?

Vim says, "Why didn't you bring your friend in, Conrad?"

"I can't stay long."

"Should your cousins out there be concerned?"

Voort sighs. "Maybe later. No one knows we're here."

"I *told you*," Spruce says.

"Yeah, yeah, I remember."

"He's ruining everything," Spruce says. "Everyone is fighting over you." She's finally addressing Voort.

"Nephew, come into the back room. Spruce, a couple minutes," Vim says, holding up his index finger. "Last time I checked, the Constitution guaranteed free speech. Or does that bother you too?"

"*We voted not to help him.* His plan is blowing up in his face like I said it would. Uncle, we voted!"

Vim seems to actually flinch at the word "we." In an odd way, Voort realizes, Spruce's opposition is helping him.

She wedges between them, furious, shorter than both men but her anger gives her a larger presence. The room is dominated by a TV the size of a small movie screen, and filled with porcelain knickknacks and crystalware on shelves. Lots of breakable glass.

Spruce says, "I sent my kids to stay with their aunt in Chicago. Teresa missed the test to get into Hunter. I can't even keep my own daughters home."

"Sorry," Voort says.

"You don't care who you drag into this," Spruce says bitterly.

"Watch TV," Vim tells her patiently. "We get over a hundred channels, not that any of them broadcast anything good. You'd think one would carry Jackie Gleason."

Bok will be calling soon, but you don't rush Vim. Conrad follows his limping uncle down a short hallway and into his study/gun room, which smells of pipe tobacco and oiled leather furniture. The weapons are arrayed on racks and in locked display cases, the glass dusted, the mahogany polished, light reflecting off surfaces as immaculately as off a patrolman's new shoes. Vim takes the swivel chair. Voort falls onto the same couch he used to spend hours on, when he lived with Vim and Maeve for months after his parents died. The room looks the same as it had in Brooklyn, before Vim retired.

"Start from scratch," says Vim.

Voort has to shake his head. He cannot recall denying a Vim request before. "Forgive me but it's better if I ask the questions, Uncle. Do you need to go to the store for anything?" he says meaningfully, hopefully. "To take a drive for an hour or so?"

Voort getting right to the point by not mentioning it. Voort needing Vim out of this house, and Vim, understanding, shifting his gaze to the gun cabinets. He rubs his closely shaved cheek. He still grooms himself daily as if going in to work.

"This has to do with the man in the car?"

Voort answers slowly so the real truth is clear.

"No."

"They're coming after you."

I don't want to incriminate you.

Vim says, "I can help. I should have already. That damn vote. Do you want to discuss anything? Plans?"

Voort says gently, "I could use advice, Uncle, but there's not time."

Vim's eyes behind the lenses are red with fatigue. He has not been sleeping. In his case this does not imply worry. It means he's been spending nights at Greg's tug yard, with one of his Remingtons on his lap.

"I think it might be better," Vim says slowly, as if imagining Spruce's distress—and not trusting her—"if you left now and came back in five, six minutes. The key's under the flowerpot. Don't help yourself to whatever you want. Don't make sure to take the right ammunition from the bottom drawers. Good luck."

"You always were a bad uncle," smiles Voort.

"You always had renegade potential," Vim says, opening the top desk drawer, holding up the gun-cabinet key, and slapping it on the blotter on his desk. "Need anything else? Want me to come along?" Vim looks embarrassed. "Your dad's been mad at me. Chewing me out."

Voort grasps the big hand. In his prime, when Vim used to get out of a squad car, the whole Ford would lift up as if relieved of tension. Vim had been so powerful Voort had once seen him pick up a VW from behind.

"You're doing plenty, Uncle. I'll pass it on."

When they get back to the living room, Vim tells Spruce that Voort's leaving. His sadness is no act. "You two used to flip baseball cards in my kitchen. This fighting is making me sick. Spruce, I've been meaning to get to Sears, pick up one of those new vacuum cleaners. Maeve says the old one's had it and frankly, this whole mess gives me splinters. I want to go out for a while."

Spruce looks suspicious.

"I didn't want this," Voort tells her.

"You could have avoided it," Spruce says.

"This is my house," growls Vim. "I went along with you so far but in the old days we *never* would have run from a threat."

"In the old days we didn't *get* this kind of threat."

Vim shakes his head doggedly. "The country doesn't bow to terrorism and neither should the family. That's what's this is, plain and simple. Maybe you think the whole city should send their kids to Chicago too."

Voort walks out and drives off. Six minutes later when he circles back, Vim, Spruce, and the other cousins are gone.

He uses the flowerpot key and hurries back into the gun room. Vim—the Korean War vet, police marksmanship champ, deer hunter, NRA member, and subscriber to every gun magazine published in the United States—used to love showing off his shotguns, semiautomatics, and old service revolvers to Voort the boy. He'd taken Voort shooting and taught him how to disassemble firearms. He'd given pop quizzes on loading weapons, on firearm safety.

Now Voort passes up the fancy stuff—Vim's double action Spectre and Ruger MP-9—and instead takes from the cabinets what he's been trained to use, either by Vim or by the department, two Remington 870s with autoload and extended magazines, an extra Sig, a 9mm Glock for Mickie, and enough double-ought shells, slugs, and cartridges to last a half-dozen cops through a shootout, in close-quarter fighting.

He wraps the ordnance in two Kevlar vests.

I wish he had a couple of helmets too. I don't know how Bok will be armed, but nothing beats a shotgun close-up, and I can fire five rounds in five seconds with this.

Voort finds the second key—a Muessler special on a leather thong—hanging on a peg fixed to the gun cabinet. A kitchen door provides direct access to the garage, so the weapons won't be visible from the street. He grabs a ball of twine off a garage shelf, and an old terry-cloth rag. After storing it all in the trunk he gets behind the wheel, and a strong urine odor hits him. Stone gazes out of the window, stiff and mortified. He's wet himself.

Good. He's quiet.

Voort needs to plan now, fast.

As Voort backs from the garage the cellular begins buzzing. He'd hoped for a bit more preparation time, but he won't be able to put Bok off any longer, it seems. He's going to have to cut things close.

"I'm a mile from the bridge," says Bok. "If you don't tell me the real place this time, send Mickie's wife a condolence card."

Voort gives directions to the little church atop the Palisades; not a great choice, he's thinking, but what is?

"A church," repeats Bok.

"It's more historical landmark. No staff. No groundskeeper. Look it up on the Internet if you don't believe me. It's so isolated it even has its own exit on the parkway. It's only open one day a week. Budget cuts."

"I just walk in with your friend, I suppose?"

"You stay outside and send Mickie in. Stone and Mickie pass each other on the way. Then you leave."

"What about taking your shot," taunts Bok. "You know. *High Noon*?"

"Getting back Mickie *is* my shot."

Voort holds his breath. Bok is thinking.

"Hey, when you win, you win," Bok says, and hangs up.

If he's at the bridge, he can reach the church in thirty-five minutes, but I hope he'll probe the grounds first. Check things out before making contact.

"Ted, what was on the *Candace*?" Voort says, driving.

Stone's head swings slowly around in the rearview mirror. What Voort sees shocks him. The mask is off. Stone's remote look has reversed itself. The black pupils are small as lasers. The open mouth shows white, sharp incisors. The jaw muscles have relaxed as if Stone's rerouted all physical force to his will. His breathing is as calm as a good decision. A few alterations of tendon and he's changed into Voort's personal Dorian Gray.

"The *Candace*, Ted."

Back on the parkway, Voort needs only four minutes to reach the old smugglers' church. The parking area is empty. Dense mist seems to be rising off the forest, ferns, grass. He bumps the Subaru over the curb and carves ruts in the slippery earth on both sides of the asphalt walkway, which winds through woods. Reaching the clearing, he drives around the rear of the church, veering close to the edge of the Palisades. The original chapel and more modern addition—containing the offices and meeting room—show their long side to the river, where the sun comes up, so light would flood in.

"You a churchgoer, Ted?" Voort asks, maneuvering around stone benches in the garden and directly up against the thick rear door. Voort takes the car key with him when he gets out. To push the Subaru away from the door, Bok will need at least two men to expose themselves out here.

"You won't hear him coming," says Stone.

Voort unlocks the cuffs affixing Stone to the car door. The lawyer allows himself to be pushed around the church to the front entrance.

Stone says, "You are so alone."

Over two hundred years ago, in this spot, Voorts struggled under wooden chests loaded with smuggled silver to buy muskets for General Ethan Allen. They peered with spyglasses at British sloops on the Hudson. They gathered in the light of whale-oil lamps to study hand-drawn maps showing the position of General Howe's Iroquois allies, and supply roads that his engineers were hacking through forests, as British forces maneuvered to slice the colonies in half.

"Leave me here," says Stone. "And go."

Voort fits Vim's new Medeco into its slot and feels tumblers opening. He pushes Stone in, punches on lights, punches in the four-digit code to disarm the alarm—connected to a private firm fifteen miles away. The numbers correspond to the date that General Cornwallis surrendered to General Washington, ending the American Revolution.

"There's still time," says Stone.

Inside, the nave is small and rectangular and about a dozen movable meeting benches sit empty. The ground-level windows—additions cut into the original stone—are sealed from outside by thick, locked wooden shutters with small diamond-shaped gun ports. The Dutch who built this place feared that Indians or British could attack them at worship, so all barriers are thick oak. In front of the church, the only original entrance, a wooden bracket is suspended from a low rafter to allow for a blunderbuss booby trap to be rigged above the door. It had been designed to be used if worshippers had to retreat to a trapdoor basement, and out through the smugglers' tunnel—now cemented up.

The church was never attacked until now.

Four small stained-glass windows—also protected by shutters—are set into a balcony that was added in 1829, as the congregation grew, and before the township seized the land. The granite draws coolness from the rock below. Voort has never been in here without other family members. He cuffs Stone to an iron ring set into stone in back of the nave. He uses the terry-cloth rag from Vim's garage to blindfold Stone, so he can't see defensive preparations. Then Voort rushes out to the Subaru and brings back the guns.

"I won't send him after you. I promise. He'll leave you alone," Stone calls out.

Voort begins dragging pews around, turning them over and rearranging them into a rough, staggered circular maze. A pew. Then a few clear feet behind it. Then another pew. As he works, he goes over the property layout in his head. The mercenaries will start in from either the parking lot or pebble beach below. Coming by water would require more time, Voort guesses.

But they might still try. Or leave that way, call in the boat.

The thick oaks and maples will conceal Bok until he reaches the clearing. Then the path splits left and right to either door.

The problem is, there's no way to see out there unless I break a window, which means they'll spot me too, up on the balcony. But it's the only way.

Voort busts out the glass on one window, shattering a picture of Roman soldiers playing dice. He's surprised to see the world unchanged out there, foggy and gray. The bad visibility will force Bok to get closer if he wants a good view, which is better for Voort's shotgun. He breaks a second window. He checks angles of fire from the balcony.

"I have to go to the bathroom," says Stone.

"You're like a goddamn old lady," says Voort.

Voort imagines Mickie and Stone passing each other out front, as he finishes arranging pews. He's drenched in sweat from the effort. The original trapdoor to the cellar is now in the open, surrounded by his makeshift, staggered barricades. He wishes the smugglers' tunnel still led out, but it was closed after a teenager got drunk and hit his head on the rock, and his parents sued the township.

Lawyers, Voort thinks.

At least the cellar is accessible.

Voort uses Vim's second key to unlock the trapdoor—all original locks have been replaced—and pulls it open. A ladder disappears into the darkness of the cellar. He curses himself for forgetting a flashlight. A cool musty smell wafts up.

If Mickie and I need to get down fast, we may not have time to open it. We can't escape that way but we can fight if Bok tries to come down.

"Leon burns things," Stone says.

"Then let's hope you get out first."

Stone twists his head toward the stained-glass images diagonally above, which he'd seen before Voort blindfolded him. "That's Daniel in the lions' den up there, isn't it? One man. Four lions. Those odds don't always work out."

Bok should reach the turnoff in about twelve minutes. That gives me twenty to forty minutes before the rough part starts.

He slips on a Kevlar vest, loads the first Remington, and places the shotgun into the old wooden blunderbuss bracket suspended by the front door. The rickety assembly creaks, the shotgun barely fits, but the apparatus holds. He loops the twine from Vim's garage around the trigger, and then up behind it, through an iron ring set into the ceiling. Making sure there is enough slack, he measures the distance from the ring to the door handle. He does not yet tie twine to handle because if he did, the shotgun would fire when he opened the door during the prisoner exchange.

If we get that far.

Stone calls out, "Do you have kids?"

Voort hurries down the aisle, past the pulpit and through a doorway, bringing him into a rear hallway lined with main office, bathroom, and meeting room. He pushes a desk to the back door, and up against it. He piles a chair and a box filled with Bibles on top of the desk.

"I love my daughter very much," says Stone, head cocked, listening, as Voort returns to the nave.

Voort loads the other weapons and leaves the Glock on a pew where it can be snatched up as he and Mickie, hopefully—retreat toward the trapdoor, or up to the balcony. The easy way in for Bok will be through the front, unless he can push the Subaru out of the way in back.

By now the mercenaries could be arriving, separating, sneaking through woods.

Maybe Bok's phoned the *Wanderer,* Voort thinks. Maybe Bok is figuring he'll get away by water, chug off with Stone.

"Everything I did was for my daughter," says Stone.

Which is what makes Voort snap.

Voort whirls on Stone from across the nave. He steps up to the man with his Sig out. When he grabs the lawyer and pushes the barrel into his mouth, Stone starts to scream.

"What was on the *Candace*?" says Voort.

Teeth break. Blood sprays onto Voort's hand and knuckles. He's slick with blood. *Click.* "What . . . was . . . on . . . it?" *Click.* Each snap of the trigger ratcheting up the high-pitched muffled cries until Stone screeches steadily. Voort jams the steel against the roof of the man's mouth.

Tears flow from beneath the dirty blindfold. Stone's face muscles seem to be jumbling, fracturing. Voort smells shit. All he wants at the moment is to hurt the man.

"Don't . . . shoot . . . meeeee!"

Voort's rage is out of control. Stone's fear fuels it, pushes Voort further into the red zone, and Stone is pleading, trying to say, "Stop! I'll tell you."

Stone tells him what was on the boat when it sank.

SEVENTEEN

"A computer?" repeats Voort.

"A laptop."

"What was in it?"

"Nothing . . . now . . . it's . . . destroyed," Stone gasps.

The lawyer is begging, trying to plead his way out of a world into which he has sent other people, but never before has he been on the receiving end. His will has collapsed along with his body. He sags. His knees buckle. Voort yanks him up by his shirt and the man tries to pull away, but with the handcuffs affixing him to the iron rings on the wall, he only jerks himself closer.

"What was in the computer?"

"My . . . records."

Voort drives the Sig into Stone's kidney area and the lawyer arches and screams. Blood sprays from his mouth, spotting Voort's hands and clothing. A sweet, hot taste is on Voort's tongue. Stone's face is streaked with tears and mucus. Blood smears four lips, as if the men have kissed.

Glancing up, Voort catches sight of the stained-glass lions. By a trick of light they seem to have crept closer. A bright, sharp attentiveness has come into their eyes.

Stone dry heaves, babbling.

"Clients came on the boat to . . . review investments."

He's learning the cardinal rule of his new world. Speech wards off pain.

"What clients?" says Voort.

"Don't . . . hit . . . me."

Stone fills in the generalities Voort had heard on tape. Names spew out, none familiar, but several preceded by titles: "General." "Colonel." "Senator."

"These people live in this country now?"

"Legally."

"War criminals."

"Business . . . people . . . I'm their banker . . . General Azima lives in Baton Rouge . . ."

The cool stone walls absorbing one more confession in a two-century-long string.

Remember these names, Voort thinks.

Stone wheezes out words as talismans against pain. "Foreign governments (gasp) can't collect taxes in the States . . ."

It's a finance lecture under torture. Torquemada's put Messrs. Smith and Barney to the rack.

Where is Bok? Outside?

But the flow of information is too enticing for Voort to stop, to take time to check the property, eye it from up top. Stone utters a Russian name. A German name.

"Ferdinand DeChase sold U.S. cigarettes in France, without licenses, but Interpol was investigating him . . ."

Voort thinking, *Cigarettes?*

The stained-glass Paul of Tarsus seems to gaze down, even though Paul's eyes are raised.

"Colonel Gallo needed to get out of Argentina . . ."

Stone taking his five percent and putting the rest into

condos on the Gulf of Mexico, forests in Montana, a donut chain in Utah, energy stock, a Hawaiian fruit company, a water-rights group. The real owners never appearing on any deed, any contract.

Just in his hard drive, which sank.

The U.S. taxes always paid, because once the money's here, Uncle Sam gets a cut.

"I kept the extra disc in a waterproof box."

At that moment, fifty yards away, Leon Bok stands appraising the chapel from just inside the tree line, beneath a large oak. The fog will make an attack easier. But it renders the defensive features of the building less distinct.

Mickie Connor lies at Bok's feet, curled on the wet ground. His wrists are bound to his ankles. He's gagged, unable to call out and warn Voort. Judging from his jagged breathing, he is in tremendous pain.

Bok—balancing contingencies—is waiting to hear that the rest of his assault team is in place before he starts moving. Just a couple of minutes more . . .

How many guys are in there with you, Voort?

If it's just Voort, things should be easy. But if it's more, Bok may have to change tactics a bit, or even leave.

His first duty is to get the client out, safe.

The modern merc travels light, aided by the finest electronics. Bok's gaze travels between the outer building and the Palm in his hand, which shows the corresponding layout inside. He's linked wirelessly through his cellular phone to the Internet. A few key-taps and he's right inside the nave with Voort thanks to the Wayne Hills Township Website. Anyone could find it. Voort himself suggested using the Internet as a way of assuring Bok the church was isolated.

Well, you were right.

Voort had probably figured Bok had no time to access the Internet. As it turned out he'd made one too many suggestions. Thank you, Voort.

A trapdoor, huh?

Bok studies a little write-up of the door and cellar and sealed tunnel below. The "Visit Historical Wayne Hills" Website includes photos of the church's "fine old meeting room," "19th-century balcony addition," "musty cellar, dug originally for defense."

I can't tell if there's a man standing by the balcony window or not. Is that shadow a person or did Voort just put a coatrack up there? Damn this fog.

He glances down at Connor. The detective gazes back dully as if focused on something a great distance away. Bok's seen the look in tortured suspects. They withdraw inside to escape pain, trying to retract their nerve endings and awareness from the surface. They grope for distraction as pain management. The strategy makes them docile, but it never works in the end, when Bok decides to push things.

Mickie's fingers are broken. His arms jut oddly, dislocated. If Mickie even reaches the church—if the trade goes that far—he won't be able to help Voort.

Bok asks Mickie, "How many people are with him?"

But it's a rhetorical question. Mickie wouldn't know. On the Palm, "Friendly," the Wayne Hills deer, is saying, "Visit ye Olde Dutch church on Saturdays, my human friends. It's the only day we are open!"

*   *   *

And in the church, in his head, Voort fills in the scene on the *Candace* as he drives questions at the lawyer. He sees Stone's "investors" dressed for a boat ride, ambling on-board in ones and twos. They've come to the Big Apple to see a show, shop, cruise on Stone's mini–floating UN of crime on the East River. The clients needing to study Stone close-up as he tracks their precious pesos, zlotys, Euros, shekels . . . converted into respectability in a new land.

These people wouldn't settle for a monthly statement in the mail. They'd want to watch his face.

Everybody smiling, doing coke, getting laid on the *Candace*. Quieting when the laptop gets switched on and the flowcharts come out.

Bacchus, god of good times, reveling on Stone's boat.

"What happened to the *Candace*?" Voort demands.

"Hit . . . the barge."

"The Mcgreeveys worked for you?"

Blood drips onto the wood-plank floor. Stone shuffles his feet and shakes his head. Smear marks streak the planks.

"I paid them not to report the accident . . . they wanted more."

"Your clients were *on the boat* when it sank?" The implications grow huger.

The blindfold swings back and forth.

"I dropped them off first."

Stone looking the wrong way when Voort speaks, as if his hearing is playing tricks on him, or Voort stands some-where else.

Voort imagines empty vodka bottles and coke residue on tables and women's clothing—a brassiere, a high-heeled shoe—in a cabin redolent with cologne, perfume, the rutting odor of sex. In Voort's mind, "Mister Five Percent" himself—half wasted on drink or drugs—steers his beloved yacht through the fog.

"We collided in Hell's Gate," says Stone.

"Why kill the cabdriver?"

Stone hesitates and Voort drives the butt of the Sig into his jaw and Stone screeches. Some third life-form seems to be in the room. Some animal that had lived inside Voort is now out, free. He knows it is the creature Bok awoke in the Mobil station.

When Stone starts talking again, his voice is muffled and a clicking sound comes out, like rubbing bones.

"We didn't know he was a cabby. He was just a treasure nut. He asked questions. We were afraid he was some kind of cop."

Bok should have called by now.

I have time for one more question, Voort thinks, the tape recorder rolling the whole time.

"After the *Candace* sank, why not just leave it there, on the bottom?"

"No guarantee . . ."

Stone throws up.

No matter. Voort understands. There was no guarantee that the boat would *stay* hidden, that it, or evidence, wouldn't wash up. Voort's learned enough to know that tugs and ferries carry sonar. Their captains know the river's contours and wrecks. A new one might easily be noticed. Sooner or later—by accident or curiosity—civilian or police divers might explore it. Stone couldn't leave proof of his activities where even a small chance existed that someone could find it.

"I need a doctor," Stone gets out.

His pants are torn, his shirt out, its tails smeared with blood. Stone's finished being sick. His face has gone slack and vomit dabs his lips. The red mist seems to be clearing from Voort's eyes. The lions have gone back to looking normal. Stone suddenly seems more pathetic than hateful. For an instant Voort actually feels a stab of pity for the man.

But then Stone says, "You can't use it."

He's rallying? Is it possible?

"You can't do *anything* to me," the lawyer hisses through broken teeth. "Not after how you got it. You know it but you don't really *have* it." He starts coughing. Or is he trying to laugh?

"Inadmissible," he wheezes.

Is Stone trying to keep me from preparing for Bok?

Resources beneath resources. Voort thought the man was through. But he steps back, feeling Stone's awareness probing from beneath the blindfold. He imagines a light has come back into Stone. He imagines with an almost superstitious certainty that Bok's presence, coming closer, has infused the man with fresh strength.

Could Stone still have an advantage here?

Voort says slowly, reasoning as he speaks, "You didn't tell me all of it. There's more, isn't there? Yes. *What did you leave out?*"

No answer.

Voort's rage is gone and in its stead he's filled with

cold hard certainty. "There's something else," he says, responding to Stone's resistance more than his words. It is the exercise of will itself that is the real message.

Stone says, "Nothing . . ."

Voort feels glass grinding in his belly.

Stone whispers, "I promissssse."

Voort can't stop himself. He lifts the Sig to hit Stone again.

"Site A clear," comes the whisper in Bok's earpiece. The Brit's reporting in from the woods near the parkway. Bok's rear guard is there to make sure police or tourists don't surprise them at the church. His crew has arrived in two vehicles. The Honda sits in plain view in the parking lot. It's the cop decoy. The SUV is in the woods with the Brit. It's the escape car, if Bok decides to leave by road.

"B site. Can't see our friend."

Which means the always reliable Oyven the Norwegian—another ex–UN peacekeeper from Serbia—has circled around to a wooded position that gives him a view of the back door, where Voort's Subaru blocks access.

I'd need a ladder to reach the upper windows. If Voort shows up there I could take him out, even in the fog. But if there are more people with him, they'll hurt Stone.

Mustn't let the client be harmed.

Bok imagines Voort loading weapons, making barricades.

That's what I would do.

Suddenly he knows how to get inside.

"Site C?" he whispers.

"I'm not a fooking bird," snaps the voice in his earpiece. Bok envisions his Aussie hiking up the cliff path from the pebbly strip beach below, and the *Wanderer*, which will be idling offshore.

"Give me a fooking minute. I can't fooking fly."

Almost ready.

Bok unconsciously pats his South African BXP—his favorite personal weapon: a black little soldier-stopper weighing only five pounds when unloaded but capable of firing nine millimeter cartridges at a rate of a thousand rounds a minute. Thirty-two-bullet extended magazine. Deadly close up, or at longer range.

The team's other armaments are sadly lighter, but you don't risk flying five mercs into the U.S. these days with assault weapons—especially not if they're coming to do a quiet salvage job. And you don't risk driving around with grenades and rocket launchers in your car or boat—not with cops doing all these spot checks on the river, and on bridges, not with four tough-looking mercs in a car fitting the profile from which cops work.

We don't look like accountants. We look like what we are, guys they want to stop.

So in the final moments before battle, Bok goes over the arsenal converging on the church. The Aussie has his .44 revolver and ankle .38, and the others a range of silenced semiautomatic handguns with extended magazines. A Beretta. A Glock.

They're experts. And they have knives too.

"C team's up, rugby fans!"

Which means the Aussie is here thanks again to the Wayne Hills Website. Bok had summoned the boat to the Hudson as soon as Voort had directed him to the George

Washington Bridge. By the time he'd learned the exact location of the meeting, the *Wanderer* had been close enough to get here after a short delay, due to fog.

Bok orders the Aussie to circle around and meet him, staying in the woods in case Voort's gazing out.

He hears a scream from inside the church. Stone.

Losing our temper, Voort?

He likes when enemies lose their temper.

He hears the vaguest rustle—so faint that an untrained ear would miss it. He shuts the PDA and smells the merc before the lithe ex–Australian Navy diver and the crew's wiseacre materializes out of the mist.

The Aussie whispers, "He snatched the client, eh? Bad for the reputation."

The Aussie always was a pain in the ass.

Another scream.

That Stone is suffering does not bother Bok. Voort will keep his hostage mobile. Stone has no capacity for pain. He complains if he gets a paper cut. You can't expect Voort not to vent a bit now.

But what enrages Bok is that the detective has the client in there at all.

The Aussie seems to guess the thought. "Losing our edge, mate?"

Bok sighs.

He punches in Voort's number. If Voort survives the initial hit he'll probably retreat to the cellar or shielded balcony or the back rooms, Bok figures.

"Ready to trade?" Bok asks casually.

He hears Stone moaning in the background. It makes Bok irritated at Stone.

*Get over it. Pain ends. In two hours you'll be on a jet.
The police won't figure out what happened. The bodies, if
there are bodies, will be gone.*

Voort's voice seems farther away on the phone, but
the shouting is audible inside the church. Voort yells,
Vince? Mike? We're starting!"

Bok thinks, Vince?

Voort tells Bok, "Put Mickie on. I want to know he's
still all right."

Bok nods as if he and Voort can see each other's faces.
I'll have a chat with Mr. Stone too."

Voort lifts the loaded Remington that had been leaning
against the wall. He checks to make sure it is ready to fire.
The second shotgun lies snugly in the ceiling-bracket, but
the twine looped around the trigger is still not attached to
the door.

As he frees Stone's cuffs from the hook in the wall, the
stained-glass lions' eyes seem particularly luminous.
Weakness of any kind draws their attention. The intensity
in their gaze is the sort humans want to avoid.

Without support, the lawyer sinks to his knees. Voort
tells Stone, "Stand up."

"My back hurts."

"If you want to stay here, that's fine with me."

Stone forces himself up. The effort sends a fresh cas-
cade of sweat down his forehead.

Stone shuffles forward, prodded by Voort. His cuffed
hands extend in front of him. The blindfold remains in
place.

In a moment, Voort knows, he will unlock the door for

Stone. The opening door will trigger a whole chain of events.

I don't want Stone to see how I laid out preparation in here, just like Bok doesn't want me knowing where he i in the fog.

On the phone he'd told the mercenary, *Send Micki across the clearing. When he's close, Stone will come out*

"So Mickie runs in and you snatch back Stone? I don think so."

Back and forth. Pay-scale mediation or hostage trad ing, the principle's the same. Send Mickie out. No, th hostages will pass each other nine feet from the door. No *thirty* feet. How about midway to the trees?

"You have the advantage," Voort had said. "You ca leave."

Bok had assured him, "Oh, we'll all go home tonight.

In the end, Bok had negotiated a slightly bette arrangement. The prisoners are now supposed to pa each other roughly twenty feet from the front door—bot walking slow.

"Pull your pants down," orders Voort.

"My . . . pants?"

Voort helps with his free hand. He roughly undoe Stone's belt buckle and pants. The church seems smalle cramped, cold, loud and quiet at the same time. Eve whispers echo. Bok will have marksmen outside, Voort fig ures. He'd be crazy to stand in the doorway, in view. Bu the only way to monitor things will be to keep Ston close—as a shield—as long as possible. That moment wi be the most naked and dangerous of all.

There's no other way.

Stone's gray wool trousers drop around his tanned, muscled legs. But his skin is stained with piss and shit. The black brief underwear is heavy as a diaper.

"There's a speed limit out there, Ted."

"I can't see."

"What didn't you tell me?"

"It won't do you any good."

Voort reaches for the lock. He forces his fingers to undo it. His heart is booming. Are Bok's people outside, pressed against the wall?

I was wrong to come here.

Voort shouts, "I'm sending him out. Vince, I'm ready downstairs!"

I'll never fool them.

Stepping to the side of the still-shut door, Voort tells Stone, "Reach out. Push it open."

Stone shakes his head. Apparently he's entertaining the same notions as Voort. He doesn't want to be the one standing there when the door swings open either.

"Open it," orders Voort.

And Stone steps forward like a stumbling automaton and extends his cuffed hands and *here we go*. The door is creaking open.

God, protect Mick and me.

Stone stands there for an instant, in the light.

No shooting erupts. No men run in.

Bok's voice calls from across the clearing, "Here comes your friend!"

Voort has no choice. *I have to look out.*

Voort extends his head a few inches around the door-jamb. Stone shields him, at least from straight ahead.

Nothing but fog fills the clearing. But then a shan
bling figure appears, alone, tottering toward the churcl

"Mickie?" Voort's hope rises with his clenching stomacl

The figure moves closer. "Con Man, he has four guy
with him."

God bless you, Mick. Can this really work?

Bok calls out, "Send Stone now."

"Go."

Groping, pants down, Stone veers left as he blindl
gropes into the clearing. Stone bumps a bench and crie
out. Mickie passes him, fifteen feet from the door.

Bok calling, "Follow my voice, Mr. Stone. How man
are in there with him?"

It's going to work.

Stone calls, "I can't see."

Mickie almost here now, something wrong with him
from the way his arms just hang down. He's slumped, i
pain. But Voort can't risk stepping out into plain view t
help him.

Mickie gets out, "They're in the woods on both side
Stay inside."

Bok repeating, "Mr. Stone? Mr. Stone?"

"Don't come out, Con Man."

Mickie's arms don't move. His elbows are angle
wrong, his fingers turned in odd sideways directions. T
hell with exposing himself. Voort moves fast, pullin
Mickie in as Stone finally answers Bok out there. "Ye
alone! He's alone!"

Voort slams the door.

Muffled now, Stone is shouting, "Alone, Leon!"

The door latches.

Mickie stands there, blinking, looking around, shaking his head and wincing.

"Don't tell me," he says, "that you're really alone."

"He made me say things," Stone says.

"I'm sure you held out as long as you could."

"He knows about the boat."

"It won't make a difference."

On the crew radio, Bok orders, "Hit the door. Now."

He hears the growl of an engine starting up in the woods, from out near the parkway. It is as if he had addressed the vehicle itself, his will so powerful that even inanimate objects obey. Bok envisions the SUV starting toward them, through the trees.

He tells Stone patiently, trying to get through the lawyer's shock, "Mr. Stone, get out of here. Go down the path and wait in the boat. I'll join you in a few minutes."

"Which airport?" Stone asks, picking up his pants.

"Newburgh." Bok's calm, concentrating on the woods. "I leased a Lear," he says as the engine sound gets louder. "Watch your step going down. It's slippery. Couple of months, and I bet you'll be back home. I bet it will all clear up."

"I . . . I . . ." Stone's humiliated, dazed and shamed, and Bok needs him functioning, so Bok lies. "I shitted myself too the first time in battle, Mr. Stone."

"You did?"

Bok sees headlights coming.

"He has guns," says Stone, turning, starting away, already a hunched figure stumbling toward the cliff. He's a shroud, a piece of past already, detached, gone.

"Having them isn't the trick," Bok murmurs as shoot-

ing erupts at the far side of the church, where the Subaru
is wedged up against the door. The planned distraction is
beginning. Bok envisions the detective in there, running
away from the front door and toward the back. Voort
charging out of the nave. Mickie the cripple trying to keep
up with him, or hiding, arms hanging like an ape's. Laurel
and Hardy. Abbott and Costello.

How could they have imagined they'd beat me.

Stone's voice comes out of the fog. So he's still up top.

"I never thought he would come back."

Here comes the SUV now, bouncing across the clearing.

Through the mist, from both sides of the church, Bok
sees his troops materialize. The Norwegian hugs the building, moving toward the side window. The SUV angles its
left headlight and grille perfectly, hurtling toward the front
door, a four-thousand-pound self-propelled battering ram.

Fuck diving, Bok is thinking. Diving is boring.

Leon Bok charges the front door, BXP up. The Aussie
will reach the entrance with him, just after the SUV hits.

This is what I was put on earth for, thinks Bok.

EIGHTEEN

Memory does not come in conscious time and neither does innovation. They're like Einstein's travelers, passing in a compressed instant that begins and ends inside a single footfall of a running policeman's feet.

BOOM.

Hearing firing outside the back door, Voort rushes down the nave with the Remington. Bok must be trying to break in past the Subaru back there—figuring Voort is still in the front. The firing means they're shooting the lock off—or trying to. Getting up close. Blowing out the wood all around the old lock. Scrambling in over the hood of the car—to covering fire.

BOOM. . . . BOOM. . . .

Voort thinking in Einstein time.

Mickie stumping along behind like a half-crippled camp follower. At least his eyes will be useful. There's no way to keep his partner back.

The engine roar doesn't register at first. But as Voort scrambles into the rear hallway he hears it inside the silence between shots.

Mickie shouts, "The front! Not the back!"

Voort reversing direction.

Too late. There's a crash from the nave and as Voort re-enters the main room—*the booby trap never worked because the door was blown in*—he sees the high grille of an SUV withdrawing from the smashed-in doorway . . .

BOOM. . . .

Voort firing now, charging blindly, the Remington spraying double ought at the backing-up vehicle and anybody trying to come through the front door.

Voort firing on automatically. Four shots left . . . three . . . and he's shouting for Mickie to get to the side.

Blood streaks the floor.

Voort rolling right.

Headlights shine in, through fog.

The car stopped, he thinks as he drops behind a pew, gasping and listening for footsteps and shoving in more shells, not waiting to run out of ammunition before he reloads.

Mickie on the floor, groaning. Mickie saying, "Windows!"

And the shutters to his left are splintering and Voort thinks, *SILENCERS*, swinging up and left but keeping the pew between him and the door . . . *BOOM* . . . Wood blows apart and he hears a spray of slapping noises—silenced nine millimeter bullets breaking the sound barrier and pinging into wood and off the stone walls.

A scream outside the window.

Voort crawling as the pew above his head splinters, but the retinal image remains of movement by the door, and *the headlights are still stopped so maybe I got the driver.* . . .

Cousin Spruce, he remembers, owns a bumper sticker that says SHIT HAPPENS FAST.

"I can move, Con Man. Are you hit?"

Voort hearing men outside, calling to one another.

Thinking, retreat to the trapdoor? Or the balcony? Decide. Fast.

Can we even reach either one?

Mickie's on the floor beside him. He's bleeding from his hand.

"Splinters, Con Man. What a laugh."

Loon Bok feels at peace. Soared, sure, on some level, but that's nothing compared to the other part. The way his whole body seems to melt into the earth, trees, landscape as he moves. The way his blood feels like it's all lit inside with electricity and nothing matters except the immediacy and this is the way it has always been for him in a fight. Battle provides clarity denied by other human experiences; love, avarice, hunger, excess. Bok has inserted himself, between ticks of a clock, into his own tissue. He has slowed mortality. Stepping through the door, past the smoking SUV and dead Brit in the driver's seat, spraying bullets, he is beyond confidence, rapture, hesitation.

Ahead is the druidlike circle of scattered half-splintered, overturned pews. The Aussie's pressed to the wall of the entrance. Blood, Voort's or Mickie's, drips back into the maze of pews, a smeared trail flowing toward the trapdoor Bok knows is back there, thanks to the Website.

You used the ladder to get down there, Voort.

Silence.

Bok calls out, "Voort?"

No answer, but even an amateur knows not to give away a hiding place.

Bok calls out, "You did well. You got the man outside. *Two* of my guys."

Nothing. No breathing. No click of a magazine being inserted into a weapon. No groans. Nada.

Bok's gaze glides left, and he nods to the Aussie, who slides toward the overturned pews, starting a little pincer action here as they penetrate Voort's makeshift maze. The Aussie glances at the blood trail, makes sure Bok saw it. When he enters the more exposed part of the nave—visible from the balcony—his eyes go right, and up. He stares, cocks his head, then resumes moving toward the pews.

Bok hisses loudly so Voort can hear, "He's on the balcony, William!"

The Aussie winks and moves two steps forward, away from the balcony, and stops. Two light steps and halt.

"Voort, I'm impressed with you," Bok calls. "How's your buddy Mickie?"

Bok staying in the shadowed area as the Aussie reaches the outer ring of overturned pews.

"Grabbing Stone, *that* was one helluva move, Voort," Bok says.

The Aussie crouches, spins, takes in the outer row between pews. The back of his head shakes back and forth. Voort's not in this circle. The Aussie resumes moving. Even Bok can't hear his gliding footsteps across the plank floor.

Bok calls, "Stay low on those steps, William."

Bok envisioning the two stooges, Moe and Larry, down there in the darkness, like scared women. A little fire will smoke them out, or seal them in actually, since the Website said the old escape tunnel is cemented up. The Aussie rounds the second row of pews and *only one more to go* and Bok keeps up the chatter.

"Stay by the wall, William!"

William's nowhere near the wall, of course.

The Aussie glides around the final, most drawn-in circle of Voort's homemade maze.

He's almost at the trapdoor now, but staying back, so they can't see him coming.

The Aussie rises and signals Bok.

BOOM . . . BOOM . . .

The Aussie blows sideways, not *away* from the trapdoor but *into* it. The explosions are coming from *upstairs*, from the *balcony*, and Bok thinks, *tricked*, even while he realizes that, astoundingly, the detective has taken out *three* of his finest.

Bok's in the nave before the echoes of shots have even died off and he's angry now, an extension of the BXP now, releasing the little black Voort-killer to do its wood-splintering, flesh-tearing best, the bullets stitching through solid wood bannister wall up there, in the direction from which Voort's shotgun blasts had come.

The Aussie's moaning, from the cellar.

Bok realizes with wonder that the blood on the floor is probably not even Voort's. It's Stone's.

You smeared his blood in a trail to sucker me in. You blindfolded him while you did it.

Bok thinking, *You want this? Me too.*

Bok's in the open. His reflexes will always be better than Voort's. The church is filled with smoke, and moans, and holes stitch across the stained-glass lions. Voort will be somewhere behind that solid bannister wall, on the balcony or stairs. He'll have to show himself to fire.

Or maybe I got him.

Stone will be down at the river by now. Worst comes

to worst, the Frenchman will start up the engine in a few minutes, and drive the lawyer up the Hudson to Newburgh, then get him onto the Lear.

Bok will have fulfilled his contract.

Stone will be safe.

Connor can't shoot, but are they together?

No more speaking now because the first sound will determine things. Bok frozen, waiting . . .

Bok hearing sirens in the distance. Wondering if he underestimated the cop that badly, thinking *Voort may have actually planned to turn himself in from the first, if it meant saving his buddy and taking me down. Is it possible he even called 911 before I hit the church?*

Bok realizes he's got only minutes to get himself out. He knows that he *can* get himself out. He sees the extent to which he has hurt himself with overconfidence. Voort's will is a living thing in here.

But I want him, thinks Bok.

The sirens get closer.

Bok straining to hear—through the noise—the inevitable whisper, scuff of sole, creak of leather, cock of a hammer, rustle of fabric because *those two guys are only cops and I am better than* . . .

"Bang!" comes from above, and Bok is so ready, so wired that even as he's moving reality hits him and he sees *it was Mickie yelling.* Bok pressing the trigger and even as his murderous fire rakes the balcony he's turning back because the stupid detectives have *split up* . . .

Voort rising from the *bottom* of the staircase.

Bok actually sees the shotgun blast before he hears it and is blown backward.

Bok, spread-eagled, is flying. He knocks over pews. The ceiling looks so high up there.

Bok smells bananas in the nave. The smell is so thick it's like a fruit stand, not a church.

Bok watching from afar as cops run in, yelling for someone . . . it has to be Voort . . . to drop the shotgun, get down, get on the floor.

Voort doesn't say, "I'm a cop."

Bok doesn't know that he *isn't* a cop.

As the faces bend over him Bok hears a policeman on the balcony shouting for a medic. "There's another one up here, alive!"

The faces come closer. He sees cop faces but behind them, other faces also. Bok realizes with wonder that they are not human faces.

This has to be my imagination.

Is it Hell's Gate?

NINETEEN

The siren sound is faint but audible on the river. The helmsman revs the outboard and backs the *Wanderer* from shore. As the pebbly beach disappears, Stone sits quietly in the stern, looking back. He hurts all over. He sees nothing but gray, thick mist.

"Leon said to get you out," the driver calls over his shoulder with a French accent. "Twenty minutes and we'll be up near Newburgh. A car's waiting. Take it easy, Mr. Stone. There's a first aid kit on board. I can take a look at you when we get farther away. You okay for now?"

Stone slumps, too tired to speak. He's dumped his soiled clothing into the river, wiped himself, and dressed in jeans and a T-shirt that the helmsman had provided. From the shooting sounds erupting up top, Stone wonders if the owner of these clothes will need them at all.

Everything that happened is Bok's fault.

"Beer, Mr. Stone? Bottled water?"

Leon should have warned me. If he had done his job better, none of this would have happened, Stone thinks.

"There's rubbing alcohol and disinfectant in the first aid box. And bandages. I can do stitches. I can give you a shot if you need something strong."

On the river they pass a looming tugboat, which seems to float along on mist, its stack hovering in air. It blasts out three warning notes on its horn. two small ones followed by a quick long. It is an animal, saying in cadence, get-out-of-the-way.

If only the Mcgreeveys would have used their horn on the night I ran into them, Stone thinks. *They were negligent. It was their fault we collided, not mine. And if they hadn't started asking questions about me later at the seaport, I would have left them alone.*

Stone gazes out at the long, low form of a barge behind the tug and then both crafts fall away into mist, swallowed-up, gone.

I gave Bok too much credit.

The pain in his face gets worse. Stone makes his way to the first aid box, opens it, rummages, and comes up with a plastic bottle of alcohol and gauze.

He doesn't know the helmsman. He's never met Bok's crew. He assumes that the man has adequate instructions and, like Bok, is a former soldier. Certainly like Bok the big man possesses a rough sort of competence. He gives his steering full attention. He's solicitous without fawning. He doesn't turn to stare when Stone groans, dabbing alcohol on the gouges around his torn-up mouth.

I'll need stitches but it could have been worse.

In fact, considering how things might have turned out, Stone realizes that he is probably not seriously injured. He upends the bottle and lets the liquid douse his gashes. The burning is rough, cleansing punishment. He is washing away Voort. Disinfecting himself of the cop.

I could have been on a beach right now, safe, if Bok had been more accurate.

Another tug approaches, veers, sends another trio of

get-out-of-the-way blasts across the water. Stone makes out the red-and-white hull, so the boat's a McAllister, moving quickly since it's not towing anything, but the *Wanderer* is faster and the tug falls behind.

Stone's growing angry at Bok now, and anger brings back dignity.

"It'll be a little rocky here, Mr. Stone. Why not take a seat."

Stone lets himself relax, lets the river take him. The scene at the church is already fading. So is the terrible feeling of being trapped. His wrists throb, and he rubs them where the cuffs clenched him. As he rides northward, the world is opening up its opportunities to him again.

What a horrible afternoon.

He even feels a bit of gratitude for the helmsman now. After all, this stranger whisking him to safety dove down into the dark river for him, groped along that filthy bottom for him, and removed evidence that could have ended Stone's family, career, life.

I'm safe.

Despite the pain he feels a lifting of cares, a shaft of optimism.

The computer is gone.

The other problem is gone.

Stone falls into speculative revelry, sees in his mind a white powdery beach, stucco-tile roofed seaside villa in Central America, air-conditioned, with a couple of guards with dogs. Palm trees. A Mercedes outside. He sees himself waiting for the all-clear to return home. He's on a stone patio, hooked to the Internet. He smells the ocean.

He's working his accounts. Soon the evening's guests will arrive. In Central America the girls are very pretty, and poor, so it's easier to find ones who are extra cooperative when Stone wants things from them.

As for Candace, he can get messages to her regularly. *Mmmmmmmm.*

Smiling, he's only vaguely aware of the rhythm of the boat horns, foghorns, river music, two short B-flats and a long each time they pass a tug. Those tugs are really out today. Fog or not. Busy, busy, busy. Blasting out notes as if sound approximates safety and each crew is handing off the *Wanderer* to the next . . . babysitting Stone and even *alerting* the next tug to . . .

Stone stands up in the back of the boat. The air is chilly suddenly.

He squints into the fog.

No, he is thinking. *I'm being paranoid. That's all.*

"What the hell," the helmsman says. *"Look* at *that. Three* of them coming. Hey! Get out of the way!"

A trio of tugs grind toward them out of the north, in mid-channel, horns sounding without stopping. Arrayed in a V shape, they're a diesel-powered blue-collar armada.

Voort had time to make a phone call. He left me alone and went into the back of the church. His damn family owns tugboats. He knows all these guys.

Stone breaking out in a cold sweat.

Horns are blowing in all directions now, like it's the Fourth of July or the tall ships have arrived. Like fireworks will go off any minute. The notes booming, combining, building into a cacophony echoing between the Palisades on the western shore and the towns on the east. People probably stopping on the waterfront in Irvington or Dobbs Ferry. People craning out into the fog, trying to imagine what could be causing the racket out there.

Stone says, "Turn the boat around."

The stupid helmsman not understanding.

Stone shouts, believing it all of a sudden, "I'll drive. Get away from the wheel!"

The helmsman can't even hear over the din of converging horns.

Stone pushes the man away, because *he* knows the river. *He's* had the *Candace* here. The whole scene has become some horrible joke, like *how many tugs can you fit in a river,* as the cordon draws closer. He sees tugs behind tugs.

Nononononononono!

Pushing the throttle up. To hell with bad visibility.

"What are you doing?" the merc cries.

Stone jerks the wheel and the *Wanderer* surges sideways over a wake, the bow plunging, and spray washed over them as he sees, to the south, more tugs coming and the lead one is turning sideways, to block him, pulling a long, low outline behind it, a barge, *just like on the night I hit the Mcgreeveys* and *it can't be happening twice* but there's another goddamn barge in his way.

The tugs are trying to hem him in.

It doesn't work.

Stone is quicker.

Stone veers expertly through the blockade. There's enough space to thread the maze. He's going to make it. He's through the cordon, in the clear! He never even sees what he hits—a big timber probably, part of a busted-up

pier, or bit of wreckage—any of a thousand pieces of debris floating down from Albany.

He hears the impact before he feels it. The *Wanderer*
is skidding sideways, and the whole boat seems to lift into
the air and plunge down with its props churning in a gas-
driven tantrum.

Water on his face now. Water on the windshield.
Water pouring *over* the windshield as Stone flies forward,
his injured face striking the wheel and his arm tangled in it
so he's crying, *"Get me out!"* and there's no explosion, just
a great awful pressure against his chest and in his neck,
with the tug turning upside down, except he sees it's *not*
the tug but *him* and *his* boat upside down. The water
rushes into his nose and lungs.

Stone swallowing water.

Stone breathing water.

Stone thrashing and being sucked down and a minute
ago he was *on* the boat but now he's under it, underwater
where the crunching noises seem louder, and in the darkness there's a *cr-ack* and something sharp and spiky digs
into his back.

Stone tries to scream, but more water floods into his
mouth.

He kicks. He claws. *I'm going to drown, going to die.*

Stone's head breaks the surface.

He's breathing. His chest burns. One leg won't move
and his clothing is weighing him down, but he is free,
alive, free.

He tastes oil and grit and realizes that the huge form
blocking his vision is the prow of a tug, looking awfully
high up there, idling five feet away. Another two seconds

and the thing would have run him over, ground him into meal the same way the Mcgreevey tug and barge cut the original *Candace* in half and then tore out its guts.

Stone gulps air, looks up past huge tire bumpers to see three men looking down at him. They're just staring. They're not even moving to help. They're just *standing* there.

"Help me," Stone sputters.

He's vaguely aware that forty feet away, the merc is being hauled from the water into a different tug. The whole river seems to be throbbing and humming, from the engines roaring, the props turning. It's all that steel moving under the surface. Those blades.

"Save me," Stone pleads.

An old man on the deck looks down toward him and then back at the other men. Stone sees they are bending down, uncoiling a rope and float to throw him.

"Thank you," he calls.

The old man's voice seems far away and indistinct, like fog itself.

"Help you? We'll help you. My name is Mcgreevey," he says.

TWENTY

The room is small but comfortable, the mattress solid, the TV reception adequate, the sink clean, like the toilet, and the view outside the mesh-covered windows shows the junction of the Harlem and East Rivers, a bit of green from the Brother Islands, an expanse of gray in the Bronx. From his cell, Voort can look out from Rikers Island prison—day or night—at Hell's Gate.

Stone's in here too. Pretty funny. Both prisoners.

Voort's in his fifth day in the special sequestered section set aside for ex-cops—to keep them safe from other prisoners. "Voort the kidnapper," the newspapers are calling him; killer of four and detective-impersonator, also accused of breaking and entering, assault and battery, and theft of police property, namely his badge.

Stone is charged only with money laundering, based on the testimony of an accused kidnapper, me. But at least the judge declined to set bail. He found out Stone had leased a jet to leave the U.S.

Vim has declined to press charges over the "stolen" weapons in New Jersey. And the Wayne Hills Township sheriff has agreed to extradite Voort to New York since the gunfight was self-defense, according to a witness and hero, NYPD detective Mickie Connor. Voort will pay back all damages to the church.

"If we file murder charges later, you'll be back," the frustrated Jersey DA had said.

Now Voort hears a key in the latch and turns as the steel door swings open.

"Visitors, Fred," says guard Antoine DuChamp, a soft-spoken, steroid-popping weight lifter—a giant whose biceps are so huge that they threaten at any moment to rip through his uniform. Antoine looks as if he could stop a riot all by himself if provoked. He calls all prisoners "Fred."

"Who's here, Antoine?"

"Not the lovely lady again. Not this time. It's your three fates, man. This time it's the suits."

Voort gives a last glance out the window. A banner strung on a passing tug out there, from stack to stern, reads WE'RE WITH YOU, COUSIN. A man waves from the pilothouse. Greg looks two inches tall through the mesh.

"The commissioner's waiting, Fred."

Camilla's come every morning so far, but it is clear that the rift between them has widened. Arrests tend to do that. This morning she'd told him, "I got a job, Voort. In Reality TV," and laughed. "Like I don't have enough reality in my life already?" But her smile had been tight, her posture stiff, the joke sad. The distance separating them had seemed a lot farther than a few feet.

What am I supposed to do, tell her everything through a prison telephone? The truth is, I still don't want anyone to know what happened to me. I don't think I'll ever tell.

"Your chief of detectives is here too," says Antoine. "She looks tough, Fred."

Cuffed, Voort accompanies Antoine down a long hall filled with the humiliated silence or hyperactive cries of the incarcerated. He's steered to the prisoner-guard elevator. He rises toward the tiers he's visited before as a guest, not a prisoner. Always before on Rikers Island, Voort's had the luxury of leaving when he pleased.

RENEGADE COP RUMORED TO HAVE UNCOVERED MASSIVE UN THEFT, reads a *News* headline under the arm of a passing off-duty guard.

I wish I could figure out what Stone wouldn't tell me.

A voice from the break-room television says, "Authorities remain close-mouthed about developments in the Voort case as they try to unravel conflicting stories. The whole episode is a fog of accusations."

Voort pauses by the door, sees that the Channel Five midday news show is on. He sees a head shot of himself on-screen. Antoine does not protest the delay this time. Antoine is curious himself.

The announcer says, "Ted Stone's lawyer has called Voort, quote, a psychotic ex-cop who fixated on his client and suffered delusions of persecution."

Antoine chuckles, "You look pretty unbalanced to me, Fred."

The well-heeled lawyer, on-screen now, says, "My client had nothing to do with the abduction of Detective Mickie Connor. He represents a company that hired divers in good faith to look for a sunken ship. He had no idea of any illegal activity, and cannot be held responsible for it. He should be released."

News footage shows a McAllister tug five days ago rendezvousing with a police boat. Stone and another man

Voort does not recognize are being handed by civilians to cops. They look wet, and slightly roughed-up.

The announcer says, "The second man fished from the river has refused to talk to police. He was released after Detective Connor was unable to identify him as one of his abductors."

Cut to the shot-up interior of the church.

"The dead men have been identified."

Cut to head shots of the dead. Labels beneath each face identify home countries. South Africa. Norway. Australia. Great Britain.

Cut to Vim outside his house angrily shooing reporters away.

"Individual members of the Voort family have acknowledged that he claimed he was threatened. But none could confirm he was."

Back to the studio now, where the anchorwoman tells the anchorman, "This is one big mystery, eh, Louis?"

The anchorman nods. "Mississippi's Republican senator Harrison Browne has said this scandal is one more reason the UN should be kicked out of the U.S. UN spokesmen countered that one incident does not tarnish a half-century of good works. Now to some new styles. Hemlines are up!"

"Your partner's here too," says Antoine.

"A whole delegation, huh?"

"I met your dad once. I was six. He saved my brother's life. Good luck."

Voort's been in the warden's office before, but as a cop. It's large and bright, with sun coming through the steel mesh on the windows, forming a shadow mosaic of

ittle squares on the cinder-block walls. The paint is insti-
utional green, and there are a few decorative concessions
o the warden's position. A yucca tree. A Lincoln Center
poster. The commissioner, seated beside the chief of de-
ectives, rises to greet Voort from a real leather couch.

"Hello, Voort." Warren Aziz shakes hands firmly, a
statement of support in itself. Voort's always liked the commissioner, a populist who dresses frugally, lives alone in an
East Side walk-up, and takes the subway to work to make
himself accessible to civilians each day.

"Couldn't you get evidence in the normal way?" says
Eva Ramirez, beside him.

"I wish," says Voort.

"I would have settled for evidence we can use," says a
third visitor from a club chair. Tommy Lamond Deans is a
deputy mayor and liaison between city hall and the police
department. He'd headed up the mayor's commission on
police corruption last year, and he and Voort have come to
respect each other after earlier run-ins.

"Actually, sir, you *can* use it," Voort says. "If I'd been a
detective when I snatched Stone anything I found out
would have been worthless. But evidence learned during
the commission of a crime—by a criminal—*can* be introduced, that is, as long as the criminal is willing to admit
what he did. I am."

"Hi, Con Man."

Mickie eyes Voort meaningfully—and warningly—
from a folding chair beneath the photo—a head shot—of
the current governor, one of those recyclable portraits that
rotate every few years on institutional walls.

"How you feeling, Mick?"

"I'm trying out for the Special Olympics this afternoon. The hundred-yard dash. Any event you don't need hands for."

Mickie winks, meaning, shit's happening. Be alert!

And both detectives glance toward the last man in the room, a well-dressed stranger occupying the power seat behind the warden's desk. He's not the warden. The man is in his fifties, Voort guesses, formidable-looking in an expensive, conservatively cut suit, white shirt, and striped tie. The shoulders are broad. The haircut is clipped. Ice blue eyes examine Voort through wire-rimmed glasses. The guy is apparently too important to be introduced yet.

"Who are you?" Voort says.

Mickie starts talking, meaning, leave the guy alone just now. "Con Man, remember what you told me about deciding to give that tape you made to the *Times*? Stone's confession? We came to ask you to reconsider."

I never told Mickie anything about the Times.

Voort snaps, picking up Mickie's cue, "If I want to do it I'll do it. It goes to my mental state."

The stranger's lips press more tightly together, but Aziz and Deans seem oddly unconcerned. It strikes Voort that they don't like the guy in the suit.

Voort turns back to the stranger and says, again, *"Who are you?"*

And Aziz says, "This is Campbell Dunn, from Washington."

"Washington State? George Washington?"

"Homeland Security," says Dunn quietly, and Voort thinks, chilled, *Could the other thing that went down with Stone's boat relate to security? Could the missile be real.*

"What does security have to do with me?"

Aziz says, "We've been having some interesting discussions with Mr. Dunn."

"Interesting," echoes Eva. If you didn't know her, Voort thinks, you wouldn't pick up the tone of disgust.

"Discussions we'll share with you," says Aziz. "As the mayor suggested. Campbell? Why not explain it to him?"

Dunn nods, steeples his hands as if creating a little fleshy church, his ice eyes hinting at weighty matters. There's something of the boardroom or military in his bearing. His voice carries a vague southern accent. Voort places its origin close to the Mason-Dixon Line. Northern Virginia, perhaps. Or southern Maryland.

Dunn starts off almost blandly.

"What do you really have as evidence? A kidnapper's testimony may not impress a jury. A tape made of Stone confessing while you beat him. A jury might discount this so-called confession made under duress. Perhaps Stone said it only to get you to stop. I'm sure this has occurred to you."

Voort starts to feel sick. Dunn is right.

"You have a video of a dead woman accusing Bok of murder—but Bok is dead too—and accusing Stone of theft, well, *that's* admissible, but there's nothing backing it up. It's merely an accusation. Bok's PDA gave us nothing incriminating, Bok's surviving crew member refuses to talk. And if Stone hired Bok to look for the *Hussar,* that's perfectly legal."

Voort the prisoner feels himself filling with despair.

Dunn continues in his measured fashion, each word falling like the beat of a judge's gavel.

"We also have a few words Stone babbled to the tug crews when he was fished from the river. But what did he *say*? He didn't confess anything! He *denied* that he'd been involved with the deaths. In short, there's no case, Detective. Just words, as you know."

"What do you want?"

"And on the other hand," Dunn continues, picking up cadence, driving points home like a good attorney summing up before an attentive jury, "let's look at evidence against *you*. *You* quit the department in front of witnesses. *You* misrepresented yourself and abducted Stone before witnesses. *You* say Bok worked for Stone, but there's nothing to tie them together or to Mickie's abduction. *You* admit that you beat the man up."

"I should have hit him harder," says Voort.

Mickie says, "You made your point, Dunn."

Mick morphs into one of his wise-guy roles, the game-show host. Voort recognizes the Monty Hall grin, hands spread wide, smile broad and white. Mickie likes to do the act when they bargain with particularly obnoxious defense attorneys.

"Let's make a *deal*," Mickie says.

Dunn glances with irritation at Aziz, not Mickie. Mickie's not worthy of his ire. Dunn is the kind of guy who goes to the boss, not the employee. Dunn's look says to Aziz, can't you keep your people in line?

"What I'm about to disclose involves national security," Dunn tells Voort.

Voort is impressed, but his experience in the Szeska case has also made him wary of the invocation of these words.

Dunn nods. "Enemies here. Enemies abroad."

"Start with here," says Voort.

"You'll love this, Con Man," says Mickie.

"Detective Connor," Aziz snaps. "That's enough."

"But before we can go further," Dunn says, leaning forward, pushing a sheath of papers at Voort across the desk, "sign this. It acknowledges that what I'm about to tell you is protected, that you're fully aware that any disclosure would make you liable for incarceration. In *Leavenworth*. Loose lips, Detective. Loose lips."

"I remember her," says Mickie. "From high school."

Voort scans the paper. Dunn has told the truth.

But he picks up the vaguest head shake from Mickie, from the corner of his eyes. It suddenly occurs to Voort that Aziz has brought Mickie along specifically to piss off Dunn.

"May I ask you something, Mr. Dunn?" Voort asks, trying hard to figure possibilities.

"Of course."

"If I sign," he says, "and you tell me things . . . if those turn out to be the *same* things I learned from Stone, the confessions on my tape, does that mean I'm no longer allowed to *use* the tape?"

Tommy Deans looks away quickly, but he seems to have relaxed.

Dunn says, "An interesting legal question, but that's not my area. I'm sure later we can find the right person to answer that very good inquiry, after you sign."

"Meaning once I sign I can't mention the tape."

"Meaning once you do, you've taken the first big step," says Dunn, "to walking out of here, free."

"What about Stone's charges against me?"

"They can be dropped."

Voort says, surprised, "You'd guarantee that on paper?"

"Why not?"

"Great invention, paper," says Mickie. "Con Man, he's not telling you that you'd be off the force."

Dunn shrugs. "Mr. Stone wanted something too. He's not fond of you. And frankly, if you're in prison you'd be unemployed anyway."

"But if Stone's going along with this, doesn't that prove I'm right?"

Dunn's look seems to concede a little sympathy. "Stone's version is, Mickie learned that Bok's crew was involved in drug smuggling. When they took him, you made the mistake of deciding Stone was involved. But he had no knowledge of their illegal activities. Now that those men are dead we'll never know who they *really* worked for. They may have worked only for themselves."

Dunn spreads his hands like a magician who has just made cards disappear. But his smile fades when Voort shakes his head.

"Why are you protecting Stone? I'm not signing your damn paper."

The bureaucrat looks surprised. In Washington, probably everyone signs disclosure papers before having any conversations at all, thinks Voort. Restaurant owners probably keep no-talk agreements under their bars, for handy use by diners.

"Everyone's offering me shitty trades these days," Voort says. "I'll take my chances in court."

"And in the newspapers," Mickie says.

"To punish who? Him? Or yourself?" says Dunn, coming back at Voort with the same bland reasonableness. "You remind me of a major I knew in Vietnam. After Charlie took him, after they had him awhile, all he wanted was revenge. When we got him back he didn't care about anything else. We had to relieve him of command. What really happened to you in that bathroom, Voort?"

"They held a gun to my head."

"Did they? Is that all? Sign the paper."

"We signed," says Aziz, but his neutral expression urges resistance. Voort wonders why no one warned him of this meeting. Then he understands. Dunn signs everyone up before he talks to them. Once you're signed up, you can't tell anyone else.

Eva suggests to Dunn, "Try without threats."

To Voort she says, "You don't need threats, do you?"

Which is when Voort decides that his bosses *want* him to make the deal but not sign the paper. The NYPD wants the leeway to reveal the tapes later on.

"No," he says. "No threats."

Dunn averts his eyes for a fraction of an instant, reminding Voort of an actor friend who does the same thing before stage performances. It helps him slip into his new personality. Dunn straightens. The transformation is impressive. The stern face has relaxed into something reasonable. The best guys can always summon up appropriate roles: demon, angel, enemy, friend.

Dunn sighs and, coming around the desk, looks approachable, full of chagrin.

Hell, he's even nodding in admiration of Voort's perception.

"Let's start another way," he says.

"Yeah," Mickie says. "Let's."

"I've lived in Washington too long," says Dunn, sighing deeply. "You forget how to talk to people. You bargain instead of reasoning. I should have appealed to your patriotism, Voort. After all, with this terrible terrorism—"

"Terrorism?"

"It doesn't stop," Dunn says.

"I don't understand. What does Stone have to do with that?"

Dunn's palms go up. "I've given the wrong impression. It isn't that he's involved, no, quite the contrary because . . ." Dunn sighs again, gropes for right words, looks grave, as if lives hang in the balance, lowers his voice to an intimate level. "He's helping us out . . ."

"Us," says Voort flatly.

"You lost family, didn't you, Detective? To terrorists."

Voort remembers with a sick feeling his cousins who died at the World Trade Center. He'll never forget that day. He also notes that Dunn has started calling him "Detective."

Dunn asks, "You want to keep the people who do this kind of thing away from our shores, don't you?"

"Dunn, are you capable of speaking plainly?"

"Yes, yes, Washington again. You can't go from A to Z in a straight line. Forgive one more question. You *do* know that after 9/11—you *do* remember that we . . . well, Treasury . . . discovered that large positions had been taken in the stock market *before* those planes hit the Trade Center.

Millions of dollars had been positioned to make a fortune if United or American airline stocks went down. The investors knew what was going to happen, Voort. And if *we* had known who *they* were, *we* might have predicted it too."

"How is Ted Stone connected to this?"

"I'm trying to underline the importance," says Dunn, a flush of emotion reddening his face, "of how crucial it is to fighting our enemies that we *follow their money.*"

"I could use money," says Mickie.

"Follow whose money?" says Voort.

"*That is exactly the problem,*" says Dunn. "How do we know when money moves electronically who really moved it? With four hundred billion dollars disappearing annually into the underground global economy every year, how do we know which monies belong to friends and which benefit others?"

"You use informants," says Voort, starting to see the big picture, "to help you keep track of things."

"No different than police using them on the street," agrees Dunn, like he and Voort are on the same team, an effective duo.

"Stone is an informer," says Voort.

"A *helper,*" says Dunn.

"You look the other way when he slips thieves and war criminals into the country because he's helping you. You don't care if murderers come in as long as they're not terrorists. One standard for us. One for everyone else."

"I don't appreciate that tone."

"Hell, more cash coming in means jobs, investments. We need all the cash we can get these days, right?"

"I find some things I have to do unpleasant too, Detective, but I'm a realist. This is *not* about investment," Dunn says, genuinely angry now.

"Yeah, I see that."

"No. You sit back and hope for safety and don't want to know how we achieve it. The world is small, Voort. Pick up a phone and move money in minutes. We like to think we can follow it. We *announce* in Washington that we can follow it. But whenever we say we're freezing assets of our enemies, how do you think we know where the assets are?"

"I'd like to know where *my* assets are," says Mickie.

Dunn nods, regaining some control. "Painstaking research, Voort. Finance is complicated business! You don't unravel the trail with a few taps on a computer keyboard. You need people who know."

"Thank you, Mr. Stone."

"Love America or hate us, they all invest here. This is where they make the money. This is where the world buys and sells. I could drive you to Westchester this afternoon and show you a new condo going up. Do you know who *really* owns it? A Chinese general! I could fly you to the Maryland shore and show you a hotel where forty percent of the financing was routed through Malaysia, by an opium lord."

"No wonder everything I invested in went down," Mickie says.

Dunn says, "When Hamas routes its drug money here, do you think they sign the papers with their real name? Bogus companies! Fraudulent IDs!"

Voort says, "Your informants help you figure out

which accounts to ignore and which to watch. Ted knows which you can eliminate. Run-of-the-mill thieves and torturers are no big deal. Letting them in is worth a good tip every once in a while from Ted. The war criminal goes free. The terrorist gets stopped."

"For the greater good." Dunn blows out air, gets up, paces with passion, agitation. "Of course we never knew about the murders *here*. Stone went too far. But yes, we let him operate. We've stopped him now. He's through. He'll leave the country."

"Then why do you care if I pursue him?" Voort answers his own question. "Because there are more people like him. Because it's a dirty war and you don't want the newspapers, Congress, the world, to know how you operate."

"Because the system works, no different than the one you use in the police. Or would you like the *New York Times* to publish a list of every informant *you* use? How long could you keep operating effectively if that occurred?"

"Lies," says Voort. His head hurts.

"You never told a lie?" asks Dunn. "*You* never told yourself it was for a better good."

Voort thinks of Camilla. He shuts his eyes.

"Computers aren't magic, Voort. In the end—no matter how good the program—you need a human being to guide you and explain what's going on. And that was Ted Stone."

Voort feels acid eating at his stomach.

Then he asks, seeing more, "And how did Stone get information about me from the police department, about my family? Through Washington? Did he go to you people with a story that we were persecuting him? Did someone in your department help out?"

"Of course not." But Dunn's face is red now. *So this is what the fight with the mayor was about,* Voort thinks.

Voort asks, "And Captain Mcgreevey? What do you tell him about why his sons died?"

Dunn sidesteps the question. He's calmed, and no wonder, because Voort realizes they've started bargaining. The fundamental question has been answered. Voort will keep silent. His stomach burns.

Dunn says, "Stone won't press charges. He'll swear you shot the men in self-defense."

"I asked about Mcgreevey." Voort envisions the old man and the tug armada handing Stone over to the police on TV. "And Rebecca Means, Colin's sister."

"The president said there would be casualties in this war. Not even one is acceptable. But better a small number now than a lot later."

"How about someone in your family next, Dunn?" says Mickie.

"Are you threatening me?"

"You'd sacrifice them for a greater good," says Voort. "Right, Dunn?"

Dunn looks away, gathers himself. He's remembering his role here as the reasonable man. "Which do you want?" he says. "To take cheap shots? To blame yourself the next time something happens and we *could* have prevented it except we lost the chance because of you?"

"I hate these questions."

"Decent people do."

"I want closure for Mcgreevey," Voort says. "You're so good at figuring out lies, so one more shouldn't hurt. For him, and for Rebecca Means. Something that makes them feel better. Turn the boys into heroes. Figure out the best damn lie you ever told, and sell it."

"You agree then," says Dunn, looking relieved. "You'll sign the paper?"

"Sell your lie. But I won't sign anything."

"Why not?"

"For later on, if I change my mind."

Aziz speaks up. "If you go too far, Dunn. If you pull this garbage again and don't tell us," he says.

"I thought you were here to help," Dunn tells Aziz. But his stern mask dissolves. He surprises Voort by nodding. The real man may be likable, or at least tolerable. And Voort has to admit to himself that he'd not do well facing Dunn's choices every day.

"Anything else?" Dunn asks.

"Yeah," says Mickie. "If Voort didn't do anything wrong, he keeps his job. Fuck Stone. We all know he did it. Voort keeps the job."

"I agree," says Eva. "If you'd done your job right, Mr. Dunn . . ." She trails off.

Dunn seems about to protest. Then he relaxes.

"I'll try. I really will. It's the best I can do."

"No, you'll do it," says Tommy Deans, finally speaking up. "I spend my days making deals with people who crawled out from under sewers. It's time I made one for someone I respect for a change. You'll do it for Voort."

And Voort holds up a finger, frowning. "A question

from me, Mr. Dunn. What else went down with the *Candace* besides the records?"

For the first time, the man from Washington looks genuinely surprised. Baffled.

Voort does not think he is acting this time.

"What do you mean, what *else*?" asks Dunn.

TWENTY-ONE

He can't believe that he's outside again, free. The sun shines directly on his face. The fog is gone. It seems unreal to Voort as he boards the prisoner ferry that the river is no longer divided into tiny mesh-sized squares, as it had looked from inside his cell.

No one has met him outside the prison, or will be waiting on the Bronx landing where the ferry will dock. He's called no one to pick him up, not even Camilla.

What do I tell her?

He puts the thought off again. He has other things to think about. The boat is lightly filled with guards ending day shifts, visitors, lawyers, and released prisoners. On the landing Voort ignores the charter buses loading for the trip back to Manhattan. He hails one of the yellow cabs usually waiting for a fare.

Back on Thirteenth Street—alone in his empty house—he showers off the prison smell and leaves his clothes in the laundry even though they are fresh. He shaves and dresses in fresh-pressed jeans, a crisp white shirt, and a Calvin Klein two-button, black-tweed light-weight jacket. His black-tasseled loafers are shiny. Here comes the wealthiest cop in New York.

He takes the Jag downtown and leaves it out front of One Police Plaza, its once-again-legal police visor down.

Mickie's on medical leave indefinitely, holed up in his new apartment. Voort accepts congratulations tossed his way in the lobby. He ignores glances directed at him as he waits for the elevator. When he gets upstairs, detectives greet him warmly. Santini waves; all is forgiven. The secretaries are smiling. The computer girls chipped in and left a gift certificate for the kayak shop on his desk.

"Stock up the refrigerator. We want Voodoo brewskis," the note from Hazel says, as if no time has passed and everything is the same as it was three weeks ago.

Mickie's desk is cluttered as always. Voort's is sparkly clean, emptied but not reassigned. Santini apparently held on to Voort's packed-up files and had them brought back in and piled in a corner by the mini-fridge and coffee machine.

Stone was afraid there would be something in these records. Maybe he was right and I missed it before.

The top box is heavy with taped-in files, books, pens, magic markers. The next box contains knickknacks and what he is looking for—notes and files relating to the deaths of Colin Means and the Mcgreevey brothers, and to the *Hussar* and Ted Stone.

He fills the Mr. Coffee with Jamaican Blue Mountain. As it percolates, the rich smell fills the room. He leans back and puts his feet up. He carefully begins to read.

Here's the map of the river.

Voort going back in his head to only three weeks ago. He sees himself happily paddling on the East River with Camilla. He sees the kayaks and the body floating. He sees the bruise pattern on the taxi driver's body and remembers how it had matched his own.

Listening to the tape of Captain Mcgreevey now.

The coffee is rich and sweet, and Voort is famished. There's no fresh food in the mini-fridge, so he buys a turkey on kaiser in the cafeteria, brings it back to the office, and piles on extras from jars. Sweet red peppers. Artichoke hearts. Cornichon pickles. Honey mustard.

Beats the food on Rikers Island.

Chowing, he goes over the notes he made interviewing Rebecca Means. Colin was quiet, he reads. Colin loved treasure. Colin liked to go to the river and gaze out in the direction where he believed lay the sunken *Hussar*, with its $600 million in gold.

No help here.

The phone rings as, frustrated, he sifts through the next box, which he sees is crammed with yellow pads, Tina Tadesse's autopsy results, the missing persons list, the xerox of the signatures that he'd taken from the guest book at the South Street Seaport.

"Detective Voort," he answers. Just saying the title fills him with gratification.

"Back on the job so soon?"

Shit, he thinks. Camilla.

I can't believe I didn't call her.

He squeezes his eyes shut. He has never in his life felt like more of a screwup. She's called on the office line—not his cell phone—so she knows exactly where he is. He feels as if she can see him.

Or is this what I wanted at some level? To piss her off?

"Where are you?" he says.

"At the prison. This is quite a reversal, isn't it? Me

here," she says, not sounding amused but tired. "I came back to visit you."

"I can explain," he says.

How many times has he heard the same words in this building, from suspects.

"No need," says Camilla. The tone and words fill him with dread.

"I might have missed something in my notes," he explains.

"Well, I hope you find it."

"Where can we meet?" he says, loathing his own sense of too-late.

"Oh, tonight. There will be plenty of time for a talk."

From the way she says it, from the deadness and finality in the tone, Voort feels the floor dropping away.

What else did I expect? Or want?

"At home," he says. "Good idea, Camilla."

"No, not at your home," she says, naming a restaurant in which they have never eaten, and an address in Soho—way south of where they live. When the meal is over, she seems to be saying, we won't stroll as usual to "your" home.

Click.

Hanging up, Voort suddenly has the most vivid feeling of another man's flesh on his thighs and back, as if it's been there all along. As if, even with Bok gone, it remains there. It will always be there.

The wave of revulsion sends Voort's hand lashing out, smashing into one of the boxes and knocking it over so it falls sideways, spilling contents.

Voort goes back to work, sitting on the floor.

Nothing I can do until tonight.

He sits amid the memo books and papers like a college student before final exam day. He tries to read. He must read. There's something here, he tells himself.

He stares down at Tina Tadesse's autopsy results and his line drawing of Hell's Gate. Then there's the missing persons list and the xeroxed copy of the guest-signature list from the South Street Seaport Museum, and the description of the divers on the *Wanderer*.

He tries to channel his emotions into concentrating. He makes his focus small. He tries to block out Camilla, but his heart is throbbing in his throat and fingers.

Voort holding up the missing persons list.

Rereading the names he'd seen once before.

Harvey Clarke.

Cleon Francis.

Beth Aarons.

His neck starts to itch.

Is this it?

Voort pulls the phone off the desk and punches in the number of Ted Stone's office. His throat is dry. What he sees in his mind is the half-hidden name plaque on the desk of Stone's receptionist . . . the one who had been out "sick" both times Voort came by.

LIZZIE A, written on the name plaque.

Lizzie Aarons?

Lizzie for Elizabeth? Elizabeth for Beth?

Voort gets through to Ms. Snob on the first ring. With Stone in the news, perhaps business is light.

He's Beth's brother, he says, calling from Seattle. There's been a terrible auto accident involving Cousin

Cynthia, and she is in the hospital. He needs to speak to Beth right away.

"I'm so sorry, but Beth doesn't work here anymore."

"Do you have a forwarding number or address?"

"I'm sorry, but she got sick and never came back. She called in and quit, I heard. Why not try her at home?"

"I will."

Traffic is light heading uptown on the FDR, and the Queensboro Bridge is clear. Lizzie Aarons lives—or lived—with her mom, who'd called in the original missing persons report. The address is in Astoria, not far from Hell's Gate. It turns out to be a small row house along a narrow street and across from a lamp factory. The air smells of glue, and the stack is spewing gray smoke into the air. Mom's home, he sees, noting an old Taurus in the weedy driveway. The chain-link gate creaks when he opens it. When he pushes the buzzer, it produces a high, wheezy whine.

Alice Aarons—Beth's mom—stumbles against the doorjamb when she sees Voort's badge. She's probably been fearing a visit from the police ever since she listed her daughter as missing—a status that Voort knows from the computer girls has not been changed.

"You're the policeman who was on TV."

"Yes, ma'am."

"She's dead," she says. "You found her."

"I'm not with missing persons, but I am trying to locate her. Can you stand a few questions? They might be questions you've been asked before?"

"Why not? I ask myself the same questions every day."

Does he want coffee, she asks. All she has is instant.

"Please," says Voort, feeling that a minor chore might soothe the woman's frazzled nerves and give him more time with her.

He follows her through the living room toward the kitchen. The house has a lived-in feel. It's furnished cheaply but neatly. The wooden floors and pine furniture are polished, the rag rugs vacuumed, the chintz curtains held back with satiny looking cords.

He halts before a photo on a wall unit—showing mom and daughter standing on Fifth Avenue, beneath the logo of the famous toy store, FAO Schwarz. As the missing persons report listed Beth as being twenty-two, the photo seems recent. It's summer in the shot, or at least hot, because both women are sleeveless. Beth looks beautiful, brunette, long-haired, dark-eyed, smiling. But her face, at least in the photo, does not appear intelligent to Voort.

In the kitchen, over coffee, he gets to the real questions after one or two minor ones.

"Does Beth have a relationship with her boss, Ted Stone?"

Alice has been lifting a cracked cup to her mouth. It stops.

"I wouldn't call it a relationship."

"What would you call it?"

"The same thing you would, probably," she says wryly. "Beth is a lovely person, but she's not a rocket scientist. She's just naive."

"You don't approve."

Voort careful to keep the questions in the present tense.

"I never met him."

"But you know *her.*"

"You think you know someone, even your own child, and then it changes when you see them fall in love," she says.

"In love?"

"In heat."

Alice puts down the cup because her hands have begun trembling.

She says, "I saw Stone on the news. And you too. She's dead. I know it. If she were alive she would have called me. She calls twice a day if she's away and she hasn't called in weeks."

"I'm sorry," Voort says.

"Everybody tells me, don't give up hope. They say she'll turn out like that girl in Canada last year who disappeared. Maybe you remember. She had a tumor in her head. One day she just wandered home. Some news to hope for, huh? A tumor."

"I remember that story. The operation worked."

Alice Aarons wipes her eyes. Voort experiences a sense of mystery coming to culmination, resolution. "Beth goes up to her room and moons about him. She cries if he doesn't call. I told her, 'He doesn't care about you.' But she doesn't want to hear it. I even wondered if she moved away, took an apartment, because I argued with her about him."

"But she would have called if she had."

"More coffee?"

"This is fine, thanks."

"Beth would sit up there and fill page after page in

her diary." Alice has suddenly switched to the past tense, perhaps not even knowing it.

"Her diary," Voort says, a liquid feeling in his belly.

"It's private," Alice says.

Voort says nothing. Just toys with the spoon.

"I read it. I don't know what to do anymore," whispers Alice.

"I think that you do," Voort says.

Minutes later he's upstairs, sitting on Beth's single bed, holding the diary. The room seems frozen in mid-transition, reflecting the incomplete passage from girl to woman. Pink walls. Rock and roll posters. Piles of *Glamour* magazines on the desk she once did homework on, in high school. It's a kid's desk, painted yellow.

The diary has a lock but Beth didn't use it. In this room, whatever else she had, she had trust.

Voort finds plenty on Stone inside, all right.

"May I borrow this?"

"Why are you here? Was Beth involved in what happened in that church?"

"I don't think so. Not in the way you mean."

"You were in jail and now you're out. They're not telling us things, are they? It's a cover-up."

"I'm not allowed to say. But I'll find out what happened to Beth."

"You'll tell me either way?"

"I promise."

Alice's lower lip quivers, and when the tears come, Voort sees more clearly the depth of this woman's loneliness, on top of her grief.

He drains his coffee and leaves the cup on the night

table near the bed. "I'll call every day," he says, realizing that this is the same promise he had made, and broken, to Camilla.

In the car outside he sits reading the diary. It's easy to spot the appropriate passages. Beth's done him a favor. She's underlined things. He eyes the little-girly loops in the writing, the purple ink highlighting the unadulterated dreams wafting up from the small, lined pages as a receptionist imagined a life with her boss.

Does he love me too?

She was as deluded as me, he thinks. Telling herself lies. Hope is much more powerful than reality. And what better place to escape into it, unchallenged, than a diary. No one to laugh at Beth here, contradict her, remind her of the unpleasant questions.

Beth writing, *I was a little shocked when he told me what he liked to do on the boat, while he drives.*

Convincing herself that domination is affection, that debasement is love. Voort changing the scene on the *Candace* in his mind as he reads. Stone's dropped the clients off, if the MO in the diary is accurate, but he's kept Beth Aarons on the boat for some special partying. Stone's pulling the handcuffs and masks and dildos from a drawer.

"Con Man," says Mickie, when Voort calls his partner's new apartment in Queens. Mickie sounds a little slurred, from painkillers, probably. But Mick's alert enough to process things.

"Thanks for helping out in the meeting, Mickie."

"The doctor said I can be back at work in three, four weeks. A gimp with the brain of steel. Hey Con Man, this new apartment isn't so bad. Who needs a pool, right? Who needs a boat? A guy should get back into the general population. Syl doesn't mind, well, she *minds,* but sooner or later I'll get out of the doghouse. When Bok had me when I was tied up, owning a fucking big house didn't seem so important, my man."

Voort tells Mickie about the diary.

Mickie is quiet a moment. Then Mickie says, "You're kidding? Blow jobs?"

"That's what she wrote."

"All this—murders, fires, the security guy—because of *that*?"

Voort back on the *Candace,* envisioning the lawyer at the wheel, not paying attention to the right things. Stone not seeing the boat or barge looming until too late.

Mickie saying, "Seven people murdered. Probably about half a million people robbed. Arson. Drownings. The church."

"The perfect system shot to hell."

"You think she's down there in the wreckage?"

"My guess is, the boats collided. Stone got out. He lied to the Mcgreeveys. He said nobody else was on board."

Both men stay on the line silently, comfortable with their electronic connection. Voort thinking about the way the extra act—the one you can't keep yourself from doing—gets you in trouble. He's seen it a hundred times. He and Mickie spend their careers sifting through the wreckage of lives ended by a single excess, often something quite ordinary.

"I'll order divers down," says Voort.

"To check near the wreck, as well as on it. There won't be evidence on it."

"Yeah, well, wherever they dragged her. If we can even find the wreck again."

"And we can't tell the press anything," says Mickie. "Or Mr. Smith comes back from Washington."

"Not other cops. Not a jury. All for the greater good, whatever that means."

"Beat the devil," Mickie says.

"But the deal with Dunn," Voort adds thoughtfully, "says nothing about talking to people who already know what Stone did."

Mickie needs a second to understand, but then Voort hears a long breath on the other end of the line. "His investors would be pissed off, all right," Mickie says. "Yep. Ve-ry angry. Guys like that would get pretty pissed off if they knew Stone reported everything they did to the Treasury Department. I wouldn't want them pissed off at me."

"Not that I would do such a thing," says Voort. "Even though Stone told me exactly where they are, what they invested. Where he hid all of their money."

"What kind of people are we?" Mickie says. "Animals?"

"Not us," Voort says. "Nope."

"I sure hope no one calls them."

"Camilla moved out, Mickie."

"Then do something about it, asshole," Mickie says.

The boy and the father sit on the rooftop, on a hot August night, looking out at the city. From below come the sounds of life, struggle, pleasure, doubt. Planes angle overhead, and seem by illusion to reach the height of stars. Lit windows provide a panorama of urban dioramas. Here's the lonely woman gazing at the street enviously, as if to absorb the lives of strangers. Here's the happy couple entwined, a portrait framed by wood and glass. Here's the cat peering out, filled with feline fears and secrets. Here's a telescope in a window. Its owner has gone out.

"Dad, what's the most scared you ever were?"

These are precious moments for a boy and dad. And the boy looks up at the man and he's filled with curiosity. Has Dad ever *really* been scared at all? Voort the boy waiting for a story about a shooting, or a chase, or about the time he heard Vim and Bram talking about last night in the dining room, when they thought he was asleep . . . about a convenience store robber who'd knifed his father in the arm many years ago.

"That's an easy one," Bill says. "The most scared was . . . before I asked your mom to marry me."

"You mean you didn't know she'd say yes?"

"She seemed so fantastic. I stayed up all night rehearsing. I knew she loved me. But for her to go the extra step, to say she'd spend her *life* with me, well, I was scared all right, pal."

And Voort, riding downtown to meet Camilla years later in a cab, thinks back to the night on the roof, and remembers the story in a way he did not before.

The sense of loss a wave now, building . . .

Voort asks the cabdriver to pull over two blocks from his destination. He's early. It's the first time in weeks he's been on time for anything with Camilla, he realizes. Strolling past the knots of tourists and revelers, he still has no idea what he is going to say. His will, when it comes to her, has been sucked away into some black dead hole.

He rounds the corner. The restaurant lies halfway up the narrow street, but he does not need to look at the addresses because he sees her ahead, standing outside.

Waiting for me. Early too.

"Hello, Voort."

She seems reluctant to go inside. She does not want to do whatever she's planning in the restaurant, he sees without asking. She doesn't want to be bound politely by a chair and table, a glass of wine, a waiter's schedule, the check coming while two people look at anything else except each other.

"You look nice," he says.

"Thank you."

Her anger has drained away, and the coldness has been replaced by exhaustion. Her look is affectionate, as if she's gazing at old photos already. It is this emotion—passion reduced to affection—that frightens him the most.

When he takes her arm, she willingly gives it, allows him to turn her west, where she probably wanted to go anyway, toward the river, and the past.

"This isn't working, Voort."

He feels his stomach dropping, his blood slowing. He feels secrets like glass grinding in his intestines

"I took a sublet temporarily, in Tribeca," she says. "I'll be working long hours in a new job."

As if employment had anything to do with her moving out of his house.

"I want to explain, Camilla."

"Hey, people change. You do. I do. Sometimes I think problems don't come from the changing, but the refusal to admit that you're not the same."

"I wish you'd reconsider."

Voort's voice seems to come from somewhere inside him, pushing out from way below his vocal cords. To get out, the words have to slice through sinew and bone. He wonders if he can make things better. He wonders if she will really hear what he says. He wonders if it will even matter. He knows he's been selfish for too long.

Whatever happens with Camilla, though, he knows the only way to banish Bok is to do this.

"Camilla," he says, "there's something I have to tell you. Something that happened. Something you need to know."

A pause. No change in expression.

Then, "All right. I'm listening," Camilla says.

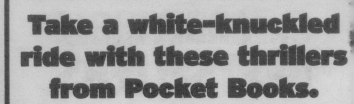

Take a white-knuckled ride with these thrillers from Pocket Books.

Heretic
Joseph Nassise
The Vatican has a secret weapon. His name is Cade. And he's
the last defense in the war between good and evil.

Blood Memory
Greg Iles
Memory fades. But murder lasts forever.

Puppet
Joy Fielding
She cut the ties to her past. But someone won't let
her forget...

The Unforgiven
Patricia McDonald
She swore she was innocent of murdering her lover.
someone doesn't believe her—and wants her to pay.

The Black Jack Conspiracy
A Department 30 Novel
David Kent
When secret government agency Department 30 is involved,
the stakes are always life and death. But this time the game
is fixed.

Voices Carry
Mariah Stewart
Her memories are flooding back. With a vengeance.

POCKET BOOKS
A Division of Simon & Schuster
A VIACOM COMPANY

POCKET STAR BOOKS
A Division of Simon & Schuster
A VIACOM COMPANY

Available wherever books are sold or at www.simonsays.com.   1345C